THE HADES TRIALS

THE COMPLETE COLLECTION

ELIZA RAINE

ROSE WILSON

Editors: Christopher Mitchell, Kyra Wilson

Cover: Kim's Covers

*For everyone who is convinced that
there's a goddess of hell inside them...*

THE POWER OF HADES

ONE

Blood. Everywhere I looked, there was blood. And fire. Flames were licking over the bodies where they lay motionless.

What have you done?

I tried to stagger to my feet but a wave of dizziness crashed over me and I dropped back to my knees. I didn't feel the pain as they cracked against the rocky ground, only saw the crimson blood as it splashed up my white dress.

What have you done?

'Persephone?' Someone was roaring my name and I turned, heat searing the skin on my face. 'Where are you?'

I made no noise. I didn't want him to find me. I couldn't let anyone find me. I couldn't face them all when they realized this was my fault. *I couldn't face him.* My gaze snagged on the body of a woman, only twenty feet from me. Her face was peaceful, even as her skin burned. Tears slid down my cheeks.

Look at what you've done to her. To them all.

Pain tore through my head, unbearable, as I heard him scream my name again. I couldn't live, while they burned.

TWO

'Persy? Isn't that a boy's name?'

I bit back a retort before it could slip from my lips, and forced them into a smile. Today was *not* the day I got sacked for swearing at a customer.

'Do you want milk in this Americano?' I asked the tall, muscular guy with the lopsided grin across the counter from me.

'Nah, I like my coffee bitter,' he said, and waggled his eyebrows at me. His gray eyes shone, and when I looked into them I found it strangely hard to look away again. I was sure I could see purple swirling around in them. 'So,' he said, pointing to my name badge. 'Parents wanted a boy?'

I sighed, snapping out of the pleasant effect his eyes were having on me.

'No. It's short for Persephone,' I said, slapping a plastic lid on the steaming coffee and sliding it over to him. 'Next!' I called.

'What time do you finish your shift? Are you busy later?' he said. I looked sideways at him as the next customer in the line, a doddery little old woman with a stick, stepped forward scowling.

'You need to move out the way,' I told him, and he bowed his head at the old lady apologetically. His pale hair flopped forward and he pushed his hand through it as he straightened, his chest muscles straining under his tight blue t-shirt.

'I'm so sorry, ma'am. I was just asking this delightful young lady if she had plans later this afternoon,' he smiled at her. I rolled my eyes as the lady's scowl vanished, replaced with a smile under flushing cheeks.

'Well, aren't you the lucky one,' she said to me.

'No, I'm not. I'm afraid I have plans this afternoon,' I said to the cocky guy.

'That's a shame,' he said, this time his smile not quite reaching his eyes and a wicked gleam forming in them instead. 'Catch you around, Persy,' he said, and strode from the coffee shop. A weird tingle skittered through me, and I shook my head as I turned back to the little old lady.

'I'd have canceled my plans if I were you,' she said, cheeks still pink. 'There aren't many men that look like that, even in New York.'

'In my experience, the prettiest men are the best ones to avoid,' I told her. 'Now, what can I get you?'

My shift at Easy Espresso lasted another two hours, and even though a steady trickle of caffeine-starved customers kept me busy, I couldn't shift those mesmerizing eyes from my mind. I'd meant what I'd said though. Well-polished men whose second sentence was to ask you out were an absolute no-no for me. Unfortunately, my type was the effortlessly cool, ripped jeans, oily t-shirt, totally-distracted-by-something-stereo-typically-male-like-fixing-or-building-things guy. In short, the sort of guy who never, ever noticed or chatted up girls who worked in coffee shops.

I'd worked in Easy Espresso for a year now. I didn't hate it, but I didn't love it either. Don't get me wrong, working as a barista in a little, local coffee shop beat working in one of the big ones, where the lines were always ten people deep and everyone was angry and in a hurry. Easy Espresso had a more relaxed vibe, sandwiched between a dry cleaners and a bakery, with only three little tables inside and the same outside. My boss, Tom, wasn't an asshole, which was rare for New York and a first for me, but I knew I wouldn't be there much longer. I only had one semester left at the New York Botanical Gardens, and when I graduated I'd be able to get a job doing what I really loved.

I felt a frisson of excitement as I shrugged on my biker jacket when Stacey arrived to take over from my shift at 2pm.

'See you tomorrow,' I called to her quickly, and raced though the door before she'd even got her ugly brown apron on. The crocuses should finally be opening in my little patch of greenhouse, and after Soil Science class I had a whole hour with Professor Hetz to go over the designs for my private garden. If I did a good enough job then he would put me forward for the landscape designer scholarship, and I'd actually have a shot at my dream career. And the way rooftop gardens were taking over the city, there was a good chance I could find enough work to stay in Manhattan too.

I grinned as I jogged towards the subway entrance, pulling my tatty slouch purse higher over my shoulder. The Botanical Gardens, and my beautiful domed lecture building, were in the Bronx, a good twenty minutes away, and I only had thirty minutes before Soil Science started. A flash of lightning caught my eye, and I cast my gaze upwards. Black clouds were rolling across the sky out of nowhere. *Weird.* It was forecast to be dry and warm all week, and after a dismally wet start to April, the city deserved some sunshine. People began to hurry around me, picking up their paces and scowling. I didn't have an umbrella and my little leather jacket wasn't going to keep much of me dry, so I upped my jog to a sprint, aiming for the cover of the subway underpass. A sudden clap of thunder made my heart leap in my chest, and I couldn't help slowing down to a stop and looking up at the sky again as the noise reverberated through the streets, bouncing off the towering buildings surrounding me. It had gotten dark quickly, and although there was still no rain falling, the sun was completely blocked by thick, dark clouds. I could see purple lightning sparking inside them, and then there was another crack of thunder. This one was so loud that an involuntary cry escaped my lips, my hands flying to my ears unbidden. Fear started to trickle through me. Outside in the city was no place to be during a lightning storm.

'You should get inside, Persy, where it's safe.' I jerked my gaze down from the lightning-filled clouds and my jaw dropped as I saw the blonde haired pretty-boy from earlier, standing ten feet away from me. And he was the only one on the streets, I realized, flicking my eyes from side to side. Where had everyone gone? There must have been fifty people bustling about not thirty seconds ago! *This was getting really fucking weird.* Panic was beginning to build inside me, and I took a step backwards. The pretty-boy smiled at me, then in the blink of an eye, he was standing directly in front of me.

I gasped, my pulse skyrocketing, and took another step back, but I couldn't take my eyes off his. Purple lightning was firing in his irises, in time with the flashes above me. It was utterly beautiful and completely terrifying. My muscles twitched as my heart hammered against my ribs. Every part of me wanted to get away from him, but I couldn't move.

'Who are you?' I breathed.

'You wouldn't believe me if I told you,' he grinned. 'But I don't like being turned down.'

A flicker of anger penetrated my fear. The pretty-boy couldn't take rejection? My mind filled with an image of Ted Hammond, who'd bullied me all through high school, making my life hell whilst anyone was looking, and worse when no one was.

'So you make flashy storms when girls aren't interested in you?' I raised my eyebrows at him. He laughed softly, and I swore he was starting to grow taller, beginning to loom over my already slight form. I instantly regretted what I'd said, the familiar helpless feeling making my insides shrink. *I wasn't strong enough to stop him.* It was the same thought that had dominated my life for years.

'Ohhhh, Persephone. I do so, so much worse than make flashy storms.' He was beginning to glow a faint purple, and I screamed as a bolt of lightning suddenly flashed from the sky, hitting him square on. Light erupted from him, and I turned and ran, my instincts finally taking hold of me. 'Where are you going, little Persy? There's no escaping me!' Booming laughter echoed around the empty streets, and my chest began to tighten, my lungs burning as I ran faster. I didn't know where I was going, panic blinding my ability to reason or think, an animalistic need to get away forcing my body to keep moving. Another purple flash blinded me momentarily and I skidded out of the way as a lightning bolt screeched down into the tarmac. The smell of burning asphalt filled my nostrils as I turned, spotting an entrance to the subway further up the abandoned street.

'Come on now, Persephone, Hades will be so upset with me if I fry you before I can get you to his realm.'

Hades? Did he just say Hades?

I kept running, my sneakers pounding the street, desperate to reach the subway. Lightning couldn't get underground, surely. But as I got closer the entrance to the subway shimmered, and my steps faltered as the world ahead of me morphed from 6th Avenue to a meadow, the subway entrance becoming a dark and gaping cave mouth. I stumbled hard and fell to one knee, landing on soft grass instead of hard asphalt. My breathing was shallow now, my mind reeling, and I scrabbled back to my feet and spun around. How the hell was this happening? *What* the hell was happening? A wave of dizziness swamped me as I tried to process the endless green turf and pretty flowers surrounding me.

'Where am I?' I shrieked, looking around for the lightning-eyed pretty-boy. Dark clouds still rolled overhead, flashing purple. 'Why am I here? Who the hell are you?' Tears of frustration and fear began to fill my eyes. I had a class to get to. I needed to show Professor Hetz my garden. The garden I'd worked on for months, that my whole future depended on... Some part of me knew that the garden should have been the least of my worries, but it had occupied every corner of my mind for months. It was a chance at a new start, where nobody would see me as weak or poor. I had to cling to something real in this twisted hallucination, or whatever the hell it was, and all I had was my garden.

There was another boom of thunder, and rain began to fall from the flashing clouds, heavy and cold. I let out a roar of anger, still turning around frantically, looking for the asshole who'd fucked my day up so tremendously.

'Where are you, you cowardly bastard?!' I screamed. As if in answer, the rain pelted down harder and lightning streaked towards the earth on every side of me.

THREE

At least ten streaks of lightning zigzagged into the earth in a ring around me, the light so bright my arms flew up instinctively to cover my drenched face. The screeching sound they made penetrated my skull so deeply I felt dizzy with fear. I had to get somewhere safe, somewhere the lightning couldn't get me. I blinked, trying to clear the light from my vision, but the only thing I could see in the empty meadow was the cave mouth. It was set into a little mound not more than three feet high, with stone steps leading down into the earth just barely visible in the darkness.

Surely that's where he wanted me to go? Which meant it was the last place I should be considering. Another boom of thunder echoed around me and my terrified body jumped in fright.

I couldn't stay where I was, I decided, and pushed my sodden hair back from my face as I ran for the cave.

I ducked low as I stepped into the darkness, welcoming the instant relief from the rain. Panting from running and shouting, I sat down hard on the top step, looking out over the meadow as I tried to organize my crashing thoughts. My hands were shaking and my mouth felt dry, and I knew adrenaline was surging through me. *This couldn't be happening,* I asserted mentally, screwing my face up. I must have had some sort of nervous breakdown, or a stroke or something. Maybe I'd been hit by a car? Clearly a gorgeous guy who could control lightning hadn't just magicked me into a meadow and blasted electricity at me to get me to go into a cave. Clearly. Because that would be batshit crazy. Next-level crazy.

I took a deep breath, and began to wring out my long dark hair. It sure was wet for a hallucination. I patted my purse, though the gesture was more out of habit than anything useful. My cell phone had no battery. And who was I going to call anyway? I was probably lying on 6th Avenue unconscious, or with any luck in the back of an ambulance by now. Hopefully the medics would charge up my phone and find my brother's number. He would sort this out. Sam was good at sorting stuff out.

I took another long breath. I was starting to feel better. There was no way on earth this was real. I wasn't in a cave, in a meadow, being hounded by a man made of lighting. *I couldn't be.* And if this was all a dream then it couldn't hurt to take a look around. After all, if I was in a coma or some shit, then I might be here for a while. Channeling my new-found confidence through my body, I stood up, surprised at how shaky my hallucinated legs felt. And how cold my hallucinated skin was.

It's obviously a very intense hallucination, I thought, squinting into the darkness below me. Those happened all the time, didn't they?

I put a wobbly, wet sneaker out in front of me, and carefully took a step further into the cave, my socks squelching. Great. What were the chances of there being a laundromat at the bottom of these steps, I wondered? To be fair, if I was dreaming the whole thing, then probably quite high. Maybe I could conjure up some other nice things to be waiting for me at the bottom, I thought, taking another step into the darkness. Maybe a lemon drizzle cake. Or a series of hot guys in dirty overalls, and a shower big enough for them all.

Before long, I was ten steps down, and my eyes were adjusting to the lack of light. The stone steps were worn and uneven, so I was moving slowly, but they seemed to go on and on. After another ten minutes my fantasies about the filthy mechanics were struggling to occupy my mind. Down I went, desperately clinging to happy thoughts as the panic deep in my gut tried to crawl its way up into my throat. Where the hell was I going? I could swear it was getting warmer, although that could have been because I was drying off and moving. Or perhaps it was the anxiety making me hot. Anxiety always made me hot.

After what felt like an hour, but was probably closer to fifteen minutes of putting one soggy foot in front of another and moving deeper and deeper into the earth, I finally saw a flicker of light ahead of me. *Blue* light. I hurried my pace, still taking care on the dodgy steps, but keen to find out what in the world could be causing flickering blue light. Maybe it was the ambulance lights, wherever my body *really* was, leaking into my hallucination. My breathing quickened as the steps rounded a bend. Sconces lined the rocky walls at intervals, each holding a torch burning with blue fire.

'What the...' I murmured, holding my hand hesitantly up to one of them, and drawing it back quickly as I felt the fierce heat. Well, I thought, raising my eyebrows, impressed. Maybe my brain was capable of more imagination than I'd been giving it credit for. *I wonder what else is down here?*

I didn't have to go much further before the steps leveled out, turning into a long flat corridor lined with more torches. I walked faster once I was on safer ground, looking up at the tunnel roof periodically. I wasn't claustrophobic, but when underground it seemed sensible to check the earth above your head was stable once in a while. I walked for about a mile before I reached a closed wooden door, carved with what looked like ancient Greek letters, all glowing the same blue as the torches on the walls. I reached out for the iron ring in the middle and pulled hesitantly. The door didn't budge. I pulled harder, dreading the thought of having to go back up all those steps, back into the stormy meadow. The door didn't move even a millimeter, and I snarled as I dropped the ring in frustration. It thudded against the wood and then bounced twice, the knocks ringing out loudly in the narrow chamber. I froze, the noise unexpected and unnerving. A slow creak sounded, and I took a quick step back from the door. It was swinging open.

If I'd thought my imagination had done well with blue fire, then it deserved a freaking award for the woman stood in front of me.

She was pale-skinned and wearing skin-tight black leather from head to foot, showing a hell of a lot of cleavage. Jet black hair run through with hundreds of tiny tight silver plaits was pulled up in a high ponytail, which showed the intricate black pattern tattooed on the shaved bottom half of her skull. Silver jewelry covered her ears, wrists and hands, all of it sharp. Earrings like daggers hung down from her lobes, and she wore finger sheaths that ended in gleaming claw-like points. A shining tiara set with a single black stone was wrapped around her forehead, which drew attention to her most remarkable feature of all. *She had no pupils.* Her eyes were pure white.

'Welcome to hell,' she said, with a grin.

FOUR

As I watched, too stunned to do anything else, the white began to leak from her eyes, and her grin slipped as electric blue irises and dark pupils began to form.

'No. Fucking. Way,' she said slowly. I moved my mouth but no words came out. I just gaped at her, and she gaped back. 'He found you. He actually fucking found you. Oh gods, Hades is gonna... Oh shit. Oh shit, shit, shit!' She stamped her foot, her silky voice rising in pitch and her hands flexing into fists.

'Who found me?' I half-whispered. 'And... why is everyone talking about Hades?'

The woman chewed on her bottom lip as her black brows drew together. She shook her head.

'Zeus. Zeus found you. I don't believe it.'

I let out a barked laugh and she leaned one hand on her hip, unsmiling.

'It's not funny, it's a fucking disaster.'

'What are you talking about? And who are you?' I said, my confidence growing at her words. I'd been obsessed with Greek mythology since I was a kid. This was *definitely* something my stupid-ass brain would make up.

'I'm Hecate. And you're Persephone. And you're not supposed to be here, that's what I'm talking about.'

'Hecate? As in the goddess of magic?'

'Amongst other things, yeah,' she said, regarding me. 'So... you remember some stuff then?'

'From classical studies? Yeah, I remember loads,' I said, frowning. 'I carried on studying Greeks and Romans after school.'

'Classical studies. Right,' Hecate said, nodding slowly. 'You remember nothing from...' she trailed off, raising one perfect eyebrow at me. I raised both of mine back at her.

'What are you talking about?' I said eventually, when she didn't speak. She blew out a sigh.

'Hades is going to lose it when he sees you. But I guess that's what you get for pissing off the Lord of the Gods. Fucking idiot.'

'Hades is a fucking idiot?'

'Yeah. But for the sake of the gods, don't say that in front of him. Or tell him I said it.'

'I had no idea I was this imaginative,' I breathed.

'What?'

'This isn't happening,' I told her. 'I've invented you.'

A lopsided smile took over her face, and her blue eyes twinkled.

'Is that right?'

'Must be,' I said. 'Zeus and Hades and Greek gods don't exist. I'm sure we'd have noticed by now if they did.' Even as I spoke the words, doubt and panic were warring with them. Something was wrong, Very, very wrong. *That'll be the fact that you're probably gravely injured or dying somewhere in the real world*, I reminded myself.

'You've been in the mortal realm a long time, Persephone,' said Hecate, quietly.

'New York,' I told her. 'And I've been there twenty-six years. *My whole life.*' I stressed the last sentence.

'Sure you have,' she said, in a voice that said I was totally deluded. 'What the fuck am I supposed to do with you now?'

'Well, you were obviously expecting someone,' I said, thinking back to her white eyes. 'You welcomed me to hell.'

'Yeah, I was expecting the last contestant for the Hades Trials. I just didn't expect it to be you.'

'The Hades Trials?'

'You know, for someone who's made all this up in their head, you have very little clue about what's going on,' Hecate said. She had a point. My stomach lurched uneasily again.

'So why don't you tell me?' I put my hands on my hips in an attempt to regain some sort of semblance of control, but the woman in front of me was clearly a hundred times more fierce than I could ever be.

'OK. Zeus has decided that Hades needs a wife. Women have been trying to earn the position of Queen of the Underworld by completing a series of Trials. I was supposed to meet the last contestant here today.'

'Can Hades not just choose someone he likes?' I asked, frowning at my own question. This was absolutely mad.

'No. He swore after his first wife that he would never remarry, but he upset Zeus in a pretty big way recently. And the big man's punishments cut deep.'

'Hades is being forced to marry as a punishment?'

'Yep.'

'So... what's this all got to do with me? And how do you know who I am?'

A worried look crossed her beautiful face, then she let out a big sigh and closed her eyes.

'What a fucking mess,' she breathed, and opened her eyes again, fixing them on mine. 'I could refuse to tell you, but I guess you'll find out sooner or later.'

'Find what out?'

'You're Hades' first wife.'

∼

My head swam for a moment as I gaped at her. Then a laugh, bordering on hysterical, bubbled from my lips, getting louder and louder as the words repeated themselves in my head.

'How the hell am I coming up with this?' I gasped through laughs. 'I've made myself the wife of the king of the dead? What the actual fuck?' Fresh laughter welled out of me, my ribs starting to ache as I leaned over, pressing my hands on my knees. 'I mean, there's being into bad boys, but Hades? Lord of the Underworld? Talk about extreme!'

'This is so not how I saw today going,' sighed Hecate. She let me laugh a while longer, tears streaming from my eyes as adrenaline-fueled instability took over my senses. 'Are you done?' she asked, when the laughter began to ebb away, and I dabbed at my wet cheeks. I nodded.

'I'm so done. Done with all of this. I need to wake up now.'

'Persephone, this isn't a dream,' she said, stepping forward and gripping my arm hard.

'Ow!' I exclaimed, my laughter dying out abruptly.

'See? You can feel that?'

'Yes,' I said sharply, tugging my arm back.

'This is real. And trust me when I tell you, you don't

want to fuck with Zeus or Hades. Or any of the Olympians for that matter. If Zeus found you and brought you here, then you have to compete in the Trials. And that has... ramifications.'

I scowled at her.

'No. No, I'm sorry.' I turned, and my stomach lurched as I bumped into a wall made from solid earth. 'Where's the corridor gone?' I asked, my voice weak. Blue light flared around me and I spun back to Hecate. Her eyes were milky white again and her hands were raised by her face. Thin wisps of purple smoke were trailing from her palms, and slowly they convalesced into a dagger, spinning gently in the air in front of me. I felt my heart begin to hammer in my chest. 'I need to sit down,' I said, feeling my legs wobble beneath me.

'Persephone, you have a past in this realm. A past I am not at liberty to divulge.' Her voice had gone weirdly formal, compared to how she'd been speaking before. 'But I can tell you that Hades will be very shocked, and very angry to see you. And there will be many others who will be less than pleased. This weapon will work here in Olympus, even on a god, and you should keep it on you at all times.'

The dagger floated towards my shaking hands, and I tentatively reached for it. It was warm to touch, and had a little green stone set in each side of the pommel. Other than that it was unremarkable.

'Thanks,' I muttered, staring at it. It felt real in my grasp. *Too real.* I squeezed my eyes closed. *Wake up, wake up, wake up. Sam, where the fuck are you? Wake me up!*

Nothing happened. That didn't mean anything though. There was no way I was the wife of Hades. I'd been watching too much Netflix.

But something in my core was straining, almost longing

for this craziness to be true. *Why? Why would I want that?* In what world would I want to compete to be the wife of a god I had apparently already been married to once, then completely forgotten? I wanted to design gardens! I wanted to grow living things! I didn't want to be in a cave with a magic dagger and angry gods!

'I want to go home,' I whispered, looking at Hecate. 'I was going to have a meeting today about my scholarship.'

A flicker of pity flashed across Hecate's face, her eyes blue again.

'I'm sorry,' she said quietly. 'Zeus is a prick. Don't tell him I said that either.'

'Can you send me back?'

She shook her head sadly.

'For your sake and Hades, I wish I could. But there's no crossing the big man.' She cocked her head at me again. 'You know, deep down, that this is real, don't you?'

I looked at her.

'I know something is wrong,' I admitted.

'Maybe when you see the realm, some of it will come back to you. Hopefully not all of it,' she added quietly. I frowned.

'If what you're saying is true, why will Hades be angry to see me? Did we fall out?'

'Something like that. Only he can tell you what happened. And he will likely choose not to.'

'Why?'

'Persy, I can't tell you, so don't ask, alright?' she said, a flicker of exasperation in her tone.

'Persy?'

She gave me an apologetic look.

'Sorry. That's what I used to call you. Before you... left.'

'Were we friends?'

'Yeah. You had cooler hair then. And much better dress sense.'

I looked down at my leather jacket and ripped jeans, then at her sleek black catsuit.

'Oh,' I said, not sure what else to say. My brain seemed to have slowed down completely, almost like it was refusing to process anymore. 'I can't think straight,' I told Hecate. 'And I feel very tired suddenly.'

'Let's get you some food and dry clothes. Maybe a stiff drink. The gods know, I need one,' she said and held out her hand.

I paused for a second, then took it.

FIVE

I followed Hecate through the wooden door and down more corridors lit with blue flames. They reflected off her silver jewelry and I let the light and patterns they made occupy my frazzled mind as we walked. I figured there was no point trying to concentrate on where we were going if walls could just appear to block the way. There was no point concentrating on anything really. This whole mad situation seemed to be far beyond my control. I was unbelievably tired and I wondered if going to sleep in this pretend place might make me wake up in the real world.

'Technically I'm supposed to present you to the gods in an hour, but I'll let them know we'll be a bit late,' Hecate said over her shoulder to me. 'Zeus won't be surprised, the asshole,' she snarled.

'Why did he come and find me?'

'I already told you, because it'll upset Hades.'

'Oh yeah. Apparently my ex-husband hates me.' I rolled my eyes. *Batshit crazy.*

'Woah now, I never said that,' she said, slowing down and looking back at me.

'You did too!'

'No, I said he'll be angry to see you. You're not supposed to be here.'

'Right. Is this one of those messy divorce things?' I asked with a sigh. None of this made any sense.

'Hmm, something like that. There'll need to be some damage limitation. I'll do what I can but...' She trailed off. She didn't speak again until we reached another door covered in glowing blue marks, which I was now positive were Greek. 'Persy, this is going to be a bit weird for you. Don't freak out on me, OK? Just... act normal.'

I looked at her.

'I'm too tired to freak out,' I told her. It was true. My thoughts were becoming more and more sluggish, and my legs felt like they weighed a ton. The adrenaline was wearing off. 'Plus I have no idea what normal is here,' I pointed out. 'I don't even know where I am.'

'You're in Olympus. Virgo, to be precise.'

'Virgo? Like the star sign?'

'Each of the Olympians has their own realm, and yeah, in your world they're star signs. Hades' realm is Virgo.'

'My star sign is Capricorn,' I said. 'Who's realm is that?'

'Artemis. And she and Hades do not get on. Also her realm is forbidden, except if you're a centaur. So unless you're hiding a horse body under those jeans, give up any ideas of visiting.'

'Right,' I said. Centaurs. Of course there were centaurs here. A little surge of panic bit through my fatigue. This couldn't be happening. *But it was.* At least there was something about Hecate I trusted. *Likely because she was a figment of my own imagination and I'd invented her for exactly that reason.* I would just try to treat anything and anyone in this place as though it were completely ordinary, I decided firmly. What other choice did I have? Freaking out wouldn't do me any good at all. As long as I could do nothing about this messed up situation, I might as well go along with it.

The room on the other side of the door was not that weird after all. It was a bit like a dressing room, with rails of clothes down one side, and a long counter down the other, with a mirror above it. The light wasn't blue anymore though, the rocky walls giving off a pale glow closer to daylight.

'Is all of Virgo underground?' I asked, then immediately wished I hadn't. I didn't expect to be here long, but I seriously couldn't handle being in a place where there was no outside. Panic fluttered through me, threatening to derail my new attitude adjustment.

'Not all of it, no,' Hecate said, bending to open a cupboard under the counter. She straightened and handed me a straight cut glass. She held onto one herself and I watched as her eyes turned milky. Red liquid began to fill her glass, and I looked down to see the same happening in mine.

'What is it?'

'Wine,' she said as the blue returned to her irises.

'You can conjure wine? I'd be drunk constantly,' I said, impressed. She winked at me.

'Who says I'm not?' She knocked back a huge gulp of the liquid, and I hesitantly lifted my glass to my lips and inhaled. It smelled divine, like black currants and cherries. I took a sip.

'Wow,' I said, involuntarily. Hecate gave me a look, pursing her lips.

'I'm actually quite jealous that you get to discover Olympus all over again. The first time you do anything is always the best,' she sighed.

'And you can't tell me why I left in the first place?'

'No. I'm not even sure myself, but even if I was, Hades would kill me.' She flicked her hand, eyes flashing white again, and a chocolate cake appeared out of nowhere on the counter, in front of the mirror. My stomach growled in response.

'Can you do anything you like with your magic?' I asked her.

'I can do quite a lot,' she shrugged, steering me towards a chair in front of the mirror. 'But it's not all fun and games. I'm also goddess of ghosts. That's a lot less fun, I can tell you.'

'Really?' I asked, as she sat me down and stood behind me. I watched in the mirror as she lifted a lock of my dark, wet hair and let it fall back onto my jacket with a slapping sound.

'Yeah. Most folk aren't exactly thrilled to find their souls stuck as corporeal beings. Sometime it feels like I'm wading though shit trying to sort out their messes.'

'Is that why you live in the underworld? Because of the ghosts?'

'Uhuh. Now, we need to do something about your hair. And eat some cake. You'll feel better.'

I thought about refusing, remembering something about not eating food from the underworld, but the cake looked and smelled amazing. This whole place is pretend, I reminded myself, and lifted a slice from the cake. What harm could it possibly do? I took a bite, sensations firing in my mouth as the richest chocolate I'd ever tasted slid over my tongue.

'Oh my god,' I mumbled around the cake.

'Gods,' Hecate corrected me. 'Twelve of them. And don't forget it.'

'Right,' I nodded. I looked at her in the mirror as she rummaged though the rails of clothes behind me.

'I'm not wearing something like...' I trailed off as she straightened and raised one eyebrow.

'Like what?'

'Like what you are,' I finished awkwardly. 'You look great in it! But I'm not quite as... confident about the bust area as that outfit requires.'

'Persy, from what I remember, that's a load of shit. But don't worry, I was planning on something a little more conservative. If you went out in front of Hades in skin-tight leather he might bust something,' she said, frowning at a green dress on a hanger. I shook my head. Maybe when I met my alleged ex-husband this would start to make more sense. Maybe not. I finished the piece of cake and glugged down the rest of the wine, already starting to feel much more alert.

'So, tell me about the Trials,' I said. 'What will I have to do?'

'Er, best you find that out later,' she answered evasively. Alarm trickled through me. *It doesn't matter, it's not real,* I told myself.

'Are they dangerous?'

Hecate shrugged.

'There've been a few casualties,' she said, sliding a pale blue thing off a hanger.

'What?' I said, spinning on my chair to face her. 'Casualties? What kind of casualties?'

'Don't worry about it, with any luck Hades will find a way to withdraw you anyway,' she smiled at me, but I knew she was lying. I took a deep breath.

'I like the green,' I said, pointing at the dress still on the rail.

'Oh. OK.'

'And can I have some more wine?'

'Hecate, why is my hair white?' I kept my voice as level as I could, but it flickered all the same. 'I've dealt with enough weird shit today, and I'm not sure I can add this to the list.'

'Shush, you've not seen it all together yet. You look amazing.'

She'd hidden the mirror from me, turning it a smoky black, but I could see the lock of my hair that had fallen over my shoulder and was now laying across my left breast. The pale green dress was a halterneck, showing only a moderate amount of cleavage, but it was tight around my waist. The bottom half of the dress flowed like liquid to the floor though, shimmering turquoise when I moved, and a thigh-high split showed off the gold lace-up sandals on my now-dry feet.

If it weren't for the little piece of white hair dominating my attention, I would have been quite thrilled with the outfit.

'OK, are you ready?'

'Do I have a choice?'

'Nope. Ta da!'

The mirror cleared, and my mouth fell open. My hair was *white*. Not like when an old person goes gray, but white. I moved my head from side to side and saw silvery strands catch the light. It was set in gentle curls and half tied up, with lots of little plaits everywhere like Hecate's. A few stray curls fell about my ears, brushing my bare shoulders. I leaned closer to peer at my reflection. My green eyes looked more green somehow, like fresh grass, dark liner rimming them and making them pop. A deep purple colored my lips, making them look fuller, and my cheekbones looked sharper too.

'What have you... How did you make me look so...' I couldn't finish any of the sentences. I looked a thousand times better than I had ever managed to make myself look.

Hecate beamed at me.

'Just wait until I get you into some of your old dresses,' she said, eyes flashing. 'Although we'll need some fighting gear too.'

'Fighting?' I raised my eyebrows. 'Other than scrapping with my big brother, I'm not really a fighter. I'm more of the 'love things, grow things', type of gal.'

'I'm sure it'll all come back.' I opened my mouth, but shut it again. There was no point in asking her what that meant. I was just going to go along with this. 'OK. I think you're ready. Finish that wine and we'll go.'

I downed the rest of my drink in one, and rolled my shoulders as I stood up.

'I'm ready,' I told her and she took my hand in hers.

'Good. I'm sorry.'

'For what?'

'This,' she said, and her eyes turned milky.

SIX

The world around me lurched, white light flashing bright around me. I squeezed my eyes closed and gripped Hecate's hand harder, then I heard the muttering of a crowd, which died away almost instantly. I opened my eyes.

'Oh my god,' I whispered.

I was in a white marble room, facing tiered rows of seated people. And the word 'people' was a loose description. Although over half of them looked human, a lot didn't. There was a woman with a severely misshapen face and leathery wings protruding from her back, and a beautiful lady whose skin looked like it was made from wood. There was a man who must have been ten feet tall if he had been stood up, his skin a shining gold color, and a creature that had furry legs that looked like a cat's and a beak for a nose. Standing at the back, just in front of the white marble wall were three minotaurs, a centaur and an incredibly curvy woman with a wooden leg and hair that seemed to be moving of its own accord. I took a deep breath. *OK. Ten, no, make that a hundred points, to my imagination.*

'I did warn you,' muttered Hecate, still gripping my hand. As I turned to look at her I realized that the sides of the room were missing, grand Greek columns lining the edges at intervals instead. And beyond them were flames. And not just any flames. Flames larger than sky-scrapers that leapt and danced and weren't only red. Purples and blues and oranges flickered amongst the crimson and I was vaguely aware of my jaw slowly dropping.

'It's so beautiful,' I breathed.

'Welcome to the Underworld,' boomed a voice.

I turned to the last wall and my knees instantly felt weak again. I was in a throne room, I now realized. There was a raised dais at the end of the room, and eleven people were seated on large chairs along the platform. These weren't people though, I knew, as my eyes flicked across them all, trying to take it in. *These were gods.* Power emanated from them, almost tangible in the air, as they each eyed me.

'It's really not Zeus's place to welcome you here,' said the most beautiful woman I'd ever seen, sitting forward in her chair. 'That honor should go to Hades, but he is... indisposed just now.' She had skin the color of coffee, and her hair was pastel pink and wrapped around her body like a dress, leaving her midriff and long legs totally exposed. Her pale lips matched her hair and her eyes were almost black. 'I'm Aphrodite,' she said.

I gazed at her, all the liquid leaving my mouth completely. Hecate squeezed my hand.

'Bow,' she said out of the corner of her mouth. I dipped my head low, taking another breath.

Get a grip, get a grip.

'I'm-' I started to say as I straightened, but a man stood up, cutting me off.

'You're Persephone,' he said, his eyes gleaming and purple energy crackling around him.

'You!' I said, anger springing to life inside me. He was Zeus! With his stupid purple lightning, and asshole laughing eyes.

'Me!' he beamed, his dark beard and hair morphing into that of the gorgeous blonde from the coffee shop. 'I'm ever so pleased you could join us,' he said. 'Some quick introductions? It would be rude for you to remain ignorant.' I glared at him, but kept my lips pressed firmly together. This was not the place to pick a fight, even I could tell that.

'This is my brother, Poseidon,' he said, gesturing to a bored-looking man with insanely blue eyes in the seat next to him. 'And this is my lovely wife, Hera.' The grand looking lady on the other side of him inclined her head at me and I returned the nod. She had inky dark skin and turquoise blue hair in a complicated looking plait that ringed her head like a crown. She had a real crown too, glittering with the reflections of the flames on either side of us.

'These are the twins, Artemis and Apollo,' he said, pointing at two slight, golden-haired figures, both sporting broad smiles. Artemis looked no older than fifteen, her brother maybe only a few years older. 'This is Dionysus.' Zeus gestured at a man dressed in clothes from my world, tight leather trousers and a Hawaiian shirt open to his navel. Dionysus gave me a lazy grin from under a flop of dark hair.

'Nice to see you again, Persy,' he drawled. I blinked thickly at him.

'This is Hermes,' Zeus said, and a red-headed man with a neat beard beamed at me. I couldn't help the small smile that leapt to my lips in return. There was something about him that slightly eased my racing pulse. 'You've just met Aphrodite, this is her husband, Hephaestus.' A man with a hunched shoulder and lopsided face was sat next to Aphrodite, his form swamped by a massive leather tabard. He didn't look at me. 'And this is Ares and Athena,' Zeus finished. An enormous man in full Greek armor glared at me through the eye-slit in his red-plumed helmet, and a beautiful blonde-haired woman in a white toga with an owl on her shoulder gave me a small smile. Athena had always been my favorite growing up. She was portrayed in my books as the goddess who was the most fair and most intelligent, but still fierce, and I'd tried to channel that every time Ted Hammond had got too close to me. *Not that I'd ever been able to stand up to him*, I thought bitterly. Even sat next to Ares' hulking form, Athena radiated power greater than his, and a respectful jealousy surged through me.

I bowed my head.

'It's nice to meet you all. I must confess though, I'm a little confused,' I said, as formally as I could, my lips slightly numb. 'Apparently you all know me from a life I can't remember.'

Athena stood up from her chair and my skin prickled with something, magic or power or anticipation, I wasn't sure.

'Persephone, you have been made to forget your past with good reason. It is highly inappropriate that you are here now, but there's nothing we can do about it. The Lord of the Gods has made sure of that.' She shot a sideways glare at Zeus, who flopped back into his throne with a lazy shrug.

'Oops,' he said.

'I know this may be hard for you, but you need to act as though this is your first time here in Olympus.'

'Erm, that's not going to be hard for me,' I said. 'I've never seen this place or any of you before in my life.'

'You misunderstand me. You will want to find out what happened in your past. But this would be folly. You must trust that the twelve Olympians made the correct decision in removing those memories from you, and leave it at that. Start again. From today.'

I frowned, confusion and anger battling against the compulsion I felt to worship this beautiful, wise woman. I knew hazily that her powers were at work. I mean, she was a goddess, she could make me do whatever she wanted. But was it right that they could remove my memories? Tell me I was married, then not allow me to know any more? *Married!* The thought was laughable. I'd never even had a boyfriend for more than six months, what the hell would I want with a husband? *None of this is real, you idiot. Who gives a shit?* The voice trickled through my racing thoughts. *Sam is going to wake you up soon, in a hospital bed somewhere.*

I smiled at Athena.

'Fine,' I said. She cocked her head at me slowly.

'You do not believe this is real?'

I said nothing and the goddess let out a long breath.

'Father, you can be cruel,' she said quietly, then sat back down on her throne.

'If Hades didn't behave like a disobedient child then I wouldn't have to be,' Zeus barked.

'And her? Do you believe she deserved this?' said Hera, speaking for the first time and gesturing at me. Zeus shifted uncomfortably in his seat.

'You forget, brother, she has the potential to be danger-ous. Your games should not go this far,' said Poseidon, his piercing blue eyes not leaving me as he spoke.

'Dangerous?' I echoed.

'Dangerous,' he repeated, something in his expression making me want to be someplace else, and fast.

'I will be her companion during the Trials, she will not be a danger to anyone,' said Hecate, stepping forward beside me. Relief and gratitude washed through me as I remembered I wasn't completely alone. Hecate had been my friend once, apparently.

'Hmmm. To be sure, I wish to assign her a guard. Of my choosing,' said Poseidon, finally taking his eyes from mine and looking at Zeus.

'I would like to choose a guard for her too,' said Athena quickly.

'As I'm sure would Hades, were he here,' added Hera.

Zeus rolled his eyes and sighed, and I looked at Hecate.

'Why the fuck do I need a guard?' I hissed at her.

'Her powers haven't been unlocked,' said Hecate loudly to the assembled gods, ignoring me. 'She does not need a guard.'

'Powers?' I gaped at her, feeling the hysteria fringing my mind again. *Of course I'd give myself powers in this mad fucking fantasy. Why wouldn't I?* 'Let me guess,' I said, feeling an unhinged smile take over my face. *If I could have any power in the world what would it be?* That was easy. 'I can make plants grow?'

Hecate looked at me, her brows drawing together.

'How'd you know that?'

'Because Hades left her love of nature when he sent her to the mortal world,' said Hera, so quietly I barely heard her.

A silence fell over the room and my head span as the colored flames danced on each side of us.

'I suggest Persephone choose her own guard. We will

present our options this evening, after the first Trial,' said Athena, authoritatively.

'Agreed,' said Zeus, sitting forward. 'Now, I do not believe Hades will be joining us now-'

'And why is that, brother?' boomed a voice. Gooseflesh shot up on my skin as the temperature in the room dropped sharply. Fear began to crawl through me, though I didn't know what I was suddenly so scared of. I felt Hecate stiffen by my side and Zeus's eyes flashed as he slouched back into his throne.

'Hades! I'm so glad you could make it after all! I have a surprise for you.'

Black smoke began to gather in the center of the dais, swirling fast into a humanoid form.

'Another contestant for your foolish competition, no doubt,' hissed the angry, slithery voice, and I felt a strong compulsion to step backwards, and keep going.

'Indeed,' said Zeus, a smile spreading over his face. The smoke was nearly solid now, but not quite, the form before me translucent and fluid and featureless.

Until it turned to me.

For a split second the world disappeared completely. The first thing I saw were his eyes, the rest of the swirling smoke flashing into human form so briefly I almost missed it. But I registered the massive shoulders, the dark trousers and shirt, the gleaming onyx in the center of a belt around his waist, before my eyes met his again. *They were silver.* Not white or grey or pale blue but shining silver, and they were filled with shock. Emotions I didn't recognize began to hammer through me, and suddenly something inside me was beating against my mind, desperate to be free. The sensation made me feel dizzy and sick.

I knew this man. All notion of this being a crazy dream, all ideas that I was hallucinating, all the rational thoughts and truths that I'd been clinging to disintegrated as I stared into those desperate pools of silver. I knew this man. *This was real.*

Anger suddenly erupted in those haunted eyes and before I could look at the rest of his face his solid form was gone. A blast of power pulsed through the room and I cried out as pure terror gripped my mind. Images that were usually relegated to my worst nightmares, blood and death and gore and fire, filled my head and blinded me to everything else. I could smell the tang of the blood, hear the fire roaring, feel the screams reverberating around me as people died everywhere I looked. *I was drowning in blood.* I choked for breath as my legs crumpled beneath me, too far gone to feel the crack of my knees as they hit the marble.

'What is the meaning of this?' bellowed Hades, so loudly I threw my hands over my ears, squeezing my eyes shut. It didn't help. All I could see were bodies, torn apart, flames licking over them. I clawed at my throat desperately, unable to get enough air. *I was drowning in fear and blood.*

'Hades!' I distantly heard Hecate's voice. 'She doesn't have her power, you're going to kill her!'

Instantly the terror melted away, a soothing calm flooding through me. I gulped down air, pressing my shaking hands to my wet face as Hecate crouched down beside me.

'It's OK,' she said quietly. 'You'll be OK.'

'Everybody, leave,' the slithery voice said. Although he spoke quietly, the words were as clear as day. 'Except you, brother. You and I need to talk.'

SEVEN

Hecate had barely magicked us out of the throne room and I was still clinging to her arm as the combination of terror and adrenaline finally got the better of me and my stomach began to heave.

'Red wine and chocolate cake is not so appealing anymore,' muttered Hecate, staring down in distaste at the mess I'd made on the dressing room floor. Then there was a fizzing sound, and the vomit vanished. 'Here,' she said, handing me a glass of water. I took it with shaking hands and she eased me onto the stool. 'I've never seen Hades lose control of his power like that. I'm sorry.'

'What's his power, scaring people to death?' I asked, my voice coming out in a bitter croak.

'Well, no, but that is an unfortunate side-effect for humans.'

'Huh.' I took a long shuddering breath.

'I saw... I saw horrible things,' I said quietly.

'Dead people?' she asked, quirking an eyebrow, her braids flashing as she cocked her head at me. I nodded.

'Yeah. Lots of dead people.'

'Hades is the Lord of the Dead. He's the most fearsome of all the Olympians, although not the strongest, and his rage would cause any human to see death. And trust me, that was Hades' real rage.' She blew out a breath, chewing on her lip. 'He let his true form show. With spectators. That's... Well, there are very, very few people in Olympus who have seen his eyes.'

Those silver orbs, deep with desperation and power filled my mind.

'I know him,' I said quietly, looking down at my glass.

'Yes,' said Hecate, and crouched in front of me, her blue eyes full of compassion.

'But... My life. My life in New York...'

My real life felt distant in my spinning head, like it had just been a game, or a dream. I could feel it slipping away. Was that because I was dying somewhere in New York? Would this all end soon too? Or was this the reality? *Hades' eyes...* I knew, more surely than I'd ever known anything in my life, that this was not the first time I'd seen those eyes. They meant something to me, down to my very core. But what? Was it love for a husband? It didn't feel like love. And how the hell could I have loved someone whose power was to fill people's minds with scenes from their nightmares?

'I'm sorry your first meeting with him turned out like that. I knew it would be pretty shit but... Nearly killing you was definitely not ideal. But you have to trust me when I tell you that I think this could all work out OK. Maybe. If you're a fast learner and we can stop you being so... human.'

I blinked at Hecate.

'Right,' I said eventually, at a loss for anything more constructive.

'There's got to be a way of unlocking your powers, but we'll need to do it slowly. And without whichever stupid guard you end up with knowing about it.' She jumped to her feet. 'You want to hope you get either Athena's or Hades' guard, Poseidon's will be a total fucking killjoy.'

'Why does he think I'm dangerous?'

'Persy, we're back to shit I can't tell you, so stop asking.'

'Stop asking?' A flash of anger bubbled through my fatigue. 'Are you serious?'

'Look, this is what Athena meant. You have to accept that the past is in the past, and that's that.'

I glared at her, feeling a frisson of satisfaction as the confident look on her face flickered. I didn't think I'd ever intimidated anyone in my life before. But then I'd never looked or felt like this before either.

'I've been kidnapped, told my whole life was a lie and that I had a husband I didn't know existed. If that isn't bad enough, you now want me to compete to marry the same man who already decided NOT to be married to me once before, in order to live in a world full of dead things when all I've wanted to do my whole life is grow things.'

I stood up from the stool, aware of the increasing pitch and volume of my voice and not caring one bit. 'How the fuck do you expect me not to ask you questions?'

'Calm down,' Hecate said quietly.

'Calm down? Are you insane? Of course you are! You live in hell and can conjure wine, why the fuck am I even talking to you?' I wheeled around, squeezing my eyes closed and pressing my hands to my face again. I was close to losing it, and I could feel the panic squeezing my chest. 'I'm not doing the Trials. I don't want to be here. I don't want anything to do with a creature who is surrounded by death, who *embodies* death.' Tears were burning the back of my eyes, and I squeezed them shut tighter. 'This is a fucking nightmare, please, let me out. Let me leave.' I didn't know who I was asking, I just desperately wanted the plea to come true. 'I can't stay here.' This was worse than school. This was worse than being taunted and called trailer trash and having stupid shit thrown at me. This was worse than Ted Hammond breathing down my neck, pawing and groping at me. Those bodies on fire, the smell of the blood, the paralyzing fear...

'I'm sorry, Persephone. You have to compete.' Hecate's voice sounded strained and sad behind me. 'I'm going to send you to sleep now. I'll wake you before the first Trial.'

'No, please-' I said, whipping around to face her, but I lost consciousness before she even came into view.

I blinked and the world around me came blearily into view. I was in a bed, on a soft mattress, and a thick downy comforter was weighing down on me, covering my whole head. It felt cozy rather than smothering though, and I gripped it in my hands and wrapped it tighter around myself as the memories of the last few hours crashed over me like a wave. A hard lump formed in my throat as realization settled heavy within my heart. Now that the panic, the adrenaline, the mild hysteria was temporarily at bay, I knew with one hundred percent certainty that when I sat up and swung my legs out of bed, I would still be in this fucked up reality instead of my own. I knew this was real. As unlikely as it was, something deep in my core, maybe even in my soul if I had such a thing, knew it.

'Shit,' I muttered. 'Shit, shit, shit.' What would I do now? I thought about Athena's words. I was supposed to let go and move on. Hecate said I had to compete in the Trials. To marry the Lord of the Underworld. I shuddered. I couldn't marry that monster. No fucking way. I mean, he was made of smoke for Christ's sake! Those deep silver eyes shimmered into my mind.

You were married to him once. How? How was that even possible? I couldn't have loved him. He was freaking terrifying. And although I didn't consider myself as a total wimp, I wasn't exactly the sadist type, into blood and torture. My mind flashed to what sex with a man made of smoke and death would be like. Probably significantly more kinky than I was used to. *Stop it,* I chided myself.

All I had to do was not win the Trials. Then I wouldn't have to marry him. And in all probability, I wouldn't be winning anything anyway. What would happen after I lost the Trials? Would I stay here in this world? Or get to go back to New York? I supposed either would be better than staying in the underworld. Did they employ gardeners in Olympus?

I lay still in the bed, refusing to peek out from the covers as I weighed up my options. One thing I kept coming back to was that panic and denial were unlikely to do me much good. If I had to fight, as Hecate had suggested I would, then I might face danger. Which meant being strong. Something I wasn't especially good at. I was good at avoiding fights, not getting into them. But I didn't want to be an easy target, not because mom and dad couldn't afford a house this time, but because I was human, and weaker than everyone else. I couldn't deal with that. Not again. It had taken six years to reach a point where I felt I could hold my own in New York. Six years to build up the confidence to follow my dreams, and actually make progress. Six years to reach a point where I could confidently turn down arrogant pretty-boys when they sleazed on me. Zeus's face filled my mind, merging with Ted Hammond's, and I scowled. No way was that happening again I thought, screwing my face up into the pillow, defiance buoying me. No fucking way.

Hecate said I used to have good dresses. And powers. I doubted I was ever as badass as she clearly was, but Poseidon had called me dangerous. Maybe instead of worrying about what had happened I should take Athena's advice, and forget about finding out what had occurred in the past and move on - become a new kind of dangerous. A new Persy, whom none of them wanted to fuck with. Especially that purple-eyed asshole, Zeus.

'Knock, knock?' came a questioning voice at the door, and I took a deep breath.

'Yeah?' I called, and reluctantly pulled the comforter from over my head.

'Good, you're up,' said Hecate, walking into the room through a massive mahogany door. I was in a windowless room, the walls all painted a rich navy blue and the ceiling giving off that same daylight glow that the dressing room walls had. I looked about, taking in the old-fashioned but expensive-looking wardrobe and dressing table, and the cabinet lined with glass bottles of colored liquids.

'Is that a bar?'

'Yes.'

'Good,' I said, and kicked the covers off. I made my way over to the grand little cabinet and poured some amber liquid from a square decanter into one of the two empty glasses.

'Do you want to know what that is before you drink it?' asked Hecate, but I shook my head, and tipped it down my throat. It burned, and my eyes began to water, but it was exactly what I needed. Fire in my belly, I thought, breathing through my teeth. I needed fire in my belly.

'Please can you dress me in the most badass thing I used

to own?' I asked Hecate, looking at her. 'I'm done freaking out.'

'Boy am I glad to hear you say that,' she beamed at me, eyes flashing. 'And badass is exactly the style you want, as you're about to fight a demon.'

My fierce new resolve wobbled as I looked at her.

'A... demon?'

'Yes, but a low grade one as it's your first Trial. Trust me, they're not hard to put on their ass.'

'Hecate, the last time I fought anyone was Sam, fifteen years ago.'

'Who's Sam?'

'My brother. At least, I thought he was my brother,' I answered, sadness hitting me in the gut like a physical punch. 'I guess I won't see him again,' I whispered.

'When you're married to Hades you can do whatever the hell you like, so don't worry about it,' she said dismissively. The silver covering her ears shone as she shrugged. I opened my mouth to tell her that I would be doing whatever it took to avoid marrying Hades, but closed it again. Perhaps it wasn't such a good idea to share all my plans just yet. And if I managed to pull them off I wouldn't have to lose my brother.

'Right. So, how do I fight a demon?'

'It depends which type it is.' She turned to the wardrobe and opened it to reveal rows and rows of dresses, in every color I could imagine. 'We don't have many of your old things here, but I remember them well enough to work some magic,' she winked at me.

'Thanks,' I said. 'But seriously, how do I fight a demon?'

EIGHT

In what seemed like no time at all I was back in the throne room with Hecate, feeling slightly dizzy from the bright lurching motion of her transporting us. I managed to keep the contents of my stomach in place this time though, which I was taking as a small win.

I was wearing my white hair up in a high tail now, a silver band decorated with emerald gems keeping it back from my face. 'So as not to hinder your view of the demon', Hecate had said. My clothes too were made for 'getting out of the way', supple leather trousers that were black, and a slightly less supple leather corset that was supposed to be thick enough to repel claws. Given that the garment barely came above my breasts I wasn't sure what I was supposed to do if any claws were aimed higher.

Just stay out of the way, I told myself, as Hecate had spent the last ten minutes doing so. I was good at staying out of the way, and I was quick. This wasn't exactly what I thought I'd been training my body for when I'd hauled my ass out running every other day for the last year but I was sure glad now that I had.

The throne room was mercifully empty, and I took the opportunity to move closer to the dais. Only two thrones were on it now, massive and imposing and breathtaking. One I assumed belonged to Hades, as it looked to be made entirely from bones. I shuddered as I took in the skulls lining the arched back, the long limb bones making up the chair legs, the curved rib bones running down the raised arms. Something black that looked almost alive appeared to be holding the throne together under the bones, and I dragged my eyes from the unnerving thing to the other chair.

As fierce as the throne made from skulls was, the second throne was almost scarier. The whole thing appeared to be made of something that looked like thick barbed wire in the form of rose vines. Large metal roses with sharp, jagged edges made up the back and the seat of the chair, and I couldn't understand how anyone could ever sit on such a thing without slicing themselves to pieces. Lethal looking thorns jutted out of the tightly wound vines along the legs and arms and I shook my head with a long breath out. The two thrones were confusing and brutal to look at and they were making my nerves worse. I turned instead to the enormous flames licking up around the sides of the throne room.

'What's below us?' I asked Hecate.

'More fire,' she shrugged.

'Is there any way into this room without the magic transporty thing you do?'

'Not that I know of.'

'No, there's no other way. But if you think this is nice, you should see *my* throne room.'

I turned slowly, already knowing who had spoken. The arrogance was unmistakable.

'Zeus,' I said through gritted teeth. Hecate was bowing her head low and throwing me a pointed glare. But I wasn't going to bow my head. This was my opportunity to ensure I wouldn't be bullied by this jerk.

'You are in the presence of the Lord of the Gods. I suggest you show some deference,' he smirked. He was in the form of the blonde boy from the coffee shop.

'You owe me,' I hissed. 'You kidnapped me just to play stupid games with your brother. Until we're even you'll get no deference from me.'

I heard Hecate's intake of breath as Zeus's eyes flashed dark, and his surfer-guy build began to expand before me.

'I do believe that you need to be reminded of who I am, little mortal,' he said, his smile no longer reaching his eyes. Purple lightning began to fire around him, sizzling into the marble, but I held my ground. At this point, what did I have to lose? If I really did have to begin these Trials today, I wasn't going to start by being bullied.

I glared at him as the purple lightning flashed closer.

'Won't you be in trouble if you kill the girl you went to so much trouble to find?' I asked in a singsong voice.

'Trouble? Me? Nobody chastises Zeus!' He was three times my size now, approaching the high vaulted ceiling of the throne room, but I stayed put. My stomach was flipping and flopping as lightning screeched into the stone inches from my leather boots, but I managed to keep the flinches from showing on my face.

'Harm a single hair on her body and we'll find out once and for all which king is strongest,' hissed a voice, at the same time as my skin felt like it was being covered in ice. A smoky form shimmered into existence beside Zeus and tension literally crackled through the air. Then Zeus slowly began to shrink, the tension easing as his size decreased.

'I enjoy a woman who can stand up for herself,' Zeus said as he reached human size again. 'This might end up even more interesting than I had anticipated,' he grinned, a new, and unnerving look gleaming in his eyes. I ignored him, my gaze fixed on Hades. I wanted to see those eyes again, desperately. They had been the only thing I'd recognized here, the only thing that made some sort of sense since I'd arrived - even if I didn't know what they meant.

But all I could see were the suggestions of features, the hint of a mouth, or the tiniest flash of silver in the dark smoke. Nothing I could hold on to. He was staring back at me though, I could feel that much.

'We haven't been formally introduced,' I said, my mouth dry. 'I'm Persephone.'

There they were. For less than a second, and I almost missed it, but those silver orbs definitely flashed into existence.

'You shouldn't be here,' he said, his voice making me think of snakes.

'Yeah. I've heard. But I am, so...'

'You are human, and mortal, so you are highly unlikely to win the Trials. When they are over, you will be returned to New York.'

Relief washed through me, so strong my knees almost buckled. Hades' plan was the same as mine.

'If she survives them,' added Zeus, who was sauntering over to the thrones on the dais. A little wave of heat cut through the cold as tendrils of smoke danced out from Hades form.

'So I was right? You can't kill me? Or hurt me?' I asked Zeus, willing my confidence to build as my palms began to sweat. Sweat was my body's default reaction to any stress. Stupid body.

Zeus looked into my eyes as he waved his hands, and eleven other thrones appeared on the dais, the rose throne vanishing. He sank slowly into his own seat.

'Not during the Trials, no. And anyway, I don't want to hurt you. There are many other things I'd rather do with you...'

A stronger wave of heat blew over me, and I thought I saw Hades' chest solidify under the smoke for a second.

'Right,' I said, flexing my fingers. 'Well, in that case, I would like to take this opportunity to inform you that you are a colossal prick.'

Hecate made a slightly strangled coughing sound and I let my smile spread fully across my face. Something fierce leapt in Zeus's eyes, but I wasn't sure it was anger.

'Oh, brother Hades. I see why you liked this one. And I can see why it was so hard to let her go.'

'Enough!' Hades shouted, and the temperature ratcheted up even higher. 'Where are the others?' he hissed, and stalked towards the thrones, his smoky legs seeming to carry more weight than should be possible. I took a few long, controlled breaths. I'd done it. I'd stood up for myself. But I wasn't sure I'd made Zeus back off. In fact I had a horrible feeling I'd just made him *more* interested in me.

'Oh, I haven't summoned them yet,' smiled the Lord of the Gods, and snapped his fingers.

The room began to morph around me, the ground rumbling and bright flashes of white light disorientating me. I was moving lower, I was sure, the ground dropping so that I was in a circular pit, stopping when I was about ten feet below the rest of the room. The dais now wrapped around the edge of the pit, the gods appearing one by one on their thrones and peering down at me. I turned slowly, seeing three new faces on the opposite side of the pit, and a man in a white toga stood next to a huge iron dish. Hecate was still standing next to me in the pit and I looked at her.

'Those are the judges,' she said, without me having to ask. 'And he's the commentator. That's a flame dish, and we use them to send pictures to the rest of Olympus - like your TVs in the mortal world.'

As she spoke, gently flickering orange flames in the iron dish above us roared up, gleaming white hot, then vanished, replaced with an image of Hades' smoky form. I glanced at where the god really sat, in the throne made from skulls. A shiver took hold of me. He was staring featurelessly back at me.

'As you all now know, this is the last entrant in the Hades Trials,' he said, and I realized with a jolt that the image in the dish was speaking the same words. It was just like a camera was on him. 'There will be three rounds, each made up of three Trials. The current leader, Minthe, won five tokens. In order to beat her, Persephone,' his slithery voice stumbled slightly at my name and goosebumps covered my skin again, 'will need to get at least six to win. Defeat the Spartae skeleton.' He fell silent, then the commentator leapt to life, making me jump.

'Good day, Olympus! So there you have it, from the Lord of the Underworld himself. Can this last contestant beat the beloved Minthe to a spot on the Rose Throne? She's starting with an easy test, a Spartae skeleton. As you all know, the Hades Trials test the future queen in the four values that our divine gods hold most dear; Glory, Intelligence, Loyalty and Hospitality. All things the queen of the dead will need in abundance!'

He sounded like a TV presenter from my world, and I listened intently to his over-enthusiastic words. So this was a test of glory?

'Well, I have to say, this newcomer sure looks the part, but who is she? So far we know nothing about her history or powers, but no doubt more will be revealed as we watch her fight!'

I frowned.

'If I was already married to Hades, how come they don't know who I am?' I asked Hecate quietly.

'The gods wiped you from Olympian history. Only they, and a handful of lower gods from the underworld, like me, know you ever existed.'

'Right.' Wiped from history? Didn't that seem a little extreme? *What the hell had happened?* Curiosity burned deep inside me as I tried to imagine a life in this place, but I gave myself a mental shake. I was moving on, like Athena said. All that mattered was the future.

'I have to go now. Good luck,' Hecate said, a sincere look on her beautiful, angular face.

'Thanks,' I answered her.

Her eyes turned milky white as the air around her rippled, then she was gone. A suffocating sense of how alone I was washed over me immediately. A rumbling snapped my attention to the walls of the sunken pit I was in, and I watched as patterns began to push their way out of the marble, as though they were being carved before my eyes. The patterns were of vines, covered in grapes and leaves and twisting together as they spread across the wall until they met the place they'd started. Something about them was wrong though, and I moved closer to the stone to look.

Some of the vines didn't match up properly, like two pieces of a jigsaw that didn't go together. I reached out to touch one of the areas where the vines cut off bluntly and heard a clattering sound behind me.

'Persephone will have no crowd to cheer her on today, as is the rules for the first Trial. But this is where she will win or lose supporters,' sang the commentator, excitement in his young voice. 'Will she make short work of her first demon? Or will she meet an untimely end and hand Minthe the throne today?'

I glared up at him, until the clattering got louder and dust started to gather in a large ball on the other side of the pit. My stomach tightened, my muscles tensing as the dust swirled faster, hardening into something. I shifted my weight from foot to foot, my heart beginning to hammer hard in my chest. Movement caught my eye, and I realized more carvings were appearing on the walls, but deeper, and not the same color as the stone.

Weapons. They were weapons. Twenty feet to my left was a huge sword, held up securely in the marble vines as though birthed from the wall itself. I couldn't make out what was behind the still swirling mass of dust, but there was an axe on my right, blade gleaming. I turned quickly, and saw a flail behind me in the white vines. It had a short wooden handle with a chain coming out of the end, topped with a gleaming silver ball covered in four-inch sharp spikes. I reached for it, the stone vines crumbling as soon as I touched the weapon, then reforming behind it. It wasn't as heavy as I thought it would be, but my hands still shook as I hefted it experimentally. I swung it gently as I turned back to the dust, my relief that I could use it with just one hand vanishing when I took in what was before me.

NINE

The dust had dissipated, and in its place was what I could only assume was a Spartae skeleton. It looked like it had been aptly named. The skeleton's jaw clacked open and shut unnervingly as it looked at me, and I braced my wobbling legs. It was like a Halloween outfit come to life, with gleaming white bones and empty eye sockets. And it was lifting a sword and starting to move towards me. I swung the flail in my hand, trying to build up some speed, and as though sensing the danger the skeleton immediately broke into a run. Adrenaline flooded my body, my fight and flight instincts warring with each other inside me. I held my ground, raising the flail as it whirled around, careful to keep it a good distance from my own body. Thank the gods it was so light. My pathetic attempts in the gym wouldn't have granted me the ability to wield much more.

If Hecate said this was an easy demon to defeat, then I would defeat it easily, I told myself as my breaths came shorter and the skeleton raised its sword above its head with a hiss. I swung out clumsily with the flail just before the thing got close enough to bring the sword down, aware that my weapon had a longer reach. The spike covered ball crashed into the skeleton's rib cage, bones flying and clattering to the ground as the top half of its body tipped backwards, no longer attached to the bottom. The sword fell with it, the metal ringing loudly as it hit the marble. I held my breath as the flail swung back towards me, feeling my shoulder wrench slightly as I flicked the lethal ball away. I'd done it! But... Unease trickled through my brief elation as I glanced up at the silent gods, then round at the judges. Nobody was moving, their eyes fixed on the Spartae skeleton.

Too easy. That was way, way too easy, I thought, as I looked back at the demon.

Sure enough, the scattered bones were starting to vibrate gently, then one wooshed back towards the still standing legs. I took a breath as the bones all began to zoom back, the skeleton rebuilding itself before me.

OK, I thought, fear trickling through my pumped up body. How do I defeat a skeleton that can put itself back together? I thought about every horror and fantasy book I'd ever read. Smash up the bones? Set fire to it? Freeze it? I glanced around the pit quickly, looking for anything that might be more useful. The weapon I couldn't see earlier was a crossbow, I now saw, but I didn't think that would help. The flail seemed the best bet for smashing bones. As the skeleton bent to retrieve the sword from where it lay on the floor I made my mind up. With a roar I launched myself towards it, swinging the flail faster this time. I hurled the ball at the thing's skull, getting a kick of satisfaction as it toppled from its body with another hiss. Its bony arm reached for me and I brought the flail down through its forearm, hoping to splinter the bone, but it just severed at the joint and clattered to the floor. I moved backwards, out of the other arm's reach, then smashed my weapon down onto the bones on the floor as hard as I could. The jolt of the ball hitting the solid marble sent shockwaves through my arm and up to my shoulder, but when I lifted the ball the bones looked completely untouched.

'How-' I started, then pain blasted through my own skull and I staggered sideways as black spots appeared in front of my eyes. I felt cold bony fingers glance off my arm as I stumbled in confusion and realized foggily that I needed to move. The fucking thing had hit me, hard. My legs carried me across the small pit quickly, and when I turned back the Spartae skeletons' skull was whizzing back into it's rightful place at the top of its long backbone.

Shit. This was going to be harder than I thought. If bone smashing wasn't an option, what else was there? I flashed on Hecate's insistence that this was supposed to be easy for someone who couldn't fight. Glory, Intelligence, Loyalty and Hospitality. Those were the things I was being tested for, according to the irritating commentator. The skeleton lifted the sword again, his jaw clacking faster than before, the sound setting my own teeth on edge. I moved slowly along the wall and he rotated to follow me. Fear began to hammer against my rational thoughts, a desperation to switch off from this crazy fucking situation growing inside me. *Come on, Persephone,* I chided myself, blinking away the dizziness. *If this is real, you have to survive. If it isn't then you've nothing to lose. Sort your shit out, now.*

Loyalty and hospitality wouldn't help me here, but intelligence... Maybe this wasn't about fighting, but about being smart. I turned quickly to the wall, and heard the demon begin to move, his bony feet clacking on the marble floor. I only had seconds.

I raked my eyes over the marble until I spotted a part of

the vine pattern that didn't match up. I reached out and ran my fingers over the marble. It was warm, and when I pushed harder, I realized it was supple too. But that was all I had time to find out, and I leapt to the side just as the sword came down where I had been stood. I was faster than the skeleton was though, and I sprinted to the other side of the pit without looking back. I moved as fast as I could, scanning the walls for anywhere the vines were broken, then pulling the weird warm marble into shape, re-attaching them. As soon as the blunt ends met up the vines turned hard and cold.

I was sure I was doing the right thing, reconnecting the pattern. After all, there was nothing else in the pit, other than the demon. I was only just keeping out of its reach, having to scan the wall fast and likely missing loads, but I was making progress.

After a few laps of the room I was pretty sure I'd got all of them, and had so far avoided the blows from the demon's sword, but nothing had happened. There must be more to find, I thought, racing just ahead of the clacking footsteps as I scanned the stone desperately. My legs were beginning to tire, my breath becoming harder to catch, and my arm that still held the flail was aching.

'Aha!' I shouted in a surge of excitement as I spotted two blunt pieces of vine just a few inches off the floor. I ducked down to fix them, almost skidding as my momentum carried me fast across the marble. I knew as I dropped that I was putting myself in a seriously vulnerable position, and my heart was pounding as I tweaked the vines into place. The sword came whistling past my ear and I held my breath as I launched myself back up and away, already running, when an echoing rumble started. Without slowing I put my back to the wall, a weird side run taking over my legs until I saw that the skeleton had stilled. I slowed suspiciously, every muscle in my body humming. Had I done whatever I was supposed to? Would the demon just crumble back to dust now?

Suddenly a hole began to appear in the middle of the pit, tiny at first, then growing fast. Huge flames in many colors, the same as the ones that licked up around the side of the epic throne room, shot up through the hole as it finally stopped growing. My stomach lurched as heat washed over me. There was now a thirty-foot hole leading to a flaming abyss taking up most of the pit I was in.

Sure, I now had a way to kill the skeleton - there was no way it would survive falling into that.

But nor would I.

Through the flames I saw the skeleton drop its sword on the marble with a clang and I scowled. Why would it do that? Then its hollow eye sockets fixed on my face and my breath hitched. It was coming for me. I fleetingly considered trying to climb out of the pit, but the vine pattern had sunk back into the wall, the other weapons vanishing too, leaving the surface smooth. I was trapped. The skeleton was running now, close to the wall and away from the hole. It was faster without the heavy sword, I realized. Running away would be pointless as I was guessing undead skeletons didn't get tired, and I was already exhausted.

That meant it was now or never. I looked at the flail in my hand. There was no way I was giving my own weapon up.

Banking on the assumption that skeletons weren't smart, I took a deep breath and stepped closer to the flaming hole, turning my back to it and swinging the spiked ball fast. I could feel my leather clothing heat up as I got as close as I dared. Looking to my right I saw the demon closing in and I swallowed hard.

Stand your ground, Persephone. Stand your fucking ground.

The skeleton turned sharply and I sent a silent prayer of thanks to anyone listening. I'd been right, it was too stupid to be cautious. It was coming straight for me.

As the demon reached me it threw both arms out, ready to push me but I ducked and threw myself to the side, flinging the flail out towards it. The weapon connected, and I heard clattering bones as I span back around. I'd only knocked off one arm, and the bits of bone were already vibrating on the floor. I didn't hesitate, flailing the weapon back at the skeleton's head. It raised its other arm to block my blow, and the ball took the thing's wrist out. I kicked out as high as I could with my foot, my stomach lurching as I felt my leather boots connect with hard bone, but the skeleton barely budged. The fallen bones were whizzing back towards it now and panic took over. With a roar, I dropped my shoulder and barreled into its rib cage.

Mercifully, it fell. But so did I. I landed on the things chest, feeling a brief satisfaction as I felt and heard ribs give way under me, then pure terror as I rolled away and almost fell straight off the edge of the pit. A purple flame leapt up beside me and for a split second my limbs froze, fear making me unable to move. The thought of falling forever swamped my thoughts, paralyzing me. Then a voice sounded in my head out of nowhere.

You have about ten seconds before that thing puts itself back together. Move, now.

It was a male voice, and unbidden, my limbs twitched,

then I was scrambling to my knees, moving away from the ledge as fast as possible. When I was a foot away I pushed myself to my feet, then turned. The skeleton's rib cage had collapsed when I'd fallen on it, its limbs scattered on the marble floor. I kicked out hard at any bit of bone I could reach with my feet, sending them flying into the flaming abyss. The demon's skull hissed as more and more bits went shooting off the edge, its detached arms flailing on the ground as I finally reached its skull. Hope shot through me as I looked down at the hollow black eye sockets. I'd won, I thought, as I gathered the last of my energy and punted the skull off the edge as hard as I could.

TEN

'Well how about that folks! Not the classiest fight we've seen, but she got the job done!' The commentator's voice boomed across the pit as the rumbling started again. The hole was closing, and the floor was rising. I threw my arms out to the side to steady myself, panting for breath as adrenaline still fizzed through me. I looked up at the gods, where Hermes and Dionysus were clapping enthusiastically, Athena and Aphrodite more slowly. The others just stared at me, Hades' smoky form flickering and Zeus's eyes gleaming.

'Now to the judges to find out what she scored!' I turned as the floor finally stopped moving, now level with the three men in grand seats. 'Radamanthus?' beamed the commentator. The man on the left, chubby and cheerful-looking, with dark bushy beard and eyebrows, smiled at me.

'One token,' he said.

'Aeacus?' The commentator asked. The second man, skin so pale it was almost blue, spoke in a cold voice, and didn't meet my eyes.

'One token,' he said.

'And Minos?' The last man, with dark skin and a shining bald head, looked intently at me. His eyes were dark too, but bright with intelligence, and I felt like he was seeing far more of me than I was comfortable with.

'One token,' he said eventually.

'The judges are agreed! One token for Persephone. And what shall your tokens be, young lady?'

Everybody looked at me.

'What?' I stammered, and the commentator gave me a patronizing smile that made me want to punch him on the nose.

'You get to choose your tokens. What would you like to win?'

'Do I get to keep them?'

'Yes.'

'Seeds,' I said, without pause.

'Seeds?' repeated the commentator, his voice shocked and his eyebrows almost lost to his hairline. 'You want seeds?' A smile twitched on his mouth and I glared at him.

'She shall have pomegranate seeds,' said Minos, and the commentator bowed to him, hiding his smile quickly.

'Of course she shall,' he said deferentially. The air rippled in front of me, then a box appeared, floating in midair. It looked like a long ring box and when I reached for it with shaking hands, the lid popped open. Inside was a series of little chambers, and in the first, suspended in some sort of gel, was a bright red pomegranate seed.

'Er, thanks,' I said. It wasn't quite what I'd hoped for when I'd asked for seeds, but I hadn't expected a reward at all, so I dropped my flail on the floor with a clatter and closed the box. Maybe they would produce something magnificent when I got back to New York. Something 'out of this world'. I clung to that idea as I heaved a few deep breaths. *I'd just defeated a demon skeleton.*

'You're welcome, Persephone,' said Minos, then the air in front of the judges rippled and they vanished.

'We'll see you for the next Trial in three days, and boy is it a good one! Persephone will have her hospitality tested to its limits very soon.' The commentator winked, then he vanished too.

'Hospitality? What am I supposed to do, have everyone over for dinner?' I said, turning back to the gods. A wave of power rocked over me, and I dropped to one knee without even thinking about it, bowing my head.

'Remember your place, girl,' I heard Poseidon say.

'Sorry,' I mumbled. Adrenaline and a sense of achievement were surging through me. I'd just kicked a demon skeleton into a multi-colored fire pit. This place was freaking crazy, but I'd done it. I'd defeated a demon.

'Now, we must assign your guard. Then you may rest, and prepare for the next Trial,' said Athena, and I raised my head to look at her.

'I'd like to throw in an option, if I may?' drawled Dionysus, and eleven heads snapped to look at him.

'Why?' asked Zeus, frowning.

'Why not?' he shrugged, a lazy smile on his face. He was wearing an open white shirt and tight black leather trousers, with huge Doc Martin boots that weren't laced up properly. The longer I looked at him, the more desperately I wanted to get steaming drunk with him.

'There are many reasons why not,' Zeus said stiffly, and turned back to me. A thought occurred to me at his words. Why wasn't Zeus putting a guard in? As if sensing my question he smiled at me.

'I don't need to assign a guard to you, dear little Persy,'

he said, emphasizing the nickname he'd read on my name badge in what now seemed like a lifetime ago. 'I can come and see you myself whenever you like.'

A blast of heat pulsed out from the dais and Zeus gave Hades a sideways glance, his mouth curled in a smug sneer.

'Let's move on, please,' said Athena, and stood up. Her owl was absent now, but other than that she looked identical to when I'd met her earlier. 'There are four feathers behind you. Inspect each, then choose one.'

I turned around and sure enough, a grand desk had appeared behind me, and I could see feathers on it. I approached cautiously, setting down my seed box on the cherry-wood surface and picking up the first feather. It was almost as long as my forearm and a rich green color, with yellow edges. I ran my fingers gently down the soft edge, feeling pretty stupid. All the gods were sat behind me, watching me stroke a feather. I wished Hecate was back.

A trickle of cold suddenly tingled through my finger-tips, and I got a sudden sense of grandeur and power. My brows drew together as I peered at the feather. Maybe there was more to this than I thought. I put the green feather back and picked up the next one, a fierce, solid red. Angst and irritability immediately invaded my thoughts and I put the feather back quickly. I didn't think I needed that in my life. The next feather was silver and gold, and by far the prettiest one, though the smallest. That made me instantly suspicious and I handled it carefully. When I picked it up I was surprised to feel lighter suddenly, like there was a lot less to worry about in the world. Past holidays, vacations spent relaxing and reading filled my mind. Hmmm. I was still suspicious. That seemed a little too disarming. The last feather looked like something I'd pick up in Central Park. It was a gray-brown, with a dusting of gold along the edge the only thing making it less plain. But as soon as I picked it up, a chuckle bubbled from my lips. I had no idea what I thought was funny, but the longer I held the boring feather, the more amused I felt.

'This one,' I grinned, turning to the gods. Athena closed her eyes slowly, and Dionysus did a little fist pump.

'Good choice, Persy love,' he beamed at me. His accent sounded British.

'You're an idiot,' muttered Poseidon to him, shaking his head. My eyes flicked to Hades. Was he disappointed I hadn't chosen his feather? Did it even matter? If I was stuck here in his world, surely he could see where I was all the time anyway?

'You may regret making that decision so hastily,' said Athena levelly, 'but it was a fair choice.' I put the feather back on the desk and immediately realized she was right. It had been an impulse decision because the feather had made me smile. *Shit, I should have chosen the one that felt like power.* I picked up my seed box and turned back to the gods.

'What happens now?' I asked, addressing Athena as she was still standing up.

'Now you rest. You'll meet your guard and start training for the ball tomorrow.'

'Ball?'

'Yes. Your next Trial is to host a masquerade ball. And that will conclude the first round.'

I felt my jaw drop slightly and I forced my mouth shut again. I fished desperately for something to say, but the world flashed white and I wasn't there anymore.

~

'I wish people would stop freaking doing that,' I snapped, as the light cleared from my eyes and I looked around the bedroom I'd been in earlier.

'Yeah, annoying isn't it,' said a now familiar voice.

'Hecate!' I whirled to see her holding two huge tumblers out and grinning like a fool.

'Told you you could do it!' she sang, and handed me one of the glasses. I took it, and on her cue we downed the contents simultaneously. If I thought whatever I drank earlier burned, then this soothed. It was like drinking honey.

'My god, that's good. What is it?'

'Gods,' corrected Hecate. 'It's Nectar.'

'As in nectar and ambrosia?'

'Yeah, except if you drank ambrosia like that it would kill you. Until you get the ichor back in your veins, at least.'

'Ichor,' I said, cocking my head at her. 'That's gods' blood, right?'

'Yup. And you're full of all that icky red human shit now,' she said, and sat down on the bed. 'Well done. I can't believe you picked seeds as your token though. You're a fucking lunatic.'

'Er, thanks?' I said, sitting beside her. 'What's wrong with seeds?'

'Well, nothing, but here you are risking life and limb, and you decide seeds are your worthy reward? Are you not worth more than that?'

'I, erm, I didn't really think about it like that. I just said the first thing I wanted. Which was seeds.'

'The other contestants all picked precious stones, emeralds and sapphires and diamonds. But you... seeds. You're an enigma, Persy.' Her bright eyes were boring into mine and I looked away uncomfortably with a shrug.

'I think I picked the wrong feather too,' I said.

'Feather? Is that how they made you choose a guard?'

It turned out that only the Trial had been broadcast via the weird iron flame dishes, so Hecate hadn't seen the feather choice afterwards, so I told her about Dionysus's feather making me laugh and my stupid impulse decision.

'Well, you could have chosen worse. Hades guard would have been strict as hell, and Poseidon's even more dull. Athena's would have been best but you could be in for something pretty entertaining from Dionysus. Just hope it's not one those randy little sprites his realm is full of.'

'Randy sprites?' I asked, slightly alarmed.

'Yeah. Did they tell you anything about the next Trial?'

'Yeah. I'll be hosting a masquerade ball,' I said, scowling. Hecate's eyebrows shot up.

'Wow, really? They've brought that one out early,' she said thoughtfully.

'Do I literally just have to plan a party?' I asked, hopefully. She gave me a look as though I were a complete idiot.

'No, Persy. You have to host a ball for some of the most disgusting and dangerous folk in Olympus. They will try to ruin the party, mostly by trying to screw or kill each other. Occasionally both. And there's always a surprise twist, something horrendous for the host to try and rectify.'

'Well, it still sounds easier than killing a skeleton.'

'It's not. Trust me.'

'Oh.'

'We'll get some specialist help in on this one. I'll send Hedone to you tomorrow.'

'Hedone? Isn't she...' I racked my memory. 'Goddess of pleasure?'

'Yup, and party planner extraordinaire. You'll love her.'

'Right,' I said.

'In the meantime, get some sleep.'

'Is this my bedroom?' I asked, looking around the room.

'Erm, yeah.'

I paused before asking, 'Was it my bedroom before?'

'No. You slept with Hades, dummy.'

'Oh.' My feelings must have shown on my face because Hecate frowned at me.

'You don't like this room?'

I shook my head, feeling guilty for complaining to her but not seeing the point in lying.

'It's just hard not having a window,' I said. She regarded me a moment, then stood up.

'I'll see what I can do tomorrow.' I gave her a grateful smile.

'Thanks.'

'You're welcome.'

'Seriously, thanks for everything,' I said, trying to impress my sincerity into the words.

'You're welcome,' she repeated.

I was asleep within seconds of my head hitting the pillow, exhaustion completely taking me over. I expected to dream about murderous skeletons or mysterious and terrifying gods made of smoke, but instead I found myself in a garden. And it wasn't a normal garden. As somebody who spent hours of their waking life dreaming up gardens, I knew instantly that this one was not born of my brain. *So whose was it?*

. . .

It was stunning, I thought, as I wandered towards an epic water feature. The word 'fountain' didn't really do the structure justice. There was a large round pool, the stone the same shining white marble from the throne room, and in its center was a statue of a man on one knee, holding a globe on his back. I recalled the ancient myth about the Titan Atlas, who was made to hold up the heavens as a punishment by Zeus. Could that be what I was looking at? As I got closer I saw that the globe was not representing my earth, but was made up of hundreds of rings, interlocking to form the sphere. Gemstones glittered in the places where the rings overlapped, and water burst from them, shining the same color as the gem until they reached the clear, sparkling pool below. I drank in the sound of the running water, the feel of the cool breeze on my face, the smell of the primroses... I turned on the spot slowly, looking at the huge array of flowers in beds lining the hedged circumference of the garden. Not all these flowers should be able to grow together. Many needed totally different temperatures and soils to the ones they were blooming right next to. I frowned.

'I heard you chose seeds,' said a voice. A male voice. Was it the voice from the Trial? The one who had told me to get up, when I'd been frozen to the spot? I realized distractedly that I hadn't told Hecate about that.

'Who are you?' I asked, quietly. It felt wrong to speak loudly in a place as serene and beautiful as this.

'I'm your friend, Persephone. I remember you well.'

'Really?'

'Of course. The Queen of the Underworld is not easily forgotten.'

'Where are you?'

'All around you. I am the garden.'

I turned on the spot again.

'Am I dreaming?'

'Of course you are. But dreams are controlled by the gods too, Persephone. I heard you chose seeds.'

'Why does everyone care so much that I chose seeds?' I said, annoyance interrupting the intense soothing effect of the garden. Another gust of wind fluttered through my hair, carrying the scent of lavender. I inhaled deeply. I wanted to stay here.

'I admire your choice. You know, pomegranate seeds can be eaten.'

I frowned.

'I'd rather plant them.'

'Trust me, my Queen. You'd rather eat them.'

I woke with a start, sitting up abruptly in the dark. Disappointment and a deep sense of loss swamped me as I looked around at the dim bedroom, the only light coming from twinkling stars on the weird rock ceiling. It was pretty enough, but now I longed for fresh air, the scent of flowers, the sound of running water. What a weird dream. I was positive I hadn't created that garden, so whoever that voice belonged to must have. *Eat the pomegranate seed?* That was my hard-earned reward. I didn't think so. I shook my head to clear it, then lay back onto my pillows with a sigh. Everything about this place was weird. The sooner I lost the Trials and got back to New York, the better.

ELEVEN

The next time I opened my eyes the ceiling was giving off its weird daylight glow, the stars gone. What time was it? I made a mental note to ask Hecate how to keep time as I swung my legs out of bed. I was wearing a silky camisole top and matching shorts that I'd found in the wardrobe, and as weird as it was going to bed in what felt like someone else's clothes, they felt divine against my skin. I sat down at the dressing table and peered at my reflection. The make-up Hecate had put on me yesterday was gone, and my now white hair was hanging loose past my shoulders, only a slight curl left in it. But the tiny braids were still scattered throughout the bright locks. I gathered it all up into a ponytail without brushing it, and used a band on the dresser to secure it in a messy bun. My eyes still looked more green, and my cheekbones more angular. It was weird, and maybe just my imagination after defeating a demon skeleton yesterday, but I looked more fierce. More competent. Would Ted Hammond and all those brats at school have been so cruel if I'd looked like this back then?

Probably.

There was a knock at the door and I turned my head. How did they know I was awake? I scanned the room suspiciously. *What are you expecting to find, secret cameras? In a world that uses iron fire dishes instead of TVs? Get a grip, Persy. Just roll with the punches. You'll be home in no time.*

'Yes?' I called.

'Can I come in?' came a woman's voice from the other side of the door. It was a husky, sensual voice, and I immediately felt conscious of my silky PJs.

'Erm, yeah,' I said, standing up. The door creaked open and a voluptuous woman backed in, holding two steaming mugs. My lips parted involuntarily as she turned fully to me and smiled. She had thick dark hair that looked like it would be heaven to touch, deep laughing brown eyes that gleamed with fun, and lips that looked... well nothing like any lips I'd ever seen. There was no better word for them than kissable.

'Apparently humans are into coffee in the morning,' she said, and passed me a mug with a smile. 'I'm Hedone.'

'Hi,' I stammered. 'I'm Persephone.' She nodded and sat down on the end of my bed, cupping the mug.

'Hecate is busy most of today, so she asked me to start prepping you for the masquerade ball.'

'Do you, er, help everyone out?'

She gave a tinkling laugh.

'No. But I think you're rather special, and I owe Hecate a favor.'

'Why do you think I'm special?' I asked, taking a small sip of coffee. It was utterly amazing, way better than anything we served at Easy Espresso.

'A couple reasons. I have a soft spot for humans, but more than that, I've not long taken part in some Trials of my own.' Her eyes darkened, her husky voice hardening a little.

'The Immortality Trials. They were tough, and I would like to help an underdog,' she said, looking at me.

'Underdog, huh,' I sighed, sitting down too. I wondered if Hedone was one of the few who knew I'd supposedly already been married to Hades. I didn't want to tell her if I wasn't supposed to, although it was almost impossible not to trust her. *That was her power though. Goddess of pleasure, remember?*

'Did you win your Trials?' I asked her.

'I'd rather not talk about it,' she said simply. 'Now, we have a lot to go over. Hecate said you needed some help with your clothes and make-up, then there's Olympian etiquette to cover, charm and graciousness after that, and we've all the logistics of the ball to plan. We'll need to look at the guest list, and try to anticipate what problems might be thrown your way. You'll also be having combat lessons.'

'For the ball?'

'Of course.'

'Why would I need to fight at a ball?'

'This is no ordinary ball, Persephone,' she said.

'Call me Persy,' I told her automatically. She smiled.

'This is a test to see if you are capable of holding the position of Queen of the Underworld. Politics and combat go hand-in-hand. You need to prove your ability to hold your own, support your husband and represent your realm. Social events have been at the root of almost every serious fight between the gods for centuries. They are of the utmost importance.'

'Oh,' I said. It kind of made sense that one of the Trials would be a party when she put it like that. 'That doesn't really sound like my sort of thing.'

'No? You don't like parties?'

'Or politics. I like gardens.'

Her pretty face creased into a frown.

'You're in the wrong place then,' she said. 'There aren't many gardens in Virgo.'

My heart sank as she spoke. I mean, I'd already suspected as much, but it still sucked to hear it.

'Are there any plants anywhere?'

'To be honest, I don't spend much time here, apart from with Morpheus, but I'll ask him to come and see you. He knows this place like back of his hand. Now, let's teach you how to do something better than...' she paused and looked at my hair with an awkward frown, 'well, better than that.'

'Will you show me how to do whatever Hecate did with my eyes that made them super green?' I asked her, a little over-eagerly. Hedone gave a tinkling chuckle.

'I think we may make a party-goer out of you yet,' she grinned.

We spent three full hours in the windowless bedroom, going over how to get fine black lines drawn around my eyes, creating fuller looking lips with tiny crayons, and how to get a gentle curl set into my white hair. At home I would never have allowed myself to spend so much time on such things. I mean, it wasn't like I left my apartment looking like a bag of shit, I always found time to swipe on a bit of mascara and make my cheeks a little less pale, but I'd never commit- ted this much time to learning how to make myself look good. I'd once watched an online video tutorial for French braiding but I'd only lasted ten minutes before I wanted to throw my laptop out of the window, screaming about impos- sible fucking hairstyles. But Hedone made it easy to learn somehow.

'There you go,' she said, as I secured the last piece of what I now knew was called a 'crown braid' to my head. It was essentially a plait that kept my hair back from my face more stylishly and securely than my crappy bun. It reminded me of Athena's and I loved it. 'I told you you could do it.'

I beamed at her, aware that I looked like a small child receiving praise, but not really caring.

'What's next?'

'Lunch, but not with me,' she answered, tweaking my braid slightly. 'I have to go now.'

Unease at being left alone skittered through me.

'OK. Well, thanks for all your help.'

'That's OK. I'll be back this evening to go through feasting etiquette.'

'Does that mean we'll be eating a feast?' I asked hopefully.

'Yes. So go easy on lunch. See you later,' she said, and let herself out of my room, closing the door behind her.

At least she didn't do the stupid bright-light vanishing thing, I thought, looking in the mirror. What was I going to do now? I stood up and looked at the wardrobe, deciding I should probably get dressed.

Just as I was deciding between a red pantsuit type get up with a low neckline, and the green dress I'd worn yesterday, a small excitable voice sounded behind me.

'Definitely the red one.' I span around quickly, nearly dropping both outfits in surprise.

A gnome was standing on my bedroom floor, completely naked, grinning up at me.

'Who the hell are you?!'

'Skoptolis, at your service,' he bowed low, bending his three foot frame in half.

'At my service?'

'Well, technically, I'm here to guard you. I've no idea what from, but it beats what I was doing before.'

'You're my guard?' I gaped at the naked gnome. He had twinkling amber eyes, thick dark hair in a mess on top of his head with a matching beard, and massive feet. I did my best to avoid seeing if his other extremities were as large, but it was somewhat hard not to look.

'I sure am,' he said, rocking on his heels.

'Could you put some clothes on?'

'Nope.'

'Please?'

'No can do. Not allowed.'

'You're not allowed to wear clothes? Why not?'

'Dunno. Is it this that's causing the issue?' He thrust his hips forward, flicking himself at me and I spluttered as my cheeks reddened.

'Yes!'

'Ah. Does this help?' With a little pop, the gnome vanished, replaced by a dog. It was a small, terrier type dog, the same color as the gnome's hair had been, and its amber eyes still gleamed with trouble.

'Skop...' I tried to remember the name he had told me.

'*Skoptolis,*' said a voice inside my head. This time I did drop the clothes in surprise at hearing its voice inside my skull. '*Hello?*' the voice said again, and I stared down at the dog wriggling out from under the green dress I'd just dropped on top of him. '*Is this better?*' He wagged his tail.

'Yes,' I said slowly, staring at him. 'But...'

'*If you want me to stay in an animal form, then I'll have to talk to you like this.*'

'It's weird,' I said, frowning. 'You're in my head.'

'*Then I'll go back to my normal form-*' he started, but I waved my hands.

'No! No, stay like that, please.' I'd rather a wagging tail than a wagging gnome knob. 'What are you?' I asked him.

'*A kobaloi.*'

'Are you, by any chance, a randy sprite?'

'*I have my moments,*' he answered, tail wagging faster as he leapt up onto the bed beside me. I automatically reached out to stroke his fur, then paused. Was that weird? He's not actually a dog, he's a naked, hairy gnome, I reminded myself. '*If you put that red thing on, you'll find out just how randy I can be.*' I snatched my hand back.

'Then I'll go with the green,' I muttered, scooping the clothes up off the floor as I stood up. I strode to the wash-room with the green dress, and heard Skoptolis jump to the floor behind me. 'Erm, where are you going?' I said, turning to him.

'*I have to guard you.*'

'In my own bathroom?'

'*Yup.*'

'No way.' The dog wagged its tail faster as I glared into his eyes.

'*But you've seen all my bits and bobs,*' he protested, his mental voice still light and laughing, like that damned feather I'd chosen.

'I don't care, you're not seeing mine!' I exclaimed.

'*Please? I bet they're really nice.*'

I rolled my eyes.

'Not a fucking chance,' I said sternly. 'Now wait here, you pervert.'

'*You can call me Skop,*' he said, tail still wagging furiously.

'Whatever,' I grumbled and slammed the door shut behind me.

I stepped back out of my washroom in the green dress a few minutes later, and jumped when I saw Hecate sitting on the edge of my bed and scowling at Skop, who was back in naked gnome form.

'Dionysus is a jerk,' she said, looking up at me.

'Let me guess,' I grinned. 'Don't tell him you said that.'

'Exactly,' she answered, with another grimace at Skop.

'I thought we'd agreed on something furry,' I said to him.

'I can make this furry if you want,' he beamed, reaching down.

'Put that the fuck away!' snapped Hecate, and the kobaloi gave an infectious giggle, before shifting back into dog form. 'What was that drunken idiot thinking, sending you a kobaloi as a guard?' she said, shaking her head.

He was thinking that you were far more likely to need cheering up than guarding, Skop said in my head, and I couldn't help but warm to him, and Dionysus, a little.

'Who knows,' I shrugged. 'I still don't know why I need a guard at all.'

'Me either. Anyway, I have good news.' I quirked an eyebrow at her as she clapped her hands together. 'I have convinced Hades to give you a new room. A new room, above ground.'

Gratitude hit me all in a rush and I flung my arms around Hecate without thinking. She gave an awkward squeak. 'There's a catch!' I let go and narrowed my eyes at her. 'It's not normal for contestants to be given the finest rooms in the Underworld. So you're going to need to earn it. Publicly. To avoid awkward questions.'

'Right,' I said, slowly.

'There will be another Trial. This evening. If you win, you can have the new room.'

'OK. Sounds fair,' I said, anxiety and anticipation skittering through me.

'Also, you have to have lunch with Hades.' She spoke so fast I almost didn't catch her words.

'What?' My stomach twisted as I gaped at her. 'When?'

'Now. Have fun!' she said, and the world flashed white once more.

TWELVE

'Damn Hecate,' I hissed, as I gazed around at the room I was in, heart racing as I tried to take it in. It reminded me of a church, massive vaulted ceilings stretching above me, all made from white marble. Intricate weaving patterns ran down the stone everywhere, depicting vines and plants and flowers, butterflies flitting amongst everything. Huge drapes, at least twenty feet tall, lined the two longest sides of the room. In the center was a large table laid for two, next to a circular raised platform. The platform was empty and something about it seemed wrong. Really wrong.

I stepped closer to it, frowning as a hollow feeling spread through my gut, something akin to grief pulling at me. Why would an empty platform make me feel such a sense of loss? Giving up on trying to work out the unsettling feeling, I turned to the table. There was nothing remarkable about it, except that it was a little large for two and dressed beautifully. There, however, something remarkable about the two chairs drawn up to it. Just like the grand thrones I had seen in the fiery throne room, these were decorated with skulls and roses. But where the thrones were bold and intimidating, these were elegant and stunning. And even more interestingly, they both had skulls *and* roses carved into the rich mahogany wood. The vines of the roses twisted around the skulls seamlessly on both chairs, and something about the pattern felt oddly satisfying. The two elements were drawn together perfectly, displaying the angry skulls and the fierce roses as equally dangerous and beautiful. They were nothing like the angry thrones.

As I reached out to touch the wood of the closest chair, a voice spoke sharply behind me.

'How did you get in here?'

I whirled around, starting at the words, then feeling a violent shiver rock though me as I saw the smoky form of Hades.

'Hecate sent me here. With the white-light-flashy thing you all do,' I said too quickly, trying to swallow the fear that leapt up inside me. 'I assumed you were expecting me.'

He let out a sigh, the smoke rippling around him.

'That woman needs to learn to meddle less.'

'Oh. Should I go?' I asked hopefully. The smoke rippled, and I caught the briefest flash of silver eyes.

'You shouldn't be here at all.'

'I didn't ask to be,' I snapped, unable to help myself. 'Why would I want to be in a place with no outside?' The smoky form rippled again.

'The Underworld is no place for you.' His voice was cold and harsh.

'Then send me home,' I said, my palms suddenly sweating at the thought that he could actually send me back. *Please, please send me home.*

'I can't,' he hissed, and the temperature suddenly shot up. 'My bully of a brother has spoken.' At the word bully, my fear receded slightly, and I cocked my head. Hades felt bullied? That couldn't be right. How could a king be bullied?

'Why don't you stand up to him?' I asked, the brazen words almost failing me as I spoke them. The temperature soared again as smoke billowed from him.

'You think I haven't tried that?' he said loudly, and images of fire began to lick at my mind, the iron tang of blood creeping onto my tongue.

'Please, please don't!' I begged, hearing and hating the fear in my voice, but not able to hide it. 'Not again.'

The fear lessened immediately, the images vanishing as the room cooled.

'This is no place for humans,' Hades snapped. 'You are likely to get yourself killed here.'

'You mean you're likely to scare me to death!' I snapped back, my nerves frayed. 'How the hell am I supposed to have lunch with you if you frighten the shit out of me every time I ask you something you don't like?'

The smoke rippled.

'Lunch?'

'That's what Hecate said.' My head was starting to pound. I'd only met the man twice and I already hated being around him.

'That infernal woman,' Hades muttered. There was a long silence, then he spoke. 'Are you hungry?'

'No,' I lied. 'You can just send me back to my room.' He paused before answering.

'I'm told you don't like your new room.'

New room? Hecate's word flicked into my head. *'You used to share a room with Hades, dummy.'* How? How had I ever shared a room with that thing? Even if you took the fact that he was made of smoke out of the equation, as far as

I could tell he had no personality whatsoever, let alone a sense of humor. Plus he was terrifying. I prayed he wouldn't mention the fact that we were supposedly married once.

'It's very nice, but there aren't any windows. I spend most of my time outside, back at home,' I said, as politely as I could manage.

'There is an outside here,' he said curtly, and I noticed the hissing sound had lessened in his voice.

'Really?' He raised a smoky hand, and the drapes along each side of the room withdrew slowly, and my breath caught in my throat. *Sunlight.* I hurried to the glass windows that had been hidden behind the fabric, and recoiled slightly. The land beyond was completely barren. Cracked, dry earth stretched for miles, and other than a few bare stubborn trees, nothing lived.

'What happened?' I breathed.

'Nothing will grow,' he said bluntly. 'But I believe it still counts as 'outside'. What is that?' I turned to him as he asked the question, and saw his smoky arm pointing towards my feet. I looked down and blinked as I saw Skop, sitting still and blinking back up at me.

'That's my new guard.'

'It's a kobaloi. Why would you need a kobaloi as a guard? All they do is play tricks on people and try to screw everything,' he said. Skop's tail wagged and a smile sprang unbidden to my lips.

'Apparently Dionysus was under the impression that I needed entertainment more than guarding,' I said.

'He was wrong.' I took a deep breath. Hades thought I needed a guard too? Some of the iciness had left his voice, and the addition of the, albeit faint, sunlight to the room was helping to ease my racing pulse. I gathered my courage, deciding to try to get whatever information I could out of the man I was supposed to have once liked enough to marry.

'Will you tell me why I need a guard?'

'No.'

'Am I in danger, or is Poseidon right, am I the one who's dangerous?' I pushed.

'Neither.'

I decided to change tack. Hades hadn't scared me for a full three minutes now, and I was feeling bolder the longer we spoke.

'Why does the temperature change when you're angry? Why is it cold sometimes and hot others?'

'That's enough questions.'

'No it's not! I know nothing about this world, surely I deserve a few harmless questions answered?'

'Deserve?' He rippled.

'Yes, *deserve*. Do I need to remind you that I've been abducted to the freaking Underworld and made to fight demons for a life I don't understand?'

The smoke form contracted quickly, almost turning solid but not quite. There was long silence, and my heart began to hammer again. Had I gone too far?

'It only gets hot when I haven't got control of my temper,' Hades said suddenly, and I was sure the hissing sound had gone from his voice completely. 'If I'm scaring on purpose, it's cold.'

My eyes snapped to where I knew his were. *He was answering me.*

'Are you made of smoke deliberately?' I asked, quickly, as though I needed to get all my questions in before he changed his mind.

'Yes.'

'Why?'

'I don't want people to know what I look like.'

'Why not?'

'I'm the Lord of the Dead.'

'That's not an answer,' I said, cocking my head at him and scowling.

'Yes, it is.'

'No, it's not. Are you trying to be more scary?'

'No. I'm trying to-' he cut off abruptly. 'I don't need to tell you this,' he said. His voice was definitely different now, deep and rich where it had been cold and scratchy. I took a long breath, and went for the question I most wanted to ask him, almost hoping he would say no.

'Can I see your eyes?'

'No,' he said, but the word was soft.

'Please?' I stepped towards him, staring into his smoky, featureless face.

'Why do you want to see them?' he asked.

'Because... When I saw them yesterday, I knew I wasn't dreaming. I knew this was real,' I said, knowing I was telling him too much, but not able to stop myself. 'They're the only thing I recognize in this world.'

Hades' form flashed, and suddenly, there they were. Those intense, beautiful silver eyes. But they were filled with sadness, and pain so evident that my breath caught.

In under a second they were gone again, and I let out my breath slowly. The desire to help him, to make him happy, to fix whatever made him so intensely sad was overwhelming me. I scrabbled for something to say but Hades spoke first.

'You must leave. I'll tell Hecate not to plan something so stupid again,' he said, the hiss back in his voice. Coldness washed over my skin, and I didn't know if it was his power or my own emotions.

'But-' I started, but he cut me off, his voice making me think of snakes when I didn't want to. I wanted to hold onto that emotion, that feeling of intensity. *I wanted to help him.* 'Do not talk to me again. You will not be here much longer.'

Anger cut through my confusion, as my feelings were doused out instantly. One minute he was making me feel all this overwhelming emotional crap, the next he was being a dick to me?

'I hope not,' I snapped.

'Lose the Trials, then leave my realm,' he said, his tone hard and arrogant and cold. Something ragged and desperate gnawed at my gut, but my conflicting feelings were resolving themselves as anger.

'With pleasure,' I spat, glaring at him.

THIRTEEN

'Well, *that was rude,*' said Skop as I threw myself
down on my bed.

'I wish they'd stop flashing me about all over the fucking
place,' I fumed. 'Why can't they just use doors and stairs like
normal fucking people?'

'*I like it when you swear,*' Skop said as he jumped up
beside me. '*Feisty women are just my type.*'

'Not now, Skop. I am seriously not in the mood. I
thought you were here to cheer me up.'

'*I am. Would you like me to take a shit in one of his
shoes?*'

A bark of laughter escaped my lips.

'Very much, but I'm not even sure he wears shoes. He's
made of smoke.'

'*Nah, he's got clothes on under there.*' I raised my
eyebrows at the dog.

'You can see through his smoke?'

'*Yeah.*'

'What does he look like?' I hated myself for asking, but I
was incredibly curious.

'*I'm mostly into women, but he's pretty tasty.*'

'Right,' I said, rolling my eyes.

'*You'll see him soon enough,*' Skop said, trotting about in a little circle on the covers, then settling down in a tight ball.

'I doubt that. He just told me never to talk to him again.'

'*Which is angry-man-god-speak for: I'd very much like to have sex with you.*'

'Don't be ridiculous,' I said, but a frisson of something skittered through my core at his words. *Smoke. He's made of smoke, fills your head with dead people and has just demonstrated that he's a total dick. Do not go there.*

Hades was definitely one bad boy too far.

I spent the next half an hour trying to learn how to talk to Skop in my head, like he did to me. I had to project the words I was thinking to him, which was harder than it sounded. After a while though, I started to get the hang of it.

'Will I be able to talk to everyone like this?' I asked him silently.

'*Nope, only sprites, magical objects you've bonded with, or powerful beings.*'

'What about Hecate?'

'*I dunno, you'll have to ask her.*'

As if on cue, there was a knock at the door and it swung open before I could answer.

'Speak of the devil,' I muttered, as Hecate strode into the room, a large tray laden with sandwiches in her arms.

'I am so, so sorry,' she said, then frowned. 'The devil? Isn't that what you call Hades in your world?'

I gulped.

'Yes. And you sent me for lunch with him without even telling him!'

'I know, I know, I thought it was a good idea for you two to catch up!'

'Well, it wasn't.'

'Tell me about it. I've just had my ass handed to me. I'm surprised I didn't get demoted,' she said, blowing out a sigh and setting the tray down. 'You look smoking hot by the way. Love your hair like that.'

Once I'd forgiven Hecate for her misguided attempts at my marital reconciliation, I got changed into leather fighting garb and she took me to where I would be learning combat. Mercifully, we did use stairs and doors to reach the training hall, the maze of blue-torch-lit tunnels rendering me lost in a matter of minutes.

'Can you remember how to get back if I ever get lost?' I silently asked Skop, trotting along at my side.

'*Course I can,*' he told me cheerfully.

The training hall was a large cavern, with the same daylight glowing ceiling as my room had, and a distinctly Greek vibe about it. Columns lined the walls, and the space behind them was filled with open crates. Hecate made her way straight to one in particular and began to rummage about.

'Did you bring the dagger I gave you?'

'Course,' I said, pulling it from the little sheath that was attached to my belt. The fighting clothes had straps and pouches and loops for weapons all over them.

'Good. Put it down over there and don't come anywhere near me with it.'

'OK,' I said, and laid it on the floor. Skop sniffed it, then trotted away quickly.

'Here,' Hecate said, straightening and holding out a similarly sized dagger. I went to her, taking it and peering into the other boxes. They were filled with weapons. 'The floor will absorb shock when you land on it, so you won't hurt yourself,' she said.

'When I land on it?'

'Yup,' she said, then out of nowhere kicked her leg out towards me. She managed to swipe both my ankles at the same time, and I yelped as I crashed to the floor, the dagger skittering away from me. She was right about the floor - it morphed beneath me into something spongy as soon as I landed, but my ass still hurt as I hit. 'Lesson number one: when you're in this room or any fighting pit, you need to be constantly vigilant.' I glared at her.

'You think you could have told me that before we came in here?'

She grinned at me.

'Lesson number two: nothing is fair.'

'Lesson number three: your teacher is an asshole,' said Skop in my head, and I suppressed a smirk.

Hecate spent the next hour teaching me how to use a dagger in close combat. It mostly involved hiding what your intentions were, or finding gaps to get the thing through, and in no time at all I was frustrated and tiring.

'I need to get back to running,' I panted, as Hecate whirled easily out of my grasp for the fifth time.

'Running? Being fast will only get you so far. We need to build up your tolerance, teach you how to take a few hits,' she said, dancing on the balls of her feet, her fists raised.

'Am I the only human in the Trials?' I asked her, mostly just to lengthen the pause and get some energy back.

'Yup.'

'What about the current winner, what's she?'

'A mountain nymph. She has earth powers.'

'Huh. So living underground's not a problem for her, I guess.' I thought about what I'd learned about my own supposed powers in the throne room. 'And my powers were to grow plants?'

'Kind of, yeah.'

'Kind of?'

'Stop asking questions, Persy,' she said, and danced towards me. I lifted my arms quickly into a defensive position, flicking my dagger out towards her.

It seemed my short break was over.

Eventually Hecate announced we'd done enough, and I should save my energy for that evening's Trial. I didn't know what energy she was referring to, I was wiped out. But when we returned to my room, Hecate produced some of the wine she'd given me when I'd first arrived.

'This will revitalize you,' she grinned, and poured us both glasses. 'We have an hour until the Trial.'

I drank some of the wine, immediately feeling more alive, more alert. Weird. Wine in my world dulled the senses.

After a while, we began to talk about what to expect in my next Trial. Hecate thought it was unlikely that I would be fighting again, so soon after the last fighting Trial, and it wasn't likely to be a hospitality test either, as that would be covered by the masquerade ball.

'So it's going to be intelligence or loyalty,' she mused. 'Or glory in a different way from fighting.'

'How do they test loyalty?' I asked. She looked sideways at me, an uneasy expression taking over her face.

'To be honest with you, Persy, that's usually the worst Trial. It'll be something you won't expect, and you won't always be told the world is watching.'

'So they'll try and trick me?'

'Yes.'

'And I won't even know I'm in a Trial?'

'Not necessarily. If there's no chance of you beating Minthe, they might let you off lightly.'

'Is Zeus designing all the Trials?' I asked, taking another sip of fortifying wine.

'No, all the Olympians are involved.'

'Do they get on with each other?'

Hecate snorted. 'Absolutely not.'

'What did Hades do to upset Zeus?' I asked the question casually, although I was burning to know the answer.

'He broke one of their very few sacred rules. He created new life in Olympus.'

'Life? But he's all about the dead.' I frowned at Hecate, and she cocked her head at me.

'Hades isn't like the other Olympians, Persy. There's far more to him than people see.'

I thought about those silver eyes, so full of emotion. But then the fire, the taste of blood, the smell of burning filled my head and I sighed.

'People only see smoke,' I said.

'He wasn't always like that,' she answered quietly. Something in my stomach tightened.

'What happened?' I asked, but deep in my gut, I already knew the answer.

'You.'

FOURTEEN

It seemed like no time at all until I was standing in front of the gods again, lined up on their thrones, building-sized flames dancing on either side of the floating throne room. I found my eyes fixed on Hades' smoky form, framed by the intimidating skulls making up the back of his huge seat. My palms began to sweat.

'Good day, Olympus!' the commentator's voice rang out suddenly, and I whirled to see him stood behind me.

'*Gods, he's irritating,*' said Skop's voice in my head, and I glanced down at him, sat by my feet.

'Agreed,' I told him silently.

'So today we have an unannounced Trial! As our little Persephone is human, and as such the only contender with no powers, she will be granted an additional reward if she completes this test.'

I pictured a room with windows, the idea of not being underground hardening my resolve. *Even if the view was of a barren wasteland.*

'*He wasn't always like this.*' Hecate's words replayed in my head. She had refused to say anymore, and my frustration at the tidbits of my past she was dropping was getting harder to suppress. Had I caused that wasteland outside too? What had I done?

'The Trial will be one of Glory,' beamed the commentator, and my pulse quickened. *Please not fighting, please no demons,* I prayed. 'Today we get to see Persephone face some of her fears,' he sang, and I felt my stomach lurch. My fears? How would they know what my fears were? If there was a single fucking spider involved, the room with windows would have to go, I thought, as anxiety ratcheted my temperature up. 'We will not be performing the Trial in the throne room though, so let us away to the chasm!'

'What?' I started to say, but that damn white light flashed again and everything was gone.

When the light cleared from my eyes, I swear my heart stopped beating for a moment. I was standing on the edge of a sheer drop. I stumbled backwards, my heart in my throat, as my knees began to wobble. I instinctively crouched down, to lower my center of gravity and to stop myself falling if my legs did actually give out. My head swam as vertigo began to swamp my working senses, nausea building as I stared over the edge of the drop. Whoever had spoken to me during the last trial had known I was too scared to move when I was flung to the edge of the hole in the fighting pit. They'd known I was terrified of heights. Was this their doing?

Get a grip. Get a grip. You're nowhere near the edge. You don't even know what you have to do yet. I forced myself to look around, taking deep breaths. I would be better once the adrenaline kicked in, and surged me past the initial fear.

I was outside. Actually outside, after days of wanting to be. There was nothing but dull beige sky above me, and the cliff edge I was crouching on was gouged out of the dry, dusty ground. There was another cliff opposite me, forming the other side of what I assumed the commentator had been referring to as the 'chasm' and all of the gods were there, lined up on their thrones, their faces too distant for me to make out expressions. I took more deep breaths, trying to feel a breeze or take comfort from the fact that I was no longer underground, but it felt no different. The air didn't move, the temperature was neither cool nor warm, there were no scents filling my nostrils. It didn't feel like any outside I was used to.

'Hecate? Skop?' I called hopefully.

'I'm on the other side,' said Skop in my head, and I was surprised by how much comfort I drew from hearing his voice.

'I'm scared of heights,' I said too quickly, as though expressing my fear might expel it. It didn't.

There was a long pause.

'Shit,' he said eventually.

'So here we are at the chasm! As you all know from previous contestant's Trials, this is a particularly nasty part of the underworld,' rang out the commentator's voice. 'Fall down there and you'll fall forever.' Bile rose in my throat. *Fall forever?* Being burned up by magic flames was one thing, but to fall forever? Goosebumps rose on my skin. I genuinely couldn't think of many things more terrifying.

'All Persephone needs to do to complete the Trial is get to the other side. Good luck!'

'What?' I exclaimed aloud. How the fuck was I supposed to get to the other side? There were no bridges, and the chasm was at least twenty meters across so jumping wasn't an option. Not that I'd have been able to jump over a freaking one meter gap, if it was over an endless void. 'How?' I yelled. I stared over at the gods, small in the distance. Nothing. I turned on the spot, staying crouched to stop my legs from shaking. The three judges were a few meters behind me, sitting on their grand seats and surrounded by empty, cracked land. 'Oh!' I said in surprise. None of them responded, their gazes boring into mine. I couldn't see anything else, so I turned back to the chasm. Maybe there was a bridge further down. But to find out, I would have to move closer to the edge.

I sat down, my insides shaking. For years and years I hadn't even been able to climb a step-ladder. It didn't matter how resolute or rational I was in my thoughts, my body betrayed my mind every time I was in a position where I could potentially fall. My legs and hands would shake, my breathing would become too shallow, and my vision would start to blur as dizziness took over.

You know what's coming, I told myself. *So you can deal with it. You can do this.*

I shuffled forwards on my butt, closer to the edge. I was only a foot away, so I didn't have to move far before my feet reached the precipice. I drew my knees up, and shuffled farther forward, forcing myself to take deep, slow breaths. I could see the chasm clearly now, and I looked left to right, trying to spot a bridge. There was nothing.

'*It's invisible,*' said Skop's voice in my head.

'What?'

'You're sort of at a disadvantage here, as you're not from Olympus and have no power, so I feel it's only fair I tell you. The bridge is invisible.'

'Then how the fuck am I supposed to cross it?' I hissed back in my mind.

'You have to feel for it. Then hope you walk straight. Or go across on your butt. That works too.'

'Feel for it? Are you fucking psychotic?' If my heart beat any faster I was sure I'd throw up. Or have a heart attack and drop down dead. Although I'd rather that than cross an invisible bridge over an endless fall. 'There is no fucking way I'm doing this.'

'Try.'

I started at the voice, my breath catching. *It wasn't Skop's.* It was the same one I'd heard in the last Trial.

'Who are you?' I yelled. I had no way of answering him in my head, as I couldn't project my thoughts at someone totally unknown.

'Reach forward, and feel for the bridge.'

'No! Did you tell them I was scared of heights?' My voice trembled.

'It's a foot to your left,' the voice continued, ignoring me.

My whole body was covered in sweat now, my back slick under the leather corset. I shuffled a foot to my left, my damp hands shaking as I put them flat on the ground and lifted myself sideways. Dust stuck to them as I drew them back around my knees.

'Good. Now, reach forward.'

I closed my eyes, but it did nothing to lessen the rising panic. *Come on, come on, come on. They're not going to let you die this early in the competition. Get a grip.* I shuffled backwards a little, then swiveled onto my belly, wishing I could hear anything other than my heart hammering against my ribs to distract me.

'This place sucks,' I hissed aloud, as I gripped the edge of the cliff with my sweaty hands. My head was too far back to see over the edge, which was exactly how I needed it to be. 'And I bet I look like a fucking idiot.' Memories flashed into my mind of me being sprawled on my front on the ground before, each time because some jerk had tripped me or pushed me, to make everyone else laugh. The thought sent a spurt of determination through me, and I moved my fingertips along the edge carefully. Then my right hand hit something hard. Slowly, I began to feel around, wriggling my way closer, but keeping an arm's length from the precipice. Skop had been right. There was a bridge. It was cool and smooth to touch, like plastic or metal and I could grip each edge with my hands. It couldn't be more than two feet wide. Very, very slowly, I drew myself up onto my elbows and knees, still gripping the edges of the bridge so I didn't lose it, and keeping my eyes squeezed shut. The muscles in my thighs were vibrating, and another wave of dizziness crashed over me as I inhaled deeply. *You've worked yourself up into this mess of nerves,* I scolded myself. *Just get on with it. You're holding the edges of the bridge, you won't fall off. Just crawl across. Olympus is watching.*

I moved one knee forward, my stomach lurching as I did so. My survival instincts were begging me to open my eyes, but common sense and fear kept them closed. It was an *invisible* bridge. There was no way I wanted to look down as I did this. I slid one shaking hand along the edge of the bridge, my skin slick against the material. I pushed gently, testing my weight. It felt solid. I let out a long breath, then repeated the movement on my other side. Knee forward, hand forward. Again. And again. *I could do this.*

And I probably could have, if my traitorous eyes hadn't flickered open.

Black dots instantly invaded my vision as the image before me swam and warped. Icy cold fear clamped onto my muscles as I stared down into black nothingness, the sides of the rocky chasm stretching on endlessly beneath me. Fresh nausea swamped my insides and I couldn't think straight. *Get off the bridge, get off the bridge, get off the bridge.* Over and over the words sang through my head, drowning out anything else. I felt my right leg spasm and jerk, and pure terror bit into me as my right hip collapsed. I had no idea how far across the bridge I'd got, blind panic obliterating facts as my body began to shut down. Pain lanced through my head as I crumpled onto the bridge and my chin banged into the hard material. I barely registered the taste of blood as I flung my arms around the bridge, squeezing my eyes closed again as they filled with tears of fright.

'Persephone! Go back the way you came, you're not far!' Skop's alarmed voice rang in my mind and I focused on his words. *You're not far.* I forced my shaking, numb legs back up, not caring one jot how I must look with my front half wrapped around an invisible bridge, shoving my butt in the air. *'That's it, you're doing great.'* I began to shuffle backwards, one painstaking inch at a time, my hands shaking so badly I could barely use them. *'You're almost there, your legs are off the bridge now,'* Skop said, his voice strained but clear.

When my hands hit a solid barrier, I knew I'd reached the cliff. Painstakingly slowly, I unwrapped the fingers of my left hand from the bridge, then did the same with the other. Tears were streaming down my cheeks as I held my breath, straightened and opened my eyes. *I was off the bridge.* I scrambled backwards, far away from the edge, and looked across at the gods through tear-blurred vision. None of them moved.

'I can't do it!' I yelled, my whole body vibrating. I felt sick. *My stupid, stupid fucking body and my stupid, stupid fucking brain won't let me do it.* A sob escaped me and I swore viciously. I hadn't wanted to look weak. I hadn't wanted to make myself a target. I was supposed to be the underdog who would hold her own.

But look at me. Sobbing and shaking like a little girl, too frightened to cross a damned bridge.

And the whole of Olympus had seen me fail.

FIFTEEN

'*This room isn't that bad,*' said Skop as he jumped up onto the bed beside me. I pulled the covers further over my head.

'It's not about the fucking room,' I snapped. And honestly, knowing that the view out of the window that I hadn't managed to win would be that awful wasteland, I meant it. 'It's about looking like a fucking idiot in front of the whole damn world.'

'*Maybe nobody was watching today,*' the kobaloi said.

'Yeah, right.' Zeus, Athena, Hades, all of the gods were watching. They'd all seen me go to pieces, fail spectacularly at a test of glory. They'd all seen the judges award me zero tokens, before I was flashed back to my bedroom, shaking and crying. I screwed my face up and shouted abuse into my pillow. I was so angry with myself. I felt like my body had betrayed me, and I couldn't do anything about it. The feeling of impotence, the lack of anyone else to blame, the memories of spending years feeling too weak to achieve anything were overwhelming me. Fury was starting to build deep down in the pit of my stomach, and I had no outlet. I couldn't hide in this bed forever. But how the hell could I show my face?

I knew very little about this world, and I had no idea just how many people had witnessed my breakdown. But even one person seeing it was one too many. My fears were exposed, and I was a failure.

'*Have you always been afraid of heights?*' asked Skop, his voice gentler than usual.

'Yes.'

'*Do you have any other fears?*'

'None so fucking debilitating,' I spat. Shame was burning inside me, fueled with anger. I wanted to escape my own body, be somebody else. Anybody else.

'*Good. They can't use the same test twice. So that's the worst out of the way.*'

I peeked over the edge of the comforter and looked at him.

'Really? I'll never have to do that again?'

'*Nope.*'

'Thank fuck for that.' A little slither of relief, or hope, cut through the shame. But I still had to go out there again. I still had to show my face, after looking so utterly pathetic.

There was a loud knock at my door, and I drew the comforter back over my head.

'Go away!' I shouted.

'You know, hiding under the covers is not really helping your image,' said Hecate, and I heard the door shut behind her. Shame shivered through me again.

'What am I supposed to do, just pretend it never happened?'

'Yes. That's exactly what you need to do. Shrug it off like you couldn't give a shit.'

'How?' I pulled the covers down and looked at her.

There was no pity in her beautiful face as she stood over my bed, hands on her leather-clad hips.

'Everyone has weaknesses. The whole point of these Trials is to expose them. You're lucky. Yours is out of the way early. You need to stand in front of the world and act like it's totally fucking normal to not be able to cross an invisible bridge over an endless chasm, and make everyone believe you're going to ace all the other tests.'

I stared at her, playing her words back. Part of me knew she was right. People were not superheroes. And nobody was fearless. *But everyone else has powers. You're the underdog, the weakling,* the other, shitty part of my brain pointed out.

'I've reminded everybody that I'm human, and inferior,' I said quietly.

'I don't mean to sound like a bitch, but they already knew that. They didn't need reminding. Nobody out there expects you to win anything at all.'

'Then why the hell am I here?' I exploded. 'Just to be made a mockery of?'

Hecate threw her arms in the air, giving me an exasperated look.

'Yes! You already know that! Zeus brought you here to piss off Hades! It wasn't anything to do with you personally!'

I let out a cry of frustration.

'Nothing to do with me *personally*?! This is bullshit! This is completely unfair and I've had enough.' I kicked the covers off viciously, and leapt to my feet. 'Where's Zeus?'

A surprised expression crossed Hecate's face, then a smile began to form on her lips.

'Persy, I'm glad to see you angry instead of wallowing in shame, but I don't think having it out with the lord of the gods, most powerful being in Olympus, is a very good idea.'

'He can't hurt me until after the Trials. I want to talk to him.' Fury was rolling through me now, fire burning in my belly.

'No,' she said flatly. I snarled and she raised her eyebrows. 'You can fight me instead. In the training room.'

I glared at her, but the more I thought about it, the more I wanted to train with her. I wanted to kick and punch and scream and shout.

'Fine. What kind of sadistic asshat designs an invisible bridge, anyway?' I hissed eventually.

'*My thoughts exactly,*' agreed Skop in my head.

The more blows I landed on Hecate, and the more I felt my skin bruising and my muscles aching, the less useless I felt. I was made of flesh and blood, and pounding my fists into training pads reminded me of that fact. Seeing the material dent when I landed a kick squarely in the center, seeing the wooden staffs strain when I smashed them into Hecate's weapon - it proved that I *did* have an impact.

'This is much, much better than this morning,' panted Hecate. 'And now I'm starving. It's late.'

We ate together in my room. We didn't talk much, too intent on devouring a meal of roast chicken and carrots.

'Did any of the other contenders fail at a Trial?' I asked as I swallowed my last mouthful.

'Yeah, loads. There's usually nine Trials, in three rounds, and Minthe only got five tokens and is in first place.'

'Usually nine?' I asked. Relief that I wasn't the first to fail mingled with curiosity. 'Is there a chance that I'll do less than nine?'

'Um, yeah. A couple girls did less,' she said evasively.

'There's only one way that'll happen,' said Skop. I threw him a bit of chicken and he leapt to his feet, tail wagging.

'Skop, don't tell her!' said Hecate.

'I swear to god, if I hear the words "don't tell her" one more time-' I started, but Hecate cut me off.

'Gods!' she said loudly, sighing. 'I'll keep correcting you until you get it right. It's *gods*, not god.'

'Whatever! Why did those girls do fewer Trials?'

Hecate dropped her eyes to her empty plate.

'They died.'

I blinked.

'Died? In... in the Trials?'

'Yeah.' I set my plate down beside me and Hecate stood up, grabbing it quickly. 'Right, well, I'd better be off to bed. Hedone is back tomorrow, helping with the ball preparations.'

'They let people die?' I said, staring at her.

'They're not allowed to intervene, Persy.'

I opened my mouth to argue that somebody kept talking to me during my Trials, but closed it again. So far, it seemed the owner of the voice was trying to help me, and if that was against the rules, I should probably keep quiet about it.

'I knew this was dangerous but...'

'Keep training like you did just now, and do what Hedone tells you and you'll be fine.'

My rational voice spoke in the back of my head. *None of this is real anyway, who gives a shit if you die in this made-up place?*

But I didn't believe the voice anymore. I couldn't, no matter how much I wanted to. I knew it was nothing but a last-ditch attempt by my rational conscious to explain the insane circumstances I'd found myself in.

But as insane as they were, I knew in my heart they were real.

I didn't think I'd been asleep long when I stepped into the beautiful, ethereal garden again. The tinkling sound of water was interrupted by the chirruping of birds, and I looked up, scanning the trees.

'You won't see them. There's much you won't see until you fully accept this world.'

The voice was deep and calm, just like before.

'Is it you who keeps talking to me during the Trials?' I asked, walking towards the Atlas fountain.

'I can only talk to you in your sleep, dear girl,' he answered. I stopped, crouching down by a patch of flowers and running my fingertips gently over the petals. A shiver of satisfaction rippled through me. This place was perfect. 'You are afraid of heights?'

The question tainted the serene feeling I was enjoying and I scowled.

'A fact you and the rest of Olympus are now aware of,' I said. 'Who are you?'

'It matters not who I am, Persephone, but who *you* are.'

I blew out a sigh, then stood up and moved to the next section of flowerbeds, inhaling deeply.

'I have no idea who I am. Nobody will tell me.'

'That's not true. You know you were once married to Hades.'

'Which I find very hard to believe. If you've invented this incredible garden, then you must understand - I couldn't live underground. Nor could I love a man whose world is death.' I gave a little shudder as I spoke.

'No. Your powers do not lend themselves to death,' the voice agreed.

'Exactly. All I want to do is plant things, give them life and watch and nurture them as they grow,' I said happily, tracing the petals of a tall sunflower. 'That's the opposite of death.'

'Indeed.'

'And anyway, I don't have any powers,' I said.

'Persephone, you can do anything you want to do. You have no idea of your potential.'

I rolled my eyes. All my life mom and dad had gone on about my 'potential.' It was nothing but a word thrown around by parents with kids who were failing. Shame fizzed through me again. *You're a failure and everyone knows it.*

'Why do you care about me?' I asked.

'You have been wronged, little goddess.'

'Goddess?'

'Eat the pomegranate seed, Persephone. You'll see.'

The garden around me faded, and my eyes flickered open with a start. These were definitely not ordinary dreams, I decided, blinking up at the star-covered rock ceiling. It really was quite pretty, I thought absently, trying to replay the conversation I'd just had before I fell back to sleep.

Was it Hades? I didn't think so. The voice sounded nothing like him, and I couldn't imagine him creating a garden like that. *Zeus?* Zeus hated me. And wouldn't be so gentle, I was sure. *Then who?*

I woke early the next morning and had a long bath. My muscles ached and the hot water felt good. After navigating my huge wardrobe and managing to select something to wear and dress myself without Skop sneaking a peek, I sat down at my dresser to try one of the hairstyles Hedone had taught me. I wanted her to be impressed when she arrived.

'What do you think would happen if I ate the pomegranate seed I won?' I asked Skop.

'*Why would you go to all that trouble to win a seed and then just eat it?*' he asked, his voice incredulous.

'Just answer the question.'

'*I don't know, but I doubt you'd sprout a tree from your ass,*' he said. I shook my head, rolling my eyes but unable to hide my smile.

'Thanks, that's really helpful,' I said sarcastically.

'*Maybe if you win another one you could find out, but you only have one at the moment.*' He made a good point, I thought. '*What made you think of eating it?*'

'We eat them back home,' I said defensively.

'*You eat seeds? Humans from the mortal world are weird,*' he said.

'How come the gods stay here in Olympus and don't do anything in my world?' I asked him.

'*Beats me. Mostly I ignore the gods, and concentrate on my own shit.*'

'Which is?' I asked, raising my eyebrows at him as I fiddled with a lock of white hair.

'*Screwing, primarily,*' he said, his tail wagging and eyes gleaming.

'I should've guessed,' I said, rolling my eyes. 'You look too cute like that to be so disgusting.'

'*There's nothing disgusting about sex. If you think there is then you've been doing it wrong.*'

'Eew,' I said, turning away from him. Truth was though, I didn't know if I'd have gotten as far as I did on that cursed bridge without the randy little kobaloi. I was becoming a little bit fond of him.

Hedone arrived a short while later, and to my delight she was very impressed with my hair and make-up efforts. She took me to a grand dining room, very Greek in style with fluted columns everywhere, and high glowing ceilings. A long table set for twenty ran down the center of the room, and we sat together as she took me through the correct order to use knives and forks and spoons and little bowls. I tried to tell her about the movie Pretty Woman, but she just smiled politely at me. I spent the next hour trying to bury an increasing feeling of homesickness, and concentrate on what she was teaching me. Eventually she announced that it was time for lunch, and that she would be back in a few hours.

'And I'm bringing Morpheus with me. He says he knows of somewhere he thinks you might like.'

'Oh, thank you,' I said. 'I assume I'm not going to be dumped on an unsuspecting Hades for lunch again,' I joked awkwardly.

'Err, no, but your presence has been requested by someone else.' She gave me an uneasy smile.

'Who'

'Zeus.'

SIXTEEN

I uncrossed and recrossed my legs under the table, looking around at the ridiculous opulence for what must have been the hundredth time. The moment Hedone had stopped talking, bright white light had consumed me, and then I'd found myself in this grand dining room. Only the word 'room' didn't really apply. There were no walls or ceiling, and stunning pastel colored clouds swirled above and around me. A gentle, temperate breeze swept through my hair, and I closed my eyes. It felt incredible. I was outside. Properly outside, where the air moved, and the sky stretched on forever.

The floor was made from the same white marble I'd seen so much of, as were the columns that ringed the circular space, but gold vines with tiny little white flowers wound their way around them. I'd walked as close to the edge of the room as I dared, but it turned out I wasn't over my last brush with heights, and dizziness swamped me before I could see anything. So instead, I'd sat back down at the table. Steaming hot coffee had been poured for two, and

I picked the cup in front of me up and sniffed it. It smelled divine, and I was sipping at it before I could stop myself. A small happy moan escaped my lips.

'You humans and your coffee,' said a voice, and Zeus shimmered into existence in the chair opposite me. He was in blonde surfer boy form. Fury filled me instantly.

'Hello,' I said stiffly. 'I've been wanting to have a talk with you, so I'm glad you've invited me to lunch.' He smiled at me, and my heart skipped a beat. I couldn't pretend he wasn't obscenely gorgeous. *He abducted you. He's an asshole.*

'So I heard. Shame about yesterday's Trial. I understand you missed out on a room with a view?' I said nothing, just sipped more coffee, letting my anger bubble. 'What do you think of the view here?' My eyes dropped to the table, shame pricking through my anger. I was instantly annoyed with myself for giving my emotions away. 'Ah, but of course,' Zeus said softly. 'You won't be able to go close enough to the edge to see.'

'As if you didn't already know that,' I spat. 'You've done this deliberately, to mock me.' I glared at him, projecting as much venom into the look as I could.

'You and I have gotten off on the wrong foot, Persephone,' he said softly.

'The wrong foot? Explain to me how there could possibly be any other kind of foot? You kidnapped me!'

'That was when I thought you were just a useless little mortal human. I can see now, you may have lost your powers, but you kept your spirit.'

I stared at him, confused.

'You're saying this *after* I failed to cross the chasm?' I would have expected that to cement his poor opinion of me.

'You were clearly terrified, yet you tried anyway. I

admire that.' I frowned suspiciously. 'Let me show you the view, Persephone. This might be the only time you're off Virgo for a little while, and I believe you will appreciate the... openness of my realm.'

'Your realm? Where are we?'

'Leo. Sky realm of Zeus, center of Olympus,' he smiled at me. Power emanated from him, and my anger was melting away. I knew, vaguely, that he was doing it, but I was struggling to care. 'We are in my personal rooms at the top of Mount Olympus. The citizens of my realm live in houses that float in the ring of clouds around the mountain, or further down the mountain itself. And they get around in wooden ships with sails powered by light.' I stared at him. 'Now tell me, surely you want to see that?' His voice was warm and seductive and I couldn't deny that what he had described sounded amazing.

'OK,' I said, standing up. Zeus stood up too, then held his hand out towards the edge of the room. Glass appeared out of nowhere, wrapping itself around the marble floor and stretching up.

'You can't fall, I swear,' he said to me, then strode to the glass. I followed him cautiously. The dizziness didn't come as I got closer, and I wondered if that was because of Zeus, or because I knew I couldn't fall. Either way, I got close enough to the edge to see beyond.

And Zeus was right. The view was spectacular. If I'd had any lingering doubt that this was all in my head, it would have been dispelled at once - there was no way I could have invented what was before me.

Beyond the circular room was a thick band of fierce black clouds, crackling with purple electricity, but nestled in amongst them were massive mansions. Many had walls made entirely from glass, presumably so that they could make the most of the view of the mountain I was on, and all had elaborate courtyards filled with greenery. In the gap between the clouds and us were four of five of the ships Zeus had described. They were breathtaking. Reminiscent of pirate ships from movies back home, they were slightly different shapes and sizes, but all had taught metallic sails that sparkled and shimmered like liquid gold. I couldn't stop staring at the one closest to us, the colors of the pastel clouds reflecting in the rippling surface.

'They're beautiful,' I breathed.

'I know. And they are a functional way to move between the realms. My daughter Athena is very good at creating things of both use and beauty.'

'Athena created them?'

'Yes. Along with your mortal world.'

I snapped my eyes to his.

'Athena created humans?' Zeus barked out a laugh.

'No, no, no. That was myself and my old friend Prometheus. Athena created the mortal world, where your precious New York is. Last time the Olympians fought she convinced me that humans should not pay the price of our disagreements, and I allowed her to create your world to put most of them. You know, as an experiment.'

'An experiment?'

'Yes. Humans are more resourceful than I realized though. The last lot managed to break the boundary into our world. Athena was most upset when I scrapped it all and she had to start again.'

My mouth fell open.

'What-' I started, but he waved his arm dismissively.

'I'm hungry,' he said.

My mind still reeling from what he had just said, I

followed him dumbly to the table. *Scrapped it all and started again?*

'I'm sensing that you don't have a particularly high opinion of humans,' I said, sitting down.

'They have their uses. And we have many half human demigods here in Olympus. In fact we even allow them in the academies to learn to use their powers.'

'So humans can live in Olympus?'

'Not unless they are born here. Which many are.' He pulled a face, and snapped his fingers. A plethora of fruit appeared instantly on the table, all laid out on shining silverware.

'So, if I were to win these Trials, I still wouldn't be able to live here?'

'If you were to win, you would be reinstated as a-' he faltered, looking up at me as he leaned over to reach a platter of watermelon.

'A goddess?' I asked, thinking of what the voice in the garden had said last night.

'Hecate told you?'

I said nothing as the god shrugged. *So it was true. I used to be a goddess.* A shiver ran through me and I did my best to keep my face impassive.

'It doesn't matter if you know. The point is, I've changed my initial way of thinking.'

I raised an eyebrow at him, then reached for a bowl of grapes.

'The mighty Zeus admits he was wrong?' I said carefully.

He laughed, and it was a happy sound, that made me feel warm and safe.

'No. But all beings, great and small, are prone to changing their minds.'

'Meaning?'

'Meaning, I want you to win.'

'Look, I'm really confused,' I said, my brain bursting with questions. 'You brought me here to upset Hades, right? Because he doesn't want me here. When you abducted me,' I paused to glare at him, 'what were you hoping to achieve?'

'Honestly, I didn't really think it through,' he shrugged, the mischievous gleam back in his eye. 'I didn't even expect to find you.'

I sighed, and rubbed at my forehead.

'Where's Skop?' I asked, suddenly realizing my kobaloi guard was nowhere to be seen.

'Oh, I didn't think he needed to intrude on our lunch.' Suspicion burned through me.

'There's not much point in me having a guard if you can dismiss him,' I said.

'I'm the Lord of the Gods. Dionysus's lapdogs will do as I bid them.'

Arrogance and annoyance were written across his face as he began to eat the fruit he'd gathered onto his plate. I matched his silence as we ate, thinking hard. So far, he had been more forthcoming in his answers than I had expected. I needed to get as much information as I could out of him. And though my anger was difficult to hold onto, my distrust of him had gone nowhere. Clearly his powers had missed that emotion.

'So, I get my powers back if I win?' He nodded at me. 'It seems like Poseidon wasn't a fan of me. Will he object to that?' Zeus made a pffff sound.

'Poseidon is a cautious old man, who gives himself too

much to worry about. And Hades' unlawful actions have brought about a word of trouble for him too. Ignore him.'

'Why does he think I'm dangerous?'

Zeus looked at me, and the fruit suddenly vanished. In a heartbeat, it was replaced by mountains of pastries, the smell divine. He reached for something covered in shining chocolate.

'You know I'm not going to answer that,' he smiled. I picked up a donut, covered in powdered sugar, and bit into it. It tasted even better than it smelled. 'I like watching you eat,' said Zeus, and my eyes snapped to his. Energy rolled off him, and it was infectious. It seeped into my own body; life and ferocity building inside me like the purple sparks in his eyes. 'I like to see a woman as beautiful as you enjoying using her senses.' His voice was low and husky, and heat flooded my core.

He abducted you! He's a god! You're not really feeling these things! The voice in my head was screaming at me, and I forced myself to listen to it.

'Is there any way I can get my powers back?' I blurted out.

'No,' he said simply.

'Please? I'd have a better chance of winning.' As I said the words, I wondered why I wanted them so much. I didn't want to win. I wanted to go home.

'No.' I let out a little snarl of frustration and Zeus smiled. 'You are quite, quite beautiful,' he said.

'Will you at least tell me what they were?' I snapped, ignoring his comments, and my rising body temperature, as best I could.

'No. I'm inclined to let your frustration build a little longer. I think watching you-' he paused, eyes boring into mine, 'explode,' he said slowly, and every muscle in my body clenched, 'would be very pleasurable indeed.'

'Send me back,' I said quickly. 'I want to go back to my room now.'

He reclined in his chair, a lazy smile on his beautiful face.

'Very well. Thank you for the pleasure of your company today. I'll see you soon,' he said, and the white light flashed.

SEVENTEEN

For a long time after I was safely back in my room, I couldn't help feeling like I'd just lost some sort of game. It made me furious that he could manipulate my body like that. Thank god my brain was harder to coax.

'You know, he thinks he's the big cheese, but he's not. That's why he's so pissed at the moment,' snapped Skop. He was really not happy about being left behind. I was surprised he was taking his guarding duties so seriously to be honest.

'What do you mean?' I asked the kobaloi.

'Oceanus is back. Which means Zeus is no longer the strongest being in Olympus,' he said cattily.

'Oceanus is stronger than Zeus? What do you mean he's back? Where did he go?'

'Gods, you're clueless,' he sighed, and flopped onto his front paws. *'The Olympians went to war with the Titans,'* he said, and I nodded.

'I remember learning that. Cronos was told that his own son would overthrow him so he ate all his children.'

'Correct. Fucking weirdo. But his wife, Rhea, hid her

seventh son, Zeus. He grew up, rescued his eaten siblings, then the war began.' I opened my mouth to ask how you could rescue someone who had been eaten, but closed it again. I wasn't sure I wanted to know the answer. *'The Olympians won, and threw most of the Titans into Tartarus, a pit of endless torture. But some Titans didn't fight, including Oceanus and Prometheus. Two of the most powerful beings to have ever lived. Titans are the original gods, they're fiercely strong.'*

'Oh,' I said.

'The Titans who didn't fight were allowed to live in Olympus, as long as they kept to themselves. Which they did, but everybody knew Zeus feared and hated them. They were seen less and less, and eventually they just vanished. Until recently, when Oceanus returned.'

'Why did he come back?'

'Some descendant of his went and woke him up, is what I heard. But he was good mates with Hades back in the day, and they've fallen in together again pretty quickly.'

'So that's why Zeus is so angry? He's scared?'

'I wouldn't say it to his face, but yeah, that's what I think.'

'How do you know all this stuff?' I asked him.

'Parties. Everything you need to know can be learned at parties. They're where all the politics of Olympus are managed.' I thought about the ball, supposedly my biggest Trial yet.

'That's what Hedone told me.'

'She's right. As well as smoking hot,' Skop said. I rolled my eyes, even though I agreed with him.

'The masquerade ball can't be as bad as the chasm,' I asserted, loudly.

'I wouldn't be so sure about that,' Skop replied.

~

A little while later there was another knock on my door and I jumped to my feet to open it. I was bored, and pent-up; anxiety-fueled energy was surging through me. The fresh air in Zeus's realm had only served to remind me that I was trapped underground here, and I was becoming more and more bothered by the fact.

'Good afternoon, Persephone,' said Hedone, but I looked straight past her at the man behind, towering over her shoulder. He must have been at least eight feet tall, and just like me he had a shock of white hair. But he also had white eyebrows, over sparkling blue eyes and his skin was a very pale blue. Glittering dust seemed to swirl across his face as I stared, and he smiled at me, a broad smile that made his incredible eyes light up even more.

'I'm pleased to meet you, Persephone. I'm Morpheus, god of dreams and permanent resident of the underworld,' he said, and held out his arm around Hedone.

'Hi,' I said, and took his proffered hand. His skin was ice cold and smooth, and I noticed he was wearing something that looked like wizards' robes, a gaping sleeve falling back and revealing deep blue swirling tattoos snaking up his muscled arm as he shook my hand.

'The lovely Hedone tells me you're missing your garden.'

Alarm bells rang in my mind. This man was the god of dreams, and he knew I was missing gardens. Did the voice in the garden in my dreams belong to him?

'I am,' I said.

'Well, I haven't sought permission from the boss, but I think I know a place you might like,' he said with another broad smile. His voice sounded nothing like the one in my dreams.

'Thank you,' I said. 'Can we walk there, instead of doing that flashy thing?'

He laughed, and his skin seemed to ripple with more blue light.

'Of course.'

We walked for ages, and I checked with Skop that he was paying attention to where we were going again. The thought of getting lost in this underground labyrinth was more than I could take. Hedone walked with her hand in Morpheus's and they frequently exchanged happy glances with each other.

'Are you two, um, an item?' I ventured awkwardly.

'Yes,' Hedone beamed at me. I thought about that for a moment. The goddess of pleasure with the god of dreams. I bet that lead to some seriously epic sex.

'So, Morpheus, do you control everyone's dreams?'

'Oh no. No, I create themes for people's dreams, then I allocate them as necessary.'

'Themes?'

'Yes. Like fear, or self-reflection, or guilt, or humor. Every individual interprets those themes differently, in their sleep. The sub-conscious is a powerful thing, and it dictates most of my work.'

'Can you... can you talk to people in their dreams?'

'Oh yes. But I'm only allowed to do that on order of Hades.'

'Oh. Can Hades do it too?'

'All of the Olympians can. They can do pretty much anything they like,' he said, with a raised eyebrow. 'Are you getting a visitor in your sleep?'

'No, no, I'm sure it's just an overactive imagination,' I said quickly, and Morpheus lips quirked into a smile.

'Well, whatever it is, it's nothing to do with me, I can assure you,' he said.

'Huh. Will you be at the ball?'

'Of course. Are you prepared for it? I've heard the tests are going to be good,' he said.

'What have you heard?' said Hedone, excited. 'You must share!'

'That would be cheating! I could lose my job,' he said teasingly, then leaned forward and kissed her quickly. 'Sorry, my love.' I felt a stab of jealousy at their cute flirting and squashed it guiltily. Hedone was nice. Why would I begrudge her anything?

'Persephone has a little more prep to go through, but mostly just conversational etiquette now,' Hedone said. 'She'll do great.'

I smiled warmly at her.

'I'll be honest, I don't see how it can be worse than the chasm,' I said quietly. Neither Hedone or Morpheus replied.

'Told ya,' said Skop in my head.

We walked the rest of the way in silence. The path was on an incline, with small sets of steps interrupting the blue torch-lit corridors at regular intervals. We must have passed a hundred doors, until eventually we stopped in front of one.

'This room doesn't get used any more, as far as I know,' said Morpheus. 'But Hades used to use it a lot. Anyway, there's some sort of magic still infused into the room and some of the plants have survived without company.'

'Plants?' My heart skipped a beat. There really were plants in this place?

'A few, yes. We call it the conservatory.' He pulled on the door handle and held it open for me, gesturing into the room. I stepped hesitantly through the doorway.

Something inside me sparked to life as I cast my eyes around the derelict room. It looked just like I would expect a conservatory to look, if it had been neglected for fifty years. The walls and domed ceiling were made of glass, presumably to let the dull light in, and beautiful once-white wrought iron bars curved up and around the whole structure, creating the frame that supported it. But my attention was drawn to the one color I had rarely seen since coming to the underworld. The one color I was always most drawn to. *Green*. Twenty feet away, sprawling and out of control was a giant yucca plant. Its long leaves were droopy where they should have been sharp, but they were still vibrant with color. I moved further into the room quickly, looking for other signs of life. I found two more yuccas, a fair few succulents, low on the ground in moulding soil, and to my sheer delight, right at the back and leaning keenly towards the weak sun, a single orchid.

'How on earth have you survived?' I murmured to it as I crouched down, inspecting it closely.

'It's nothing to do with earth, I assure you,' said a slithery voice, and I leapt to my feet, my stomach lurching.

'Hades!' I heard Morpheus say, his voice filled with surprise. I turned to see him hurrying towards me, a smoky cloud forming before him. 'I'm sorry boss, I didn't know you would be here.' He was talking quickly, his smooth demeanor and confident grin gone.

'And why, exactly, *are* you here?' Hades' voice made my

skin crawl, as though something cold was slithering all over me.

'Persephone was missing her plants. I thought this place might cheer her up.'

The smoky form was now humanoid, though void of features as always. Hades said nothing, and I looked for Hedone. She was nowhere to be seen.

'Since when have you befriended this human, Morpheus?' asked Hades eventually. Morpheus dropped his gaze to the dirty floor.

'I was just doing a favor for someone. I didn't think it would do any harm. I'm sorry, boss.'

'Leave,' Hades said. Morpheus turned and I hurried towards him, trying to skirt as far around Hades as I could. 'Not you, Persephone,' he said though, as I drew level with him. Fear and something unidentifiable skittered through me on hearing him say my name. Morpheus threw an apologetic glance at me over his shoulder, then disappeared through the open door. I gulped. 'I heard you had lunch with my little brother,' Hades said. *Oh god. This could get awkward.*

'Not through choice,' I replied, trying to keep the wobble from my voice. There was a pause.

'Did you enjoy it?' My eyebrows shot up in surprise. Not only was it not the question I was expecting, but the tone of his voice had changed. The iciness was gone, and he sounded almost nervous.

'It was nice to feel the breeze on my skin,' I admitted. 'But I dislike Zeus intensely. So no.'

To my astonishment, Hades chuckled.

'Good. I dislike him intensely too.'

'So I've heard,' I said cautiously.

'I...' Hades started, then tailed off. 'I never thought I

would see you in this room again,' he said eventually, quietly. The slithering was gone from his voice completely, his tone now rich and deep. This was nothing like the way he had been with me at the end of our last conversation. What had changed? Suspicion filled me, and despite my efforts to ignore it, so did hope.

'It doesn't surprise me that I've been here before,' I told him. 'I feel something strong about this room. But I don't know if that's just happiness to see something growing.' Hades snorted.

'I wouldn't say growing. More like *not dying*. It takes all my power just to keep that one damn flower alive,' he said, and a smoky arm gestured at the orchid. 'The other plants are feeding off the residual magic left over I think.'

He was keeping the orchid alive? I definitely hadn't expected that.

'Well, it's beautiful,' I said carefully, stepping back towards the orchid. It was too. It was a slipper orchid, the shape of it round and sensual. It was a vivid purple, with yellow accents softening the petals.

'You planted it,' he replied, his words barely audible. Something pulled at my gut, and for a brief second I felt something so strong it took my breath away. It was a desperate, desperate desire to be somewhere, but I didn't know where.

But the feeling ebbed away fast, and was replaced with that same crushing sense of being trapped. Not physically trapped here in the underworld, but trapped somewhere deeper and infinitely more painful. I felt separated from my own emotions, and I knew I was being kept apart from something more important than anything else I knew. Was it him?

'Why did you send me away? What happened between

us?' I asked quickly. 'It's killing me not knowing.' I looked pleadingly at where I knew his face was, flashes of silver cutting through the dark smoke.

'Nothing happened between us,' he answered, his voice sad. 'Circumstances beyond my control meant you had to leave.'

He didn't hate me. Relief and happiness crashed through me, at the same time as my rational brain screamed at me. *Why do you care? You don't know this man, and he's made of fucking smoke and death!* But rational thoughts were no good to me here. When I wasn't around Hades, the thought of ever being with him was intolerable. But once I was in his presence...

'Hades, I need to know what happened. Please, give me my memories back.'

'I can't. It is not safe.' Exasperation filled me, and I clenched my hands into fists. 'But, if it helps, I'll stop making your life harder,' he said gently. I raised my eyebrows. I didn't even know he could speak gently.

'How?'

'Well, for a start, I'm sorry I got angry with you before. Hecate kind of threw me through a loop. I wasn't ready to see you alone. I'm normally excellent at controlling my emotions, but you're...' I waited, my breath held. He shook his smoky head and carried on. 'You're the one thing my asshole brother knew would cause me pain.'

'Pain? I'm sorry,' I whispered. And I was, though I wasn't sure why.

'No, I'm sorry. You didn't choose any of this. It's my fault. And to say sorry, I'd like you to have this room.'

'Really?'

'Yes. Just until you lose the Trials and go home, that is.

You must understand how important it is that you don't stay here.'

A flicker of indignation ignited in me, and I spoke before thinking the words through.

'If what you're saying is true, why don't you want me to be your wife again?' Saying the word wife out loud felt weird and I instantly regretted it.

'Persephone, please. I can't answer that.' His voice was strained, and I felt a little guilty about pushing him when he was clearly making an effort.

'Fine,' I muttered.

'Good. In the meantime, take care of that fucking flower for me so I don't have to.' My eyes flicked between the orchid and him and I couldn't help grinning at him.

'Why are you suddenly being nice to me?'

Hades blew out a sigh, the smoke around his face rippling.

'Seeing you here, in this room... It's impossible not to be. And if you are only to be here a short while longer, then you may as well enjoy it.'

'Thank you, Hades,' I said sincerely.

This time I saw more than a flash of silver. Hades solidi-fied, and I swear, my knees actually went weak, like I was in a slushy romance novel.

He was *beyond* beautiful. His eyes were swirling liquid silver, and the emotion pouring from them was written across the rest of his face. Jet black hair curled past his ears, and he had a thick covering of dark stubble spreading across his chiseled jaw. His lips were soft and full and parted slightly. My eyes darted down his body, taking in a black shirt stretched tight across massive shoulders, open at the neck and showing a smattering of curly chest hair, a heavy duty leather belt, and ripped navy jeans.

I don't know what I'd expected Hades to look like under the smoke, but my gods, it wasn't this.

'I'm sorry,' he said quietly, and I watched the words form on his lips, before his image vanished under black smoke again. 'I struggle to control myself around you.'

'Please,' I half-squeaked. 'Please, stay like that, instead of the smoke.'

'No. I must go.'

'Wait, before you do,' I said quickly. My heart was racing. 'Have you been talking to me? In my head?' The smoke flickered.

'I want you to lose the Trials, but I don't want you to die doing so,' he answered eventually.

'Is that a yes?'

'Goodbye, Persephone. Enjoy the conservatory.'

The smoke vanished.

EIGHTEEN

I stared at the empty spot Hades had vanished from for a long time. Emotions were crashing around in my head, that feeling of being separated from something rising and falling inside me. It didn't matter what Athena had said, I couldn't ignore my past. Not when I was apparently now living in it again. I almost wished I hadn't seen Hades under the smoke, because now that I had, I couldn't get his image to leave me. Those fierce cheekbones, sensuous lips, his bulging chest... Every other man I had ever seen paled into nothingness next to him. And it was more than physical attraction. I knew him. I knew that offhand humor, that rich version of his voice.

He kept the orchid alive for you. It's all he had left.

I knew that's what the flower meant. What this room meant. And he had known when I entered it today. *He still cares.* Then why did he want me to lose? Surely, if he had another chance of being with the woman he didn't want to leave in the first place, he would welcome it? What had happened? Why had I been made to leave? Frustration welled inside me.

It wouldn't work. I didn't want to live underground, in a place with no proper outside, and a glass conservatory the only garden I could access. I didn't want to be tied to a man whose dominion was death. I didn't want to live in a world without windows, for gods' sake. He may be beautiful, and I may have a connection to him, but whoever I'd been when this was my home, I wasn't that person any more.

Hades was right. I should try to enjoy the time I had here as best I could. I scanned the room, looking for a trowel. I spotted a pile of tools stacked against the glass, and when I went to investigate I found a rusted faucet on the end of a creaky copper pipe in the ground. Good. I had everything I needed to immerse myself in a few hours of gardening, and try to forget about this crazy infatuation.

Skop tried to talk to me a few times while I worked, but I gave him one word answers. Before long I had managed to lose myself to the soil, and the hours flew by. Too soon, Hecate came into the room, telling me it was time to train. I reluctantly left the conservatory with her, half listening to her berating me for getting my nice clothes 'covered in crap', but mostly just trying to keep Hades' face from invading my mind.

'I saw Hades today,' I told her, after we had beaten the shit out of each other for an exhausting hour, and were tucking into roasted beef in my room.

'Oh?'

'And I mean, I saw him. Like under the smoke.'

'Ohhhhh.' She looked at me, a wicked gleam in her eye. 'I knew he'd slip up if he spent enough time around you.'

'So is that his true form then?'

'No, if a god showed you his true form you'd die, you're human. But it's the non-lethal version of it.'

'Oh. What does his true form look like?'

'Erm, glowy. And sort of terrifying.'

'Right. So, do you see smoke Hades, or...' I paused, trying to think of what to call non-smoke Hades.

'Hot Hades?' offered Hecate. That worked, I thought, nodding. 'I see hot Hades. Everyone who lives or works in the underworld does. But Virgo is one of the four forbidden realms. Hades is by far the most secretive and private of the Gods.'

'So, he must not be enjoying all this Trial stuff being shown to everyone?'

'No. He's not. The gods ran a competition for Immortality a while ago, and each god hosted a Trial. Hades tried to refuse having his here on Virgo, but Zeus made him. And I think that's why Zeus is making him hold his Trials for a wife here. Because Hades made it so clear he didn't want to do it before.'

'Zeus really is a dickhead,' I said.

'Yup.'

'Why does he dislike Hades so much?'

'That's a really long, difficult question. And one Hades could answer better himself.'

'Huh. Maybe you should set up another date,' I said teasingly, but I half hoped she would say yes. I was longing to see him again, even though I knew I shouldn't.

'No way, the ball is tomorrow night, and you don't need any more distractions.

'Fine,' I said on a sigh.

'Hedone is having a dress and mask made specially for you, they'll be here tomorrow.'

'OK.'

'And make sure you take your dagger. It's the only weapon you have that will work against gods, remember that.'

'Why would I need to harm a god?' I asked her, alarmed.

'Persy, are you learning nothing? You must always be prepared.'

~

I slept badly that night, and for the first time I didn't visit the beautiful garden with the Atlas fountain. Part of me wished I had. Its calming serenity was just what I needed, even if I didn't know who was taking me there. I sighed as I rolled out of bed, the ceiling lit with the daylight glow telling me it must be morning. The last three or four times I'd woken it had still been covered in twinkling stars.

'So, what's the plan for today?' asked Skop, yawning.

'Finalize the food for the feast, and go over greeting and conversational etiquette,' I told him with a scowl. My idea of a nightmare. If I had my way it would be beef burgers and a cheerful hug, but apparently that didn't cut it if you were trying out for queen of the Underworld. 'I hate this place,' I muttered as I stomped into the bathroom and started the water running in the shower.

'It's not that bad. You know, I was thinking that you should name that dagger Hecate made for you.' I gave him a look from the bathroom door before I closed it and pulled off the long silk camisole I'd slept in.

'Why?' I asked him mentally as I stepped under the water. I instantly felt less bad-tempered, the weary grogginess dissipating as the water flowed over me.

'Because all proper weapons work better if they have

names. *Hecate made that blade for you, it's one of a kind. And probably magic. You might be able to bond with it if you name it.'*

'Oh. OK. What shall I call it?'

'Name it after something you love. Or miss.'

'Light,' I said immediately, without thinking about it. 'I'm fed up being underground.'

'You didn't like it much better outside,' Skop retorted.

'That does not count as outside. Zeus's place had a proper outside. Wherever that chasm is...' I tried to think of a word for the still, temperature-less, beige void but gave up.

'There's plenty of light down here.'

'Not real light.'

'Fine. How about... Faesforos?'

'What does that mean?' I asked, and repeated the word aloud. I liked how it sounded.

'It means bringer of light,' Skop answered. A little shiver ran through me, although the water was still hot. Bringer of light. *'Maybe you can bring some real light to the under-world,'* he said.

'Do you think I can win this, Skop?' I asked him slowly.

There was a long pause.

'I know there's more potential in you than you know there is,' he said eventually.

There was that fucking word again. I hated it. *Potential.* Always so much potential, but never, ever fulfilled.

'I thought you were here to offer comedic relief,' I sighed. 'Not deep and meaningful pep talks.'

'Your wish is my command. Did I tell you about the time Dionysus tricked Poseidon into having sex with a tree?'

≈

The rest of the day with Hedone flew by. The ball was starting at eight, and she'd packed the day with last-minute preparations. To my delight, she had decided to celebrate my human, mortal heritage by serving a feast of food from my own world, specifically New York. Hot-dogs, pastrami sandwiches, smoked salmon bagels, cinnamon rolls, powdered donuts, and more were on the menu, and for the first time I actually began to look forward to the party a little bit.

That was until I had to start practicing how to greet people. Hedone had persuaded Morpheus to assist, and he entered the grand doors of an empty dining hall over and over again for an hour, looking surprised and delighted to see me each time. My acting skills were no match for his though, and my awkward hand shakes and uneasy smiles were not up to Hedone's standards at all.

'Watch me do it, darling,' she told me patiently. Morpheus left the room, then re-entered, a cocky look on his handsome face.

'Morpheus, it's such a pleasure to see you,' enthused Hedone, stepping towards him and holding out her hand. He took it gracefully, bending and kissing it.

'I'm honored to have been invited,' he said.

'But of course you were! And may I say, you look magnificent. How are your family?' She managed to keep her voice sincere and sultry, and her eyes were fixed on his the whole time.

She turned to me. 'You see, Persephone? Don't sound bored, don't sound over-excited. Just try to be elegant, and regal. Don't shake hands, hold yours out to be kissed, like you're more important than they are.'

I frowned. This was so not my thing. Like not even

close. But it was one evening, then it would be over. I could do it.

'Right,' I said.

'Always ask about their family, and never forget that flattery will get you absolutely everywhere in Olympus. Try to pick out something specific to compliment your guests on.'

'OK,' I nodded. 'Let me try again.'

Eventually Hedone decided she was satisfied with my level of 'enthusiasm and sophistication'. I felt like a total fake, but she said my carefully plastered on smile was acceptable, and I was willing to accept that she knew best. We ate a brief lunch, consisting mostly of fruit, 'so that we had room for the feast', then we went through table etiquette again, followed by socially acceptable levels of swearing. Apparently the Olympians were entirely exempt from these rules, but the rest of us were expected to abide by them.

'There is one more thing I wanted to talk to you about,' Hedone said to me as we walked back to my room.

'Sure,' I said.

'It's about... well it's about sex.' I stumbled slightly as I looked at her in alarm.

'I'm not expected to-' I started, but she waved her hands quickly.

'No, no, of course not. But you should be aware, when lots of beings with powers get dressed up and drunk together, sex is pretty inevitable. And I don't believe attitudes to it here are quite the same as you'll be used to.'

'Please tell me I'm not attending an orgy,' I groaned. Hedone gave a tinkling laugh.

'No, although they're pretty frequent too. But gods, and

demigods for that matter, are very good at disappearing for a short while, then reappearing later.'

'So you're saying that if someone vanishes, they're probably at it somewhere?'

'Yes. Part of the game at these parties is watching for who disappears at the same time.'

'It sounds like bad reality TV,' I muttered. Hedone gave me a small frown, then continued.

'Zeus and Apollo are probably the worst for it, and if Hera is present it can cause sparks to fly. One of your jobs as hostess is to cover for people who have irate or worried partners.'

My mouth fell open.

'I have to cover for folk cheating on their partners? No!'

'It's all part of the politics, I'm afraid. And when Aphrodite does her thing, nobody is really to blame anyway.'

I thought about how Zeus had affected me the previous day, the desire my traitorous body had felt. Did Aphrodite do the same thing?

'Can the gods make someone have sex with them, even if they don't want to?' I asked, aware that my voice was betraying my fear. That was seriously not OK.

'Technically, yes, but it is strictly forbidden.' Some relief washed through me. 'You must remember that gods have enormous egos. Most will try to win you over. There is no satisfaction in taking something they haven't won.'

'What did you mean by Aphrodite doing her thing?'

'Ah, she would never make anyone do anything against their will,' Hedone smiled at me. 'Quite the opposite. Her presence tends to exaggerate all desires. A tiny crush or curiosity becomes heightened. Hence an increase in wandering eyes and hands.'

That sounded dodgy as hell to me, but I said nothing.

'You'll get used to our ways, I'm sure,' Hedone said as we reached my door. 'Try not to worry, and if you can, try to enjoy it.' She laid a hand on my shoulder and I felt a surge of gratitude towards her.

'Thank you so much, for all your help. You really didn't need to give me so much of your time,' I said. An oddly bitter look flitted across the beautiful woman's face.

'Time is a funny thing,' she said quietly. 'Good luck, Persephone. I'll see you tonight.'

NINETEEN

'You can do this,' I breathed, brushing my hands down my skirt for the hundredth time. I was standing before an enormous stone archway sealed with deep purple drapes, and I was starting to struggle with my nerves. The memory of me clinging to the bridge, sobbing and shaking, kept interrupting my confidence, and the longer I waited the more I just wanted the big entrance part to be over and done with.

The main counter to my last public failure, and the reason I wasn't already a quivering wreck, was my absolutely unbelievable outfit. Hedone had freaking excelled herself, and I was positive that I'd never looked so good. To be honest, I probably never would again, and I was determined to enjoy it while it lasted. The dress another fitted halterneck but this time with no plunging neckline, rather it tied around my throat. There was no back to the top of the dress at all though, the fabric of the skirt resting perfectly across the small of my bare back, then falling to the floor. The skirt itself was made up of hundreds of flowing ribbons of chiffon, all overlapping and slightly transparent, and they parted tantalizingly when I walked, showing flashes of skin and making my legs feel a million miles long. But my favorite thing about it was the color. Every ribbon making up the skirt was a different shade of green. The deepest reminded me of evergreens and Christmas, and the lightest was a powdery teal. When I moved the colors blended and merged, making it look as though the dress were alive. The bodice was white, and tiny green flowers snaked up and around my ribs, accentuating the shape of my breasts. Long, ridiculously soft white gloves covered my arms, reaching well past my elbow and making me feel Marilyn Monroe levels of glamorous.

I had fixed my hair in an elaborate style involving lots of curls and braids, and the white ringlets that fell about my face to my shoulders made the black mask around my eyes stand out even more. There was something thrilling about wearing something so delicate, yet fierce. It looked and felt like it was made from lace, and magic kept it perfectly on my face, un-moving. The lace pattern was of tightly weaving vines, and a swirling green feather stood up proudly on the right side of the mask, forming a statement flourish. I loved it. I had also strapped *Faesforos* to my thigh, as Hecate had instructed me to. I would have preferred it to be strapped to my ankle, but I was wearing the gold, heeled sandals that criss-crossed their way up my calf again, plus the dress would have revealed the weapon. I wasn't especially comfortable having a blade that close to my important parts, but I trusted Hecate enough to risk it.

'I think this is it,' said Skop beside me, as the drapes rustled. My heart rate quickened, my palms beginning to dampen as I realized he was right. The curtains were opening.

'Citizens of Olympus! Please welcome your hostess for the evening, Persephone!' But the commentator's words were lost to me as the room beyond the curtain was revealed. Hedone had told me what she had planned, but I could never have imagined something so utterly stunning.

The room didn't look like any of the others I'd seen in the Underworld so far. Its vaulted ceiling was twinkling with stars, and the huge space was dotted with Greek columns, but the similarities ended there. There were no windows, but the walls were the same as the ceiling, deep navy and sparkling with stars. It was as though the floor was floating in the night sky, but I wouldn't have described the room as dark. Atop all of the columns were flames, burning in various colors and casting a soft glow over everything. They were seemingly staying put by magic. Running from the archway I was standing in all the way across the room was a long red carpet, ending at a raised dais. The gods' thrones were all present, and all empty. But the room itself was far from empty. Everywhere I looked I could see people and creatures all dressed in beautiful, grand clothes, and every one of their imposing, masked faces was fixed on me.

Shit. I dropped hurriedly into a curtsy, and a slight applause rippled through the crowd. I took a hesitant step into the room.

'*Fucking own it, Persy,*' said Skop's voice in my head. I raised my chin and took another step along the red carpet. If I was ever going to walk a red carpet, it would be looking like this I thought. My confidence grew the farther into the stunning room I got. The columns were short enough that the torch-light carried, but tall enough that they were still grand. Delicate gold vines, with little buds that glittered like diamonds, wound around them, reminding me of Zeus's dining room. They were perfect for breaking up the large space, and hiding behind, I thought wryly. Satyrs and tiny women I assumed were nymphs moved between the guests holding trays of drinks and tiny canapés, and the whole room smelled divine. Kind of like strawberries but musky. Excited energy thrummed through the air, an anticipation that was almost tangible. When I judged that I was in the middle of the long carpet, I paused and turned slowly on the spot, making a show of scanning every one, and squashing the relief I felt when I spotted Hedone and Morpheus. *Channel what Hedone taught you,* I thought. *A little arrogance, a lot of grace.*

'Thank you all so much for joining me tonight,' I said loudly, and a touch aloofly. 'I am honored you have all made it. Once I have a drink I will be happy to receive you all.' A satyr appeared out of nowhere, holding up a saucer-shaped stemmed glass full of clear liquid. 'Oo,' I said, my formality slipping. 'Thanks.' He grinned at me, then shot off towards the back of the room, between the legs of the silent crowd. I took a grateful sip of the cool drink, a delightful fizz lingering on my tongue.

I could do this.

One by one the guests approached me, and I soon became very grateful for my gloves. There were only so many people you wanted to kiss your skin, and some of the guests were positively freaky looking. I had no idea what they were, but many seemed to be hybrids of animals, and a fair few had wings. The majority looked human though. I kept my practiced smile plastered on my face, and complimented most people on their masks. They were all so striking that it was hard to focus my attention on anything else. I tried to remember everyone's name as they introduced themselves, but it was impossible to keep them all straight.

'Are you remembering all these names?' I asked Skop silently, as I drained my glass. The satyr appeared immediately with a new one.

'*I already know most of these douchebags,*' he muttered back. '*None of them have recognized me though.*' He had a mischievous tone, and I sent him a warning glare.

'Don't fuck this up for me, Skop. It's serious.'

'*I'm glad you finally think so,*' he answered.

After fifteen minutes of introductions a gong sounded, and a hush descended over the room.

'Honored guests, citizens of Olympus, please welcome your gods!' sang the commentator's voice, and white light flashed over the dais, drawing everyone's attention. The room as a whole dropped to their knees, and I followed suit quickly. I only lasted a heartbeat before lifting my bowed head though, my eyes seeking out the one god I really wanted to see.

Hades was in his smoke form, of course, but like everyone else he was wearing a mask. *And he was letting his eyes show through it.* They fixed immediately on my own, and my breath caught as my emotions responded automatically. Something deep and true and almost painful flowed through me and I grasped unsuccessfully at the feeling. Too soon his eyes flicked away from mine and I released a ragged breath, before realizing that his mask was incredibly similar to mine. It was jet black and the same shape, but I didn't think the pattern was vines. I was too far away to tell. Had Hecate done that on purpose? Where was she? I scanned the other gods as they gazed over their assembled crowd.

Aphrodite stood out the most, in a completely sheer gown that had a hint of pink to it, her skin the color of chalk and her hair and lips a vibrant red. Hera was dressed far more conservatively, in a teal toga that made her dark skin glow, but her mask was the most elaborate, an enormous peacock feather fanning up and over her piled-high up-do. Zeus was sporting an older look today, dark hair shot through in the right places with gray and a traditional toga that showed off most of his taut, muscled chest.

'Thank you for attending. Please announce the first test of the evening,' Hades said, his voice the nasty slithery one. My skin crawled and I screwed my face up in conflicted confusion before a loud noise drew my attention behind me. Shimmering into existence with a scraping sound was a giant hourglass. The top half was filled with sand, but it wasn't falling. Apprehension trickled down my spine like ice.

'Tonight Persephone will face three tests,' boomed the commentator, and I realized with a start that the cheerful blond man was standing a few feet from the hourglass. 'And the judges will decide whether you get zero, one or two tokens.' Two? The leader only had five, and I already had one. Wait, why was I excited? I didn't want to win, I reminded myself sharply. Lose, but don't die. That's what Hades had said. So far nothing felt particularly lethal about the ball. 'There are a few rules that apply to the whole evening, so let me make those clear.' He looked intently at me. 'You may not ask for direct help with a single test. If you require information, you must acquire it naturally via conversation, or that test will be forfeit.' I nodded. 'You may not leave the ball.' I nodded again. 'And you may not drop any of your duties as hostess. If at any point you are deemed to be behaving inappropriately, the test will be forfeit.'

'Understood,' I said.

'The first test is a scavenger hunt,' he beamed, looking around at the whole room again, and there was a smattering of applause and excited chatter at his words. I narrowed my eyes suspiciously. I was pretty good at those as a kid. 'Persephone needs to find four clues, that will lead to a key to unlock the hourglass. If the hourglass runs out, then that test is over and lost.' Why would I need to unlock an hourglass? A sick feeling gripped my stomach, and my breath became shallow as something began to shimmer inside the large hourglass. No... Surely they wouldn't... To my horror, the shimmering stopped, leaving a man standing in the bottom half of the hourglass. He was dressed in a simple toga, and didn't look more than my age. His eyes were closed and he appeared to be asleep. A trickle of sand began to fall from the top of the timer, running off his dark hair onto the bottom of the hourglass. 'Here's your first clue,' the commentator said, and a small scroll appeared in my hand.

'You can't do this!' I said, ignoring the scroll and turning to the gods. 'What happens to him if I fail?'

'What do you think? Could you breathe if you were drowned in sand?' answered Zeus lazily. Bile rose in my throat and my head swam slightly. No, this wasn't fair.

'These Trials are supposed to be dangerous for me, not people I've never even met!' I exclaimed. 'Let him go!' I heard gasps around me, and Athena stood up. She looked identical to when I'd first seen her.

'Persephone, the ways of Olympus are new to you, but you can not change them. The only way to save this man is to complete the test. You are wasting time.'

I gaped at her.

'*She's right. Get the fuck on with it,*' said Skop in my head.

'Your little pet can't help you on this Trial,' said Poseidon suddenly, and Skop gave a little yelp of pain.

'Leave him alone!' I shouted.

'Yeah, leave off,' said Dionysus indignantly. With a little flash, Skop vanished and reappeared by Dionysus's side and a tiny bit of relief washed through me. The wine god would look after him.

But now I was on my own and a man was depending on me for his life.

TWENTY

My hands shaking, I passed my glass to the little satyr who was hovering next to me, then unrolled the scroll that had appeared out of nowhere. There were two lines written on it.

Adorned with a blue feather and lined with white lace
*   This is a magnificent way to hide one's true face*

I read it twice. It had to be referring to a masquerade mask, surely? So I just needed to find one matching the description. A blue feather and white lace. I looked around the room. Everyone was staring at me. I heard a loud cough, and spotted Hedone giving me a pointed look. *You must carry out your duties as hostess or the test will be forfeit.* The commentator's words rang in my mind, and I scrambled to remember what I was supposed to do once everyone had arrived.

'We shall be seated for food in one hour!' I said

triumphantly, as I remembered what I had been taught. 'Let the music commence!'

The melodic sound of a harp filled the space, and I turned in surprise. The thrones had vanished from the dais and now a beautiful woman with silver hair was teasing the delicate tune from a harp twice the size of herself. But she didn't have a mask with a blue feather and white lace, so I dragged my attention from her. Eyes flicking to the unconscious man in the hourglass, sand beginning to pool at his feet, I set off towards Hedone.

'Good evening, Persephone,' she said formally as I reached her.

'Good evening,' I replied.

'Were you able to receive everyone before the gods arrived?'

'No, not even half. But I am on my way round the rest of my guests now,' I beamed, as people began to crowd around me. I turned, the smile still fixed on my lips. I scanned their masks, trying to slow my heart rate. No blue feathers. *Shit.* I held my hand out to each in turn, thanking them for their attendance, letting their names go in one ear and out of the other, before hurrying on. I managed to spot a few blue feathers, but none of the masks had white lace on them. It sounded like a feminine mask, so I started trying to approach women more. Skop could have really helped out here, I thought ruefully.

Just as I spotted a lady in a puffy pink dress that I had yet to talk to, I felt gooseflesh raise on my bare skin. I turned around slowly, already knowing what had caused the temperature to drop.

'Hades,' I said, as I came to face-to-face with his smoky form.

'Persephone,' he replied, his silver eyes swirling. My rational thoughts scattered.

'You look...' I trailed off, biting down on my lip as I struggled to find a word to finish the obligatory compliment.

'Smoky?' he offered. My mouth quirked into a smile at the unexpected comment.

'Yes. Smoky.' I felt my shoulders relax a little.

'If this wasn't being broadcast to the whole of Olympus, I would have been willing to lose a bit of the smoke.'

There was no ice in his voice.

'Why do you not let them see what you look like?'

'The King of the Underworld isn't especially popular. They expect a monster, so I give them one.' His swirling shoulders shrugged.

'But... You're not really a monster?' I asked hesitantly. *Hopefully*. Hades paused before answering.

'I'm every bit the monster they believe me to be.'

Part of me didn't want to believe him, but the memory of when we had first met, the screaming, burning bodies and the blood, filtered through my mind. He was the lord of the dead. Surely monster came as part of the package. I mean, these gods put innocent people's lives in danger for entertainment, I thought, glancing at the man in the awful hourglass against the far wall. Couples had begun dancing to the harp music in front of him, as though he was just part of the decorations. I shuddered.

'I... need to greet everybody,' I said. I wanted to ask Hades if he'd seen a mask with a blue feather and white lace, but I was pretty sure that would earn me a disqualification and seal the poor man's fate.

'Of course,' he said, inclining his head slightly. 'You-' he faltered. 'You look incredible.'

'Oh. Thank you,' I said, unable to stop the wave of

happiness that spread through me at his words. *Totally inappropriate happiness,* I scolded myself. *Seriously, get your priorities straight!* I turned away from him with an effort, looking for the lady in the pink dress. I spotted her, but when I introduced myself I could see that she was wearing a matching pink mask around her bright blue eyes.

'Hello,' said a woman's voice as a beautiful tan-skinned man with short dreadlocks apparently called Theseus took my hand. I nodded politely at Theseus and turned to the voice. Red mask. Dammit.

'Good evening,' I smiled at her. She was wearing a skin-tight scarlet dress, had ink black hair and she was beautiful. 'Thank you for attending tonight. Your dress is lovely,' I said.

'Well, it's not like I had a choice in attending,' she said with a smile that stopped before it even reached her cheeks. 'I'm Minthe.'

'Oh!' *Minthe as in the current forerunner for Queen of the Underworld?* What the fuck was she invited for?

'Apparently it's good form for me to show up. And to be honest, I wanted to find out what all the fuss was about,' she said, looking me up and down with a sneer on her face. All my bully alarms sounded at once in my head. Instinct made my shoulders start to contract and my eyes drop to the floor. As they did though, I caught a glimpse of my shining gold sandals, and the liquid like movement of my skirt. I looked fucking awesome, I remembered. And this was my damn party. 'As I expected, I don't really get why you're such a big deal,' Minthe said, in a bored voice.

I raised my chin slowly, forcing my shoulders back. The satyr I was coming to love appeared at exactly the right moment, and I swiped a saucer glass up from his tray.

'Ditto,' I said simply, then took a long swig from the

glass. 'Do enjoy your evening,' I said coolly, then strode away from her, as her expression morphed into a scowl. I desperately wished Hecate was there to high-five me, or at least Skop to call Minthe something rude, but the surge of pride I felt was enough for now. I knew her sort through and through. And instead of cowering, I had held my own. I could do this.

When I finally spotted the woman in a mask with a blue feather and white lace, another ten minutes had passed and the sand was up to the unconscious man's thighs. I babbled my way through greeting the petite brunette, who was called Selene apparently, scrutinizing her mask closely. A rich blue feather curled from the left side of her mask, standing nearly a foot high, and a complex border of white lace rimmed the mask itself. It was very pretty, but I realized with a lurch that I had no idea what I was supposed to do now that I'd found it. *Just ask her! Ask her for the next clue!* But what if that counted as inappropriate and I was disqualified? I couldn't take risks like that with someone else's life at stake. 'That's a stunning ring,' I said on autopilot, pointing at an enormous milky-white gem on her delicate finger, while I scrabbled for an idea of what to do next.

'Why, thank you,' she beamed at me. 'It's a moon-stone.'

'How lovely,' I replied. Were her words a clue?

'Here, why don't you try it on?' She slipped the ring off, and I started to tell her that it would never fit on my finger, when I noticed the slightly intense look on her face.

'Thank you,' I said instead, and held out my hand. With a little poof, the ring turned into another scroll the second she laid it on my palm.

'You're welcome,' she beamed at me, then turned away,

to talk to her handsome partner. I hurriedly unrolled the scroll.

Standing out in a room full of regular shapes
This unusual vessel will hold that made of grapes

Made of grapes must mean wine, I thought. And a vessel would be a goblet or glass. So I was looking for an unusually shaped wine glass? I instinctively looked over at where Dionysus was surrounded by tall women, his black sequined shirt catching the torch light. He hadn't even got one button done up on it, and I couldn't help the little smile that sprang to my lips. Skop was at his feet, and from where I was standing it appeared that he was looking straight up a pretty dryad's skirt. I rolled my eyes, then scanned their hands. All their glasses looked normal to me.

I strolled casually amongst the guests, smiling and trying vaguely to recall their names as I peered at the glasses in their hands. I didn't remember seeing one odd-shaped glass so far this evening. With a nervous look back at the hourglass, I thought hard. Where would I find the most wine glasses? The kitchens?

It took me a few moments to work out where exactly the serving satyrs and nymphs were appearing from and disappearing to, but as I watched I realized that one of the walls of the room had no twinkling stars at the base, rather a mass of shadow that obscured any details. I approached slowly, and to my fascination, the closer I got, the less I could see.

'I have a way with light and shadow,' said a silky smooth voice, and a very tall man stepped out of the darkness. He was at least eight feet tall, but impossibly slender. He had onyx skin, a bald head, and was wearing a long black robe.

'I see you wear the color black well,' I said politely. He inclined his head at me.

'Can I help you?' he asked.

'Oh, I, erm, wanted to check on the serving staff.'

'Why is that?' He tilted his head at me, his dark eyes probing. I found him distinctly unnerving.

'A good hostess likes to know that she's on top of everything,' I smiled. 'I don't believe I'd had the pleasure of your name?'

'I am Erebus,' he said.

'Persephone,' I replied, holding out my hand. He didn't take it, so I retracted it awkwardly.

'Erebus,' I repeated, wracking my brain. 'I am new to Olympus, so forgive me if I'm wrong but, are you the god of darkness?'

'And shadows, yes,' he said.

'Do you live in the underworld?'

'I do. Hades is my master.'

'So you must be following this competition keenly,' I smiled.

'The whole of Olympus is following this competition keenly. They are starved for entertainment.' His tone was dry and sarcastic, and it made me want to step away from him.

'Well, I must get on and check in with the staff. It was a pleasure to meet you,' I said.

'You will need permission to cross the shadows.'

'Oh. And who would grant me that permission?' I asked tightly, knowing the answer, and feeling irritation grow inside me.

He gave me a creepy smile.

'That would be me.'

There was a man drowning in fucking sand behind me, and this idiot wanted to play games? I plastered my most ingratiating smile across my face.

'May I cross the shadows, please? I would like to check on the feast plans and stock of wine.'

'But of course you may,' he gestured at the void in front of me.

'You have my gratitude,' I lied, and stepped into the darkness.

TWENTY-ONE

I blinked, the light bright after the gentle ambiance of the ballroom, and the pitch darkness of the shadows. Just like kitchens would have been at a function in my world, long stainless steel counters were covered in bowls and platters, and there was activity everywhere I looked. Nymphs and humans alike, wearing white aprons, spooned food into dishes, bustling back and forth between the counters and a huge bank of clay ovens at the back of the room, shouting to each other over the sounds of clanging and more chatter. I inhaled deeply, and to my delight smelled hot-dogs. I looked to my right and saw rows and rows of different glasses laid out, with more nymphs filling them fast with different drinks, before servers refilled their trays. I walked over to them, my heels clicking on the tiled floor.

'Excuse me,' I said, and the pink-skinned nymph I addressed looked up from pouring a bottle and squeaked. 'I didn't mean to startle you,' I said quickly, as she spilled something blue and fizzy onto the counter.

'What do you need, my lady?' she said, avoiding my eye, and mopping quickly at the spillage.

'It's an odd question, I'm afraid, but do you have any strangely shaped wine glasses?' Her eyes snapped to mine and she tilted her head.

'Actually, yes. It was brought in here about half an hour ago. We thought it must belong to someone here, as it's not one of ours.'

'May I see it please?'

'Of course, my lady.' She hurried away behind a row of tall metal cabinets, and returned less than a minute later with a *square* wine glass. The base, stem, and cup all had perfect right angles.

'How peculiar,' I said, taking it from her. Her mouth fell open when it vanished with a poof, a little scroll replacing it. Relief and excitement tingled through me. *Two down, two to go.* 'Thanks for your help,' I grinned at the nymph.

'You're welcome, my lady' she said nervously as I turned and raced back towards the wall of shadows I'd entered through. I unrolled the scroll as I went, reading quickly.

This week's most desired thing of all
There's no other way to get to the ball

No other way to get to the ball? I crossed through the shadows, and for a brief second it was impossible not to notice how beautiful the ballroom looked with its soft, glittering light and stunningly dressed guests twirling and swaying to the music. I forced my attention back to the scroll. The most desired thing just this week? What would people want this week that meant they could get to the ball? The answer came to me immediately. *An invitation.* It had to be. I scanned the room for Hedone, and my heart did a little leap when I finally spotted her and Morpheus talking to Hecate.

My friend looked knockout, in a white leather catsuit that looked like it had been painted onto her skin, and neon pink shot through her high ponytail. She looked like something straight out of the eighties. I hurried towards them.

'Persy!' she exclaimed when I reached her, and leaned forward to give me a kiss on the cheek. Was that allowed? Hedone hadn't covered that. I glanced at the sultry goddess and she gave me a reassuring smile. 'You look sexy as fuck!' Hecate exclaimed, holding me at arm's length and looking me up and down. I beamed at her.

'I'm glad to see you, Hecate,' I said formally. Hecate rolled her eyes.

'Oh gods, you gotta be all proper here. Rather you than me.' What I wanted to say was, *they put an innocent man in a fucking hourglass and they'll kill him if I don't win a stupid game, what the fuck is wrong with you people,* but instead I gave a little shrug.

'You did warn me,' I smiled. I had to word my next question carefully. I didn't want to break the rule about asking direct questions, so I'd already come up with a bullshit reason to ask for what I needed. 'Hedone, I never got to see the invitations for the ball and I just want to double check what time they said the first course of dinner was. You don't happen to have one on you do you?'

Hedone gave me an apologetic smile, and looked down at her slinky black dress. It made her look as curvy as that damn hourglass.

'Nowhere to put an invitation in this dress,' she said, her husky voice somehow accentuated. 'Sorry.' Just as my heart began to sink, Morpheus spoke.

'I have one,' he said, and reached into the inside pocket

of his navy blue dinner jacket. He was one of a handful of people wearing clothes from my world. He frowned as he dug about, and I held my breath hopefully. 'Aha!' he said eventually, and passed me a black piece of card.

'Thank you!' I said, and before I could read the gold embossed words, the invitation vanished with a poof, a fourth scroll in its place. Hecate raised her eyebrows at me, and I gave her a quick smile. 'See you at dinner!' I said, and moved away from them, unrolling the paper. My heart was beginning to beat faster now. I was three clues down, and that last one was the easiest yet. I looked over at the man in the hourglass. The sand was past his hips, and fast approaching his chest. I looked back at the scroll, a surge of adrenaline sharpening my focus.

Serene and melodic, giving spirits a lift
  Apollo and Hermes gave the world this gift

I couldn't help the groan that escaped my lips. The last three clues had been quite obvious but this one... Serene and melodic suggested music. I looked up at the dais. The harp player had been joined by a plethora of musicians, and I couldn't even name half of the instruments I could see. *Shit*. I was going to have to talk to Apollo or Hermes.

Remembering what Hedone had mentioned about Apollo being as sleazy as Zeus, and recalling the genuinely friendly words Hermes had given me when I'd been introduced to the gods, it seemed clear who I should seek out. I scanned the crowd, looking for the red-haired god. All of the Olympians, other than Hades, stood out - they all glowed slightly and they were all completely surrounded by fawning masked folk. Consequently, it didn't take long to spot Hermes. I smiled and nodded my way through the beings around him, trying not to let my alarm show as I accidentally brushed up against a very hairy thing with ten arms.

'Persephone! Great party,' Hermes beamed at me when I finally got in front of him. His close cropped hair and beard glittered in the low light and his elaborate mask was the same bright shade of red, with a yellow feather. He was wearing a traditional toga in black, that much like Zeus's showed most of his chest. I bowed deeply.

'I am honored to call you my guest,' I said respectfully. He flicked his eyes around at the folk still crowded close to us, and suddenly the chatter of the room fell away. It was like I was wearing earplugs.

'You and I were friends, once. I know you don't remember that, but I won't forget it,' Hermes said, his voice crystal clear and his face open and cheerful. As soon as he finished speaking, the sound in the ballroom rushed back, the string instruments casting a mellow, relaxed tune across the chatter. I smiled at Hermes.

'I was hoping to ask you about the sorts of things you preside over as a god,' I said. I needed to be very careful with how direct my questions were. I didn't think I could ask anything about musical instruments, so I would have to work the conversation around to them. This would be a test of my powers of party conversation, I thought, trying not to roll my eyes. Fucking pretentious asshole gods.

'Fire away,' Hermes said, and took a long swig from a tankard.

'Well, I know you're the messenger god, and that you work for Hades sometimes collecting souls,' I said, reciting what I remembered from my classical studies. 'And I know you're famous for playing pranks.' Hermes chuckled.

'I sure am. That little kobaloi friend of yours is a sprite after my own heart.'

'He's not played any pranks on me yet, as far as I know,' I said.

'No, I don't imagine he's allowed to. But he's got quite a colorful history,' Hermes said, eyes glittering with mischief.

'So, what else are you a god of?' I asked.

'Thieves, and wealth,' he said, waggling his eyebrows at me. 'Your own Hades has access to all the underground minerals and gems though, so he is technically richer than I am. But who doesn't love a little heist now and again?'

I raised my eyebrows at him, trying to ignore the term *your own Hades*.

'You'd steal from the king of the Underworld?' Hermes barked a laugh.

'I steal from everyone, dear girl! In fact, I was only made an Olympian because Zeus was so impressed with me stealing from Apollo and getting away with it!'

Apollo? I forced my face to stay impassive as excitement bubbled inside me. Did Hermes steal an instrument from him?

'What did you steal?' I asked quickly.

'His prize cattle,' sighed Hermes, staring wistfully into the distance. I felt my shoulders deflate as disappointment washed over me. 'Those were the days.'

'Oh.'

'He was so mad. I only won him around by appealing to his love of music.'

'Music?' My attention snapped back to the god.

'Yes. I invented the lyre, and played it to him. He liked it so much he forgave me in return for the instrument.'

'The lyre,' I breathed. That must be it. I turned to the dais, trying to recognize a lyre in the hands of one of the musicians. How was I going to find a subtle way of getting onto the stage and getting my hands on one though? I couldn't even be sure if anyone up there had one.

'Yeah. I made it out of a tortoise shell and bits of sheep gut. I don't reckon any of them up there would be too impressed with that now,' Hermes laughed, following my gaze. His laugh cut off abruptly, and I looked at him as his eyes widened. 'That's just given me a great idea. Watch this,' he grinned. The air over his hands shimmered, and a large empty tortoise shell with slimy red string tied across it appeared out of nowhere. I screwed my face up at the smell, and stepped backwards. 'Sheep gut strings,' he said, his eyes dancing.

'What are you-' I started to ask him, but with another wave of his hand it vanished, replaced by a beautifully carved wooden lyre. There was a yelp and a jarring sound and my attention snapped to the stage. A woman standing amongst the musicians was holding out the tortoise-shell lyre, staring at the red on her fingertips in disgust and confusion. 'You- you swapped them!' Hermes started to laugh, an infectious giggle that I couldn't help emulating. 'That's gross! And completely unfair!' I spluttered.

'It sure is,' Hermes replied, and downed his drink. 'But I also find it highly amusing. I need a new one of these,' he said, raising his empty glass. 'Can I leave you to sort this out? One of the duties of a good hostess is to sort out other god's mischief.' He held the lyre out to me with a wink.

'Y-yes!' I said, doing my best not to snatch it from him.

As soon as I touched it, it disappeared with a poof, a small metal orb in its place.

'Aha!' barked Hermes. 'I'm so glad to have helped! It was brief, but a pleasure, Persephone,' he beamed, then strode past me.

TWENTY-TWO

I turned the little metal ball over in my hands, hope and anticipation filling me. Honestly, if there wasn't an unconscious guy drowning in sand, the test would actually have been quite fun. The orb had three simple rings carved around it, but other than that gave me no clues. What was I supposed to do with it?

The clues will lead to a key to unlock the hourglass, the commentator had said. I looked at the hourglass. The sand was just falling past the man's shoulders. The orb didn't look like any sort of key I'd ever seen, but that meant nothing. This place was as weird as weird could get.

I walked quickly towards the hourglass, apologizing to people as they stepped up to talk to me.

'I'm sorry, I won't be a moment,' I said politely, over and over again, causing the time it took me to cross the hall to be doubled. Stupid damned manners. Eventually I reached the hourglass. A hush fell over the room and nerves skittered through me as I looked back over my shoulder. Everyone was watching me, now they had realized where I was going. They knew I had solved all the clues and got the key. There was no way I could do this bit naturally, but surely this wouldn't get me disqualified? The commentator had said I needed to unlock the hourglass. I paused, holding my breath, waiting for his booming voice to reprimand me, but only the sounds of the harp carried through the ballroom. I dropped into a crouch, my relief short lived. The frame of the hourglass was made of what looked like brass, including the thick base which bore a broad plaque in the middle. There were two round holes in the plaque and a short inscription underneath each.

Innocent and *guilty*.

I frowned. What did that mean? Was it referring to the man inside? I stood up, peering through the glass at the man's sleeping face. He had deep creases around his eyes but he was too young for them to be wrinkles from age. He had sandy colored hair that was tidy and short. How was I supposed to know if he was guilty or innocent? And of what? I let out a hiss of annoyance and took a deep breath. There must be a clue somewhere. Even these twatty gods wouldn't make a puzzle unsolvable.

I put my hands on the glass and looked again. He was wearing something around his neck, I realized. It was on a leather band and it was small and metal. Some sort of charm. It looked like... a feather? I squinted, trying to see details through the slightly warped glass as the sand began to cover the man's throat - and the necklace. *It was a dagger,* I finally realized. Why would he have a dagger charm around his neck? Did that mean something in Olympus? I clenched my jaw. As an outsider, I was at a disadvantage, once again. *Think, Persephone.* Daggers are not generally associated with innocence. Could the answer be that black and white?

Discomfort rolled through me at the thought of

deeming a stranger guilty of anything. Except these Olympian assholes for making me play their stupid games. I took a deep breath. All this time I had been thinking of the guy in the hourglass as an innocent bystander, put through this for entertainment. But what if the gods were not that cruel? What if they actually had chosen someone who deserved it? Not that I was convinced anyone deserved to be drowned in sand.

With a swift movement, before I could talk myself out of it, I dropped my little orb into the 'guilty' hole. There was a metal rolling sound, and then a click. I stepped back, heart hammering as I watched the hourglass. Slowly at first, then faster, the sand began to move the other way, shooting back up the little gap it had come from, quicker than it should be able to.

'Congratulations, Persephone!' The commentator's voice made me jump. 'You've just saved the life of a convicted murderer!'

'What?' I span around to look at the blonde man, standing only ten feet behind me.

'Part of the Titan Brotherhood, this man killed over fifty others, before he was brought to justice by the magnificent Theseus,' he beamed, and gestured at the gorgeous guy with dreads I'd met earlier. Applause erupted through the room, and Theseus nodded and smiled at everyone, raising his glass. 'We'll have a short break for the feast, then your second test will begin. Enjoy!'

Hecate sauntered over to me, her glass raised, as everyone turned back to their partners, talking excitedly.

'Nice one, Persy,' she said as she reached me.

'He's a convicted murderer?' I gaped at her.

'Yeah,' she shrugged. 'What's the problem?'

I opened and closed my mouth a few times. I wasn't sure exactly what I wanted to say, only that this was all really wrong somehow.

'That's not how we deal with criminals in our world,' I said eventually.

'Well if this offends you, I would discourage you from visiting some of the darker areas of the Underworld,' she said, raising one eyebrow. 'The Olympians are rather well known for their colorful punishments of the guilty.' I blew out a breath, and looked about for the serving satyr. I needed some more of that fizzy wine.

'My lady,' said a little voice, a tray appearing out of nowhere.

'Thank you,' I said, and swiped up a glass. 'How do they know when we want a drink?'

'That's their job and they're good at it. Speaking of which, you completed the first test fast. The judges should be impressed.'

'Hmm,' I said, taking a long swig of my drink. Thank the gods for alcohol. Although at the rate I was drinking, I wouldn't be sober enough to last all three tests.

Over Hecate's shoulder I saw that lots of round tables had appeared, ornately dressed in scarlet red tablecloths and each set for eight guests. Relief that I'd gone through feasting etiquette washed over me when I saw the number of pieces of silverware surrounding the grand black plates and bowls. A loud gong sounded, and people began to make their way to the tables.

'Top table,' said Hecate, as I moved my head side-to-side, trying to work out how they knew where to sit. 'You're on the top table.' She pointed to an oblong shaped table in the middle of the room.

'Where are you sitting?' I asked her.

'With you,' she grinned at me. 'Perks of being the boss's favorite employee.'

'Thank the gods for that,' I breathed. Having a familiar face nearby would definitely boost my confidence.

'Well done, you said gods!' Hecate clinked her glass against mine with a grin. 'We're making progress.'

'Speaking of the gods... Will they be sat at the top table with us?'

'No, they don't eat with us inferior folk. Feasting with the gods is the highest mark of respect a citizen can be given.'

'What about lunch with a god?' I asked quickly, thinking of my donuts on Zeus's mountain-top. There was no way he'd have been showing me respect, surely? Hecate laughed, presumably at the confused expression I must have had on my face.

'Don't worry, a god trying to get into your pants over a little light refreshment isn't the same. I'm talking feasting, like this, with all of them.'

'So where do they eat?' I asked as we made our way to our table.

'Who knows? Or cares?' she shrugged, pointing to a chair. I saw a prettily inscribed name card on the onyx colored plate. *Persephone*. Hecate moved to the other side of the table, and sat down but I remained standing, as I had been taught. I needed to greet all of my table guests.

'Persephone, it's a pleasure to meet you,' said a man, reaching for my hand. My lips parted and I felt heat rush to my face as my fingers touched his. He was *gorgeous*. And not mysteriously good looking like Morpheus, or pretty-boy good looking like Zeus, but panty-dropping, mouth-drooling, dizzy-making gorgeous. He was built like a football player, a white shirt emphasizing his broad shoulders, and low slung pants drawing my eyes inexorably to his hips. I dragged my attention back to his face, where his dusty blonde hair curled around his ears and his eyes shone blue.

'H-hello,' I stammered. 'Thank you for coming.'

'Wouldn't miss it for the world,' he beamed, and I swear my knees wobbled. His full lips were mesmerizing. He started to move towards a chair, but I stopped him.

'I didn't catch your name,' I said quickly.

'Oh, I'm sorry, I'm not allowed to tell you.' He gave me an apologetic smile.

'Why not?'

He shrugged.

'Hate the game, not the players,' he said with a wink. My initial captivation with him vanished, and I suppressed a growl. Now what were those bastards up to? Was this part of the test?

One by one people came up to me, kissing my hand or curtsying politely, and none of them would tell me their name. The only one of the five I recognized was the woman who was wearing the mask with the blue feather and white lace on it. I cast about for her name, but there had been so many introductions that evening that I couldn't remember it.

'Let the feast begin!' rang out a voice, and a colorful assortment of fruit suddenly appeared on all the plates. I sat down on my chair, picked the correct fork from the array available, and took a breath. I wasn't going to let my guard down for a second - something was definitely going on here.

TWENTY-THREE

'So,' I said, as cheerfully as I could. 'Where are you from?' I turned to the woman sitting on my right. She was pretty, like everyone at the ball, with tight silver ringlets falling about her shoulders and a flush of freckles across her full cheeks.

'Leo,' she smiled at me. Leo. That was Zeus's realm.

'Are you a goddess?' I asked.

'Everyone here is a god. Except you.' I looked across at the woman who had spoken. She was sitting next to Hecate, who was glaring at her. Her mask was black and red, bold lines breaking up the colors, and I couldn't help thinking of Mexican wrestling masks. She had a mountain of black curly hair piled high on her head, and she was wearing a ball gown that had a perfectly fitted corset to accentuate her massive breasts. It took a serious effort not to stare at them.

'What are you the goddess of?' I asked her with a forced smile.

'Can't tell you that,' she shrugged, and stabbed at a piece of salmon. We'd moved on from the fruit course. 'What is this? Is it from your crappy world?'

I felt my eye twitch, but kept the smile on my face.

'It's smoked salmon. And yes, it's quite popular in the mortal world.'

'Well, it tastes like shit,' she said.

I inhaled slowly through my nose, and turned to the only other man at the table, who had yet to say a word. He was the most unassuming person I'd seen at the ball yet. He was a normal size, was wearing a traditional style toga that didn't show too much of his chest, had close cropped brown hair and a simple silver mask with no feather or adornments. He wore an impassive expression on a forgettable face.

'Hello. Where are you from?' I asked him. He looked up at me from his food, and fire leapt to life inside me. Screams penetrated my skull, distant at first, then louder, as flames licked around my vision. Then as quickly as they'd started, the thoughts receded, leaving me with a white knuckled grip on my cutlery, and no idea what he'd just said to me. 'I'm-I'm sorry, could you repeat that?' I said, blinking, my pulse racing. Had Hades just got angry with someone somewhere? Why would that affect me if he wasn't even here?

'I'm from a place you are as yet unaware of,' the guy said, his expression still neutral but his brown eyes swirling with something seriously other-worldly. Something *dark*. Had he just caused that?

'Oh,' I said, unsure what else to say.

'Gods, you sound so dramatic,' the big-boobed lady said to him, rolling her eyes. The man gave a her a small smile, and carried on eating his salmon. She let out an exaggerated sigh. 'I'll level with you, Persephone, I'm a bit disappointed.'

'I'm sorry to hear that,' I said, trying not to grit my teeth. 'How can I improve your evening?'

'Well, I had hoped Oceanus would be here. There's a

big gathering next week, and the rumors are that he's at the center of it all. I wanted to get some inside info.' Her eyes shone amber behind her mask, and the more I looked at them, the more annoyed with her I got.

'I would have liked Oceanus to be here too, but I'm afraid I can't control the Titans.'

'Well you seem pretty friendly with this one,' she said, jerking her thumb at Hecate.

'Wait, what?' I stared at Hecate as she swallowed her mouthful of food and shrugged. 'You're a Titan?'

The big-boobed woman snorted.

'She's one of the most powerful beings in this room, of course she is.'

'Why didn't you tell me?' I asked her. I wasn't sure why it mattered, but somehow it did. I felt betrayed, even though she had no reason to have mentioned her heritage. But the Titans were all supposed to be in a pit of torture weren't they?

'Erm, you never asked? Why does it matter?'

'Oh Hecate, even pathetic mortals from the human world know that Titans are losers,' said big-boobs. I glared at her, but Hecate coughed, and gave me a look.

'I'm descended from Titans, yes. Hades gives a lot of Titans jobs. Let's move on to something else shall we? How's your mother?' She turned to the beautiful man, who was beaming at the hot-dog that had just appeared on his plate.

'What's this?' he asked, looking at me.

'It's a hot dog,' I told him, my face flushing as soon as I laid eyes on his lips.

'What's the yellow stuff?'

'Mustard.' He picked up his knife and a small laugh escaped me.

'No, like this,' I said, and picked up my own hot dog. It

tasted divine, and a pang of homesickness bolted through me. *I would be home soon enough.* Everyone around the table picked up their own hot dogs and started to eat, appreciative murmurs ringing through the group.

'Mom's great thanks,' the hot guy said suddenly, turning to Hecate. 'She's been looking forward to tonight. She's got something planned for later I think.'

'Who is your mother?' I asked.

'Ah, lovely Persephone, it seems so mean that I'm not allowed to answer any of your questions,' he said, and something fluttered in my stomach as he gazed at me. 'I guess it wouldn't be cheating to tell you she's an Olympian though,' he said, and winked at me again. *Guys who wink are not your type. Guys who wink are not your type.* I clung to the chant in my head, and gave him a thank-you nod.

'So, you lived in New York?' said the lady in the blue mask I'd met earlier.

'Yes, do you know it?' I asked her excitedly. It was the first time someone had mentioned anything from home to me.

'Yes, very well. It is a realm that comes alive at night.' I liked the thought of New York being its own realm, and I smiled warmly at her.

'Well if you win the Hades Trials, you can kiss goodbye to seeing cities lit by moonlight,' said big-boobs. 'In fact you can kiss sunlight goodbye too.'

Why was this woman being such a pain in the ass? I bet she was one of the ones Hedone warned me about, that would be sneaking off with some married man later on, I thought. I'd be damned if I was covering for her.

The gong sounded suddenly, pulling me out of my thoughts, and the commentator's voice swiftly followed it.

'Good evening Olympus! I hope the guests are enjoying

their meals? Well, they're going to have to wait for their desserts, as we have a short interlude... Persephone's second test!' A new hourglass shimmered into existence next to the first, which still had the unconscious murderer in it. I peered at the new glass, trying to see inside. It was much smaller than the first, and it seemed to be empty, until with a shimmer, a woman appeared in the bottom half. She was on her knees, her head lolling to one side so that a mass of dark hair tumbled down over her chest. My gut constricted, and any enjoyment I had begun to get from the ball slipped away, replaced by renewed disgust of these games. It was too easy to forget how fucked up these people were, and I had begun to relax. That was a mistake.

'As you can see, this is a smaller hourglass, and the sand will fall much faster. You don't have long for this test, Persephone.' He beamed at me, then vanished, reappearing with a little flash of light right next to me. I tried to keep my nerves from showing on my face as he handed me a golden orb. 'To complete this test and save that woman's life, you must take apart this key, and match the correct piece to the correct guest on your table. You may not ask any questions at all. Are you ready?'

'Erm-' I said, but before I could finish speaking he cut me off.

'Good, let's begin!'

I instinctively looked at the hourglass, and my breath caught, panic rising in me as I saw how fast the sand was falling. The hole in the middle was larger than the last one, and the base of the hourglass was already completely covered. I didn't imagine that I would have more than five minutes before the sand reached the woman's head. I turned back to the table, lifting the orb to my face. The room was completely silent as I inspected the ball. There was nothing on it all, no markings or inscriptions or patterns. What was I supposed to do with it? The last one had three rings carved into it. I gripped each side in my hand and twisted, imagining the rings on the last orb. To my relief there was a click and I felt movement, then I fumbled with the metal as the whole thing broke apart in my hands. Two pieces dropped onto the table in front of me, hitting my plate with a clang, and I felt my face flush. *Act like you don't give a shit*, I thought, trying to channel Hecate's fierce attitude. *It doesn't matter if the rest of Olympus thinks you're clumsy; what matters that you save this woman's life.*

I laid all the bits out on the table, turning them over in my hands and looking for clues. It reminded me of cracking open an Easter egg, the center of the orb hollow. There were five pieces, which made sense as I had five unknown guests at my table, plus Hecate. I was assuming she wasn't part of this test, as I already knew who she was.

'Aha,' I mumbled, as I lifted one of the broken bits of shell to my face, wishing there was more light in the ballroom. Painted on the inside, tiny and delicate, I could just make out a crescent moon. Whipping my gaze out over my silent table guests, I picked up the next piece, looking closely until I found a tiny heart with an arrow through it. I checked the other three pieces as quickly as I could, finding a tiny skull, a cracked bowl, and what looked like a fountain. *Come on Persephone, work it out.* Five symbols and five guests. None of whom would tell me their name or what they were gods of. The guests *must* match the symbols. I turned and looked at the hourglass. The sand was already at the woman's waist. *Concentrate!*

Well, the heart and arrow was the symbol for cupid in my world. I couldn't remember the Greek name for him, but I knew he was the god of lust, and Aphrodite's son. There was no question that he had to be the gorgeous guy, as that would explain the conversation about his Olympian mother, and the fact that I couldn't talk to him without thinking about him doing filthy things to me. I picked up the piece with the heart on it, and held it out to him across the table. He grinned at me as he took it, and the commentator's voice rang out across the room, although I couldn't see him anymore.

'Correct! Eros, god of desire and sex!'

Thank the gods for that, I thought, but felt little relief. That was the only easy one. *OK, what next?* The skull... My eyes darted to the plain guy. The plain guy whose gaze had made me see fire and hear screams. Without giving myself time to second guess my decision, I held out the skull piece to him. His lips barely moved as he took it and the commentator's voice boomed once more.

'Correct! Thanatos, god of death!'

A shiver ran through me. I'd been eating next to the freaking god of death and not known? I pushed the unhelpful thought aside, and picked up another piece. The moon. I looked at the three women, and a memory of a conversation earlier that evening flashed into my head. *'It's a moon-stone,'* the lady in the blue mask had said when I admired her ring.

'Selene!' I exclaimed out loud, as I remembered her name. She said she liked New York because it came alive at night. Surely that would make her goddess of the moon or night? With a deep breath, I passed her the piece of orb with the moon on it. She gave me a big smile, and this time I did allow a little relief to wash through me as the commentator spoke.

'Correct! Selene, goddess of the moon!'

I looked over at the hourglass. The sand was just

starting to cover the woman's chest. I only had a few minutes more, I was sure. My palms were beginning to sweat, and adrenaline was making my insides feel like they were vibrating as I picked up the last two pieces. A broken bowl and a fountain. I looked between the pretty young woman from Leo and the big-breasted jerk with the stupid hair, and bit down on my lip. I didn't know what either symbol meant. The bowl was broken... Was there a goddess of broken things? And the fountain... It couldn't be goddess of the sea or water, as that was surely Poseidon? I tried to think of famous fountains, but nothing came to me. What could the broken bowl mean? Could it just represent stuff being messed up? In which case it surely had to be the miserable trouble-maker? *If you get this wrong, a woman dies.* I closed my eyes. I was sweating profusely now. I didn't know what the correct answer was.

TWENTY-FOUR

Go with your instincts, Persephone. The pretty young woman didn't match something broken, surely. But the rude, abrasive woman I could definitely see as broken somehow. With a massive breath, I opened my eyes and held out the broken bowl piece to big-boobs. The scowl on her face as she took it made me sag in relief. If she was scowling then I'd got it right. I turned and passed the last piece to the other lady and she grinned.

'Correct! Eris, goddess of discord, and Hebe, goddess of youth!'

Each of the gods held out their piece in turn, and I watched as they glowed a faint purple, then left their owners outstretched hands and floated towards the center of the table. With a little burst of light they rejoined, but this time the golden orb had the three rings carved around it. I stood up and reached forward, plucking the key from where it was hovering, and hurried towards the hourglass. The sand had reached the woman's shoulders and was only inches from her chin. I dropped into a crouch as soon as I reached the hourglass, looking for the hole to put the key in, expecting more inscriptions. But there were none. I screwed my face up, searching for the place to put the orb.

'Where do I put the key?' I asked aloud, panic starting to flood me as I stood up, scanning the frame of the hourglass desperately. There were no holes, no inscriptions, nothing. Silence met my question and my eyes darted to the woman's face. The sand was moving past her chin, and would cover her mouth in seconds. 'Where does it go?' I shouted, my stomach tensing so hard it hurt as I started to run my hand over the metal. As my fingertips reached across the top of the hour-glass they felt hot and I paused my frantic movements, feeling more carefully. I could only just reach the top, and there was no way I could see what was up there, but I was sure I could feel a channel carved along the edge of the metal. With a last look at the woman's face as the sand covered her bottom lip, I reached up and pushed the key onto the top of the hourglass. I held my breath as I heard the sound of metal on metal, sure it was the sound of the ball rolling. Then there was a clunking sound, and the sand in the timer began to rush upwards all at once. For a second I thought the woman would suffocate from all the sand moving in the opposite direction, but before I could do anything, the bottom half of the hour-glass was clear. My heart felt like it was stuck in my throat as I watched her chest, relief making my knees feel weak as I finally saw it move. She was breathing.

A smattering of applause filled the room, and I heard Hecate give a loud whoop. What the fuck was wrong with these people? I clenched my fists at my sides, trying to rein in my emotions. A person just nearly died and they were clapping like they were watching tennis or something? Even Hecate, my only friend here, didn't seem to grasp how messed up this was. *You're in another world now. Just get on with it, and get home.*

I turned, knowing the smile I'd fixed on my face must look more like a grimace, but unable to conjure up anything better.

'This is bullshit,' I said through gritted teeth, hardly moving my smiling lips but needing to say the words out loud. I felt a bit better.

'I know it is. But you're doing a good job,' said a voice in my head, and my smile slipped.

'Hades?' I projected the thought at him, using the image of his smoky form to send the word.

'Yes.'

'Where are you?' People were tucking into huge bowls of frozen yogurt, and none of them were looking at me anymore.

'Watching.'

'Are you coming back?'

'Yes.'

'You... you helped me with the other Trials.'

'Yes. Eat your dessert.'

I let out a long breath, and walked slowly back to the table.

'Nice job, Persephone,' beamed Eros.

'Thank you,' I said absently.

'Oooh, someone isn't happy with this set up,' said Eris, her eyes flashing behind her mask. 'What's wrong, perfect Persephone?'

'Seriously Eris, give it rest,' said Hecate, rolling her eyes as she spooned yogurt into her mouth. 'Persy, this stuff is awesome, I can see why you miss American food.'

'It is very delicious,' said the woman I now knew to be Hebe. I turned to her, deliberately ignoring the goddess of discord.

'I wonder if you could tell me, Hebe, how does the fountain represent you?' I asked her, politely.

'Oh, it's the fountain of youth,' she said cheerfully. 'A little obscure perhaps, but I'm glad you worked it out.'

'Thank you,' I said, and dipped my spoon un-enthusiastically into my own yogurt. My appetite had vanished. 'I didn't, really. I just knew you weren't the broken one.' There was a collective intake of breath, and I looked up, directly at Eris. Her expression was dark, her lips twisting in a snarl and venom in her glare.

A week ago a look like that would have terrified me. A week ago I would have been groveling and apologizing for what I'd said. Hell, a week ago, I wouldn't have fucking said it.

But I was done.

I was angry and scared and sick of being used as a twisted puppet for the entertainment of others, and the only person I could take it out on right now was the bully across the table. So I was going to.

'You're right, I am broken,' Eris said, her voice almost a purr. 'You've no idea how broken I am. And how much I enjoy breaking others.'

'I do have an idea,' I told her. 'I've met plenty of people like you. Hell, I've met quite a few since coming here.'

'Oh naive little Persy. I'm afraid you're wrong. You haven't met anybody as fucked up as me yet. With one exception that is, but you're competing to marry him. So what does that make you?'

Defensiveness sparked in me out of nowhere. Hades wasn't a bully. He may be pretty scary, but he wasn't like her, or Minthe, or Erebus, or Zeus. I *knew* he wasn't. I opened my mouth to respond, but common sense kicked in just in time. I was the hostess of the ball. And Eris was smart as she seemed cruel. I knew what she was trying to do, and I wasn't going to let her bait me into making a scene at my own party. I wasn't going to let her win.

'That makes me a fucking mystery,' I smiled at her, and stood up, pushing my chair back. The whole room turned to me and I raised my glass before Eris could say another word.

'Time for dancing!' I announced loudly, and this time I got an actual cheer, instead of the pathetic applause when I'd saved two people's lives. I needed air, but this stupid underground place had nowhere to go, nowhere to breathe. Claustrophobia began to press in on me, and the rules made clear at the beginning of the evening echoed in my head. *You may not leave the ball.* I was stuck here, with all these freaking lunatics. My heart began to skitter in my chest, my breathing too shallow. *Stay calm, don't freak out,* I instructed myself, my eyes darting around the room. There must be a quiet corner I could hide in somewhere. I walked towards the far wall, the one opposite the hourglasses, smiling at everyone I passed as sweat began to trickle down my spine, my anxiety ratcheting higher. I only stopped when I found an area where the columns seemed closer together, and for a merciful moment, I couldn't see anybody. I leaned gratefully against the cool marble of the nearest column, taking a long, slow breath. I probably only had minutes before somebody showed up, but I would take whatever I could get. I just needed a couple minutes to get my shit together, that was all.

If I didn't think too much about the fact that I was trapped underground with a load of well-dressed murderers, then I was OK. But as soon as the knowledge that I couldn't leave worked its way through any positive thoughts I tried to fill my head with, the room seemed to close in around me again. If I was at home and my surroundings got overwhelming I would do what anyone would do - go outside. Get some air. Air. Just a few breaths of cold air to clear my head. But even something that simple was unattainable.

'Stupid, stupid place,' I hissed aloud. 'How the fuck does anywhere not have an outside?'

'I told you, there is an outside. You've been out in it.'

Hades' voice made me jump, and for a split second I thought it was in my head, but then dark smoke rippled in front of me.

'Yeah, on a fucking invisible bridge! What kind of asshole invents one of those? And it's shitty outside, there isn't anything growing, or even a breeze!' I barked the words before he could materialize fully, feeling braver when I couldn't properly see him.

'We don't need a breeze,' Hades replied eventually, a touch of defensiveness to his tone as the smoke stopped rippling, his humanoid form complete. There was no slithering sound to his voice.

'Well I do,' I muttered, casting my eyes down and staring angrily at the floor. A pulsing beat had begun, the melodic orchestra replaced by music far more reminiscent of my home world.

'You are upset?' Hades asked me eventually.

'Yeah. Yeah, I'm upset.'

'Why? You are doing well.' I looked up, searching the smoke for his eyes, as hot tears began to burn the back of mine. Frustration was causing them, and I cursed my body. Tears wouldn't help me, just make me look more weak.

'Who is she?' I asked, my voice barely above a whisper.

'Who?'

I gaped at him.

'Who? Who the fuck do you think? The woman you all nearly killed for entertainment!'

He turned, looking towards the hourglass.

'I don't know,' he said eventually. My mouth fell open, my stomach roiling.

'You don't know? Would you have cared if she had died?'

'No. I do not know her.'

I shook my head, the last of any tolerance I had for this place fleeing me.

'What is wrong with you people? How can you be so self important, so callous, so.... murderous?'

The smoke flickered, and I saw a flash of silver. When he spoke, the iciness was back, and images of snakes poured into my head, my skin crawling.

'You are speaking to the King of the Underworld. Lord of the dead. Ancient and all-powerful and witness to deeds you can't even imagine.' I shrank back against the column involuntarily as the smoky form grew. 'If you had lived through what I have, if you had seen the things my fellow gods have done to each other, have done to those around them... You would hold a different opinion.'

I stared at him. He was blaming the other gods?

'So you aren't as barbaric as them?' I whispered.

'Oh yes, Persephone. Yes I am. In fact, I'm worse than most of them.' Eris's words flicked into my head. *You haven't met anybody as fucked up as me yet. With one exception that is, but you're competing to marry him.'*

'Why? Do you... enjoy death?' I barely got the words out. I knew I didn't want to hear the answer. Hades flashed solid so quickly my brain hardly registered it.

'I never asked for this role. But it is mine. And I will fulfill it.' What did that mean?

'That's not an answer.' There was a long pause, and I swear he must have been able to hear my pounding heart over the music.

'No,' he said eventually, his voice quiet and the anger lessened. 'I do not enjoy death. But it is my world. It is who I have had to become. If I were as sensitive to it as you humans, I would be a very poor king indeed.'

I frowned, straightening against the column slightly.

'You humans...' I repeated. 'But I wasn't human before.' The claustrophobia pressed in on me again, that feeling of being separated from a part of my own self building inside me. 'I can't have been as indifferent to death as you are. I can't have been.' I could hear the pleading tone to my voice, and I realized at that moment what I was so afraid of, what I feared even more than him and this world.

What if I was once like these people?

This is where I was from, this man was once my husband. Did I ever find entertainment in people's suffering? I felt sick as I stared into Hades' face, and a single hot tear leaked from my eye, sliding down my cheek.

Suddenly, the smoke leapt out from where he was standing, and the next thing I knew I was in a black, hazy bubble. I looked around myself quickly, aware that I could no longer hear the music, or anything else, nor could I see beyond the thick smoke barrier surrounding us.

'What-' I started but my words fell away as I laid eyes on

Hades. *It was him.* The real him, under the smoke. My breath caught and desperation filled me as I stared at his face, into his swirling silver eyes. *Home. He was home. He was mine.*

I shook my head, trying to clear the words ricocheting around my brain.

'You were never cruel, Persephone. You were fair and kind and I...' he trailed off, hopeless sadness pouring from his beautiful face. I stepped towards him before I could help myself, and he lifted his hand to my cheek. Ever so slowly, he brushed his thumb across my skin, wiping away my solitary tear. Electricity shot through my body at his touch. His touch was warm, and for some reason I had expected him to be cold. Frustration welled inside me again. I knew so little, and I needed more.

'I hate this place,' I whispered and he flinched. 'Please, please make me understand how this was once my home. Because I know it was. I know you were.'

'It wasn't always like this. It was before you came, and it was again after you left. But when you were here...' His eyes bore into mine. 'You brought light, and life, to a place where I thought none could exist.' He spoke hoarsely, and his words crashed through all the mental armor I'd built up since coming to Olympus.

He loved me. I could see it in his face, hear it in his broken voice, feel it in his electrifying touch. All this time, all those years alone in New York, and someone, somewhere, loved me this much. And I never knew.

TWENTY-FIVE

I stared at Hades, my mind spinning. He was a god. King of the Underworld, Lord of the dead, and he'd just wiped a tear from my cheek.

'Light and life,' I repeated, my stomach feeling like it was filled with butterflies. 'Are those things you wanted here, in this place?'

'Not at first. I just wanted you.' Desire skittered through my core at his words, and I saw his eyes flash with something new. 'Damn Aphrodite,' he muttered. I raised my eyebrows at him and he sighed. 'Her music, her power. She always does this at balls, and the smoke can only keep so much of it out. She's powerful.'

'Love is powerful,' I murmured. The side of his mouth quirked up.

'See? That's her power. Making us both... soft.'

'Soft?' That's the last word I would have used to describe him. He was wearing the same clothes as he was before, jeans and a black shirt open at the neck. His skin glowed, and I wanted more than anything in the world to touch it.

'Yes. Soft and... passionate. That's what she does.' I tilted my head, trying to clear the image of him lifting his shirt over his taut chest.

'What do *you* do?'

'That's a big question.'

'You won't answer any of my others.'

'That's not fair. I've answered loads now.'

He smelled of fire and wood-smoke.

'You smell like campfires,' I told him.

'Do you like it?'

'Yes.' I stepped closer to him, the low beat of the music filtering through to me now, my hips beginning to sway of their own accord. 'I don't like that I'm not in control of my body though.'

'Aphrodite's power won't make you do anything you didn't already want to,' he said quietly. I looked up into his face. His eyes were alive with hunger now, deep and shining and breathtaking. Slowly, I reached up, and touched his jaw. A thrill pulsed right through my whole body, making all my muscles clench and heat pool deliciously inside me. I wanted him. More than I'd ever wanted anything in my life. He drew a ragged breath, then his hand was on my face, lifting it to his. Our lips met, and fire exploded in my core. Pleasure engulfed me as his tongue snaked between my lips, and desire so strong that I physically ached completely took me over. I pushed my hands into his hair, pulling him into me, desperate to taste him. I was standing on my tiptoes to get as close to him as I possibly could, pressing my body hard against his. His arm wrapped around my back and then he was lifting me, his lips moving from mine and kissing hungrily along my jaw, down my throat. I tipped my head back as I wrapped my legs tightly around his waist, the pleasure from his touch making me tremble. Waves of need pounded between my thighs, and I couldn't think straight as I entwined my fingers in his hair, his lips moving back up my neck.

'I missed you,' he murmured into my skin. 'Gods, I missed you.' A small moan escaped me, even as part of me railed against the fact that he wasn't kissing me for the first time, but I had no recollection of ever having done this before.

'I need you,' I gasped. And it was true. At that moment, I would have done anything in the world to feel him inside me, to meld his body with my own, to find a release for this ferocious desire.

Abruptly, he pulled back, his eyes slightly wild as they met mine.

'But you don't love me.' I stared into his face. The desire I felt for him went as deep as any feeling I'd ever experienced, but love? No. I didn't love him. I barely knew him. And what I did know was conflicted and confusing. I had clearly left too long a pause, as his expression hardened, and he lifted me from his waist, setting me back on my sandals unsteadily. Confusion rolled through me. 'Of course you don't. You are not the woman I married. You are someone new.'

I blinked, my physical response to him making it impossible to work out his words properly.

'I'm Persephone,' I said thickly.

'We must not do this to ourselves. You can't stay here and this would be folly.'

'What?' I felt like I'd been punched in the gut, a hollow feeling of loss and rejection making anger spike inside me, fueled by the passion still making my pulse race. 'You're mad at me because I don't love you? A man I've just met? A man surrounded by death?'

His lips parted and something jet black flashed in his silver eyes. I took a step backwards before I realized I had, the hair on my arms standing up as the temperature plummeted. *It's cold when I'm scaring on purpose*, he had told me.

'And that, little human, is why you can not stay,' he hissed. And I mean hissed, as though he were actually a reptile. The dark smoke around us billowed suddenly, and rushed back towards him, the music and sound of the party smashing into me like a physical hammer.

'Hades!' I shouted, but it was too late. He had vanished.

Unspent desire and tension ripped through me, and I barely contained the scream trying to crawl its way out of my throat as Hecate stumbled towards me.

'I know that smoke bubble,' she slurred. 'You and Hades were getting it ooooon.' She waggled her eyebrows at me, a stupid grin on her face.

'Are you drunk?'

'Yep.'

I rubbed my hands across my face, trying to dispel the lingering taste of Hades, the little pulses of excitement still rippling through me, and the surges of anger and fear that had followed them.

'Hecate, tell me what happened before. Why did I leave? Why did the gods take away all my memories?'

'Persy, please-' she started but I shouted over her.

'Hecate, I'm fucking serious, I've had enough!'

Her face morphed into a frown and she put one hand on her hip.

'It didn't go well with lover-boy then,' she said eventually. I gritted my teeth, exasperation making me feel like my body wasn't big enough to contain what I was feeling. I was ready to fucking explode.

'Tell. Me. What. Happened.' I spat the words out one by one, and Hecate grimaced.

'Alright. But if Hades-' her words were cut off abruptly by the sound of the gong.

'No! No, no, no!' But the commentator's voice bellowed across my fury.

'Is everybody ready for the third and final test? This one's a really good one, I promise you! Where is the lovely lady? Come on over Persephone!'

I closed my eyes, trying desperately to slow my heart rate, to calm down. One more test. Just one more. I had to do this, or some poor bastard would drown in sand. But after that, I wasn't giving up until somebody told me what I needed to know.

I walked slowly and serenely to the middle of the room, trying to look the complete opposite of how I felt. A new hourglass had appeared next to the first two. It was as large as the first one, and currently empty. I glared at it. *And this is why you can't love him*, I reminded myself. He doesn't give a shit about people dying. *You still want to fuck him though,* the contrary part of me chimed in. Stupid damn bad-boy attraction. But I knew, deep down, that it was so much more than that. I'd never felt anything this intense before in my life.

'So, are you ready?' the commentator asked me, from where he stood by the hourglass. I nodded at him. It didn't matter one jot if I wasn't. 'For your third test-' he began, but a resounding crash drowned him out, and everyone snapped their attention to the source of the noise. From the darkness Erebus had been guarding earlier came a flash of orange fire, and a distant scream. *Kitchen fire*, was my first instinct but then I remembered we were in a world of gods and magic. Kitchen fires wouldn't cause this much disruption, would they? There was another flash of fire, then a bird erupted from the shadows and I wasn't the only one who gasped.

Its wing span was massive, easily three times my size, but that wasn't what was most attention grabbing. The whole creature was on fire. It wasn't a bird at all, it was a phoenix, I realized. With a mighty beat of its wings all the tablecloths nearest it burst into flame, and the people stood closest darted out of the way. There was a white flash and Hades' smoke form suddenly appeared in the middle of the room, an arm held high. The phoenix froze in mid beat of its wings, and my heart leapt into my throat.

'What is the meaning of this?' Hades roared, in his cold hissing voice. 'This was not the Trial we agreed upon!' There was another flash of white, and Zeus appeared next to him, his eyes alive with crackling purple lightning.

'Oh but this is much, much better! It appears you have a gatecrasher, big brother. I forbid you to get involved,' he sneered. The temperature plummeted.

'You forbid me to deal with trespassers in my own realm? Who do you think you are?' Hades hissed.

'I am your King,' Zeus replied, growing fast so that he towered over Hades. 'Fill the hourglass! Persephone's new test is to rid her guests of this pest!'

'What?!' I exclaimed, and span to see a tiny form in the hourglass. I swear my heart stopped beating for a second as I recognized the figure.

It was Skop.

TWENTY-SIX

'Wait, you can't expect me to fight that, I'm human!' I yelled, as I turned back to the two gods, the phoenix still frozen in mid-air behind them.

'You are a human competing to become an immortal queen. You will do as you are bid,' said Zeus, his eyes narrowed and a sneer on his beautiful lips.

'Brother, this is too far!' Hades' words had an edge of desperation to them, and Zeus's smile slipped for a beat as he turned to face him.

'You are the one who went too far, Hades,' he said quietly, and fear gripped at my insides as the tension grew between the two gods, venom in their locked gazes. Zeus wasn't going to back down. I was going to have to kill a phoenix before Skop drowned. My throat seemed to lock up at the thought of the kobaloi dying, heat burning behind my eyes again. He would die because of me, because I chose his feather. That wasn't fair, he'd done nothing wrong. His job was to make people laugh, for fuck's sake, why should he be punished for being my friend?

'I'm sorry,' I thought desperately at him, knowing he couldn't hear me but needing to tell him. 'I'm sorry, Skop.'

'*Don't fucking apologize yet, get me the fuck out of here!*' his desperate voice replied.

'Skop! You're not unconscious?' I whirled to look at the hourglass, where he looked for all the world like he was fast asleep, in naked gnome form.

'*It's damned difficult to knock out a sprite completely. My body is useless, but you can't keep a brain like mine down for long.*' My heart swelled on hearing his defiant words, and determination started to battle with my fear. A bright flash made me turn again, and Hera was there between Hades and Zeus, regal and stunning with her peacock feather.

'Enough,' she said, her voice melodic and soothing. 'Olympus is watching, and we have promised them entertainment. Good luck, Persephone,' she said, and then the three of them vanished. I blinked in the bright light, then a wave of heat blasted over me as the phoenix was released from Hades' spell and its huge wings beat towards me.

'*Move, move, move!*' Skop's voice spurred me into action, the shot of adrenaline shooting through my system making me feel sick, but adding a speed to my legs I didn't know I had. All the pent-up tension from my moment with Hades seemed to be pouring itself into my muscles, and I felt strong as I raced towards the stage area, as far from the bird as I could get. It gave a screeching squawk, and then flapped its wings harder, lifting itself high into the cavernous ceiling of the room. What was it doing? I took the few seconds I had with it so far away to study it, searching for any signs of weakness. It was fierce looking, with a bright yellow hooked beak and eyes the same color. The bulk of its body was scarlet red and the flames rolling from its feathered wings burned through an orange ombre to an almost white tip. It straightened in the air, facing me, its massive tail feathers pointing down and flames dancing from them towards the ground. People were scattering across the ballroom, many glowing different colors, and I assumed they were calling their own powers, ready to defend themselves if they needed to. None would be able to help me though. And I had no power. Slowly, I moved my skirt aside, hooking *Faesforos* out of the sheath on my thigh. It felt good in my hand, but as I held it up towards the enormous flaming bird, my positivity took a nosedive. How the fuck was I supposed to use a weapon like this on that? A tiny part of my brain piped up, giving voice to the thought I was trying to ignore. *It's too beautiful to kill.* A mindless skeleton was one thing, but this? It was freaking magnificent. And to be fair, right now it was just hovering, staring at me, doing me no harm at all. Why should I kill it?

'Hello,' I called out to it, trying not to feel stupid. I heard a laugh somewhere in the room. Most likely that big-boobed witch Eris. The phoenix pulsed its wings. 'Please could you leave?' I asked, as politely as I could. This time I heard a louder laugh, and it was male voice. The phoenix's eyes turned inky black suddenly, and a voice boomed through the room.

'You think you can return here, after all these years, and it would be OK? That you would be forgiven?'

My skin felt like it was contracting around me, ice-cold dread trickling through my insides. This person was here for me. And they knew something I didn't.

'I don't know what you're talking about,' I shouted back. 'This is my first time in Olympus.'

'Lies! You deserve to rot in Tartarus for what you have done!'

'I don't know what you're talking about!' I couldn't keep the fear from my voice. My terror was not of the beast before me or the owner of the voice, but of the words he was saying. *What had I done?*

There was a bark of anger, and when he spoke again the voice was a disbelieving hiss.

'If what you say is true, then rather than punish you for your crimes, the gods let you drink from the river Lethe to forget your past? The injustice is unrivaled!' The last sentence was so loud I involuntarily clapped my hands to my ears. The phoenix let out another piercing screech, then dove towards me.

'*You need to find whoever is controlling the phoenix and kill him, you can't stop the bird itself!*' Skop's voice sounded in my head as I began to run.

'You can't talk to me, I'll get disqualified and they'll kill you!' I told him frantically. There was no reply, and for a sickening moment I wondered if they had done just that. I skidded as I turned, the phoenix roaring down behind me and I felt searing heat against my back. I pelted towards the hourglass, my worst fears confirmed as I neared it. Sand was falling so fast that Skop would be dead before I reached it. With a scream, I drew the arm back that held *Faesforos* and launched the dagger at the thin glass center of the hourglass, the neck where the two halves met. The sound of metal on glass was followed by a splintering crash, and relief coursed through me. As I'd hoped, I'd hit the weakest part of the structure, and the sand now gushed out of the broken hourglass onto the floor. Skop remained slumped inside but his head was clear of sand. He could breathe. I ducked down as I reached him, only stopping long enough to scoop up my blade from amongst the bits of broken glass, then veered off to my right. I couldn't worry about how the gods would deal with me breaking the sand timer now, I would have to face that later.

Another blast of heat told me the bird was just behind me, and I scanned the room desperately as I ran. Skop said someone was controlling the bird, but who? There were about eighty people here. Could it be Eris, or Minthe, or Erebus? All of them had made it clear that they didn't like me. But that voice... So full of unsuppressed hatred and anger - none of them could have interacted with me all evening and then blown up like this, surely.

My eyes were drawn to the people in the room who were giving off faint light, and there were a number of them, all moving hastily out of my way as I charged through the room, my skirt flying and the phoenix on my tail. I ran past Eris, who was beaming, a deep red energy crackling around her. Even if this wasn't her doing she was enjoying it. I passed Hecate, still standing at the back of the room where I had left her. She had a blaze of purple emanating from her, her eyes milky white. What was she doing?

The shadows. He's in the shadows. The voice was faint, but it was Skop's.

'How do you know?' I said, altering my course and heading for the kitchens I'd visited earlier. There was no reply. As I got closer I could see yellow sparks in the darkness, and I raised my dagger arm again. But I must have slowed, because pain lanced through my wrist and I almost dropped *Faesforos* as I looked up. The phoenix had its sharp talons wrapped around my arm, and the breath left my lungs as I was jerked off my feet. I tried to reach around with my other arm to prize the talons off but the bird twisted to the side and I was thrown the other way. We were moving higher, and I looked down at the shadows. The yellow sparks were getting brighter and I realized there was a figure emerging. It was a man, and he looked completely ordinary, save for the murder in his eyes. The power around him could have been fire or energy or electricity, I wasn't sure, but it crackled bright along his skin, leaping and dancing from him like the flames on the phoenix.

'Time to die, Persephone.'

I swung my free arm up, passing the dagger from my immobilized hand to the other, and jammed it as hard as I could into the bird's massive talon. It didn't react. Thinking fast, I tucked my legs under myself and tried to kick out hard to launch myself higher. It worked, giving me a few extra inches to slash at the bit of fiery leg above the black claw. With a squawk, the thing released my arm.

Shit, was all that went through my head as I began to fall, repeated over and over until I smashed into a table. The wood splintered and folded beneath my weight, and for a heart stopping second the tablecloth engulfed me and I couldn't see a thing. I rolled, gasping for the breath that had been knocked out of me, and sending silent thanks that the bird had only lifted me five feet off the ground. Heat sprang up around me as I fumbled my way to my feet, and panic bolted through my body as I saw that the tablecloth still tangled in my legs was on fire. I jabbed *Faesforos* into the material and ripped it quickly apart, stumbling away from it, trying to get my bearings. There he was. The man with the yellow magic, slowly walking towards me.

'Why don't you face me yourself?' I called out, my words coming between gasping pants.

'You're suggesting I'm the coward? You who ran away from the result of your atrocities?' Fury rolled off his words and the yellow energy around him danced out further, but the bird stayed where it was.

'I can't pay for something I don't know I've done,' I said, shifting my weight and gripping my dagger. Fear that he might tell me, and the whole world, what this awful thing was, warred with my need to keep him talking and keep the phoenix at bay.

'You are a murderer,' he hissed. His words hit me like a sledgehammer. No, there was no way that was true. How could it be? I couldn't hurt an insect or plant, let alone kill a person. *You are not the woman I married. You are someone new.* Hades' words sliced through my denial, and bile rose in my throat. Please, please, no. It couldn't be true.

'I don't believe you,' I choked out, and the man bared his teeth at me.

'You took her from me. You took everything that I loved from me.' Pain and grief and madness filled his eyes, and I had no doubt that whether or not his accusation was true, he believed it.

'I'm sorry,' I said, as he reached me. 'If it is true, then I am sorry.'

'It's too late to be sorry! Unless you can bring her back, you must die!' The yellow energy burst out from around him, and agony consumed me. It was like an unending electric shock ripping through my muscles, causing spasms so violent I couldn't stand. But before I could fall to my feet his arm shot out, and he grabbed me by the throat, holding me as I jerked and screamed. 'You deserve worse than this.' I barely noticed as he sucked in air through his teeth, drew me closer to him, then spat on me, his saliva sliding down my cheek. Through the blinding pain, I was only able to process one thought. *Make it stop.* Everything else inside me was shutting down, but my survival instinct was refusing to give up. My arm was rising inch by inch. As the man's eyes blazed with retribution and the pain intensified so much I could no longer see, I buried *Faesforos* into his ribs.

TWENTY-SEVEN

He dropped me with a gurgled shout, and I slammed to my knees with a hard crack that I barely registered. I fell forward onto my hands as my stomach began to heave. I didn't know if I was sick from the pain, or from the fact that I'd just stabbed a man, my head was spinning so fast. I tried to gulp down air between retching, the pain subsiding but my vision still blurry. *Murderer.* He had called me a murderer. I couldn't be and yet... I'd just tried to kill him. *He was going to kill you!* The rational voice in my head tried to drown out the guilt and fear, but it couldn't. I couldn't live with myself, I couldn't draw breath every day, knowing I was the reason somebody else wasn't. *Please, please don't let him be dead*, I prayed, turning my head towards him slowly. He was on his back, dark red blood pooling under one side of him. I crawled towards him, tears filling my eyes.

'I'm sorry, I'm sorry, I'm sorry.' The words tumbled from my mouth, tasting like the acid that filled it. He groaned and I paused. Then he moved, rolling onto his uninjured side. *He was alive.* Thank the gods, he was alive. I sat back on my heels, letting the tears come. 'What did I do?' I croaked. 'Tell me, who did I take from you?'

'My wife,' he said, his voice hoarse. 'You killed my wife.'

A light flashed so bright that pain seared through my head again, and for a moment I was sure I was going to pass out. I had reached my limit.

'No!' A female voice shouted, and I blinked furiously, trying to clear the tears and blurriness from my eyes. Slowly, the room came back into focus.

Athena was standing before us, in front of smoke Hades and Hecate. Purple energy still rolled off Hecate, and Hades was three times his normal size and his smoke seemed to be vibrating.

'You must be judged, Persephone. The Trial is over,' Athena said, her voice like a balm to my pain, calming my mind. The three judges shimmered gently into existence before me.

'But what about him? You have to help him!' I pointed desperately at the man bleeding on the marble. Hades' smoke flickered and Athena smiled at me and waved her hand towards the man. 'His judgment will come too, but for the moment he is safe.'

'Wait, what does that mean?' I asked her, but the commentator's voice boomed across the room.

'Well we really have been treated tonight folks, who would have thought it?' As if in response the phoenix beat its wings, moving higher above everyone. Treated? This shit-show was viewed as a treat? 'Now let's see what the judges think of Persephone's controversial actions tonight. Radamanthus?'

'Two tokens,' the chubby judge smiled at me.

'Aeacus?'

'Zero tokens,' Aeacus said, his blue skin reflecting the soft torchlight in the room.

'Minos?' The piercing look the wise man gave me was totally lost on me. I just gaped back at him, doing my best to contain the roiling emotion tearing my insides apart.

'You broke the rules, Persephone. You saved your friend.'

'That's not his fault, please don't punish him,' I whispered.

'We will not. You have shown loyalty. And that is valued higher than hospitality.' He gazed at me a second longer, then spoke.

'Two tokens.'

A box appeared in front of me, the lid open. It was the seed box, and inside were another two pomegranate seeds. I stared down at them, then back up at the judges. How could they not see that these didn't matter? I'd just stabbed a man who had accused me of murdering his wife, and these maniacs were handing out fucking pomegranate seeds?

'Give me my memories back,' I said, my voice louder and clearer than I expected.

Minos gave me a small smile, and the three judges faded away.

'There you have it folks! It's the end of Round One of the Hades Trials and Persephone is not only still alive, but she has more tokens than the current leader did at the end of her first round. Who would have guessed! We'll be visiting a new realm for Round Two, and I know you're going to love it!' The commentator vanished and Athena stepped forward.

'Hades, you may deal with your intruder.'

'Wait-' I started to say, but suddenly the temperature

plummeted and I was skidding across the room on my knees, along with everything else in Hades' path.

Pure terror gripped me as swirling smoke moved towards the injured man. Screaming started in the back of mind and the now familiar smell of blood filled my nostrils, churning my already empty stomach.

'Stop!' I tried to cry the word but nothing came out. I was pinned against the wall of the ballroom, and tears spilled from my eyes as Hades reached the bleeding man. With a hiss, he threw his smoky arms in the air, and the man flew up, blood spraying from his wound. My skin was so cold I could hardly feel it, and I was vaguely aware that everyone else in the room was shrinking away, melting into the walls as best they could. Everyone except Hecate.

'Hades-' she called, but the King of the Underworld roared, and the man screamed.

'You dare enter my realm, and try to kill her?' His voice carried so much power, so much terror, so much danger, that my limbs collapsed. 'You dare to try to take her from me?' The man whimpered as he hovered in the air, and black spots danced in front of my eyes as the screaming in my head grew louder, and flames began to obscure my vision.

'Please,' I said, but the word didn't make a sound. There was a cracking noise, and the world swam as the man shrieked in pain. His arms and legs went completely taut, then began to pull away from his torso. Nausea rolled through me, followed swiftly by dizziness so intense my head lolled to one side.

'Hades, stop!' It was Hecate's voice, but I couldn't see

her any more. I could only see the man I'd almost killed, and fire.

'She deserves to die,' croaked the man's hoarse voice, and black erupted through the room. In slow motion, I watched as the man's body exploded, his head and limbs flying through the air, blood spraying the very solid form of Hades. But it wasn't the Hades I'd thrown myself at that evening. This... this was something that would haunt my nightmares as long as I lived. Massive and hulking, the monster before me had onyx, soulless eyes, and as I stared, blue waves of light rolled off his enormous armor-covered body, solidifying on the ground as corpses. Corpses that were burning. Corpses that were screaming.

I couldn't breathe. *I didn't deserve to breathe.* Fear like I'd never, ever known was crushing me to death, and I deserved it. I had to die.

∽

'Well, I'd hoped to see you here.'

I blinked as I looked around the garden, the Atlas fountain trickling pleasantly before me, and birdsong warming my cold skin.

'I thought I only came here when I was asleep?' I asked mildly. It was impossible to be anything but mild in this place.

'Unconscious counts as well, my dear.' I tilted my head, then dropped to my knees and ran my fingers around a budding young crocus. 'You do not have long before Hades' rage kills you, Persephone. There is only one way you may survive.'

'Did I kill that man's wife?,' I asked the voice.

'Eat the seeds, Persephone.'

A jolt like lightning shot through my body and I opened my eyes with a jerk. I was back in the ballroom, surrounded by blood and fire and bodies. Screaming so loud it drowned out my own thoughts swamped my mind, and all I could see through my stinging eyes was death.

'Persephone!' shouted a voice. 'Hades, you're going to kill her!'

I forced my eyes closed, so I didn't have to look at the bodies around me. Was I a murderer? I couldn't organize the thoughts, couldn't make sense of anything through my paralyzed fear.

Eat the seeds.

Would eating the seeds make this stop? I opened my streaming eyes a crack, and fumbled at the floor, recoiling as I knocked the little wooden box skidding through slick blood.

Eat the seeds.

I snatched at the box, my fingers numb and shaking as the screaming got so loud I thought my head would explode. Tipping the lid open with a snap, I scooped up a pomegranate seed, and clumsily forced my hand to my lips.

Eat the seeds.

The sharpness made me gag, but I closed my eyes and took a breath through my nose, the metallic scent of blood almost making me retch again. With an effort, I swallowed the tiny seed.

The fear receded instantly, my body going completely limp as I collapsed to the cold floor. The screaming faded away, replaced by Hecate's voice, loud and shrill.

'Hades, you've fucking killed her, stop! You have to stop.'

An unbelievably peaceful calm spread through me, and I felt all of my exhausted muscles relax. This was it. This was the end. And it was surprisingly more comfortable than I thought it would be.

Something fluttered in my stomach. Then it fluttered up to my chest. I felt my body jerk as my heart responded to it. Once. Twice. A third time. Then light, green and vibrant filled my vision and something incredible flooded through my veins, sending pulsing energy to every part of my failing body. Something rich and strong and fierce. Something alien and familiar all at once.

It was power. I had my power back.

THE PASSION OF HADES

ONE

PERSEPHONE

My head swam as I sat up, the sudden movement making me feel sick. But the nausea was replaced almost instantly by a surge of energy as I looked around myself, memories of what had just happened crashing over me in an endless wave. I was no longer in the ballroom, or the beautiful garden. I was in a plush bed-chamber, on sumptuous purple and teal cushions, sheer material draped decadently around the four poster frame that surrounded me.

I should be dead. Hades' true form should have killed me. But the pomegranate seed...

'The judges must like you,' said a deep, lyrical voice. I snapped my eyes to the source of the sound, and Hera smiled back at me from the foot of the bed.

'What-why am I here? I need to get back to help that man,' I stammered. Hera's eyes flashed with fire.

'That man is long past your help. As he should be.'

'He just wanted revenge,' I whispered. 'A life for a life... I took someone from him.' My skin crawled as the image of the carnage in the ballroom floated before me. I felt sick again.

'Persephone, as the goddess of revenge I have an understanding for what drove him, but my empathy does not extend to those who would cross the gods. No mortal should be that foolish.' Her face was set and fierce and I felt a ripple of something deep inside me respond to her power.

'Are the gods really that much more important than everyone else?' I asked, my voice small. I knew I was being rude, but I was unable to keep the question inside. 'Are you really all so arrogant?'

Hera stood, the heels of her shoes clicking loudly as she did so. A blast of power rolled through the room and I suddenly wanted to worship her.

'If you are to retake your place as Queen of the Underworld someday, you need a serious attitude adjustment,' she said. A lump formed in my throat as the fears that had built up over the course of the ball welled to the surface.

'When I was a Queen, was I like the rest of you?'

'Yes.'

'I would have pulled that man apart, limb from limb?' I whispered, my eyes filling with burning hot tears.

'Your wrath had a less gruesome air about it, I'll admit,' Hera said, tilting her head to one side, 'but you were as vengeful as any of us.'

No. No, I couldn't believe her. But why would she lie? *It doesn't matter what you were before. What matters is what you are now.* I clung to the thought, forcing myself to calm down, holding my tears back.

'Well, I'm unlikely to win, so you needn't worry,' I said eventually, struggling to sit in the mass of soft cushions. I needed to get out of there. I needed to see Skop; make sure he was safe. I needed to work out what the fuck had happened and get my shit together.

'Oh no, Persephone. You are just as likely to win as Minthe. The judges must like you indeed, to give you the chance to win your power back.'

'They put my power in the seeds deliberately?'

'They must have, yes. How did you know to eat one? You clearly didn't know before the last Trial or you would have done so sooner.' Her gleaming eyes bored into mine, and distrust caused my shields to slam into place. I didn't know this woman. And even if she was Queen of the gods, I didn't need to tell her anything. Could my new power keep her out of my head?

My feelings must have shown on my face, because Hera gave a tinkling laugh, then sat down on the end of the bed again.

'If you don't want to tell me, fine. And in case you're wondering, Hades has a spell on the underworld that means nobody can invade another's mind. It's really quite annoying.'

My eyebrows shot up.

'Why has he done that?'

'Hades is not the god most think he is,' she said softly, and I was sure I could hear compassion in her voice. 'He has more respect for living creatures than you would imagine.' Hecate had said something similar to me, about Hades not being what people thought he was. And more than that, I had seen a side to him completely at odds with... whatever he had become when he slaughtered that man. A shudder rocked me.

'He would have killed me,' I said quietly. 'If I hadn't eaten the seed.'

'Yes. Temper is an uncontrollable thing, for mortals and

immortals alike. He would never have forgiven himself either, which would have been a complete pain for everyone. I'm glad you survived.'

I frowned. What was her angle? I didn't believe for a moment she cared about me, but I wondered if she did care about Hades.

'Why am I here? With you?'

'I thought it best to remove you from harm's way. Hades will take a long time to calm down. And my husband, Zeus, is good at taking advantage of chaotic situations. I wouldn't want you caught in his web.' This time there was a dangerous glint in her eyes, and her voice held an edge to match. I imagined Zeus' glee at seeing Hades lose it so spectacularly, and anger pulled at my gut.

'How long do I need to stay here?' I asked her.

'Why, are you not comfortable?'

'I... I just... I wanted to see Skop.' There was a flash of white light, then the kobaloi, butt-naked and sporting a look of complete confusion, appeared on the bed. He whirled, his bearded face sagging in relief when he saw me.

'Oh, thank fuck for that,' he said, then shimmered into his dog form. '*I thought you were dead.*'

'I'm touched you care,' I told him.

'*Are you shitting me? You saved my life.*'

'And you mine. I wouldn't have known what to do with that phoenix otherwise.'

'*Nor did I, Hecate told me to tell you. She couldn't reach you herself.*' I remembered seeing her during the chaos, her eyes milky, and blue power glowing around her. Gratitude heaved through me. She had been there, with me when I thought I was about to die. Begging Hades to stop.

Skop flopped down onto the bed with a massive sigh. '*I could sleep for a week after that,*' he said, his eyes closing.

'What a strange thing to grow attached to,' said Hera, one eyebrow raised as she looked at the little dog.

'He and Hecate are my only friends here,' I said, following his lead and leaning back on the cushions. If I was stuck here, I may as well get comfortable. I wanted Hera to leave, so I could work out this new energy flowing through my body. I didn't feel any different, but I knew it was there.

'Hades is your friend.'

I snorted involuntarily.

'Yeah, If you're into friends who can kill you, or like to wind you up to the point of exploding and then...' I trailed off, realizing my anger had made me say too much. A knowing smile crossed the goddess's dark, sumptuous lips.

'Well, now that you have a modicum of power, you might be able to survive long enough to make friends with him properly,' she said, far more gently. 'This place was very different when he was happy. I should like to see that again.'

Frustration simmered inside me, making my skin feel hot when it wasn't.

'Why won't anyone tell me why I left? Or what I did to that poor man's wife?'

Hera let out a long breath.

'He was telling the truth about you drinking from the river Lethe, you know. It is one of five rivers of the Under-world, and it will obliterate the memories of any who taste its waters. Only the King of the Underworld can reverse a power like that.' My hopes sank even farther into the pit of my stomach. Hades wouldn't tell me what had happened. He'd made that abundantly clear.

'Fine. Athena was right anyway, I should just move on. Worry about the future instead of the past,' I said, not able to give the words the sincerity I had hoped.

'He might tell you, you know. Should I send him to you?'

My jaw dropped slightly as dread trickled down my spine, flames already licking at the edges of my vision at the thought of how I had last seen the King of Hell.

'No! No, I... I think I should rest,' I said, too loudly.

'You can't avoid him forever. You're competing to marry him,' she said, then disappeared with a flash of white light.

I swore as I blinked the bright spots away. I was competing to marry a freaking maniac.

TWO

PERSEPHONE

As soon as I was done swearing about self-entitled douchebag gods, I sat upright again, and closed my eyes. If I had gained power, I needed to know what I could do with it. I concentrated hard, trying to feel something inside me that wasn't there before, that surge of life and vibrancy that I'd felt after eating the seed.

But I could feel nothing.

I knew it was there, the hairs on my skin rose when I thought about it, and Hera had confirmed it, but I couldn't feel that same surge of energy within me, or grasp anything tangible. Maybe I needed to try to do some magic? Feeling pretty stupid, I held out my hand.

'Light?' I awkwardly asked my own hand. Nothing happened. Why did I think I could create light? Hecate had said I had been able to 'grow plants, amongst other things.' I could feel, instinctively, that my power was connected to the earth. It was that same sureness I felt whenever I saw Hades' liquid-silver eyes, that same knowledge that everything I was experiencing wasn't a dream.

Hades' eyes... What in the name of the gods was I going

to do? Panic fringed my thoughts as I pictured his face, remembered his passionate embrace, then saw that awful blue light roll off him and form corpses on the ground. I dropped my hand to my lap. I had been desperate to give every inch of my body to the man, less than an hour before he had turned into a freaking death monster, tore a man apart and nearly killed me. Worse, I was competing to *marry* him. This was no good. Like seriously, no good. I had to stay away from him, and I had to lose the Trials and get back home.

I couldn't ignore the surge of fear that accompanied that assertion, but it wasn't the fear I'd felt up to now. This was different. A brand new fear.

How the hell can you leave? This place is amazing! Maybe not the Underworld, but Zeus' mountain? Flying ships? Kick-ass outfits, magic everywhere, and a friend who could conjure wine for fuck's sake! Why would I ever go back to New York now I know Olympus exists?

'Because everyone here is fucking mental!' I said out loud, shaking my head and forcing the ludicrous thoughts out of my mind. 'Murderous fucking maniacs. And apparently, so was I!' I screwed my face up as I rubbed it hard with my hands. It was ridiculous to think I would even entertain the idea of staying somewhere so dangerous and unpleasant. *Somewhere I may once have existed as a monster.*

My brother Sam's face flashed into my mind, smiling and soft. My parents, dad tending to the garden and mum sewing and rolling her eyes constantly, swiftly followed. I called up my more recent memories of Professor Hetz and my awesome garden design and the beautiful botanical gardens. I missed them. All of them.

'Manhattan roof gardens,' I said firmly. 'You're going to

make this work, Persephone. You're going to become a world famous garden designer. Not Queen of the Underworld.'

But the last thing I saw, before falling asleep alongside Skop's snoring, furry little body were those desperate pools of silver.

~

I wasn't the least bit surprised when I found myself dreaming that I was in the Atlas garden. I walked slowly towards the fountain, inhaling deeply and filling myself with the scent of wildflowers. A warm breeze moved strands of my loose hair around my face, and it felt good.

'Thank you,' I said, as I reached the marble edge of the pool. Vivid green lily pads covered in shocking pink water lilies floated gently on the surface. 'You saved my life.'

'You're welcome,' the voice said. '*I am glad you are here. I must tell you something important.*'

'Of course I'm here. You bring me here,' I answered, dipping my fingers into the water. It was cool and welcoming.

'*I wish that were true, Persephone.*'

'Oh. Well who does bring me here then?'

'*I don't know.*'

I tilted my head to one side, and felt the sun on my cheek.

'Who are you?'

'*Your only friend. You must not eat all of the pome-granate seeds in one go. Do you understand me?*'

'Yes,' I nodded.

'*You deserve your powers back, dear girl, but you must not risk overwhelming yourself.*'

'I don't feel overwhelmed. In fact, I don't know how to

use my magic at all,' I said, reaching out and drawing a lily pad towards me while perching on the edge of the fountain.

'You will learn. Do not worry about that. But Persephone, you must trust nobody.'

'Except Hecate and Skop,' I said.

'No, nobody.'

'But Hecate and Skop saved me too. They care about me.'

'You are naive, little goddess. Hecate is an agent of Hades, and Skoptolis works for Dionysus. Only I work for you alone.'

'Why? Why are you helping me?'

'You were wronged, by my worst enemy, and you paid the highest price. And now only you have the power to make it right.'

A small shudder cut through the tranquility of the garden. His words carried weight that even this place couldn't lighten.

'I was wronged?'

'Yes. The only person who can tell you about your past is Hades. And what he knows is incomplete.'

'So... How do I find out the truth?'

'When you are stronger, we will continue this conversation. Keep winning seeds, and gain more of your power back.'

I nodded. That sounded like good advice.

The dream was vivid in my memory when I woke up in the opulent bedchamber, and I replayed the conversation repeatedly as I sat up in the mass of colored cushions, still wearing my ballgown from the night before. I rubbed my aching neck and tried to get the stranger's words straight.

Could I really not trust Hecate and Skop? I struggled to believe they would bring any harm to me. I touched my parched lips as I looked down at the sleeping dog, sprawled across the end of the bed.

You were wronged, by my worst enemy, and you paid the highest price. And now only you have the power to make it right.'

A little shudder rippled through me as I recalled the stranger's statement. If what he was saying was true, then was someone else involved in whatever I had done to get thrown out of Olympus? Did that mean it wasn't all my fault? A tiny bud of hope blossomed in my chest. But who? And why didn't Hades know about it? I blew out a sigh and stared at the glowing rock wall. At the thought of Hades, images rolled through my mind again, flipping between exquisite pleasure, and unbridled terror. Talk about an emotional roller-coaster.

'Well, this is nicer than your room,' said a voice, and my eyes snapped to the door.

'Hecate!' She smiled as she sauntered over, carrying two cups of coffee. 'Thank you, for telling Skop how to defeat the phoenix, and... for trying to stop Hades.'

'No worries,' she said with an overly casual grin. 'How you doing?'

'A bit confused,' I said.

'No doubt. But heh, at least your powers are working.'

'What?' I frowned at her. 'What do you mean? I was going to ask you how to get my magic to work; I can't do anything.'

'Persy, you got lifted five feet off the ground by a giant burning bird, fell and crashed into a table, and nearly got electrocuted to death. Don't you think you should be feeling a bit sore this morning?'

I stared at her.

'My neck aches,' I said eventually.

'That'll be these stupid fucking cushions,' she said, her lip curling as she picked one up and launched it across the room.

'So... My magic has healed me?'

'Yup.' She took a long swig from her coffee and I did the same, my mind spinning. I could heal?

'How?'

'It just happens while you rest. The stronger you are, the quicker you'll heal, and you'll learn to heal big wounds on the spot eventually. You were always a good healer. Comes with the territory I guess.'

'What territory?'

'Goddess of Spring. New life. Growth and fertility and all that.'

My mouth fell open.

'Goddess of Spring?' I repeated, and heard a bark from Skop.

'Uhuh. No point keeping it from you any more, not if you can get your power back.' She was beaming at me, her eyes dancing with excitement. 'You can win this now, Persy. You really can.'

'Woah, woah, woah. You're the goddess of fucking Spring? I thought you were just some pretty human?' Skop's voice rang loud in my head.

'Erm, it's sort of a long story. I was married to Hades before. Then cast out of Olympus and removed from history. And I don't remember any of it.'

'What the actual fuck?'

'Yeah, I know,' I said to him with a look, then turned back to Hecate. 'What about what happened at the ball?'

'What about it?' she shrugged.

'Hades nearly killed me! I'm not marrying a god made of corpses!'

'Oh, he only lost his temper because that dude hurt you. When you're back up to full power his true form won't bother you at all.'

It felt like ice was sliding down my spine at her words. How could that monster, surrounded by dead bodies, ever not bother me?

'I *want* to be bothered by corpses, Hecate' I told her. 'I don't want to be like him. I don't want to be with him.'

Hecate's smile slipped.

'He's just freaked you out a bit. You'll work it out, I'm sure.'

'Hecate, seriously, I'm not cut out for the Underworld. I want warm sunshine and a cool breeze, and trees as tall as buildings stretching into endless skies. I'm not meant to be here.' I could hear the pleading tone of my voice. 'Even if I was once happy here, I'm not that person any more. And Hades knows that.'

'*You are not the woman I married. You are someone new.*' That's what he had said to me, when I was practically delirious with lust.

Hecate stared at me for a full minute, then downed the rest of her coffee.

'When are you eating the other two seeds? We need to practice using your magic.'

I sighed.

'You can't just ignore me,' I told her. 'And I'm not eating them.'

'What?' she exploded, leaping to her feet. 'What do you mean you're not eating them?'

'Not yet anyway. I want to get my power back slowly.'

Hecate narrowed her eyes at me.

'Are you trying to lose on purpose?'

'No, but up until recently I was just a human, with no notion that magic even existed. You'll forgive me for being a bit cautious,' I snapped. She eyed me suspiciously.

'Fine, but I think you're making a mistake. The next round starts tonight, and you need all the help you can get.' My stomach twisted at her words.

'The next Trial is tonight?'

'No, not the actual Trial, it's just a little ceremony thing to start the second round and announce what's coming next. But Minthe will be there.' I groaned. Brilliant. Just what I needed. 'And... so will Hades.'

THREE

PERSEPHONE

Hecate zapped us back to my own room, and I gratefully stripped off my gown and stood under the hot water of the shower until my skin pruned. I tried again to access my supposed new powers, but other than a tingling awareness I couldn't get anything to happen.

'Was one of my powers making light?' I asked Hecate as I walked out of my washroom. She was sat at my dresser, one ankle crossed over her knee and her head back, singing something pretty.

'No,' she answered without looking at me.

'Oh.' I rubbed at my wet hair with a towel.

'I can't make light either,' said Skop in my head.

'You're not a god,' I told him.

'I'm a god in bed,' he answered, tail wagging. I rolled my eyes.

I got dressed in my fighting garb quickly, unable to keep still, my palms itching. I needed to do something physical; there was a pent up energy building inside me that was making me feel restless and uneasy.

'How long until this second round thing starts?' I asked.

'Ages, it's not until this evening'

'Good. I'm going to the conservatory,' I said.

'Oh. I thought you'd want to train,' Hecate said, tipping her head forward to look at me. I shook my head.

'Maybe later.'

'Fine, have fun. See if you can get those green fingers working some magic,' she said, and winked at me before shimmering out of my room. I looked down at my hands, wiggling my fingers. Could I get them to work actual magic?

It turned out that Skop had been telling the truth about paying attention to the routes through the underground maze I was living in. I would never have been able to find the conservatory without his directions. As we walked, I filled him in on what I knew about my past, which was a depressingly short conversation, and about eating the seed and my powers returning. I didn't tell him why I ate the seed, and he didn't ask.

I knew we were at the right door for the conservatory before I even laid my hand on the wood to push it open. Something was sparking inside me, and I could almost feel the plants on the other side of the wall, joyous energy rolling off them. My pulse quickened as I stepped into the glass room and inhaled the smell of soil. The restless energy thrumming through me transformed as I ran my fingers along the nearest yucca leaf, frustration morphing into excitement. *I could feel more than just these plants in this room.* Almost like little sparks of light in my mind's eye, I could sense seeds, unable to grow, trapped under invisible barriers that held them deep in the soil beds around me. I dropped to my knees and began to dig frantically in the nearest bed, hunting for what I knew was hidden there.

'Yes!' I pulled my hand up triumphantly, clutching a hard little seed.

'*What is it?*' asked Skop.

'A sunflower,' I said instantly, then looked sideways at him, drawing my brows together. 'How did I know that?' I asked slowly.

'*You're goddess of Spring. You probably should know a few things about flowers,*' he answered, then cocked his head at me. '*Can I do some digging too?*'

Together we dug through the huge space, turning almost all of the soil beds over in our hunt for seeds. There were so many, all hard and cold, as though they had been frozen in time. I found a tin tray stacked with the other tools and within an hour we had filled it with our unearthed treasure. They were mostly seeds for flowers; pansies and chrysan-themums and poppies, but a couple were more exciting. One I was pretty sure was an azalea but that would take years to grow. I certainly wouldn't see it reach maturity.

'Persephone.' Hearing my name made my body freeze as I knelt in the dirt, dread crawling up my throat as I recog-nized the voice. It wasn't the hissing tone, but I still had no doubt that it belonged to Hades.

'I thought you gave this room to me,' I said without turn-ing. I knew my confidence would crumble as soon as I saw his dark smoke. 'Please go away.'

'Persephone, I'm here to apologize.'

'I don't care,' I lied. 'I have nothing to say to you, and there's nothing I want to hear from you.' All the hairs on my skin were standing on end, and the compulsion to turn around and look at him was almost too strong to resist.

'Please. Look at me.'

'No! Last time I saw you, you damn near frightened me to death.'

'I... I was angry. I lost control. You make me do that.'

'So it's my fucking fault?' I couldn't help the flash of rage, and I leapt to my feet as I whirled round. My anger dissipated instantly. There was no smoke. It was just him, his beautiful silver eyes glowing with sorrow. *Make it better. Make him happy.* The thoughts galloped through my brain and I snarled. Why was I so damned attracted to him? I tried to call up the image of the blue light turning into corpses around him, but he held out his hand to me and his lips parted, and heat rushed through my body. *Stop it! You don't fancy the lord of the dead, stop it!*

But my traitorous hand reached for his of its own volition, and he pulled me close to him.

'I thought you were going to die. I thought that man would kill you. And Zeus wouldn't let me stop him.' His voice was so low I wouldn't have been able to hear him if his mouth wasn't inches above mine.

'Well, he didn't kill me. But you nearly did.'

He flinched and his grip on my hand tightened.

'A god's temper is his worst enemy. There is only wrath, no rational thought. I... I would never have forgiven myself if you had...' He trailed off, and his expression was so intense that I couldn't speak for the sadness that lodged in my throat. It was as though he was passing the emotion directly to me, through those incredible eyes. 'How did you know to eat the seeds?'

Alarm bells rang in my head at his question, snapping me out of the intense melancholy. *Trust nobody.*

'Never you mind. You need to tell me what happened before, Hades. I can't do this any more. I can't live a life I'm half blind to. It's not fair and it's driving me insane.' Hades lifted his other hand to my face, and very, very slowly drew his finger down my cheek. Pleasure coursed across my skin, and I tried to stifle my sharp breath.

'Would it make any difference if I told you that you chose to drink from the river Lethe yourself? You begged to forget what happened. And I promised you that you would never hurt like that again.'

Something fierce and painful surged inside me and I shook my head. *It was true.* I knew what he was saying was true.

'I don't care. It makes no difference now. I need to know.'

'I won't break my promise, Persephone. I can't.'

I expected to feel the familiar sense of frustration at being denied my own past once again, and opened my mouth to argue. But it didn't come. Standing so close to him was making my resolve soften, my distrust lessen, and my fear of him disappear completely. He loved me. I didn't know how or why, but nothing could be clearer as I stared into those swirling silver orbs.

'You said I wasn't the woman you married,' I whispered.

'Maybe not. But the bond between us is still there. And I can't fight it, no matter how hard I try. Especially not now you have your power back. You're like a damned beacon down here, impossible to ignore.' He ran a hand through his hair in frustration, looking for all the world like a normal, if impossibly sexy, guy.

'Bond?'

'Don't tell me you can't feel it,' he said, his eyes locking on mine. I wanted to tell him to stop being so arrogant, but I couldn't. He was right. There was definitely something between us, deep and real and damned inconvenient. *Corpses. King of the Underworld. Fire and ash and death. You do not fancy Hades!*

'Well, I don't think I've got it quite as bad as you,' I said as casually as I could. Fire flashed in his eyes, and I regretted my words immediately.

'Is that right?' he said, his tender, open expression vanishing and a predatory hunger replacing it. He seemed to grow in front of me, his shoulders filling out, his eyes flashing with desire. 'Let's put that to the test, shall we?'

Before I could begin to respond he had my face in his hands, and his lips met mine. Desire exploded through me, the hunger in his kiss even deeper than the last time. His other hand snaked down my back, his touch through the fabric of my shirt electrifying. I pressed myself into him, my back arching, my hands scrabbling at the buttons on his shirt.

But he stopped the kiss abruptly, stepping back and gripping both of my small hands in one of his. I started to protest but a wave of power rolled over me and all words abandoned me as I looked up into his face. Actual flames danced in his irises as his gaze raked over my body. The desire in his expression alone was enough to make my core heat, a low ache building inside me.

'I do believe, Beautiful, that we started on the wrong foot,' he said, his voice low and rich and sensuous. 'It appears that you have no idea what being fated to Hades, King of the Underworld, all powerful god, actually entails.' I stared up at him, panting slightly. *All powerful god.* My stupid, lust addled brain allowed my thoughts to slip between my lips before I could stop them.

'Does that mean magic sex?' I breathed. His mouth quirked into a smile.

'Magic sex,' he repeated, then a wave of pleasure began to trickle exquisitely across my body. It started at my neck, like the kiss of a feather, and as it moved lower across my chest I felt my nipples tighten and a gasp escaped my lips. Hades watched me, eyes dark and hooded, as the feeling rolled further south, the divine sensation dancing around my thighs but never quite reaching their apex. The ache was becoming unbearable, the need to be touched building into something that was making my legs shake.

Was this right? Was he making me feel this against my will? No. Hell, no. There was nothing I wanted more, and the longer I looked into his beautiful face, the more sure of that I became. *Fated.* The word he had used pulsed through my brain, interrupting the pleasure gripping my body.

'Stop,' I forced myself to say, and his expression flickered, before he let go of my hands, the waves of tingling pleasure, slowly lessening. He'd done as I asked. So he wasn't forcing his powers on me. 'Fated. You said I'm fated to you; what does that mean?'

He stared into my face, and I knew I must be flushed as I breathed hard. Desire was still gathering urgently between my legs, pounding and pulsing.

'The marriage of an Olympian god is not like a normal marriage. Hera, as goddess of marriage, has a special ceremony purely for us twelve.' I raised my eyebrows at him and he continued slowly. 'There's a test. And if both people pass, then they are granted the ceremony.'

'What test and what ceremony? Can you not answer anything properly?'

Hades clenched his jaw.

'I can't see the benefit of telling you.'

'How about because I fucking asked?' I said, the pent-up energy and tension inside me slipping quickly to anger. The corner of Hades' mouth quirked up into a smile again and I bared my teeth. 'Do I amuse you?'

'You just... Nobody other than you has ever spoken to me like that.'

'I don't care, just tell me about this ceremony.'

'No. Not unless you ask me nicely.'

My mouth fell open. Hades, the King of the Underworld, was teasing me. Well, two could play at that game.

I stepped close into him, standing on my tiptoes so that I could just reach his ear. He smelled like wood smoke.

'Pretty, pretty please?' I whispered, and flicked my tongue over his ear lobe. I felt him tense against me, then he gave a low chuckle and leaned his head towards mine.

'Oh, Beautiful, until you get your powers back, you'll lose this game every time,' he said, and suddenly that trickle of divine pleasure from earlier rolled over my entire body at once. Slick heat rushed my center, and my legs began to buckle. Hades wrapped one strong arm around my back, and as my hard nipples pressed against his chest I moaned again.

'Please,' I gasped.

'Please what?' His voice was hoarse and low.

'Please, touch me.' I was desperate for him, sure that only the slightest pressure would tip me over the edge.

'Not yet, Beautiful,' he breathed. 'I've waited twenty-six years for this, you can wait a little longer.' He brought his lips to mine, soft and full and intense. And then with a flash of light, he was gone.

~

I wobbled on unsteady feet as I blinked at the space Hades had just occupied. The waves of pleasure rolling though my body had vanished with him, but my burning need for him was still painfully present.

'For fuck's sake!' I exclaimed, digging my nails into my palms as I clenched my fists. 'Why did I let him do that?'

'*Let him do what?*' Skop asked eagerly, and my fired up body jumped in surprise at his voice. Embarrassment flared in me and I looked over at him, ten feet away in a soil bed, paws filthy.

'Oh gods, you must have seen everything?' I whispered, feeling my face heat.

'*No, he put me inside a freaking smoke bubble. You look like you had fun though,*' he said, and his tail wagged.

'Well, I didn't. And you're a weird little pervert,' I told him, relieved my encounter had been private.

'*You've got no idea,*' he answered, and launched back into digging up the soil.

'Skop, what happens when Olympian gods are married?'

'*Mostly they cheat on each other.*'

'Do they get divorced?'

'*Nope. Never been an Olympian divorce.*'

'So they just put up with the cheating?' A fierce stab of jealousy gripped me as I thought of Hades with another woman, and I scowled. Why the fuck would I care who he was with?

'*Yeah.*'

'Why? Why not leave?'

'*Dunno. Guess it's to do with them being immortal. It's not like they can just start hanging around with different friends, they all die after a bunch of years and then they're left with their ex again.*'

He had a point. That would be pretty awkward.

'I guess any affairs are temporary, for the same reason. The god would outlive any but their spouse,' I thought aloud. 'Wait, are all gods immortal?'

'No. Only the Olympians. And the original Titans. Some of the strong ones, like Thanatos and Eris, can live until they are killed, but they're not true immortals.' Well, that was interesting to know, I thought. The other gods could be killed. *'You know that's why the competition for Queen of the Underworld is so fierce?'* Skop said, his frenzied front paws stilling for a moment as he looked at me. *'Immortality is the most coveted thing in Olympus. And it's one of the perks of the job.'*

A strange feeling slid through my belly as I processed his words. Immortality? My brain seemed to fizz and cloud as I tried to imagine living forever, the idea too huge for me to deal with.

'People would marry someone they didn't love in order to live forever?'

Skop snorted and resumed his digging.

'They'd do a hell of a lot worse than that.'

I realized with a jolt that the strange feeling in my gut wasn't to do with the notion of *me* becoming immortal at all, it was to do with someone else marrying Hades for it. Righteous indignation swelled in me, and anger made me stand up straight. Hades didn't deserve a woman like that. He deserved a woman who loved him, who would worship him as the king he was, who would make his every dream a reality....

Oh good gods, where was this coming from? He was made of death and smoke! *Come on Persy, death and smoke! He tore that man apart! Your brain is in your head, not between your legs!*

But he'd said fated... Could I be destined to be with

him? Or did that just apply to the old Persephone, the one who had apparently killed another man's wife? A shudder rolled over me. This was all madness. I needed to stick to my plan. Lose the Trials, stay alive, and get back to New York.

FOUR

HADES

I paced up and down the breakfast room, flexing my fists and breathing hard.

Gods, I wanted her. And I knew how stupid it was to play with her, teasing and flirting and getting close. She would just be ripped away again.

But I couldn't stop myself. Even now, all the way in my rooms, I could feel her magic, a shining green light in the squalid sea of gloom I called home. I looked over at the platform where her tree had once stood, the branches blossoming over the table that was always set for two. For years it had been painful for me to come into this room. It had been our room. The place where we drank and ate and talked. And laughed. Her tree had softened the rocky room, bringing life and color and scent to the stillness. It had died the day she left, turning instantly to ash.

When Hecate had sent her here for lunch, and I'd seen her examining the rose and skull chairs, I'd wanted to seal the doors and never let her leave. *She was back.* The one woman I had ever loved, and had thought I would never see again.

. . .

A moan of frustration left me, and I pushed my hand through my hair yet again, wishing my arousal would lessen so that I could concentrate. But her body, responding to me like she had...

She may not be the bold, confident Persephone I had married, but the kindness, the sense of right, the fire in her belly was all still there. As was Hera's bond. My destiny was as written in stone as hers was, but I had the advantage of knowledge. She had nothing but a load of gods telling her what to do, in a world she didn't recognize. I hated the idea of her anger and frustration, but how could I tell her what had happened? It had broken her once, and even if I hadn't made my promise to her, there was no way I would cause her pain like that again. And it wouldn't help her anyway.

There was a sudden urgent humming in the back of my mind, and I sighed.

'What is it?' I snapped. A voice in my head responded quickly.

'We have information on the man with the phoenix.'

Rage flamed inside me at the mere mention of the man who had tried to kill my soulmate, and I flashed myself out of the breakfast room. That was not a place for anger. *It was our place.*

I took my position on my throne, then summoned the speaker to me. He was the captain of my guard, a severe and enormous minotaur called Kerato. In fact, most of my staff were severe, and I often thanked the gods for Hecate and her much needed sense of humor.

'Tell me,' I said.

'He was named Calix, my Lord. He lost his wife in the incident and had begun a faction of sorts. He and an indeterminate number of others who lost loved ones call themselves the Spring Undead and it seems they spend their time looking for ways to avenge their fallen.'

Anger made my form swell automatically, fury edging the colossal power that burned permanently hot inside me.

'How the fuck do they even remember her? She was wiped from Olympian history!' Just saying those words was painful. *I wiped my own wife from history.* But I kept my face stoic in front of Kerato.

'We have been unable to find that out. It shouldn't be possible.'

'Unless they have access to the river Lethe.' Which would mean it was someone who was allowed to enter Virgo; one of the four forbidden realms and the most secretive place in all Olympus. That should narrow the pool of suspects down.

'We have only captured one more conspirator so far, and he died before we could get much out of him. We will keep searching for answers, my Lord.'

'Search faster, and next time you capture someone involved, I want to meet them personally.' Visions of tearing that man apart filled my head, and the heavy melancholy I normally felt when considering the dead was replaced with a gleeful wave of retribution. This was the part of myself I disliked most, but relied upon the heaviest.

This was all Zeus' fault. The thought of my brother only added more heat to my boiling blood.

He brought her back. *You got to kiss her again, feel her skin, hear her voice and see her glow.*

And I would have to lose her all over again. Just like the man I'd torn limb from limb, my heart would be torn apart, for a second time. Persephone had been right when she'd called him a colossal prick.

I waved my hand, dismissing Kerato. I needed to go and fuck something up, burn off this raging tension. I needed to get her out of my head. I was already regretting our encounter, the sight of her parted lips, closed eyes and heaving chest now impossible to shift.

I had to stop. It wasn't fair, on her or me. *Remember what happened. You can't keep a light that bright in the dark.*

FIVE

PERSEPHONE

B y the time Hecate came and got me from the conservatory, Skop and I had found every buried seed. I'd spent a blissful hour sorting them into groups, then planning the flower beds. Lots of the seeds were useless, as they couldn't be grown indoors in the warm, or alongside other greedier plants, but a complex design was forming in my head that I was positive would be stunning if I could pull it off.

I had to shower again as I was covered in dirt, and then I got dressed in a gown that Hecate had chosen for me. It was a deep mossy green color, and had shoulder straps that slid down across the top of my arms and a boob-tube type bodice that skimmed the top of my breasts. I clutched at them, looking in the mirror.

'Are they actually bigger?' I asked Hecate as I peered down at my chest. She laughed.

'No. I told you when you first got here, you just needed better clothes.'

'*Or none at all,*' Skop chimed in. I ignored him. Working in the conservatory had definitely relieved some of the tension in my body from my encounter with Hades, but I still felt hugely restless. As soon as the word naked entered my head I was picturing Hades, bare and glistening and hard and...

I squirmed and shook my head.

'What do we have to do at this thing tonight?' I asked.

'Just have a few drinks, talk to a few folk, and find out what you have to do next in the Trials. It'll be a few hours, tops.' Hecate was wearing an electric blue dress that barely covered her ass, and had some sort of leather collar attached to the top. I wouldn't have been surprised if she produced a whip and handcuffs at any moment.

'Do you have a...' I tailed off, looking for the right word. 'Lover?' I finished a bit lamely.

'Hundreds,' she grinned at me.

'Anyone I know?'

'Nope. Now, are you ready?'

The Second Round Ceremony was being held in Hades' throne room, and when Hecate transported us there I felt a strange comfort in seeing the enormous colored flames licking up the open sides of the room. My eyes flicked to the thrones. There were only two empty chairs on the dais; the skull throne, and the rose throne. My gaze settled on the carved roses intertwined with the brutal thorns, and that spark of energy I thought might be my power rippled through my veins. I raised my eyebrows in surprise and stepped closer.

'Where you going?' hissed Hecate, and yanked my arm, spinning me around. I sucked in a breath. Fifty people or more were filling the rest of the throne room, all holding saucer shaped glasses and dressed in finery. Many I recognized from the ball, and Eros, that sexy-as-hell god of lust, stood out the most as he gave me a finger wave.

'Uh, hello,' I said, and a rumble of chatter started as they all turned back to whomever they were talking to before we had arrived. A few made their way towards us though, and Hedone and Morpheus were first to reach me.

'You did so well at the ball!' Hedone said, kissing me on the cheek. Pleasure rippled through me at her touch and I blinked, trying to dismiss the awkward feeling.

'Thanks,' I said, and took a glass from the little serving satyr's tray that had appeared beside me.

'It didn't go exactly to plan, but you handled it well,' said Morpheus, taking my other hand and kissing it.

Didn't go exactly to plan? It was a complete clusterfuck! A man was literally torn apart, because of me. I swallowed my real thoughts, plastering my practiced smile across my face and hoping it wasn't a grimace. This little get-together was going to be just the reminder I needed that these people were freaking nuts.

SIX

PERSEPHONE

'So, do you guys have any idea what's coming up next?' asked Hecate, and began to gulp from her glass of the divine fizzy liquid. I copied her.

'None. Although we have heard a little rumor about the last Trial of the Second Round,' said Hedone, eyes shining with excitement.

'Ooo, do tell?'

'I couldn't possibly,' Hedone said coyly. I clamped my teeth down on the inside of my cheeks to keep my smile in place. I seriously couldn't handle this shit. It was like secrets were currency in this place, nobody told anyone anything without making a great big deal of it first. A gong sounded and the chatter broke into a fevered buzz before dying out completely. I looked around the room for the smug pretty-boy commentator, and spotted him in front of the dais.

'Good evening Olympus!' he sang out. My eye twitched. 'Tonight we mark the start of Round Two of the Hades Trials. Now, we'd better keep you all in the loop on what's been happening... Those seeds little Persephone asked for weren't just any ordinary seeds, folks! She's not as simple as she looks!'

'Hey!' I protested, but my words were instantly drowned out by his booming, amplified voice.

'Those seeds contained power! So our only human contestant is no longer at quite such a disadvantage.' He beamed at me as my mind raced at a hundred miles an hour. He knew about the seeds? He hadn't mentioned who I really was though, so whoever had told him was pretending it was new power, rather than my original powers returned. But why had they told everyone who was watching? The answer came to me straight away. If I suddenly did something magical in front of the world they would have a hard time explaining it. It would look like they had lied about me being human.

'And now, please welcome your gods!' With a blinding flash of light, the gods appeared behind him, their respective thrones shimmering into existence. My eyes were drawn immediately to Hades, his dark smoky form translucent and unnerving. I scanned the smoke for any glimmer of silver and found none. Shoving my disappointment deep into my gut, I looked along the row of thrones as I dropped to my knees and clapped with the rest of the crowd.

Aphrodite was impossible not to stare at, this time with snow-white skin, black lips and eyes, and baby blue hair cascading down her shoulders in a poker-straight sheet. She was wearing a sheer blue dress that split almost at her hip, and it was clear she had nothing on underneath. I felt heat in my cheeks, and forced myself to look on. Athena and Hera were dressed as they had been at the start of the First Round, traditional and serene looking, and Artemis and Apollo were both wearing gleaming gold armor in the style ancient Greeks wore in my books at home. Enthusiastic smiles shone out of their youthful faces, their amber eyes alive with excitement. Ares too was fully clad in war gear, as he had been before, and Hephaestus shuffled backwards in the same leather tabard.

But Poseidon looked completely different. Instead of the serious man with cropped hair and simple toga, I found myself looking at a fierce tan-skinned man, with long white hair that should have aged him, but instead made him look dignified and extremely attractive. He was still wearing a toga, but I could swear it was made from the ocean itself, greens and blues and whites crashing together across the fabric in rolling waves. A gleaming silver trident shone in his fist, easily three feet taller than he was. I couldn't help gulping. This was a god who had made it clear he didn't like me, and today he looked like he did not want to be fucked with. Had he done that on purpose? I dragged my eyes from him, and found Hermes and Dionysus both grinning at me, and both wearing matching Hawaiian shirts with bright orange palm trees and parrots on them. A smirk leapt to my lips and they flashed me the thumbs up.

At the end of the row, and just as imposing as Hades' swirling smoke and Poseidon's glowing trident, was Zeus. He seemed to have merged the pretty boy image from the coffee shop with the dark haired older man I'd also seen him as, and the result was quite breathtaking. He looked like a retired football player who hadn't stopped training, his muscles bulging and experienced confidence emanating from him. Even from where I was standing I could see the purple lightning in his eyes, and feel his infectious energy. Something in my blood responded to him, like it had with the rose throne. But instead of feeling drawn to him, I felt a heat that I was pretty sure wasn't passion. I didn't know what it was, but it made my body hum, and that restless sense of urgency crept through my muscles and made me fidget.

'And now, for the announcement of the next Trial,' boomed the commentator and every god but Poseidon sat down on their throne.

Oh shit.

'You may rise,' said the ocean god, his voice lyrical and strong. I stood up, glancing to each side of me at Hecate and Skop as nerves skittered through me. 'I have agreed to take some pressure off my dear brother's realm, and host the next Trial in Aquarius.' I looked at Hades. His smoke was rippling steadily. 'All I will tell you now is that you can expect to get wet,' Poseidon said, and I looked back at him to find his eyes locked on mine. I gave him an awkward smile and bowed my head. 'We will begin at midday tomorrow, and if you survive, I shall host a feast in your honor.

If I survive? Gods above, what did he have planned for me?

'I look forward to it,' I lied, wondering if he would be more likely to celebrate if I didn't make it.

'I'm sure,' he said, and I could hear the thinly veiled malice in his voice. What was his problem?

'Well, there you have it, folks! We'll see you tomorrow at midday for the next of Persephone's Trials!' the commentator said, and Poseidon sat back down as Dionysus rose.

'How's it going?' he said to the room at large, a wonky grin on his face and his dark hair screwed up in a bun on top of his head. 'I've sorted us out some entertainment, enjoy,' he said, and waved his hand in front of him. He looked every bit like a stoned seventies rock star, and each time I saw him I desperately wanted to hang out with him. The air shimmered a gorgeous green color, and then four impossibly tall girls appeared, wearing different colored little tutu skirts. A cheer went up from the crowd. As I looked closer I realized they all had pale tattoos covering their deep brown skin, of vines and flowers. A drum beat ricocheted through the room, making me start, then more drums began to beat along with the first. It was a tribal sound that both set me on edge and made me want to move at the same time, until a beautiful flute began to play over the top. A wave of happiness washed over me, and the four girls began to sway their hips in a synchronized dance. Slowly, the crowd began to chat again, some dancing too, some just staring at the girls.

'Dionysus's party dryads,' said Hecate at my side.

'They're very beautiful,' I said.

'*Ohhh,*' moaned Skop.

'You alright?' I asked him.

'*Not that hanging round with you all the time isn't fun, but this used to be my daily view,*' he said, staring at the four girls, his tail wagging furiously.

'Oh. Sorry,' I said. 'I can see why you would miss them. They're quite mesmerizing.'

'*Not as mesmerizing as you.*' The voice was in my head but it wasn't Skop's.

'Hades?' I whirled, and found him stood behind me, smoky and translucent. Everyone around him was giving him a wide berth, hushed and watching.

'Evening, boss,' said Hecate, then touched my shoulder. 'See you in a bit,' she said, and sashayed off into the crowd.

'*You look stunning tonight,*' Hades said, still inside my head.

'Thanks,' I replied, pleasure tingling through me at his words.

'*You should answer me silently, or tongues will wag.*'

'Fuck 'em. Let them hear one half of the conversation,' I said loudly. 'I'm not hosting or being judged today.'

My belligerent statement was rewarded with a flash of laughing silver eyes, and a glimpse of his soft lips in a broad smile. Heat pooled in my core. Those lips... Gods, I was like a randy teenager!

'As you wish. I think you will like Aquarius. You used to love it.'

'Well, I love swimming,' I told him.

'That is good. Poseidon will not make this easy for you.'

'Why does he hate me?'

'He does not hate you. He fears you.'

'What?'

'With all your power, you were a formidable goddess.'

Formidable? I would have liked the sound of that, if it didn't come with the knowledge that powerful Persephone had killed someone's wife.

'Well, I'm just little ol' human Persephone now, with only enough power to heal myself and survive your temper,' I shrugged. I got another flash of his face, this time pinched and serious.

'I wish you wouldn't remind me of that,' he said, voice low.

'Well, I wish you hadn't gone all monster and corpses on me, but we don't all get what we wish for.' I wasn't backing down on this. He deserved to feel bad for what he had done. And saying the words reminded me that as intoxicating as he was, I didn't belong here.

'I am a monster. I told you that.'

'Yes you did, but then you kissed me anyway,' I shot back. There was a collective gasp around us, and I scanned the onlookers as my cheeks heated. My eyes fell on one furious face in particular, and my stomach clenched. Minthe. And her glare was so loaded with venom I might have dropped down dead on the spot if looks could kill.

Hades chuckled in my mind.

'I told you we should have kept this conversation private.'
I stood up straight, and flicked my loose curls dramatically over my shoulder. There was no way he was winning this one. I would give them something to gossip about.

'Yes, Hades, I know being with me blew your mind and I know you cried like a baby afterward, but we're not doing it again. Now, please stop bothering me.'

I heard his deep, booming laugh in my head as I spun on my heels and marched away from him.

'Well played, Beautiful. Well played.'

SEVEN

PERSEPHONE

I f I had thought his voice was sexy, it was nothing compared to his laugh. Desire throbbed through me as I stomped blindly into the crowd. I wanted to listen to that laugh for the rest of my life. Longer, if possible. I wanted to be the cause of his laughter, to light up his face with that exquisite smile...

Gods, this was impossible! I screwed my face up and forced myself to look for someone I knew. Eros caught my eye and I changed direction immediately. The last thing my aching body needed was a conversation with the god of lust. The scent of salty sea air suddenly cascaded over me and my steps faltered as my head filled with images of endless, life-giving ocean. *What I wouldn't give to spend the day on the beach right now.*

'Hello, Persephone,' said a lyrical voice, and Poseidon shimmered into the space in front of me. I stopped, and bowed.

'Poseidon,' I said, my stomach flipping. How was it that I now found the ocean god more scary than the King of the Underworld? I needed to revisit my priorities. 'I'm very much looking forward to seeing Aquarius. I've heard it's beautiful.'

'You've heard correctly. I want to offer you some advice.'

'Really?'

'Your powers were removed for a good reason. You would be wise to keep it that way. An ability to heal and feed plants is plenty enough. We both know that you will not win this competition.'

'How do you know that's all I can do?'

'Girl, I am one of the three strongest gods in Olympus,' he said, the waves now crashing across the material of his toga, a deep rumble building in his voice. 'There is nothing I don't know.' My heart began pounding in my chest as a primal fear crept over me.

'Right,' I whispered.

'My brother made his mistakes with you once already. I will not allow him to make them a second time.'

At his mention of Hades a defensiveness flashed up inside me out of nowhere, and I felt my face tighten into a scowl.

'Are you telling me you're trying to protect your brother, one of the *other* three most powerful gods in Olympus, from me? Seriously?'

'Watch your tongue!' he spat, and a gust of damp air lifted my hair from my shoulders. 'I have no personal grudge against you, Persephone, but I will do what needs to be done.'

'I didn't ask to be here!' I'd meant to put force into the words, but I hadn't meant them to come out as the shriek they did. It was like something had finally snapped inside me, the anger and frustration and injustice of everything that had happened breaking free from the fragile container I'd built around them. 'I was fucking kidnapped! From a life

I loved! And now you're threatening me? Do you have any idea at all what you people have put me through?'

'You are the same,' Poseidon hissed, his eyes glowing an intense blue. 'Your wrath is no less as a human, your temper as hot and unpredictable as it ever was.'

'You'd lose your fucking temper if you'd had your memories and power stolen!' Rage was burning through my blood, heating my whole body, and sending almost painful tingles across my skin. 'Everyone is happy to talk about my past, but nobody will tell me what I did! I'm being forced to risk my life, and the lives of strangers and the only friends I have here, for your entertainment! And nobody even expects me to survive, let alone win! Do you understand that I am not here to make your life difficult? I don't want to be here!'

Something black burst from my hands as I threw them in the air angrily, and I stumbled backwards in shock. *Vines*. Black vines were curling from my palms, barbed and glowing.

'What the-' I started, but in a flash Hades was there, between me and Poseidon. The sea god grew, his trident pulsing with blue light, and Hades smoke flickered and danced outward, matching Poseidon's size.

'Goading her into losing her temper isn't very fair, brother,' said Hades calmly. I barely heard him over the rushing in my ears as I stared dumbly at the vines still coiling from my hands towards them.

'Stop,' I pleaded quietly, but they kept growing.

'You need to see that she is still a threat. You are blind to the danger she poses,' Poseidon said loudly.

'Zeus brought her here, not me. Go and take it up with him.' Black spots were creeping into my vision now, the vines almost reaching Hades.

'Fine. But you've not heard the last of this,' snapped Poseidon, then vanished.

'Shit, shit, shit,' muttered Hades the second he left, the smoke disappearing from around him as he turned to me. 'Persephone, you need to lose the vines, now.'

'I'm trying!'

'They'll go if you calm down, take deep breaths and think about something that doesn't make you angry.'

'Everything here makes me fucking angry!' I shouted, and the vines burst out further, curling around his feet. Frustration crossed his face as he pushed his hand through his hair, then the world flashed white.

When the light cleared, I instantly felt the surging rage inside me change; a brighter, optimistic feeling forcing it out of my veins. I was in the conservatory.

'Vent. Use your power, give it to the earth,' Hades said. I didn't need to ask him what he meant, his instruction felt like the most natural thing in the world. I flicked my wrists towards the closest flower bed, and the vine glowed as a vivid green color snaked over the black. It spread fast, turning the whole vine green in seconds. The end of the vines hit the soil, and a joyous feeling made my chest expand, the vines burrowing deeper.

I didn't know how long I stood there, channeling all my rage and pent up energy into the soil, but Hades said nothing the whole time. Eventually the vines melted away, and I felt a pang of loss as the blissful feeling faded. Being connected to the earth like that was more than incredible. It was as though I'd finally found a place I had always yearned for but didn't really know existed.

I turned to Hades and almost took a step back at the hunger evident on his face.

'You're beautiful,' he breathed.

'Erm, I just offended Poseidon, showed everyone I can't control my temper or power, and had some sort of out-of-body experience with a flowerbed. I fail to see the attraction just now,' I said on a long breath.

'When you use your power to grow things, to create life, you... You become practically irresistible.' He ground out the last word, like he really was struggling to resist something. *To resist me.*

'But... doesn't creating life kinda undermine what you do here?'

He let out a long breath.

'Yes. I have never understood it either.' A wave of exhaustion rocked over me before I could reply, and I stumbled, dizzy. Hades was there in an instant, his strong arms supporting me.

'You smell awesome,' I told him, my vision clouding. He tensed.

'Do you have any idea how hard it is not to rip your clothes off right now?' he hissed. 'I can't be this close to you.'

It was the last thing I heard him say, before I passed out.

EIGHT

PERSEPHONE

When I woke up I was in my bed, and Hades' silver eyes were boring into my bleary ones.

'What happened?' I mumbled thickly.

'Your powers are returning. You lost your temper.' The fight with Poseidon came back to me clearly, and anxiety gripped my gut.

'Oh gods, that was in front of the whole room,' I groaned, rubbing my hand across my face.

'Nobody but the gods saw. Remember how I can hide us in smoke?'

'Yeah, the smoke bubble,' I said, remembering the blissful stolen kiss in that haven he had created at the ball.

'Well, Poseidon can make his own. He didn't want anyone but me to see your exchange.'

'You said he fears me. Why?'

Hades blew out a long breath.

'Persephone, your powers and your wrath were... unique.'

A sick feeling crawled through me, and I didn't want to be having this conversation any more.

'Well, I only have a bit of my power now, and I don't intend on getting any more. I'm sure I'll stay perfectly harmless,' I said, pushing myself up to a sitting position. 'Where's Skop?'

'On the floor. This asswipe won't let me on the bed,' I heard his voice say in my head.

'You're not going to eat the other seeds?' Hades stared at me.

'No.' I dropped my gaze to my lap.

I hadn't been sure before, but now I was positive. There was no way I needed this dark, angry kind of power running through me. I knew it was part of a terrible past, and I needed to concentrate on the future.

'Persephone, look at me.' I lifted my head and did as he asked. His skin glowed and his eyes shone bright. He was *unfeasibly* beautiful. 'You must never be scared of your own strength,' he said quietly.

'I've never had any strength,' I answered him, unable to keep the bitter edge from my voice. 'I've let other people treat me like shit for years, because I've never had any strength.'

His jaw tightened, and fury flashed in his eyes, orange flames leaping then vanishing in his irises.

'They made me take your strength, when I sent you away. You were scared, and I wasn't allowed to fix it. I prayed the fear would leave you when you started again in the mortal world.' His words were hardly more than a whisper, but they carried a sorrow that was unbearable to hear. My hand went to his face automatically, the need to comfort him, to relieve this heart-breaking burden from him, overwhelming me.

'I got there in the end,' I told him. 'I learned, and I

started to stand up for myself. In fact, until you lot showed up, I was doing pretty well.'

'There is a Queen inside you, Persephone. My Queen.'

Heat rushed me all at once, and there was nothing in the world that could feel better than hearing this man call me his queen. I sucked in a breath as I felt my cheeks burn.

'Well, I think I was starting to find her,' I said.

'I hope she stays with you when you get back.'

Physical pain seemed to blossom in my chest at his words, and I clawed about in my mind for the cause.

I wanted to leave. I wanted to go home. So why did it feel like he was betraying me by talking about sending me back?

'You still want me to leave?' I asked, before I could stop myself.

'I never wanted you to leave in the first place. But you can't stay here.'

I closed my eyes and flopped back onto the pillows. This was a conversation with no ending, just endless frustration. *Move on, Persephone.*

'Why did I pass out?' I asked him, opening my eyes.

'The power drained you. You'll need to make sure it doesn't happen in a more dangerous environment.'

'Like in the middle of a Trial?'

'Yes.'

'How?'

'You'll train with me from now on.'

'What?' I sat up again, eyebrows high.

'Every day. In combat and magic.'

I was going to see him every day? It was already getting hard to stop thinking about him all the time, how the hell was I going to stop myself from lusting after him if I spent *more* time with him? *Smoke and death, smoke and death!*

'Fine, but no magic sex,' I told him firmly. The corner of his mouth lifted.

'Agreed. No magic sex.' I shoved the disappointment that he'd agreed so readily deep down and nodded. 'Good,' he said. 'Now, get some rest before the Trial tomorrow. It's going to be tough.'

'OK. And... Thanks.'

'Always,' he said, and then he was gone.

I didn't visit the Atlas garden in my dreams that night. I wished I had, the calming, serene place was exactly what I needed, and the stranger often left me with more information than I'd had before visiting.

Instead, I dreamed of fire and blood. Screams filled my ears, until the roar of a beast began to drown them out. Then Hades burst through the flames, huge and monstrous and blue, his eyes burning with fury and everything around him turning to ash.

I woke up panting, fear making my heart hammer in my chest as I sat upright.

'You OK?' Skop asked, lifting his head from his paws. I nodded at him in the faint starlight coming from the ceiling. Since both Poseidon and Hades had flouted his guard duties, he had been extra protective the rest of the evening.

'Just a nightmare.'

'You want to talk to Morpheus about that,' he said, then settled back down.

There was no need for that, I thought, laying my head back down on my pillow. I knew exactly what the dream meant. It was my subconscious reminding me that Hades was dangerous.

I dressed in fighting garb the next day, and tied my hair up in a braid that kept it out of my face. If I was to be swimming, I didn't need my vision obscured by loose hair. I also left off the leather corset I normally wore over my shirt. It was heavy, and whilst it offered some protection from the blows of weapons, I was guessing that maneuverability would benefit me more in this Trial.

While I sat and waited for someone to come and get me, I stared at the open box of pomegranate seeds on the dresser. They pulled at me, and I thought about the black vines that had shot from my hands. *Strength.* They had felt strong and useful and deadly. I'd never had power like that at my disposal. Ted Hammond flashed into my mind, followed swiftly by an image of the black vines wrapping around his throat as he groped at me. An ugly, alien satisfaction filled me at the thought. *Stop it. You're not petty or vengeful,* I told myself sternly. I forced the image away, replacing it with the memory of when the vines had turned green, and that joyful feeling of being connected to the ground, of feeling the sparks of new life embedded in the earth. And that had just been in the starved conservatory. The idea of connecting like that with a real garden sent shudders of excitement through me.

I had my hand on the box before I'd even realized I'd moved.

'Woah there,' I scolded myself, jumping up from my stool and snapping the lid closed. 'I have *got* to get better at avoiding temptation.'

'*You're doing a good job so far, you've managed to resist me,*' said Skop.

'Gnome dogs really aren't my type,' I told him.

'I could try and change your mind?'

'Nope.'

'It was worth a shot.'

I was relieved when Hecate finally knocked on my door. The wait was making my nerves worse.

'You ready for this?' she asked, handing me her now customary gift of coffee. I took it gratefully.

'Nope. But water is better than heights or demons,' I said. 'And to be truthful, I'm excited to see Aquarius. Is it underwater?'

'Sure is. The city is spread across loads of underwater domes. It's pretty cool.'

'How do people get between them?'

'Tunnels. Or they swim. Lots of water nymphs and merfolk in Aquarius.'

'Merfolk? Like, actual mermaids?'

Hecate laughed and shook her head.

'There you go again, looking like a kid who has just had a wish granted. Honestly, you should see your face.'

'You try living in New York all your life and then finding out this is all real,' I retorted, and took a drag of my coffee. *Mermaids.* Gods I wanted to see one.

'You've seen a Spartae Skeleton, minotaurs, a freaking phoenix, and the gods know what besides. Why are merfolk a big deal?'

'I don't know,' I lied. I'd be damned before admitting my deep-rooted love for children's animated movies to her.

'Weirdo. Finish that up, we need to go.'

. . .

The room she flashed us into followed a pattern, I realized as I stared around it. I knew it was a throne room immediately, and not just because of the dais covered in huge seats, but because, like Hades' throne room and Zeus' dining room, there were no walls, just riveted columns holding up the ceiling. But the view here... Turquoise-blue water surrounded us completely, and beyond I could see hundreds of glowing gold domes. Floating at different levels, they were all connected by tunnels, and I could just make out buildings inside most of them, colored white and bronze. In the distance, behind the city, I could see a pod of massive whales meandering past.

It was stunning.

I was standing on a marble floor that at first I thought was white, but when the rays of light filtering through the water hit it, looked the palest blue. The ceiling was painted with the most incredible underwater scene I could imagine, pastel corals hiding hundreds of brightly colored fish, and images of creatures that looked like they had come from another planet surrounding them. The empty thrones were all plain, except the one in the center, which was shaped like a tidal wave, smooth and fierce and perfect.

'Wow,' I breathed.

'I know. Grumpy he may be, but Poseidon has taste,' Hecate said quietly.

'I appreciate that,' boomed Poseidon's voice, and Hecate winced.

'Shit.'

The twelve gods flashed onto the dais, and when the light cleared I saw the commentator standing in front of them, his white toga as crisp as his smile.

'Good day Olympus!'

I looked straight to Hades, his smoke rippling. A flash of silver in the darkness found my eyes and I suppressed my shiver of delight. *Gods, I was getting worse.* 'Welcome to Aquarius! I'll waste no time in handing you over to your host.'

Hecate bowed low, and I followed suit as Poseidon stepped forward, and the other gods lowered themselves into their seats. The sea god looked as he had the previous night, trident resplendent as it towered above him.

'I have devised a test fit for the Queen of an Olympian. You must get the gem back in the trident. You must complete the trial alone. Other than that there are no rules.'

Put a gem in a trident. That didn't sound too bad, I thought, trying to ignore the bit about a test fit for a Queen. And at least I knew what I had to do this time. No running around guessing and trying to decipher stupid clues.

'You will be granted the temporary ability to breath underwater, and a steed,' Poseidon continued, and my mouth dropped open.

Say what? Breathing underwater and a freaking steed?

'But by no means will you be immune to any other dangers of the ocean. Understood?'

'Erm,' I said, but he banged his trident on the floor before I could say any more.

'Let us begin!'

NINE

PERSEPHONE

I gasped as cold water enveloped me, the world turning upside down as my feet were swept out from under me. The sound of rushing water drowned out my yell, and I tumbled over and over as waves crashed all around me. Instinct made me clamp my mouth shut as I inhaled a mouthful of salty water, then I was completely submerged. The light dimmed and panic and disorientation gripped me. I kicked out, feeling for the floor or anything solid, unable to see. My lungs were burning as I flailed my limbs desperately. Then the swirling motion flinging my body about stopped abruptly, and bright light began to seep back through the water. I tried to steady myself, treading water, chest aching as I looked around.

I was at the bottom of the ocean.

Directly ahead of me was a huge sunken marble trident, jutting out of the sandy ocean-bed, its three points stabbing majestically towards the surface. I started to turn to look for more but dizziness made my eyes roll. I needed air.

'Breathe. You can breathe under here.'

'Hades!'

'Breathe.'

Gods, this was messed up. I closed my eyes, and forced out every instinct in my body screaming at me to keep my mouth shut.

I inhaled.

Instead of water, cool air filled my throat, then my lungs, and I laughed aloud in relief as my eyes fluttered open. *I was breathing underwater.* Unreal. I kicked myself around in a slow circle, taking in everything I could.

To the right of the fifty-foot tall trident, high up and floating on a platform, were the twelve gods, and a little way apart from them, the three judges. I threw a pointed scowl at them all, and moved my gaze on.

The ocean bed was littered with ruined buildings, white marble and lumps of bronze nestled in the sand. Only one structure looked like it had survived whatever had sunk it, but it wasn't in good shape. I guessed the gem that I had to hunt out and put in the trident would be hidden down there. I was quite sure there would be more to it than just finding it though. A treasure hunt wasn't exactly perilous enough for these sadistic bastards.

Didn't Poseidon say something about a steed? As soon as the thought entered my mind, my legs began to feel tired. With a final glance at the gods, I kicked myself down, swimming towards the intact building. There was no point tiring myself out treading water and achieving nothing.

The water was cool but not cold, and it felt good to be swimming. I'd swum in pools all my life, but swimming in the sea was a luxury I could seldom afford while living in Manhattan. I was glad I'd left the leather corset off, my arms pulling me easily through the water.

As I reached the entrance to the building, the hairs on my arms stood up and I slowed. It looked like I would expect an ancient Greek temple to look, with a triangular facade topping cracked columns. It was single story, and half of it seemed to have sunk into the sand, leaving it severely lop-sided. I peered through the columns into the darkness.

Something rushed at me from the gloom, and I shot backwards, drawing *Faesforos* from the sheath on my thigh instinctively. But as I saw the thing, my knife arm dropped to my side limply, and my jaw dropped.

It was a seahorse. And not the kind of seahorse that I'd seen in aquariums back home, but an actual horse, with a fish's tail curled underneath him instead of back legs. In place of hair he had a solid covering of tiny iridescent scales that shone and caught the light like mother-of-pearl, and he rocked and whinnied as he bounded in circles around me. Unbridled joy filled me as I watched him, and I felt like a child falling in love with ponies again.

'It's a hippocampus. They're not the most intelligent creatures, but tame enough,' said Hades voice in my head.

'Are you allowed to talk to me?'

As soon as I projected the thought to him, a hot swell of water lifted me, and Poseidon's voice echoed in my head.

'Enough help!'

I'll take that as a no then, I thought, and reached a hand out hesitantly to the hippocampus. He bumped his large, cold nose against my hand and gave a gleeful little whinny. A smile split my face, and I noticed a simple strap over his back, with a stirrup on either side. I swam up and over him, and he stayed perfectly still in the water as I maneuvered my feet into the stirrups. I couldn't see how the strap was staying fixed to his back, so I guessed magic was involved. The cold scales weren't as comfortable as a saddle would have been, but this would definitely beat swimming. I tried to ignore the creeping worry that I might be down here some time if they expected me to need to ride this fella to keep going.

As soon as I set my sights on the ruined building again, a deep rumbling started beneath me, and the hippocampus kicked in alarm.

'Easy, buddy,' I said, soothing his neck and looking down. The sand in the clearing in the center of the building was vibrating, dust clouds lifting into the water. 'Let's not wait and find out what that is, eh?' I said to the hippocampus, adrenaline beginning to surge though my veins. Something bad was coming, I knew it. The hippocampus made a loud clicking sound in response. 'How do I make you go forward?'

My words were lost to the water around me, only audible as a bubbly mess of noise to me, but it seemed my steed understood them perfectly. He darted forward, and I gripped his neck in surprise at his speed, then squeaked in alarm as I realized he wasn't slowing down. 'Slow down!' He did, immediately, and I let out a long breath, bubbles rising around my face. 'Left a bit?' I asked him tentatively, and the rumbling grew louder. He swerved left. Good. 'And right?' He changed course, heading right. 'Excellent,' I told him. 'Let's go get this gem.'

I couldn't help glancing over my shoulder as we charged towards the gloom of the temple.

I wished I hadn't.

The sand in the clearing was beginning to churn, and I could just make out giant black claws peeking up through the ground, tips sharp and lethal looking. If whatever it was had claws bigger than me, I shuddered to think how huge the rest of it was.

I snapped my attention back to the job at hand as we zoomed between two columns, and into the temple.

'Slow down a bit, buddy,' I said, straining to see in the darkness. The hippocampus did slow down, but he also made a funny squeaking sound, before beginning to glow. A soft blue light started emanating from him, casting just enough illumination about us for me to make out more columns and what was left of a cracked marble floor, sinking into the ground. Something large scuttled on my right, and I jumped in surprise.

Trying not to think about what else might be in there with me, I urged the hippocampus on. 'That's a neat trick. I'm going to have to give you a name,' I told him, as we floated cautiously through the room, me scanning the ground beneath us for anything that looked like a gem. 'How about Buddy? I keep calling you that anyway.' He snickered and I nodded. 'Buddy it is.' A loud screech from outside the temple carried through the water to me, and I shivered. We needed to do this faster.

We did a full circuit of the room, finding nothing but more broken rock and marble, and lots and lots of large crabs. I grimaced as I realized we were going to have to go further into the temple. There were two dark doorways at the back of the room and we hovered before them. Choosing the one on the left arbitrarily, I directed Buddy towards it, and we swam through.

It was pitch black, and Buddy's soft glow failed to penetrate the darkness. A primal fear of not knowing what was in the dark crawled over my skin. Heat swept over me as I blinked and I realized that being completely submerged in water was a much, much more suffocating feeling when the water wasn't nice and cool. A budding panic started to blossom in my chest as Buddy turned in a slow circle, and the water around me heated more. Despite every breath I took being dry air, my lungs were straining, and it felt like I couldn't fill them enough. Tightness was spreading across my whole chest now, and I knew the signs of oncoming panic in my body too well. Big black spots would come soon, along with the dizziness.

'We'll come back to this room,' I said, even my blurry underwater voice sounding breathless. Buddy seemed to agree, wasting no time at all speeding back to the doorway. The gloom of the main hall seemed positively bright compared to the dark room, and the water we moved through was mercifully cool, almost like a balm over my skin. I took long breaths as Buddy slowed, petting his neck absent-mindedly as I reassessed the hall, my racing pulse calming. 'Let's hope the gem is in the other room,' I said to him. 'Cos I do not want to go back in there. Ever.'

The ceiling in the second room was cracked, and the gaps were letting in shafts of blue light that shimmered over an array of rotting wooden crates. We were on the raised side of the building, the side that wasn't sinking, and I couldn't have been more grateful for the extra light.

'OK. Let's see what we've got,' I said nervously, and slid my feet from Buddy's stirrups. Swallowing my trepidation, I kicked myself over to the nearest crate and reached for the lid. I'd half expected the wood to crumble under my touch, but it felt sturdy as I eased the lid up. There was no hinge, and the lid slid off, hitting the sandy marble and causing a wave of dust to lift from the floor. I heard a distinct slithering sound and froze, trying to tread water as gently as I could while looking slowly around myself for the source of the sound. Nothing was moving though, and I let out a long breath as I swam over the top of the open box to look inside.

Books. Piles and piles of books, probably submerged in water for centuries. I felt a pang of sorrow that they were ruined, then another distant screech made me focus. I needed to check the next box.

I went through them all and whilst I found some pretty awesome stuff, none of it was a gem. There was an unbelievably sharp looking sword, a large box full of rusted armor, and a whole host of cooking paraphernalia, but nothing that looked like treasure. Swimming back over the top of the boxes towards Buddy, I sighed. 'Guess we'd better go back to the room of panic,' I told him, then froze.

Wrapping itself tightly around the first crate I'd opened was a snake. An enormous freaking sea snake. Documentaries I'd seen about how reptiles flashed bright colors as a warning to other animals popped into my head as I stared at it. This thing was neon-bright, don't-fuck-with-me orange. It was also massive, looping itself three times around the box already, with more tail seeming to come from nowhere. And it was between me and the doorway and my hippocampus.

Would it care if I just swam over it, or would it attack? A thought stopped me from kicking up higher and trying though. What if it was wrapped round that particular box for a reason? Was there such a thing as a guard snake? *But that box was full of books, not gems.* Although... I hadn't removed any of the books. Or looked underneath them.

Pulse racing, I swam back to the box with the sword in it, and hefted it up out of the crate. It weighed a ton and I screwed my face up, dropping it again immediately. There was no way I could wield it. Besides which, I didn't really want to kill or piss off the snake. Just get it to move out of the way. I began to dig through the crates, tossing things out as I hunted for something that might distract the serpent. It didn't move from the box of books, but its head lifted warily, beady black eyes fixed on me as I launched bits of ancient sunken trash through the water.

My eyes fell on the rusted armor, a new plan forming quickly in my head as yet another screech from outside reverberated through the building. I reached into the box and lifted out a dented shield with a sun carved on it. It was heavy, but nowhere near as bad as the sword, and it seemed solid enough. I fought with the straps on the inside, eventually looping my left forearm through so I was wearing it properly. It was large enough that when I held my arm in front of me it covered my whole body, down to the waist. It wasn't ideal, but it was the best I had. It would have to do.

'Here we go,' I told Buddy, and swam towards the snake and the box of books.

TEN

PERSEPHONE

The snake's head reared back as I got close and it hissed, a purple forked tongue flicking from its mouth. A frisson of fear skittered through me but I swam on, covering myself with the rusted shield. I swam high over the snake, staying well out of reach of its head as I got over the top of the box. I squinted down, scanning for anything that looked out of place and my gaze snagged on a leather-bound book that had a bright orange cover, just visible under a few of the others. *Orange like the snake.* Was that a clue?

Steeling myself, I focused on the book and tipped my body in the water, so that I was pointing head-first at the box. Raising the shield I took a deep breath, and darted downward.

The snake went for me the second I was within its range, hitting the shield with such force that I rolled hard through the water. Gasping, I tried to angle myself down, sending a million silent thanks to the gods that the ancient shield had held. I felt water swoosh past me as I frantically reached into the box, lifting my shield arm around my back to protect myself. Shoving other books aside, I managed to close my fingers around the bound edge of the orange book just before something slammed into the back of my legs. I crashed hard into the crate, hitting my chin on a mercifully squishy book, the impact of the shield hitting the wooden sides of the box sending shockwaves through my arm. I rolled as best I could, still clutching the book, and saw the end of the snake's glowing tail coming for me just in time to bring the shield around to block it. There was another hissing sound, and adrenaline sent a surge of strength through my legs. I tucked them under myself and pushed hard against the side of the box, launching myself up and out of reach of the snake.

I wasn't fast enough though. I felt searing hot pain in my ankle as I kicked furiously, and looked down to see the creatures jaws wide open beneath me, red blood on the end of one of its fangs. *My blood.*

Praying it wasn't a venomous snake, I bolted towards the door and Buddy, trying to shake the heavy shield off my arm as my heart hammered in my chest.

'Let's go!' I called to the hippocampus as I shot straight past his rocking body, back through the doorway and as far away from the hissing neon snake as I could get. Once I was back in the gloomy main hall, I whirled, raising the shield still stuck on my arm, but mercifully only Buddy had followed me out of the room.

Grimacing, I managed to get my arm free from the shield straps and gripped the book with both hands, treading water and trying to ignore the pain spreading up my calf. If this was just a normal, boring book I was going to lose my shit.

I opened it, holding my breath.

There, glowing bright with every color of the ocean, was

a wide, flat gem, nestled in a hollow cut out of the book's pages. Relief washed through me, and I grabbed it triumphantly, dropping the book onto the floor. 'Nailed it,' I told Buddy, allowing myself a smile as I held up the gorgeous stone to show him. A pulse of pain from my leg transformed my smile swiftly into a scowl though. I lifted my knee to my chest in the water and twisted my leg, so that I could get a good look at the wound the snake had given me. It was a small cut, but it was shining with blood and was giving off a faint orange glow.

Shit. That did not look normal. I could heal though, right? As I tried to feel for my powers a wave of fatigue came over me, and I didn't know if it was from my physical encounter with the snake, or something worse. Like venom.

Putting the gem carefully into my pocket I kicked myself over to Buddy and wrestled my feet into his stirrups. It felt good to rest my legs as I sat down on his cold back, and I sagged a little, the adrenaline from both the terrifying pitch black room and my face off with the snake starting to ebb away.

'Let's see if I can use these damn powers,' I muttered, and closed my eyes, concentrating on the feeling I'd had in the conservatory.

After a full minute of trying, all I could feel was a pathetic tingle somewhere in my chest, and I was fairly certain I wasn't healing myself. My ankle still throbbed painfully. 'Fine. I give up. Let's get this over with,' I snapped, opening my eyes and patting Buddy on the neck. We bobbed together in the water as he whinnied. The best thing I could do was to finish the Trial, then get help. A piercing screech from outside echoed through the chamber and I gritted my teeth, feeling my pulse spike as I mentally geared up for what was coming next. 'Alright, alright, I'm going!' I yelled and directed Buddy towards the cracked columns at the front of the temple, and whatever it was that making that awful sound.

~

'Shit. Shit, shit, shit,' I breathed as we left the sinking building and emerged into the bright blue ocean.

The thing between me and the trident statue made the sea snake look positively tame.

My skin crawled as I stared, every part of my mind telling me to turn and run, and for the sake of the gods, don't turn back. The center of the clearing was now a swirling mass of sand, as though there was a whirlpool embedded into the ocean floor. And emerging from it like some sort of worm from a hole was the most hideous creature I'd ever seen. It was the same shape and color as a worm, but it was as wide as a house, and its head... Its whole head was a mouth. Needle-sharp teeth ringed its circular jaw, and huge claw-like black horns circled the outside of its head. Its skin was repulsive looking, cracked and rotten and leathery, and big drops of something the color of blood flicked out from it as it rolled and flailed through the water. It was about twenty feet out of the churning sand and I realized as the hippocampus reared back suddenly, that I was only just out of its reach.

'Now you face Charybdis!' boomed Poseidon's voice, and the creature screeched on hearing its name.

A surge of adrenaline wiped away the pain from my leg and the initial paralysis at seeing something so alien. My vision focused sharply, and I reached down to Buddy, who was vibrating with fear beneath me.

'I need your help, Buddy. We're way faster than this

thing,' I told him, loading my voice with a confidence I prayed I could back up. 'But we need to go right now, before that thing gets out any further out of the sand. Go!'

The hippocampus burst to life, zooming up and over Charybdis so fast I could feel the skin on my face pulling against the force of the water. I glanced down as we soared over the monster, a flurry of excitement building inside me. We were doing it. We would reach the trident statue in no time.

But my breath caught and the excitement sank like a stone to the pit of my stomach the very next second. The thing was dropping back down into its hole, its massive round mouth forming the epicenter of the sand-whirlpool below me, and a jet of water blasted up from it, slamming into us and freezing Buddy's progress completely. He squealed beneath me, and panic flooded my system as I looked down and saw a second layer of razor sharp of teeth slice out under Charybdis' first set, jagged and stained and as big as I was. We were trapped in the beam of water, and like quicksand, it was sucking us downward.

'You can do it!' I urged the hippocampus, my heart hammering as I looked up at the trident statue. But he couldn't. Slowly and inexorably, we were being dragged towards the creature's terrifying maw.

I looked desperately between the trident and Charybdis, sand and ocean water swirling faster and faster around us. Buddy was moving backwards now, his frantic tail unable to keep beating at such a fast pace against the mighty pull of the monster. I felt utterly useless sat on his back, but if he couldn't break free of the whirlpool's force, there was no way I could.

272 ELIZA RAINE & ROSE WILSON

I needed to do something else. Something that wasn't swimming. Whatever it was that I did best.

I fixed my sights on the center spike of the trident, and concentrated hard on Poseidon. I thought of what he had said to me, how he blamed me for being here, for posing a threat to Olympus. I thought about the way Eris had treated me at the masquerade ball, patronizing and cruel. I thought about Zeus, and his fucked up, inflated sense of entitlement and the shit he was putting Hades through.

Black vines burst from my palms, and a feeling like electricity burned through my entire body. There was no fear this time, no terror of what was happening. This time I was in control. This time I *wanted* the vines. I launched them at the trident, bone-deep strength filling my body to the brim as I sent them snaking further through the water to wrap around the central spike.

Buddy squealed again and I snapped my attention down, dimly noticing that my arms were glowing green.

We were too close.

Charybdis was only ten feet below us, and a tremor of fear shuddered through my new found strength as I looked down past those insanely sharp teeth, into the black, rotten gullet of the beast.

No fucking way was I going down there.

I pulled hard on the vines, willing them to hold, willing them to be stronger than the whirlpool.

They were.

I cried out in pain as my wrists were yanked up hard, both of them making an awful snapping sound as we shot up through the sea. I squeezed my legs tightly around Buddy as we were dragged higher, tears streaming from eyes I couldn't keep open against the powerful flow of water. I didn't see the trident until it was too late, Buddy and I slamming into the cold marble. The pain in my wrists was so excruciating that I hardly noticed though, and I struggled to get my bearings as I belatedly realized we had come to a stop. I heard that hideous screech again and shook my head, blinking. Buddy tipped me forward with a whinny, so that I was looking down, and through my haze I saw Charybdis launching himself up from his hole.

The sight was all I needed to snap back into action. I shoved my hand into my pocket, noticing first that the vines had gone, then yelling involuntarily at the pain. Gasping through the agony, I withdrew the gem. I had seconds before the beast reached us.

'Go!' I urged the hippocampus, and we pelted up, towards the tip of the central spike, the only one missing a gleaming blue gem. Heat engulfed us and I knew it was Charybdis' rotten breath as the light around us faded. His huge teeth moved into my peripheral vision as he reached us, and adrenaline flooded my body.

This was it. Now or never.

I screamed as I launched myself up from Buddy's back and slammed the gem into the empty recess, and the ring of teeth began to close around us.

ELEVEN

PERSEPHONE

The blood-stained teeth were barely a foot from us when white light flashed. For the first time since coming to this damned forsaken place, I couldn't have been more grateful for that light. It meant I was being transported somewhere else, and there was literally nowhere at that moment that could be worse.

I found myself on Poseidon's throne room floor again, dry and on my ass. I moved to stand as the light cleared from my vision, but immediately dropped back to the stone floor. My leg...

The wound on my ankle was turning black, the torn leather of my pants revealing how swollen it was. As I reached out to touch it new fear and pain blazed through me. I couldn't move my hands, and pain was lancing up my arms from my wrists with such intensity I could barely focus on anything else.

'You used the wrong gem,' boomed Poseidon, and I blinked up at him. He was standing in front of his throne, the eleven other gods behind him, just as they had been before I'd started the Trial. His face was different somehow, like he was straining against something.

'Where's Buddy?' I asked, before I could stop myself. Poseidon inclined his head a touch. 'The way you treated my hippocampus was commendable. He is safe.'

'Good. What do you mean I used the wrong gem?' I said through clenched teeth, trying to flex my fingers. Nothing but pain, shooting up my forearms. I felt sick.

'That gem was not the same as the other two in the trident. They were turquoise and the one you found was blue. The correct gem was in the other room. You may now be judged.'

My mouth fell open, but as I started to argue I was cut off.

'And so to the judges!' the commentator's voice sang out from behind me. I swiveled around on my butt, not giving a shit how it made me look. I couldn't stand, and I couldn't use my hands. Standing and falling on my face would look a lot worse. My head swam as I looked at the judges, fresh waves of pain stabbing through me. 'Radamanthus?'

'No tokens,' the cheerful judge smiled at me. I felt the fury morphing my face.

'Aeacus?'

'No tokens,' the serious man said.

'Minos?'

'No tokens.'

I glared at them as they vanished, injustice pounding through me, then the world flashed white once more.

I wasn't in my own room when the light faded. I was on a bed though, and I looked around warily, anger still rolling through me in waves, every pulse of pain tearing through my arms and leg making it worse.

I got past a snake and that freaking sea monster and got nothing at all for it? This was complete and total bullshit! *You don't want to win, what the hell are you angry about?* The rational voice inside me cut through the fury. And it was right. I didn't want to win, I just wanted to survive. This was a good outcome.

But it didn't feel good. In fact, I didn't feel good.

A fuzzy feeling overcame me as I tried to take in my surroundings, and my vision abruptly turned bleary.

'Is she alright?' said an urgent male voice, and I tried to look for the source but instead felt the top half of my body collapsing on the pillows behind me.

'I don't know, get out of the damned way!' answered a female voice that my brain barely registered as Hecate's, before I blacked out completely.

'You know, you should stop passing out after every Trial. It's not a great look.'

I sat up quickly, and Hecate leaped backwards before I accidentally head-butted her.

'My hands!' I said, fear making my skin crawl. I hadn't been able to use my hands... I raised them fast, and watched my fingers flex in relief. They were working, and they didn't hurt at all.

'They're fine now. Your vines broke both your wrists, that's all.'

I looked at her incredulously.

'*That's all?* Are you serious?'

'Yeah I'm serious. You just needed a rest to fix those, the

venom in your ankle was a totally different story. That shit nearly killed you.'

'R-really?'

'Yeah. Good job one of the most powerful gods in the world has a soft spot for you,' she said, with a little wink.

'Hades?'

'He healed you. He'll get in some serious shit if anyone finds out, but to be honest I'm not sure what else Zeus can do to him.' She sighed and sat down on the edge of my bed. It was narrow and I looked around as I processed her words. *Hades had healed me.*

'Where am I?'

'Infirmary.'

I nodded. That explained the metal cabinets lining the walls and the three other single beds.

'Where's Skop?'

'Hades wouldn't let him in here. Doesn't want Dionysus to know he healed you.'

'So... Are the other gods expecting me to die from the snake venom?' I asked. My tummy rumbled loudly. I was freaking ravenous.

'Nah, he'll make up some story about an apothecary having the right antidote. Which will exist somewhere, but we didn't have time to find it.'

'Thanks. Again. For saving me.'

'I did nothing. This one was all up to the boss,' she said, but the smile she gave me was as real as any I'd seen. 'I know you're not gonna like this, but we have to go to Poseidon's party.'

'You're fucking kidding.' My stomach twisted as I stared at her. I needed some time to get over the fact that I apparently almost died. Again.

'I'm not. He told the world publicly that if you survived

he would host a feast in your honor. So that's what he's doing, and you have to be there.'

'I got no damned tokens! I failed!'

'But you did survive. So get dressed.'

~

Hecate gave me a long yellow dress to wear, which was fairly plain except for the white daisies that adorned the skirt. I accepted her offer to magic my make-up and hair into something presentable, and sat still while her eyes glowed milky white opposite me.

This was ludicrous. They would have let me die for this damned competition. And they tricked me with a fucking fake gem. I mean, seriously, who would have noticed that it was a slightly different color? *Anyone who took the time to look properly,* answered the critical voice inside me that I'd spent years trying to squash. I felt my eyes narrow as I huffed.

'They're a bunch of fuckwits,' I announced, and the white leaked away from Hecate's eyes.

'Yup. You're all done.' There was no mirror to hand, but I trusted her. She'd made me look great before. 'Except Hades,' she added, moving to the door. 'He's less of a fuckwit than most of the others.' A thrill danced across my skin at hearing his name and I stopped myself from rolling my eyes. I needed to get over this. Now.

I followed Hecate through the door into a long corridor lit with torches. They burned a normal orange color, no blue fire, like the Underworld.

'Did you know it was the wrong gem?' I asked Hecate, unable to shift the anger I still felt about being duped.

'Well, it was pretty obvious that you had to get something from the dark room. The other one was too easy.'

'Easy?' I stopped in my tracks, eyebrows raised as high as they would go. 'Easy? That snake nearly killed me!'

'Yeah but the dark room was so bad you couldn't stand it for more than a minute. It was obviously the worse of the two.' I resumed my stride down the corridor, almost stamping after her, my fists clenched.

'This place is bullshit,' I seethed.

'So you keep saying. You know, you might end up offending some of the inhabitants if you carry on like this.'

'Most of the inhabitants are dickheads,' I snapped.

'I'm gonna take it you don't mean me,' Hecate answered slowly, blue light flickering around her dangerously. A trickle of alarm ran through my anger.

'No! Gods no, of course not.'

'Good. Although I *can* be a total bitch,' she said, with a small shrug as her blue light faded.

I didn't doubt it.

At the end of the corridor was a short flight of stairs leading down, and when we reached the bottom my rage abruptly abated as I took in where we were.

We were entering one of the tunnels I had seen earlier that connected the domes of Aquarius. And it was truly breathtaking.

The whole tunnel was clear, offering an unhindered view of the glowing gold domes all around us. I could see much more clearly what was inside the closest one now; white and bronze buildings surrounding a bustling courtyard filled with stalls. Most of the people I could make out were humans and they were wearing Asian style clothing, brightly colored saris and fabric everywhere.

'Aquarius is famous for jewelry markets,' Hecate said, stopping to let me stand and stare. 'We're on the east side, which is the shopping district. The west side of the city is more formal, all meeting halls and grand temples. And in the north the domes get bigger and more sparse because they're all farms.'

'Farms?'

'Yeah. Poseidon likes to be self-sustaining down here, so he has farms. I don't know how much of his power it uses growing stuff down here, but that's what he does. He doesn't trust the other gods.'

'He doesn't trust me either,' I mumbled, staring through the water at the beautiful underwater city. 'Why is he so moody?'

'I'm guessing being Zeus' brother will do that to anyone after an eternity. Hades-' she started, but stopped. I turned to her and she bit down on her lip.

'Go on...'

'Hades deals with Zeus in a different way,' she said slowly. 'And he has more reason to dislike Zeus than Poseidon ever has.'

'Why?'

Hecate sighed.

'It really should be Hades telling you this,' she said, but continued. 'When Zeus rescued his siblings from Cronos and led the war against the Titans he became Lord of the Gods by default. And when handing out almighty roles in the new world, he made sure he became ruler of the Skies. The two most powerful remaining realms he gave to his brothers. The Ocean and the Underworld. One a place of life-giving, flowing power, the other a place of dark and terrifying misery.'

'Hades didn't choose to be King of the Underworld?' I breathed. Hecate shook her head sadly.

'No. He didn't. Zeus made the decisions. The three brothers took on the epic powers required of them to rule their domains. Poseidon gained ultimate control of water, Zeus of storms and sky and Hades... He is not a god of death. Thanatos is the god of death. But Hades was forced to become the only thing that could rule over and control the kingdom of the dead.'

'A monster,' I whispered, the hairs on my arms standing on end.

'Yes. He had to become more feared than any other god. It's not just the dead that reside in the Underworld, it's also home to the world's most dangerous gods and monsters, who have been trapped in Tartarus. If they or the dead rose... Olympus would fall.'

My mind was spinning as I tried to imagine a Hades who wasn't surrounded by smoke and death, a Hades who ruled the seas or the skies instead of the Underworld. Would he be different? Hell, I hardly knew anything about him now, how would I even know? And it wasn't like Zeus and Poseidon weren't terrifying in their own right. To an extent, they were all monsters.

'So, does he hate his brothers?' I asked. Was he an outcast? Memories of crying in my bunk in my parents' trailer flickered through my mind unbidden. I knew how it felt to be an outcast. I knew how differently people treated you.

'You'd have to ask him that. I certainly wouldn't call them friends. But Hades isn't stupid. Over the years he's aligned himself with the few beings in this world stronger than Zeus.'

'Oceanus?' I said, remembering what Skop had told me about Zeus being pissed that the ocean god was back.

Hecate looked at me in surprise.

'Yes. How'd you know that?'

'Skop. Oceanus is a Titan, right? Like you?'

'Yeah, except like a bazillion times more powerful than me. He, Prometheus, Atlas, Nyx, Helios, and a bunch of other Titans stayed neutral in the war. They mostly keep a low profile or have vanished though. Zeus despises Titans. But Oceanus returned recently.'

'So how come he hasn't taken the sea back from Poseidon?'

'It doesn't work like that,' Hecate said, and began walking down the tunnel. I followed after her. 'Poseidon rules this realm, not all the oceans. Sure, he has power over water, but he doesn't own it. Hephaestus' realm is under the sea too, made up of huge volcanic forges.'

'Oh. Can a god have more than one realm?'

'Funny you should mention that,' she said. 'No.' I waited for her to go on, but she stayed silent, our sandals on the glass tunnel the only sound.

'Why is it funny?' I prompted eventually.

'Talk to Hades about it. I'm sure you'll understand it better coming from him.' I rolled my eyes, but the truth was that I was secretly longing for any excuse to talk to him.

TWELVE

HADES

Why was she not here yet? The last time I had seen her, Persephone had been as white as the marble beneath my feet, the black poison from that cursed snake most of the way up her leg. Even with the ability to go anywhere instantly, I hadn't dared try to find the antidote. I hadn't known how much longer she had before the venom reached her heart, and then it would be too late.

Dread coiled its way through my chest at the thought of her death. This is why she was sent away! This was why I'd ripped a part of my soul out - to keep her safe. And now, here she was, at death's door every other damned day.

I realized the temperature was rising and took a slow breath, calming myself. Poseidon was acting cagey since the Trial, and I hadn't seen Zeus yet. Both would goad me tonight, I was sure. I needed a better handle on my temper. *I needed to see Persephone, alive and glowing and healthy.*

The feast in her honor was being held in the courtyard of a small dome, and it was decorated beautifully. A huge circular pool filled the middle of the pale brick ground, and female merfolk and ocean sprites splashed and played and batted their eyelashes at the other guests. Not that anyone was looking at merfolk's faces; they were all as naked as the day they were born. I barely noticed them as I scanned the dome yet again. Many lesser gods were present, talking and laughing under twinkling golden lights, the blue of the ocean casting a favorable light over them.

'She'll be here soon, Hades,' I heard Hera say in my mind. I looked sideways down the row of thrones at her, but her gaze was fixed on the crowd.

'I know,' I answered gruffly.

'I spoke with her, you know. After the masquerade ball.' My heart skipped a beat. 'She is an enigma. So much of your fierce Queen has been buried too deep to resurrect.' I thought of Persephone's own words, and anger and pain gripped me. *I've let other people treat me like shit for years, because I've never had any strength.* I'd done that to her. She had been one of the strongest women I'd ever known, and I'd left her defenseless and alone.

'She will not be in Olympus long,' I said to Hera, forcing my emotions down. This was the way it had to be. I had already accepted that twenty-six years ago.

'I wouldn't be so sure about that. Strength born from overcoming trauma is very different to blood-born arrogance. It is true strength.'

'What?'

'Her experience as a human has changed her. Instead of being born to power, she's had to earn it. And the more we put her through, the stronger she may become. Stronger even than she was before.'

'No,' I snapped, but conflicting feelings of excitement and fear rippled through me. Stronger than she was before?

Was Poseidon right to fear her? But imagine her with true power, ruling by my side...

My body responded immediately to the vision blossoming in my mind. Persephone on the Rose throne, resplendent in one of her fierce black corseted gowns, an onyx crown atop her head and black vines coiling from her palms as she glowed with power. Arousal throbbed through me.

She walked into the dome at that exact second and she couldn't have looked less like the woman I was imagining.

She was wearing a yellow dress, with white daisies on it, and she was wide-eyed with awe. She looked delicate and young and vibrant and innocent and... *And I wanted her even more.*

Her eyes found me almost immediately, and a bolt of something deeper than desire tore through me. I couldn't handle it. All my resolve to avoid her and merely lust after her from afar disintegrated, and I was standing in front of her within a second.

'Oh! Hello,' she said, and I could hear the nerves in her voice. Was she still afraid of me?

'Hello. I'm glad to see you looking so... healthy.'

'I hear you are to thank for that,' she said. I could see her eyes scanning my smoky exterior, and I deliberately dropped it from my face just long enough to let her see me. Something leapt to life in her green eyes, hints of her power shining through. My arousal throbbed again.

'You're welcome,' I said, the words gruffer than I'd intended them.

'I, erm,' she started, then bit her bottom lip. I almost groaned aloud as my attention was drawn to her mouth. 'I was talking to Hecate earlier and she said I should ask you about something.'

'OK.'

'It's sort of private.'

'Oh. Right.' I threw up the smoke bubble, and she looked around herself frowning.

'Won't this look really suspicious?' she asked me.

'No. To everyone else it looks like you're talking to an over-enthusiastic griffon.' A smile crossed her face.

'Let me see you?' I dropped the smoke that hid me from the world and saw her chest swell as she took a breath. 'How come you wear clothes from the mortal world instead of a toga?' she asked me.

'It pisses Zeus off,' I shrugged. 'Plus I look good in it.' I gave her my most wicked smile and she rolled her eyes at me.

'You think so, huh?'

'You'd prefer this?' I asked, and made my shirt vanish. Color leapt to her cheeks as her eyes widened. And I knew I wasn't imagining the lust I could see in them.

'Put your shirt back on!' she squeaked. My cock was throbbing painfully now, and I let my own desire show on my face as my shirt reformed around my chest.

'You said no magic sex!' she chided, and I bowed my head.

'So I did. I apologize profusely.'

'Liar.'

'What did you want to talk to me about?'

Her face changed, a seriousness settling over her beautiful features.

'Hecate said something about gods not being able to

have more than one realm, and I should ask you about it because you can explain it better.'

'Hecate shouldn't be telling you anything about Olympus, because you're not staying here,' I snapped, the subject of her question causing the reality of the situation to slam back into me like a hammer.

Hurt flickered across her face, but she folded her arms and lifted her perfect chin.

'In that case, there's no harm in telling me,' she retorted.

The desire to talk to her like I used to, to have someone to share my problems with, made me want to tell her every secret I had, but I couldn't act on it. What good would it do? 'Tell me,' she demanded, and as I looked into her resolute face, my resolve crumpled a second time.

'Fine. Zeus is punishing me because I created a thirteenth realm and filled it with new life. I was able to keep it hidden from the other gods for a while, but eventually they found out. Zeus destroyed every living thing in it when he found it.' I was aware that my voice had gone hard with fury as I ground out the last sentence. Horror filled her eyes.

'Why?'

'As a punishment to me. But he fucked up. I was able to hide one of the creatures I had made. A sea creature who was turning out to be incredibly powerful. And once a realm has been created, it can not be destroyed, so I gave it to Oceanus before Zeus could work out what to do with it. Oceanus is one of the few beings he can't argue with.' I remembered the fury on my brother's face as he had agreed to the suggestion. He'd had no choice. And for a short time, I thought I'd won.

Until I'd seen *her*, standing in my throne room. 'Zeus announced the Hades Trials the next day, knowing how little I wanted to be married. His final act of revenge for my insolence was to find you and bring you back, knowing I'd either have to lose you again, or watch you die as a human.'

'What a complete fucking asshole,' she breathed, still wide-eyed.

'Yeah. Lord Asshole.'

'What happened to the sea creature you saved?'

'She's living under Oceanus's protection. It will be announced to the rest of Olympus that there is a new realm after these Trials are over. I think Zeus is still trying to find a way to stop it, but short of declaring war on Oceanus, I don't see how he can.'

Persephone stared up at me, her face intense and thoughtful.

'Why did you do it? Why risk his wrath like that?'

I pushed my hand through my hair, debating. Should I tell her the truth?

'After I lost you, I couldn't deal with the darkness,' I said quietly. 'You brought light and life to this place, and I became obsessed with replacing it.'

'So you made new life? Out of nothing?' She was staring at me now like I was crazy.

'Well, yeah. I didn't know if I could actually do it, and I had to have a lot of help from Hecate, but she's a Titan and much stronger than she lets on and-' I stopped talking as I realized I was babbling. Not a great trait in a king. I straightened, trying to reassert some dignity, but when I looked into Persephone's eyes they were filled with emotion.

'You literally created life to replace me?' she whispered.

'Yes. The hole you left in my heart was impossible to fill with anything less.'

'Did it work? Did it fill the hole?'

'No.'

. . .

She was in my arms in a heartbeat, her lips on mine with fervent desperation. Electricity sparked through my body, the mass of power I was permanently tempering deep inside me flaring to life. I pushed my hands into her hair, pulling her as close to me as was physically possible, every ounce of willpower deserting me completely as her desire swept through me.

'I need you,' she murmured onto my lips, lifting her hand to my jaw and pushing me back slightly, to look into my eyes. Hers were shining and intense, her pupils dilated. I moved one hand to the small of her back, pressing her against my hard body, and she tensed as she felt my arousal.

'I need you more,' I breathed, and a wicked gleam crossed her face.

'Is that right?' she whispered, and dropped her hand to her skirt. I was so hard I was beginning to worry that I wouldn't be able to contain myself.

Inch by tortuous inch, she began hitching up the long flowing material of her skirt. I took a deep breath as I watched more and more of her beautiful thighs being revealed, inhaling her divine scent. Just before she reached the top of the skirt she stopped, and moved her hand between her legs, out of view.

Oh gods, I was going to explode. I had to touch her. And this was the wrong place. She was too special, *this* was too special.

'You deserve to be worshiped,' I breathed. 'And I can't do that here. When I finally touch you I want to hear you scream my name, watch you come over and over.'

Her face flushed deeper red, her lips parting further. I ran my fingers along her jaw, drawing her face close to mine and kissed her again, deep and slow. She moaned softly as she kissed me back, and pleasure pounded through me. Or I could just take her here and now...

'You're right,' she said breathlessly, stepping back from me, her skirt dropping to the floor. 'We're supposed to be at a party.'

THIRTEEN

PERSEPHONE

I tried to concentrate on what people were saying to me, but it was almost impossible. I nodded absently as a wood-nymph told me for the fifth time that she thought it was super unfair that there had been a fake gem in my last trial. My mind was firmly stuck on Hades. He was like a freaking magnet to me, my rational thoughts turning to mush whenever I saw him. Although to be fair, I reckoned most girls would kiss a guy who created an entire world, life and all, to try to replace them. There was no question he had loved me. And there was zero doubt in my mind that any sexual chemistry we may have once had was still there.

'Persy!'

The voice was in my mind, and other than Hades' it was the one I had been most desperate to hear all evening.

'Skop!' I turned quickly, startling the girl who had been talking to me, and dropped to my knees as the little dog bounded towards me through the crowd. He skidded to a halt and wagged his tail furiously.

'*Stop nearly dying! You're fucking killing me!*'

I laughed loudly.

'I think you'll find I'm killing *me*,' I told him.

'They're total dicks for not giving you any tokens, you know. Total fucking dicks.'

'I agree. But at least I'm still alive.'

'You know, you really should eat another seed. Maybe with more power you'd be able to-'

'Slow down, hotstuff,' I said, standing again. 'My power was strong enough to break both my damn wrists. I don't need any more of that shit just now, thank you very much.'

'If you had more power, maybe you wouldn't have broken them. Or you'd be able to heal them faster if you had.'

'Let's not talk about this just now,' I said, noticing that the girl who had been talking to me was raising one eyebrow quizzically. 'Sorry,' I smiled at her. 'Just got to sort out my dog. It was nice to meet you.'

Skop followed me as I moved away from her, scanning the crowd for Hecate. I spotted her talking to Hedone and Morpheus. 'Where've you been anyway?' I asked Skop.

'Oh, erm, the water nymphs in the pool don't have any clothes on. I got a bit distracted.'

'Right. You were so glad to see me alive that you only ogled some naked women for half an hour before coming to talk to me.'

'Exactly. That's a pretty big deal. Half an hour of breasts is really not long enough to truly appreciate them.'

'Huh.'

'Especially when there are many breasts. In fact, now that I have ensured your safety I might just go back and check on them again.'

'Check on the many breasts?' I repeated.

'Yes.'

'See you later,' I sighed, and he trotted off towards the pool, tail wagging.

. . .

'That kobaloi is a menace,' I said as I reached my friends. Morpheus laughed and Hedone gave me a sympathetic look.

'They are known for being pests. I hope he's not giving you too much trouble?'

I immediately felt bad for moaning about Skop and shook my head quickly.

'No, no, he's fine really, as long as you're not a naked mermaid. I actually think he cares about me.'

'Really?' Morpheus raised his eyebrows in surprise.

'Yeah. As long as there are no breasts between him and me, I reckon he'd do whatever he could to keep me safe.'

'Well, he is your guard,' said Hecate. 'Did you chat to the boss?'

'Erm, yeah,' I answered, trying to keep any emotion from showing on my face.

'Oooo, always nice to spend time with the man you might end up marrying,' beamed Hedone, and Morpheus wrapped his arm around her bare shoulders.

I stuck close to the three of them for the whole party, talking politely to anyone who came up to me, and doing my best to avoid Minthe and any of the gods. Hades flicked in and out of my view, always in smoke form, and always looking at me long enough to give me a glimpse of his silver eyes. I was already regretting doing the right thing and ending our brief encounter.

I listened to Hedone's husky voice as she pointed out various domes in the ocean, telling me about their famous inhabitants or shops. A huge group of turtles swam right up to us at one point, and I reached out delightedly as a little one turned somersaults. The dome was cool and solid, and could easily have been glass, though I suspected it was something more mysterious or godly than that. The little turtle bumped his head against the dome on the other side of my hand, then hurtled back towards his family, who were drifting away.

'This place is awesome,' I said. *And it could have belonged to Hades, if the brothers had been given different realms by Zeus...*

'Yes, it is one of my favorites,' Hedone replied.

'Where do you live?' I asked her.

'Pisces, Aphrodite's' realm.'

'What's it like?'

'A tropical paradise. It's very beautiful. And exclusive; not many are allowed to live there. But parties are frequent so many folk of importance have visited.'

'It sounds great,' I said. Hedone gave a soft laugh.

'I'm not sure it's the right place for someone who dislikes parties, or sharing their partners,' she said.

'Huh,' I answered. No. Maybe not my thing after all.

As amazing as Aquarius was, I found myself grateful when Hecate flashed us back to my rooms at the end of the evening. I was exhausted. And my head was still buzzing with what I had been told about Hades that night. One of the first things Hecate had said about him when I first got here was that he was different from the other gods, that he wasn't what he seemed. And she had been right.

'Skop, what does Dionysus think of Hades?' I asked the kobaloi as I climbed under the covers.

'Bit of a weirdo. And grumpy.'

'Hmmm.'

'Why, you starting to like him?'

'I might be, yeah.'

'Well that can't be a bad thing, if you're going to marry him. Although why anyone would get married is beyond me.'

'Limiting the number of breasts not appeal to you?' I asked him.

'Nope. Definitely not. Unlimited breasts all the way, please.'

I'd never thought about marriage much. I wasn't one of those young girls who had a vision of their wedding day all planned out by the age of ten, but I also never gave it much consideration as a teenager, or even an adult. I'd never had a serious boyfriend before, because I simply never desired the company of any of the men I'd dated enough to keep seeing them. My brother said I was picky, and that I should keep it that way. He wanted the best for his little sister. I wondered what Sam would make of the King of the Underworld as my prospective partner, and the thought of his face if he ever saw Hades caused a bittersweet smile to settle on my lips.

Was the reason I'd never been interested in anyone before because I was meant to be with Hades? The passion I felt for him was so intense, I'd never felt anything like it before in my life. *Fated. Bonded.* If I went home, to New York, would I be destined to spend the rest of my life alone? Or with someone who would never make me feel... whatever it was Hades was doing to me?

Or was that just lust? If we gave in to our feelings, and got it all out of our systems, would the reality of the situation then just crash back in, leaving nothing but the death and darkness and secrets?

I let out a long breath. *Lose the Trials, stay alive, get back home.* That was plan and I had to stick to it.

Despite the fact that a mind-bendingly gorgeous god wanted to worship me.

~

Fire. There was fire. And pain. Someone had their hand around my throat... I blinked and tried to thrash my head, and realized with a start that it was the man whose wife I had killed. His eyes were wild with madness, and my body was convulsing with pain. But I was lifting my hand, *Faesforos* ready to strike. I was going to kill him.

'No,' I tried to moan, but no sound came out of my mouth. I tried to stop my wrist. I deserved to die for what I'd done. Let him kill me. Let him take my life, in forfeit of his wife's. But the dagger kept moving, and my stomach twisted as I felt the tip pierce his flesh, then sink between his ribs.

I woke with a shout, gasping for breath and for a brief moment, I had no idea where I was.

'Persy?' Skop was on his feet in front of me and I stared at him, my pulse racing and sweat soaking my neck and back. '*Persy, what happened?*'

'A nightmare,' I breathed, bile in my throat. 'Just a nightmare.'

I'd been ready to kill that man. And not in the dream, in real life. In the ballroom that night. My body had responded without my head's intervention, my will to survive stronger than my revulsion at what needed to be done.

I was everything they said I was. There was a monster inside me, one that would kill to keep me alive.

I felt sick.

It was you or him. You did what anyone would have done, I tried to tell myself, my skin crawling.

I knew there was no way I could go back to sleep, my heart still hammering in my chest and the feel of the blade entering flesh so vivid in my mind. I stamped to my washroom and turned on the water on the shower, letting it run as hot as I could stand.

But it didn't help. Water couldn't wash away what I'd done to that man. I may not have actually ended his life, but I had been prepared to. And I had been the one who deserved to die if I really had killed his wife, not him.

The desire to hear that it wasn't my fault, to be absolved of my guilt, made me think of the Atlas garden. I needed to talk to the voice. *I needed to hear it wasn't my fault.*

'You OK?' asked Skop as I marched out of the washroom and back towards my bed.

'I'm going back to sleep,' I said firmly, pulling back the comforter and climbing into bed.

'*Erm, yeah, good idea,*' he said, jumping up with me. But rather than spin round in circles on the covers, then flopping onto his side as he usually did, he lay on his front, head resting on his paws alertly.

'I'm fine, Skop,' I told him. 'Just confused.'

It took what felt like hours to fall asleep again. My restless mind took me over and over things I couldn't make sense of, or didn't have enough information to understand.

But eventually, I heard birds chirruping, and the soft trickle of water, and the beautiful garden materialized around me. A wave of relief washed over me, cleansing the guilt and fear instantly. I walked towards the fountain, and saw that there were hundreds of butterflies on the rings making up Atlas's huge burden.

'They're stunning,' I murmured as I got close.

'*They are more than they appear to be,*' the voice answered.

'Yes. I imagine they are. Everything is.'

The voice chuckled.

'*You are learning, Persephone.*'

'I am angry,' I told him, sitting down on the fountain's edge.

'*Yes.*'

'I need to know if I should have died, instead of the man who attacked me.'

'*Little goddess, you are not to blame for the events in your life. Nor can you punish yourself for defending your own life. You are strong inside. Stronger than you allow yourself to be. And that is not wrong or bad.*'

'But I didn't know I could kill someone. I don't want to be able to kill someone.'

'*Olympus is not the same as the mortal world. You must not apply the same constraints.*'

'Surely death is death, wherever you are.'

There was a long pause, and I swirled my fingers through the water. The butterflies leapt into the air as one, and I stared up at the mass of colors as they beat their tiny wings.

'*The only way to find out about your past and reconcile yourself with your future is to get your memories back.*'

'How? Hades won't tell me.'

'*The river Lethe.*'

'Where is it?'

'*I do not know, but if you have your powers, you will be able to find it. Why have you not eaten another seed yet?*'

'The vines frightened me,' I admitted, looking out across the garden. The sunflowers were swaying slightly in the breeze.

'*You will be less frightened the next time. And those around you will teach you how to use them safely.*'

'You told me not to trust the people around me.'

'*And you mustn't. But you can learn from them.*'

I nodded.

'OK.'

'*Thank you for visiting me, little goddess,*' he said, and the garden vanished.

FOURTEEN

PERSEPHONE

'I honestly don't know why it's taken you this long,' said Hecate, staring at the pomegranate seed in my hand. When she had knocked on my door the following morning, I had asked her to stay with me while I ate the next seed. Just in case.

'I told you, I didn't want to overwhelm myself,' I told her.

She rolled her eyes at me.

'Fine, whatever. Just eat the seed.'

'And you'll stop my power doing anything crazy? If I lose control?' I asked her, peering seriously into her face.

'Yes, yes, I already told you, I will make sure you don't do anything crazy.'

'Good.'

I took a deep breath, and looked at the little seed. The vines had helped me on Aquarius, without them I probably would have died. And the feeling when they had turned green in the conservatory... If I could be taught how to use my powers properly, and safely, then they might be what I needed to survive the next five Trials. *And find the river Lethe and get my memories back.*

Before I could talk myself out of it, I popped the seed into my mouth. Last time, I'd been too out of it, too desperate and in pain to notice the taste, but this time... It was sharp and sweet and completely delicious.

'Mmmm,' I mumbled.

'Feel any different? Like you wanna blow some shit up?' Hecate's eyes were alive with excitement.

I swallowed.

'No.'

Apart from a very slight tingle, I felt nothing. Hecate's face fell.

'Oh. How disappointing.'

'I worry about you,' I told her.

'Probably wise.'

I sighed and looked around my bedroom, restless and nervous. I hadn't really expected a burst of power on eating the second seed, but I now felt relieved and frustrated in equal parts.

'I'm sick of this room, can we go somewhere else? How about a tour of the Underworld?'

'No-can-do, I'm afraid.'

'Why not? If I'm competing to live here, I should probably know more about it.'

'I agree, but you're not allowed out until Round Three.'

I scowled.

'Of course I'm not. In that case I'm going to the conservatory.'

'OK. But don't forget the next Trial is being announced this evening.'

'How the hell am I going to forget that?' I said, opening

my bedroom door and frowning at her, but she was looking down at my feet. I followed her gaze.

Ice cold dread slid down my spine as I stared at a child's doll on the floor, just outside my door. It was charred and burned, and a note was pinned to its front, the word written on it clear as day. *'Murderer.'*

Hecate was next to me in a flash, her eyes turning white as she looked at the doll. I felt my heart begin to pound, fear and revulsion crawling up my throat.

'It's not magic, or dangerous,' she said as Skop appeared on my other side.

'It's... It's a message,' I whispered.

'*It's fucked up,*' said Skop, his usually playful voice hard.

'Did I kill a child?' I looked up at Hecate, unable to keep the hot tears from burning the back of my eyes. 'Please, please tell me I didn't kill a child.'

The thought was utterly unbearable, my head spinning as I formed the plea.

'Of course you didn't. Someone is trying to scare you, that's all,' Hecate answered, her face more angry than I'd ever seen it.

'Who?'

'I don't know. But Hades needs to know about this. Stay in your room,' she said, and reached down for the doll. Images flashed into my mind as I stared at it. Images from dreams I'd had all my life. Bodies burning around me, men, women and children alike. 'Skop, guard this door,' Hecate said, then slammed the door shut and vanished, taking the awful burned doll with her.

'What if I deserve this? What if I am a murderer?'

'*Persy, I haven't known you very long, but I seriously doubt that,*' said Skop.

'You don't remember me from before though. When I

was married to a god who rips people apart, and spent time with twisted lunatics who torture and play with folk for fun. They tried to drown you in fucking sand, for entertainment! And I used to be one of them!'

Tears were streaming down my face as my voice rose, and Skop finally looked from the closed door to me.

'*Olympus is dangerous. Anyone born here accepts that. If you play with fire, you'll get burned. I knew the risk I was taking when I accepted the job of guarding you. And you need to accept that who you used to be isn't who you are now. Move on.*'

'How can I move on when it's on my fucking doorstep?' A black vine burst from my palm, smashing into the aforementioned door with the power of a freight train. The wood splintered as I screamed, and Skop bounded out of the way as the vine whipped back towards us.

A wall of black smoke shot up in front of me, the vine slowing abruptly, like it was moving through treacle.

'Send the vine away, Persephone,' rang out Hades' voice. The anger and fear inside me had built up too much momentum now though, and I was no longer thinking clearly.

'Don't tell me what to do!' I roared, and pulled on the vine. The smoke held it, and a bolt of rage made me yank harder. 'Stop fucking toying with me! All of you!'

Hades stepped through the smoke, and locked his eyes on mine. The rage inside me stuttered and he closed his hand slowly around my trapped vine. Black lines instantly began to spread from the vine across his skin, snaking around his fingers, then the rest of his hand. I watched, open-mouthed, as they flowered in front of me, tiny black leaves forming like tattoos, now disappearing under the cuff of his shirt.

A new energy began to hum through me, dark and strong and deliciously powerful.

'What are you doing?' I whispered, the feeling exquisite, but some part of me knowing it was wrong.

'I'm doing nothing. You are doing this.' With his other hand he reached up and deftly unbuttoned his shirt. It fell open, revealing the black vines now spreading across his chest, coiling around his hard muscles. 'When they reach my heart, they'll try to take my power.'

I recoiled at his words, and the vine vanished from my palm instantly. The blissful, powerful feeling ebbed away fast, the tattoo snaking across Hades' body fading to nothing just as quickly.

'Take your power?' My breathing was shallow, and I was already dizzy.

'Yes. You would never be able to; I am too strong and my power is too well guarded.'

'Is that what that feeling was? Your power?'

'My defensive power, yes. You've exerted yourself again, you need to sit.'

I wanted to argue, but my legs felt weak. I'd passed out from using my powers twice before, and I wasn't stupid enough to deny his words. I stumbled backwards until I felt my bed behind me, and sat. Hades flicked his hand without his gaze leaving my face, and a new door appeared behind him, in place of the shattered one.

'Why did my vine try to steal your power?'

'All gods have weapons, Persephone. That is yours.' He approached me slowly, then waved his wrist again, a goblet appearing in his hand. He offered it to me and I took it with shaking hands. Without even looking inside it, I gulped it down, the sluggishness slowly receding as I tasted wine.

Hades sat down on the bed beside me. 'We all have

different types of power. Your black vines are aggressive. But you have other powers too. Like the green vines, that give life to things that grow.'

I stared at him, tangled emotions still bubbling inside me.

'The blue light around you when you killed that man. The one that turned into corpses...' He nodded.

'That is my aggressive power. I draw it from the dead.'

I shuddered. It sounded like something from a horror film.

'Who left that doll on my doorstep?'

'I don't know yet. But I will find out.' His jaw was tense and his eyes glittered with ferocity.

'Is the note on it true? Was I a murderer?'

'No, Persephone.'

'But I stabbed that man.'

'He was choking the life from you. Anyone in this world would have reacted as you did, and anyone in your world too.'

'Not if they deserved to die.'

Heat seared around me, Hades' eyes turning from silver to electric blue.

'Don't you dare say that, Persephone. That piece of shit who tried to kill you, and his friends, are enemies of mine, not yours. Once again, you are being targeted as a result of my misdeeds. I am sorry.'

Hope blossomed through me at his words. Could that be true? I drained the rest of the wine, trying to order my chaotic thoughts and slow my racing pulse. Hades would find whoever had left the doll. And the voice in the garden had given me a somewhat vague plan, but a plan nonetheless, to get my memories back. Right now, my most pressing issue was these damned vines.

'You said you would teach me to use my magic,' I said, handing him back the goblet. His eyes melted back to silver, the temperature dropping again.

'Yes. And I will teach you to fight. Starting now.'

'Now?'

'Yes.'

FIFTEEN

PERSEPHONE

'So how is it you keep showing up when I need you?' I asked as I walked alongside Hades through the blue torchlit corridors. I had insisted we walk to the training room. The less flashing about, the better, in my opinion. I felt small as we walked, his broad shoulders filling the space and his height so much greater than mine. But I felt safe, rather than intimidated.

'I told you, your power is like a beacon to me.'

'What does it look like?' He looked sideways at me.

'Green light.'

'You and Hecate both glow blue,' I said.

'Yes. Most of the time. That's the color I chose for Underworld power.'

'Who chose green for me then?'

'Your mother. She chose green for all nature powers.'

My steps faltered. *My mother*.

'But I already have parents. At home.' My words were slow and Hades stopped walking, turning to me.

'I know. But before that... You had a mother here. The goddess of the harvest,' he said gently.

'Demeter?' I asked slowly, remembering my classics lessons.

'Yes.'

'Where- where is she now?'

'She hasn't been seen in Olympus since not long after you were born.'

'Oh. Who was my father?'

'Nobody knows.'

So to add to the long list of things my head wouldn't properly process, I now had the fact that my parents weren't really my parents.

I expected to feel sadness, or anger, but instead all I felt was a kind of hollow indifference. I mean, on some level I must have realized I had a family in Olympus when I accepted that this place was real, I just never properly put the two together or let myself consider it. What did it matter? As far as I was concerned, my real family were in New York, safe and sound, and there was no way I would ever entertain the idea of anyone else being my parents or brother. Maybe I was birthed elsewhere, but that was just biology.

'Who brought me up, if my mom and dad were missing?' I asked Hades.

'Wood and forest nymphs. On Taurus.'

'Taurus? Who owns Taurus?'

'*Dionysus,*' Skop answered in my head at the same time Hades said the wine god's name. I looked down at the little dog.

'So that's why you're here? That's why Dionysus volunteered a guard?' He wagged his tail.

'It took years for you to tell me that, by the way,' Hades said, resuming walking. 'I don't think you ever told anyone else. You just arrived at one of Aphrodite's parties one day, looking outrageously gorgeous, and announced yourself as Demeter's daughter, goddess of Spring.'

'Seriously?' I hurried to catch up with him, tearing my eyes from where they'd involuntarily glued themselves to his ass.

'Yup. I knew there and then that you were no normal goddess.'

'How long were we married for?'

He paused before answering.

'Four years.'

'That's not long for an immortal god,' I said slowly.

'No. It is not.'

Sadness rolled from him, and I felt a pull in my gut as though I were physically wired into his emotions. I tried to think of something helpful to say, but nothing came.

We walked in silence the rest of the way to the training room, Hades opening the door for me when we got there.

'Now, you realize that I will have to make you angry in order for us to do this?'

'Angry is fine. But try not to scare the shit out of me again,' I said, walking onto the training mats.

'I won't,' he said quietly. 'As I told you, we all have our powers. One of mine is to make people feel their worst fears. In fact, I have a dog who has the same power.'

'You have a dog?' I turned and gaped at him.

'Yes. Several, actually. But Cerberus is the most important.'

'Wait, doesn't he have three heads?'

Hades nodded.

'Yes. I assume he exists in your human mythology?'

'Yeah, and he's sort of terrifying.'

'He's about as terrifying as I am,' Hades chuckled, rolling up his sleeves. I cocked my head at him.

'You realize that's pretty terrifying, right?'

His beautiful face turned serious as the smile slipped away.

'Yes. I do. But not all of my powers revolve around fear.' He held his hand up, palm facing me. 'Give me your dagger.'

I pulled *Faesforos* from the sheath around my thigh and hesitated, before handing it to him. In a flash he had taken the knife and drawn it across his raised palm. I gasped as gold blood ran from the wound, trickling down his forearm.

'What are you-'

'Gods' blood is called ichor. And it is gold. But that's not what I want to show you.' The cut began to glow silver, the same color as his eyes, and then the skin was knitting back together, sealing the wound. 'Healing is something you must learn as these Trials get more dangerous. Your body will do some of the work while you rest, but you must learn more immediate healing.'

'What other types of magic are there?'

'Many, many types. You already know, and dislike, the power that transports us places. Only very powerful gods can do that. Lust and love are commonly held gifts though. As is the power to make others angry.'

'What powers do I have?'

'Your black vines defend you both by their physical use and their ability to drain other's power. Your green vines make things grow, adding strength to nature. Your...' He trailed off, his eyes locking onto mine. 'It's probably not worth going into that until we know if you have regained that particular power.'

I felt my face crease into a frown.

'What? What particular power?'

Hades whole body had stiffened.

'We'll go into that if it comes up,' he repeated, his voice stern. Indignation rose like a tidal wave through me.

'I'm not a child,' I snapped. That dangerous spark flared in his eyes.

'I am your King,' he replied, voice cold and hard. 'You will do as you are bid.' Black smoke began to flicker around him.

I didn't know if he was deliberately goading me to get me to use my power, or being an actual prick, but either way, it was the only trigger I needed.

'Will I fuck,' I answered, and lifted my palms, willing the black vines into existence. They burst from my hands and I felt a surge of delight as they went exactly where I wanted them to.

Hades stood his ground as they hit him, instantly beginning to coil around his shoulders. He narrowed his eyes at me, a small smile spreading across his lips as he spoke.

'I like this shirt, and I have a feeling you're going to try to make a mess of it.' With a little blue shimmer his shirt vanished, and I felt my vines go slack as my concentration vanished, the sight of his bare skin taking all of my focus.

Then a wave of power hit me and I stumbled backwards. I jerked my wrists, making the vines taut again and pulling on them to stop myself falling.

'Bastard,' I growled. 'That's not fair.'

His eyes were dark with something that could definitely have been lust, and a tight black t-shirt suddenly covered his perfect body and I squashed the stab of disappointment.

'Better?' he said, and another wave of power slammed into me. I gripped my vines harder, trying to work out what I could do next.

'Much,' I lied, and tried to remember what it had felt like when the vines had turned into the tattoos.

But I'd been furious and scared then. I still had plenty of pent up frustration and tension roiling through me, but when I was with Hades like this, I couldn't access that primal rage, that fear that drove me to lose control. The only thing I was going to lose control of here was my grip on my desire for him. Especially if he lost his shirt again.

A little bolt of anticipation charged through me as I glared at his impossibly beautiful face, remembering his words. 'I want to worship you.' I saw his eyes flick to the vines wrapped around his chest, then widen as he looked back at me. His expression changed completely, a predatory hunger filling his face. His lips parted, and he reached up with both hands and pulled on the vines. I stumbled towards him with a yelp, then my breath caught.

My vines were gold. Shining, glittering gold.

'I guess it's time we talked about your other power after all,' Hades said, his voice deep and low and so loaded with desire it made my core clench. 'Your gold vines do the opposite of the black ones. They share your power.' He was breathing hard, and slowly reeling me towards him.

'What do you mean?' I asked, making a show of trying to pull against him, but it was a half-assed attempt. The truth was, I wanted nothing more than to be pulled into him completely.

'When your gold vines do this,' he said turning his forearms towards me so that I could see the gold vine tattoos swirling around them, 'I can feel what you're feeling.'

I stopped tugging, and my mouth fell open. Heat leapt to my face.

'You can feel what I'm feeling? Like mind-reading?'

'Let me show you,' he said, barely audibly.

Blue light began to shine along the gold vines, starting at his body, then whizzing along them, back towards me. When they reached my palms, I gasped.

I could *feel* his desire for me. More, I could see it. Images flashed through my mind of the two of us in the largest bed I'd ever seen, but I barely noticed the beautiful posts and black drapes adorning it because oh my gods, I was seeing and feeling it through his eyes. He was staring down at me laying on the sheets before him, naked and holy fuck, I looked a million times better than I really did. A series of images began to flash before me, so fast I couldn't hold onto a single one; me sinking onto his lap, him burying his face between my thighs, me bending over before him and spreading myself, his length hard and pounding and ready.

'Oh gods,' I moaned aloud, and the images stopped abruptly. I opened my eyes and saw my own lust mirrored in Hades' wild eyes. 'You said no magic sex!' I panted.

'You started it!'

'What?'

'That's what these do,' he said through gritted teeth as he lifted my gold vines. 'You're sending me images like that right now.'

'What!' I yelped, and the gold vines vanished instantly. Hades sagged slightly, before standing straight again, eyes still wild. 'Why didn't you tell me I had magic sex powers!' I demanded, trying and failing to ignore the urgent need between my legs.

'Because I didn't know if they were back or not.' My eyes flicked to his groin. I'd just got a glimpse of what was in his jeans, and now I couldn't shift it. I didn't just want him. *I needed him.* The pounding was becoming painful, and I squirmed where I stood. Either we were going to fuck right now, or I needed to be wherever he wasn't.

'Maybe we should try the training later,' he ground out. Guttural disappointment hit me in the gut. *But I need you.* 'Hecate can teach you healing before the next Trial.'

'Right,' I said tightly. He looked into my face.

'I'm sorry, Persephone. If I stay here a second longer, I won't be able to stop myself.'

Then he vanished before I could tell him he didn't have to.

SIXTEEN

HADES

For the love of all the fucking gods, the gold vines were back. That was me done for. There was no fucking way I could resist her, glowing green and gold and showing me every delicious thing she wanted me to do to her. I turned the temperature in the shower down even further, blasting my body with freezing water. It wouldn't work, but short of fucking Persephone senseless I didn't know what else to try. There was no way I was going to relieve myself with someone else, and doing it myself had stopped working centuries before.

It was getting harder and harder to believe that I was going to be able to let her go. If she regained all of her power, if those gold vines ended up able to share more than just her sexual desires...

Memories of her wrapped around me, of our bodies entwined, those beautiful vines filling my monstrous heart with life and light. I'd told her that she had changed the Underworld when she had been here, made it brighter. I had told her that I had tried to create life to replace the hole her absence had left inside me. But she couldn't know that she was the only chance I had at reversing the damage this place had done to me. The damage my brother had done to me.

I hadn't started out as a monster. I had found taking life more repulsive than most of my siblings, in fact. Which was why Zeus thought me weak, and favored Poseidon. For the first few decades of my new role, dealing with the dead had saddened me. I felt pity and empathy for the souls arriving in my realm. But that was unsustainable. As King it was my job to judge the guilty. I wasn't expected to bother with petty thieves or remorseful adulterers, but I had to deal with the scum of Olympus, the worst of every species alive. Day after day I saw and heard of the increasing levels of brutality mortals were capable of, their motives always shallow and selfish. The more punishments I had to dole out for their unspeakable acts, the less I cared for them.

And as my brothers' realms flourished, and they both found wives, my sadness turned to bitterness.

Those punishments started to become a way to vent my building anger. I started out telling myself that those receiving them deserved them, ignoring the fact that I was now enjoying watching men flayed alive, or flesh burning from skin. Ignoring the fact that the well of power that had always burned hot inside me was darkening, twisting, dirtying.

The more horrific my punishments of the guilty became, the more my brothers seemed to respect me. Before long, they left me alone, content that I was doing the job that Zeus had bestowed on me. I surrounded myself in smoke, banned everyone from my realm, and let myself become the monster the King of the Underworld needed to be.

But then I met Persephone. Somehow, she alone recognized what was buried deep inside me. And the same life-giving power she used to nurture and grow plants had flowed into me through those gleaming vines for four years, healing parts of me I thought lost forever.

Until she was ripped away.

Before I knew what I was doing I had slammed my fist into the marble wall of the shower. It cracked, collapsing completely, water spraying across the room.

'For fuck's sake!' I shouted, and stamped my foot. It instantly repaired itself. *What was I going to do?* I wasn't sure I could cope with losing her again.

The rest of the day dragged painfully slowly, my mind slipping back to the images Persephone had sent me almost constantly.

'Boss, pay attention, this is important,' said Hecate, snapping me out of an intense vision of Persephone's soft lips wrapped around the tip of my cock.

'Sorry, what?' I asked, shifting uncomfortably in my seat. Stupid fucking erection.

'Kerato says he has news. On the Spring Undead faction.' I sat up, immediately alert.

'I'll see him in the throne room now.'

'My Lord,' the minotaur bowed low as I flashed onto my throne.

'What news do you have?'

'We have captured someone known to be closely associated with the attacker.'

'Where is he now?'

'*She* is in the holding pits.'

'Bring her to me.'

Rage simmered inside me, the memory of what that man had almost done to my Queen making my blood boil in my veins. And under the rage danced the twisted excitement that accompanied the knowledge that I was about to inflict primal terror on a living being. That I was going to become their worst nightmare, their whole world, that I held their pitiful life in my hands.

I glanced at the rose throne. When Persephone had been seated beside me, I had been able to control the excitement. Subdue it, even. But in the time she had been gone the excitement had returned, the monster inside me able to rear its ugly head again, to feed off fear and death.

A greedy thrill went through me like a tremor, the dark well of power rippling in anticipation as Kerato marched back in five minutes later, a bedraggled woman following him in chains.

'What is your name?' I asked her, making my voice sound like a thousand slithering serpents and the smoke surrounding me icy cold.

'Daphne,' she answered, as she sank to her knees in front of me. Her voice was too strong, too defiant. Dark tension gripped my body.

'And you knew Calix?'

'He was my brother.' She kept her gaze on the floor, hunched low over her knees. Dirty blonde hair obscured her face from my view completely.

I hated her.

'Your brother tried to kill Persephone.'

'Yes.'

'Why?'

'She killed his wife.'

'How do you know that?' This was what I needed to find out, before I ended her miserable life. This was what made no sense to me, what posed a real danger. Nobody should remember Persephone, outside my closest advisors and the other eleven Olympians.

'I-I just do,' she said.

I sent out a tendril of smoke towards her and my magic dove inside her mind, gleefully tearing through it to find what was buried deepest, what scared her more than anything else in the world.

She shrieked, tipping her head back, eyes wide with fear.

'Stop! Please!'

'Tell me how you know about Persephone.'

'When we saw her in the Hades Trials we just suddenly knew,' she gasped, tears streaming down her face. 'Please, please make it stop.'

'How did you know?'

'We saw it. Calix and I saw what happened and he remembered his wife.' Her skin had gone as pale as snow but I was too focused on my questions to care what she was seeing.

'What about the rest of the so-called Spring Undead?'

'They all saw too, as soon as she appeared in the flame dishes. They all remembered who they had lost.' I was struggling to understand her words through her sobs, and I retracted my smoke just a little. She fell forward immediately.

'How many are there?'

'I've only met two others,' she choked.

'Name them.'

'Nicos and Lander.' I looked at Kerato.

'Lander was the first man we captured, he is dead,' the minotaur said gruffly. The woman wailed. 'We shall search for this Nicos now.'

'Good. Take her back to the pits, and keep her alive. We may be able to use her.' If there were more of these fools then she might come in useful as bait.

I barely heard the woman's sobs as Kerato hauled her out of the throne room. How had these people remembered what had happened? It was impossible without the water from the river Lethe. And the location of the river was one of closest guarded secrets in Virgo. The thought of someone within my own realm conspiring against me made my body burn with anger, the unspent tension inside me crackling to life. The colored flames around the edges of the room leapt up, all flashing brightest blue in unison. I would crush every last member of this Spring Undead, and I would make sure whoever was behind it spent an eternity in the living hell that was Tartarus.

SEVENTEEN

PERSEPHONE

It was a good thing, really, that Hades had left before anything had happened, I thought, sending a little green vine from my palm into the soil of the flower bed. A delicious energy hummed through me, making my skin tingle. An image of Hades, eyes dark and deep with lust as he looked up at me from between my legs, flashed into my mind. I felt a surge of power from the vine and gaped as a shoot leaped up in front of me. I pulled the vine back and the pale green shoot slowed to a stop.

'I'm gonna guess that was a result of you thinking about loverboy,' said Skop. I turned to him, too surprised to argue. He shook his little dog head, and resumed digging in the dirt. For a dog that wasn't really a dog, he sure loved to dig.

'Knock knock,' sang Hecate's voice from the doorway of the conservatory. I stood up quickly.

'Hi,' I called, and turned to see her sauntering between the flowerbeds towards me.

. . .

'It doesn't look much more green in here yet,' she said as she looked about herself.

'Well, I think I just found out how to make things grow quicker,' I said, gesturing to the shoot.

'Ooh, what is it?'

'A sweet pea.'

'Nice. The Trial announcement is going to be made over the flame dishes tonight, so no showy ceremonies or dicking around.' I tried to stop my face from falling, but must have failed because Hecate frowned at me. 'I thought you'd be pleased? You always say you hate all that shit.'

But now I wouldn't be able to see him again tonight.

'Oh, yeah, I just...' I scrabbled for something to say, but Hecate looked sharply at Skop, then back at me, a slow smile spreading across her face.

'You were hoping to see Hades tonight,' she said, glee in her voice.

'Skop! You snitch!'

'*I told her nothing,*' he said, without looking at me.

'Bullshit.'

'*Well, she's practically his best friend. She'll know soon anyway that you two are hooking up.*'

'We're not hooking up!'

'*Then why does he hide you or me in smoke literally every time he's with you?*'

'Privacy from perverted gnomes,' I said, my face burning.

'*Cos you're banging.*'

'We are not banging!' My protest was so enthusiastic that I said the words out loud by accident and Hecate gave a bark of laughter.

'You and I, dear Persy, need to have a catch up. With

wine. How about we watch the trial announcement at my place tonight, and have a few drinks? A girls' night.'

'That sounds awesome,' I said, surprised by how much I meant it. That really did sound like exactly what I needed. An evening with Hecate, and no Hades anywhere. A chance to clear my head.

Hecate's rooms were significantly nicer than mine, though not my taste. She had to flash me there, because I wasn't allowed anywhere other than the conservatory and the training room, and we arrived in a large sitting room. Rocky walls and the high ceiling glowing with dusky daylight provided illumination, but the room had a dark, elegant feel to it. The floor was covered in deep plush carpet in a dark grey and two black gothic style couches with ornate detailing over the curved wooden frames dominated the room. The wall on my right was made up of a giant black bookcase, full to the brim with leather-bound volumes. The opposite wall had a long counter running along it, made of a dark wood and similarly gothic in style, and abstract geometric art in hundreds of shades of blue hung on the wall above it. The counter was covered in exotic looking objects, and I was half way to picking up a glowing skull before Hecate stopped me.

'Do not touch that,' she said sharply, and I froze.

'OK. Why not?'

'You'll wake up Kako. And I am not dealing with his shit tonight.'

'Kako?'

'The evil spirit that lives in that skull.'

'Riiiight,' I said, staring at the skull. 'Of course there's an evil spirit living in your sitting room.'

'Well, I am the goddess of ghosts,' she shrugged, and bent to open one of the many cupboards under the counter.

'Is there anything else I shouldn't touch?' I asked, looking along the row of shiny, glowing items. There was a vial that had something neon orange in it, a curved blade with tiny swirls etched all over it, a large pearl that shimmered in the low light coming from the wall behind it, and many other things besides. I wanted to touch it all.

'Everything. Leave it all alone.'

I pulled a face but backed away from the counter. The back wall of the room was missing, a large archway in its place, and I could see a massive four poster bed draped with black sheer material in the room beyond. A memory of the bed I'd seen Hades and I in popped into my head and I turned away quickly, sitting down on one of the couches.

'So, where's your flame dish?' I asked.

'Oh, yeah,' she said, straightening and setting two glasses on the counter. Her eyes turned white as she glowed blue, then a massive iron dish on a short stand appeared in front of the couch. A gentle orange flame flickered to life in the center. I peered at it.

'So these are like TVs? Do they always have something showing?'

'You can use them to talk to each other, like your video phones, or the gods can broadcast on them. That's it.'

'And people in Olympus have been watching me in the Trials so far in these?'

'Yup.'

'Mental,' I breathed.

'So are your video phones. Athena is so proud of your current civilization. You've got pretty far pretty quickly.'

'Huh,' I said. I couldn't think about my world as an

experiment of a bored god. It made my head hurt too much, so I changed the subject.

'What are we drinking?'

'My specialty cocktail,' she said. 'But I'm missing something. Wait here. And don't touch anything!'

Hecate flashed out of the room and Skop immediately jumped onto the couch with me.

'*Touch the skull! Please, please touch the skull!*' His tail was wagging at a million miles an hour as he looked pleadingly at me.

'No! Not a chance,' I told him, avoiding looking at it. I wanted to touch it very much.

'*You're so boring,*' he humpfed, and sat down.

'You know, Skop, of the many words I could use to describe myself right now, boring isn't one of them. I have magic sex power for fuck's sake.'

'*What?*'

'Yeah.'

'*I want magic sex power,*' he said.

'I thought you were already a god in bed.'

His tail wagged.

'*I sure am.*'

Hecate flashed back into the room holding a large metal jug before he could elaborate, thankfully.

'How come you couldn't just conjure whatever that is?'

'I can conjure wine, not this,' she said, a wicked edge to her voice. I raised my eyebrows as she poured something lime green from the jug into two glasses. I swear there was smoke coming from it.

'Are you sure you've made this before?' I asked tentatively.

'Yup. And now you have your power back, you can drink it.' She added more things, with her back to me so I couldn't see, then strode over to the couch and handed me the cocktail. It was still green, but it smelled like cherries.

'What's it called?'

'Spartan spirit.'

'Well, cheers,' I said, clinking my glass against hers then taking a sip. There was an explosion of fruit in my mouth, bitter cherry and sour blackberry and sweet strawberries all at once, tingling across my tongue. 'This is amazing!'

'I know,' she said, taking a long sip of her own as she sat beside me. 'Oooh, look!' I raised my eyes from my new favorite drink, to see the flames in the fire dish leaping high and burning white hot. They faded as a crystal clear image of the commentator appeared in the center of the dish.

'Good evening Olympus!'

'Urgh, I hate him,' I muttered.

'Yeah, he's fucking irritating,' agreed Hecate.

'I'm sure you're all dying to know what our little Persephone is going to be facing next!' *Our little Persephone?* Gods, I wanted to smack him in the face. 'She has mostly faced tests of glory or hospitality so far.' Apprehension skittered through my belly. The other two values were intelligence and loyalty. 'Well, the wait is over! Tomorrow afternoon she will be facing her first intelligence Trial!'

'Does that mean no nearly dying?' I asked, turning to Hecate. She screwed her face up apologetically.

'Probably not, no.'

'Here is your host to tell you more,' the commentator said, and faded from view. My breath caught as the black smoke of Hades shimmered into existence, his throne room visible behind him. It was strange now to see him made of smoke, translucent and rippling, when I knew what perfection lay underneath.

'As Queen of the Underworld, Persephone would be expected to abide in my realm,' he said and his voice was tight and cold. A shiver rippled over me. 'We must therefore test her ability to survive in dangerous environments. She will be trapped in a deadly part of Virgo and must escape.' He made a small hissing sound, then vanished.

I looked at Hecate, nerves crackling.

'Where will they trap me?'

'I don't know, but he sounded seriously pissed. There is no way this was his idea.' Hecate looked worried. 'This is Zeus' doing, he's forcing Hades to expose more of his realm to the world. Gods that guy is a dick.'

I took a long swig of my drink and nodded.

'Yeah. He really is.'

Neither of us spoke for a long few minutes, then I cleared my throat.

'I probably shouldn't drink too much, if I have to compete tomorrow.'

Hecate snorted.

'You have healing power now, you won't get a hangover.'

'Are you serious?'

'Yeah.'

'No more hangovers? Ever?'

'Uhuh.'

'How the hell is everyone here not permanently drunk?'

'Some are, to be fair. Me included.' I laughed and had another big gulp of my spartan spirit, just because I could. 'If they're going to trap you somewhere, we should probably try to work out what you might need to take with you. Are you claustrophobic?'

'No more than the next person,' I said, thinking. 'Like if

you trap me in a burning room, I'll panic.' I smiled, but Hecate didn't. 'Oh. Are they going to trap me in a burning room?'

'I'm not going to lie to you, Persy, quite a lot of the Underworld is made up of burning rooms.'

'Shit.'

'Yeah. Take *Faesforos*, and use your vines. If it's an intelligence test then you'll need to solve some sort of puzzle or answer a riddle to get out.'

I groaned.

'If it's like the ball and it's all gods and stuff, I won't be able to do it.'

'Honestly, it could be anything.'

'Should we go over some basic god stuff now, just in case?' I asked her.

She raised one eyebrow at me doubtfully.

'Persy, do you have any idea how long it takes to learn the history of the gods? There are literally whole schools here to teach that.'

'Oh.' I thought about that. Schools in Olympus must be pretty different to the hell-hole I'd attended. 'What was your school like?' I asked her.

'I didn't go to school. I'm a Titan.'

I frowned.

'So?'

'So, up until recently, Zeus wouldn't let Titans be trained in the academies. Athena has since convinced him that us dangerous Titan offspring are safer under their supervision, but he still hates us. As do a lot of Olympus.'

'Why? I mean, I know about the war and stuff, but that was forever ago wasn't it?'

'Titans are strong. They are the original gods. So when

they turn nasty, they're like, seriously nasty. And that scares people.'

'Aren't all the really bad ones in Tartarus though?'

'Yeah, and there hasn't been a genocidal Titan in thousands of years, but it doesn't stop stories being told to fuel the fear.' Her eyes were tight and frustrated, and I thought about what Hades had said. *Hecate is much stronger than she lets on.*

'Do you hide your power so that people don't fear you?' I asked hesitantly. Her eyes locked on mine, and it took her a while to answer.

'I used to, yes. But over the time I've lived here with Hades I've come to trust him. And I've built up a reputation in Virgo. People don't fuck with me anymore.'

Any more? Was Hecate bullied too? The way Eris had spoken to her at the ball, mocking her Titan heritage, flashed into my memory. How in the hell could Hades and Hecate, two of the most badass people I'd *ever* met have been victims of bullying? Determination filled me, sending strength and courage coursing through my veins. If they had overcome their past and their enemies, and become as powerful as they had, then so could I. And I bet they had both put up with worse than Ted Hammond's groping hands and taunting jibes. *Have they not gone too far though?* The doubt constantly present inside me forced the question to the surface, but I shoved it back down again.

'I'm starving. What are we eating?'

EIGHTEEN

PERSEPHONE

'So, is Skop right, are you sleeping with Hades?'

Hecate asked the question so casually I almost choked on my beef.

'No! Skop is not right!'

'You want to though,' she ginned.

'Hecate, what happens when Olympians get married? Hades said something about a bond, but he was infuriatingly vague.'

'I dunno,' she shrugged. 'I'm not an Olympian. They marry for life though. No divorces at the top.'

'*Told ya,*' said Skop, gnawing on a steak at my feet.

'You know, you two were a great couple.'

'He's kinda... intense,' I said carefully.

'No shit. You should have seen him when you left.'

A bolt of pain gripped my chest at the thought, and I was surprised by its strength.

'He said you helped him. With the thirteenth realm.'

Hecate's face changed slightly, a less sassy smile replacing her usual expression, something deeper peeking through.

'He told you about that?'

'Yes.'

'Good. I want you to win this, Persy. I don't know what happened before, or why you left, but I swear whatever it was can't be as bad as you leaving again. I've known Hades a long time. Like, a really long time. The few years you were together, he almost became his true self again.'

Her words seemed to physically pound into me, as though hearing them from someone other than him made them even more real, more undeniable. How was it possible that I could have had this much of an impact on someone's life, and up until now I hadn't even known they existed? And not just anyone, *a freaking god.*

'I'm drawn to him in a way I've never felt before,' I admitted. 'I can't explain it.' Hecate stood up, gathering our empty glasses.

'Well he is sexy as fuck,' she said, as she strode to the counter.

'I think it might be more than that. I'm worried... I'm worried that now I've met him, nobody will ever make me feel like that again.'

She gave a soft laugh.

'Gods help us when you do actually screw him.'

'That's not happening,' I said firmly. 'It won't help either of us when I leave-' I broke off and she turned to me.

'When you leave? Do you still not believe you can win this?'

Trust nobody. The voice from the Atlas garden rattled through my mind.

'Well, nothing is certain,' I said evasively.

'Hmmm,' she said, and turned back to the cocktails.

I needed to change the subject again.

'So what about you? Do you have anyone that makes your brain go wonky?'

She sighed heavily and I frowned. That hadn't been the reaction I'd expected.

'Persy, I'm gonna tell you something,' she said, bringing two full glasses back to the couch.

'OK.'

'You know when I told you that I had hundreds of lovers?'

'Yeah.'

'That was a lie.'

'OK,' I said, cocking my head at her.

'I don't have any lovers.'

'Then why lie?'

'Because I don't have any lovers, ever. And never have.' She took a long swig of her drink, looking away from me.

'Oh,' I said, trying to hide my surprise.

'People judge me when they find out I'm celibate, so I lie.' Her tone was defensive and my mind churned into gear, trying to imagine what a life without sex would be like. I mean, I wasn't exactly an expert, but it had certainly livened up the last few years of my life, even if the guys had been temporary.

But that was my life, and Hecate must have her reasons for not wanting sex.

'Who the hell am I to judge you?' I said to her. 'You choose what to do with your body.' She glanced at me, her eyes more emotional than I'd seen them before.

'I wish it was my damned choice,' she muttered.

'It's not?' I frowned.

'It's complicated.' Her easy cool was returning now, and she leaned back into the couch, hooking her ankle over her other knee and sipping from her drink. 'One of my more unpleasant powers is necromancy,' she said. An involuntary shudder took me at the thought. Zombies had always scared the shit out of me. 'In an ideal world,' she continued, 'I would never have to use that power. But in the event of a cataclysmic fuck up it might be extremely important. Because, out of all the gods, only Hades and I can do it. Thanatos and the Fates can incite actual death, but we're the only ones who can animate corpses and control the souls of the dead.' I worked hard to keep the revulsion from my face.

'What kind of fuck up would require you to do that?'

She let out a long breath.

'Hades losing control of the Underworld. Or being removed from Olympus completely. The undead are one of the few things that could topple the gods.'

My breath caught. Hades removed from Olympus... Was that god-speak for him dying? I thought he was immortal?

'Could... Could that happen?'

'In Olympus, anything could happen,' she said a little bitterly. I took a steadying gulp of my cocktail.

'So you're his back up?'

'Kind of, yeah. And a power that dark must be balanced out. Hades has sacrificed parts of his own soul, physically lost pieces of himself to the Underworld. He is too strong, the demands on his power too high for him to live any other way. But for me, I learned that I could make a personal sacrifice, and keep my soul intact.'

'So you gave up sex?'

'I was a virgin when I came here, and physical love was what I wanted most back then. It was the greatest sacrifice I could make to save my soul.'

'But you didn't give up love? Just sex?'

'Persy, point me at a man who will love you without touching you,' she said, and this time her voice was full of bitterness. 'And besides, why put myself through the temptation? Why fall in love with someone and never be able to physically express it? The moment I gave in and lost my virginity, I would lose my most valuable power.'

'Shit,' I said quietly.

'Yeah.'

'But what if you never need to use that power? Surely Hades isn't going anywhere, he's like one of the super-gods isn't he?'

'Hades is the most volatile of them all. We can never know what might happen in the future. That's like weighing up my desire for a good time against the possible destruction of the whole of Olympus,' she said, looking disdainfully at me. 'Not really a risk worth taking.'

I blew out a sigh.

'Well, I hope Olympus knows what you're giving up for them,' I said. Hecate snorted.

'Do they fuck. I'm Titan scum as far as they're concerned.'

'Then why do you do it?'

'Persy, I may have an attitude problem, but I'm not going to risk watching the world fall to the undead when I could have stopped it. I told you, Titans aren't genocidal anymore.' She gave me a wry smile. 'Besides, there's no-one I want to screw that much anyway.'

By the time Hecate flashed me back to my own room, I was hammered. Like properly, well and truly, drunk. After her big revelation, and my admitting my confused feelings for

Hades, the conversation had turned to lighter topics. Hecate had demanded to hear every awful and embarrassing encounter I'd ever had with a man, and Skop had provided a number of highly entertaining anecdotes too. We'd talked about what dicks Zeus and Poseidon were, and the bitching had felt good.

'You know what, Skop,' I called, as I pulled off my leather trousers in my washroom.

'You've changed your mind and want to try out gnome knob?' he answered hopefully.

'No. I was just thinking that maybe I need to see Hades.' I pulled on the silk nightwear that always appeared clean in my wardrobe every evening, stumbling as I stepped into the little shorts.

'That's because you're drunk and randy,' he said.

'Well, some people don't get to have sex at all. I should be grateful. I should make the most of it.' In my inebriated state, this seemed like the most sensible statement I'd ever made. Why deny myself when I didn't have to? Especially to a freaking god. 'Now, how do I make him come here?'

NINETEEN

HADES

'You know what you are?' I bellowed, power bursting from the end of my pointed finger. Zeus smiled lazily back at me as he flicked his hand up and blocked it. He needn't have. He was easily strong enough to absorb my outbursts.

'What am I, Hades?'

'You're a colossal fucking prick, just as she said you were!'

Danger danced in my brother's eyes.

'I had no idea she was going to provide this much entertainment when I brought her back,' he said, strolling to the edge of my throne room and peering down at the endless flames. Rage was thundering through my body, that dark well of power desperate to expend itself.

'Zeus, without me, Olympus will fall. Do you really think putting me in my place is worth that risk?' I hissed, trying to calm myself.

'Is that a threat?' he said, raising his eyebrows as he turned to me. He was in his true form, as was I. Ancient and glowing with the barely containable power of the sky, his face was lined with as much fury as I felt. 'You caused this, Hades. You broke the laws. You deliberately defied me. Did you expect me to let you humiliate me and belittle my rules in front of the world?' Lethal rage dripped from his words, and I felt the smoke pouring from my skin as I glared back at him.

'You killed them all. An entire innocent realm, save one. Was that not punishment enough? Did you really need to risk bringing her back just to see me suffer?'

His eyes narrowed.

'So you share Poseidon's belief that she is still dangerous?'

'She can't stay here.'

'I'm well aware of that.'

'So now you are forcing her into a Trial where my own realm will kill her? Do you despise me that much?' The smoke rolling off me was starting to burn, flames dripping like liquid from my body onto the marble floor.

'She's stronger than you think, Hades.'

'That's what your wife said,' I snarled. Zeus didn't deserve Hera. He never had. His eyes flashed with purple lightning, and the roar of thunder rumbled through the floating throne room.

'We're not talking about my wife, brother, we are talking about yours.'

'You need me, Zeus. Remember that. Sky, Sea and Underworld. If any of those three fall, Olympus falls. And then who will you have to rule over?'

'You, dear brother, are immortal. Where the fuck do you think you could go that I wouldn't find you?' He flashed and reappeared inches from my face. His fierce electricity burned through my body and jet black magic coursed through my veins in response. My monster was wide awake and ready to unleash hell. 'Desert the Underworld and I will make your life even more miserable than it has been for centuries,' he hissed.

He thought I was threatening to leave? I barked out a laugh.

'You have me all wrong, Zeus. All wrong. I won't leave Virgo. Ever. I will remain here until there is nothing left. All of Olympus will burn around me, the undead will flood the world, drowning the living with their rotting corpses, and I will be here, exactly where you put me.' *Alone. Broken, twisted and unable to contain the darkness inside me any longer.*

For the briefest of seconds I saw doubt flicker across my brother's face. But then it was gone, a smug sneer twisting his features instead. He folded his arms and stepped back from me, tilting his head.

'That is quite a threat.'

'It's not a threat. It is the consequence of pushing me too far.'

'Are you telling me that you are unstable, little brother?'

'No, Zeus,' I lied. 'I am as in control of my power as I have ever been. But I would advise you not to test me.'

He regarded me a moment longer, then sighed.

'We shall see how your little human fares tomorrow. Her Trials are no more dangerous than those the other contestants experienced.'

'Bullshit,' I snapped. He smiled at me.

'See you tomorrow, brother,' he said, and vanished.

I roared, and the room lit up with flames.

They crawled over the dais, and I felt the darkness building inside me as they reached my throne, the skulls flaring blue as the fire touched them.

Then a shaft of light pierced my own skull, and my rage skittered as my focus shifted. *Persephone.* It was her light, her magic. I closed my eyes and sent my senses through the palace, seeking her green flare. And there it was. In her rooms. Why was she using her magic now? Was she just practicing? Or had whomever left that doll on her doorstep managed to get inside? The thought was enough to re-trigger my rage, and I flashed myself to her side instantly.

'Woooah, you look really mad,' she said as I whipped my head around the small room, looking for the threat.

'What?' I focused on her, my instincts telling me nothing dangerous was here, but my heart was pounding all the same. 'Why...' I trailed off. She was wearing a pink silk vest and shorts, and her white hair was loose around her shoulders. Her pupils were dilated, and I could smell cherries. 'Have you been drinking?' I asked her slowly.

'Spartan spirits.'

'I thought I recognized the smell,' I said, and let the smoke fade from around me, feeling my racing pulse start to slow. 'Hecate's cocktails are lethal, you know.'

'Ah, but it turns out that my new powers can heal hangovers,' she said, excitement in her slightly slurred voice. 'Which is just about the best news I've had since coming here.' I couldn't help the smile that was tugging at my mouth. She was happy. I wanted nothing more than to see her happy. Well, maybe there was one thing I wanted as much... My eyes dipped to the low neckline of her silk top.

'What were you using your magic for?' I asked her.

'I, um, wanted to see you. But I kinda broke the dresser.' She gestured to her dressing table, which was splintered completely in two. I raised my eyebrows.

'Magic wielding whilst drunk is never advisable,' I told her, and flicked my wrist. The dark wood of the dressing table began to knit itself back together.

'Why not if you can just fix whatever I mess up?' Her words, though meant teasingly, were far, far too close to home. How I wished I could fix everything.

'Well, I'm not going to fix your mess for free,' I said, folding my arms, and shoving the dark thoughts down. I was here now, and she wanted my company. I couldn't turn that down, no matter how much power was still swirling danger-ously close to the surface of my skin.

'Oh yeah? What do you charge for dressing table repairs?'

'I want to see you,' I said, dropping my voice and locking my eyes on hers. She gulped.

'You can see me,' she said.

'I want to see all of you.' Her pale skin colored but she held my gaze.

'Are you trying to take advantage of my drunkenness?' she said, pronouncing each word carefully.

'Isn't that why you wanted me to come here?'

Her eyes dipped from mine and I knew I was right. She wanted me as much as I wanted her, the gold vines had shown me that. But she didn't feel the bond yet. She didn't feel the dying cord that had crackled back to life when I had seen her in my throne room, and had been glowing a tiny bit brighter every day since. I would know if she felt it too. It would burst into life, safe and solid and present and eternal.

'It might have,' she said, and swayed on her bare feet.

'I'll tell you what,' I said, my anger from earlier now

merging with my arousal, pent up energy crashing around inside me like an ocean storm. I couldn't take her like this.

But there was no fucking way I was leaving with nothing.

I flicked my hand and the kobaloi barked as a smoky bubble enveloped him. I wasn't sharing this view.

'Let me see you, and maybe I'll do the same.'

TWENTY

PERSEPHONE

I raised my eyebrows as Hades stood before me, his words reverberating around my fuzzy brain.

'I'll show you mine and you show me yours?' I said, staring at him. He was so beautiful. The strong lines of his jaw, his sharp cheekbones and angular nose, the dark stubble - it was like he had been designed with as much 'man' as was available from the ingredients.

'Yes. I'll show you mine, if you show me yours.' A wicked smile was pulling at his lips and his silver eyes were dark.

'Seriously? Like we're teenagers?'

'Yes. And I guarantee I'll ruin any memory you have of anything you saw as a teenager. Or since.' I gulped. I didn't doubt it.

I wasn't exactly shy when it came to be being nude, but he was Hades, King of the Underworld. Did one just strip casually in front of an all-powerful god?

But my word, did I want to see him without those jeans on.

The thought had my hands moving before I could stop

them, and I slowly drew the thin straps of my camisole off my shoulders. Without them to hold the top up, it slid down to my hips, catching on the little shorts and leaving my breasts and stomach completely exposed. I kept my eyes on his, drinking in his change in expression as his eyes raked over me. My nipples hardened as desire pulsed through my body. The all-powerful god wanted me, and it couldn't be more obvious. Or confidence-inducing. I let a coy smile dance over my lips as I ran my fingers inside the waistband of my shorts, delighting in how his breath quickened.

'I think it's your turn to lose a shirt,' I breathed. His black shirt dissolved instantly, the hard planes of his abs utterly perfect, his huge shoulders and the V of his stomach prompting shivers of pleasure through me. *Please don't drool, please don't drool,* I chanted drunkenly in my head as I pictured those divine arms lifting me, my legs wrapping around his solid waist.

I inched the shorts down.

His hand moved to the top button of his dark jeans.

Yes. Yes. Unbutton the jeans.

I wiggled my hips, easing the shorts down further. He deftly undid the first button, then the next. I realized with a small moan that he wasn't wearing underwear. Another couple of buttons, and I would see *him.*

My hands began to shake as I moved one side of the shorts down another inch.

A resounding crash from outside my room snapped both our attentions to the bedroom door, my lust and booze addled brain protesting wildly at the sudden interruption. But before I could even consider what to do next, Hades had shifted into something unrecognizable.

He grew in size, muscles bulging, electric blue light glowing from him, and I saw his face, twisted with unbridled fury before he whirled around. My bedroom door blew apart as he raised his arms, black smoke shooting from him in curling tendrils and snaking through the open door.

'You won't escape me this time,' he hissed, and his voice was like knives slicing through flesh. *Who was out there?*

A distant screaming began to grow louder in my ears, and the tang of blood crept into my nostrils as the temperature plummeted.

No, I could stop his power affecting me, I thought as I hoisted my top back up. I dug deep inside me, hunting for my power, trying to drag it up to the surface. Vines slowly emerged from my palms as Hades stalked to the door, following after his streams of smoke. The vines were gold, and they only grew about ten inches, but a light seemed to emanate from them, and the blood and the screams died away.

'Well done, vines,' I muttered, and hurried after Hades.

He had stopped in the doorway, and was standing frozen, still pulsing with blue light and dark smoke. I ducked under his arm and stepped out into the corridor. There, against the rocky wall, was a huge broken mirror. I frowned as I looked into it. I couldn't see Hades behind me. Just my own reflection, skin flushed and silky nightwear disheveled, the image distorted by the many cracks.

'What-' I started to ask, but my words caught in my throat. I was bleeding. Scarlet red blood was seeping from my reflection's eyes. Nausea rose in my gut and my hands flew to my face, my vines brushing my cheeks as I touched them. I looked down at my fingers. There was nothing. But... When I looked back at my reflection it wasn't just my eyes that were bleeding. Blood poured from me, my skin cracking like the glass in front of me, the thick ooze gushing onto the floor.

Words began to appear across the mirror. 'You will drown in the river of blood you created.'

I stumbled backwards, starting when I hit something ice cold and solid. I whirled, tearing my eyes from the hideous mirror and staring up into Hades' furious eyes.

He was almost harder to look at than the mirror was. His beautiful features were torn and ragged, his eyes filled with black fire, the silver gone completely. Pure fury poured from him, and I could see the shapes of bodies forming in the blue light around him. Screams crept back into my ears, primal fear trickling through my whole body and forcing me to step back from him. His rage-fueled power this close up was too strong for my defenses.

'I will destroy whomever is doing this,' he snarled. 'Death is too good for them. They will burn for all eternity.'

'You're scaring me, Hades,' I said, trying to keep the growing terror from my voice. He fixed his eyes on mine, and they were almost black now. He gripped me by my shoulders, lifting me bodily off my feet and turned, depositing me back in my room. His touch was ice cold and visions of corpses littering the ground flew through my head until he let go.

'I must go,' he said, his voice hard as stone. With a flash he was gone, my bedroom door shimmering back into existence.

I stared at it, my whole body shuddering as my vines vanished. Bile burned hot and acidic in my throat, the cocktails now seeming like a very bad idea. I held my hand up to the wood of the door, feeling its sturdiness. Was the mirror still there, on the other side?

'I hope he gets the bastards. You know, if he didn't keep

blocking me out I might have been able to help,' said Skop. His voice was hard too. Warmth was beginning to seep back over me now, and I dropped my hand, taking a step away from the door. The shaking was easing.

'Did you see the mirror?' I asked quietly.

'No. What happened?'

I told the kobaloi what I had seen in the glass, as I poured myself some water and sat down on my bed.

'Who is doing this?'

'Hades will find out,' Skop said reassuringly, jumping up beside me.

'What if I deserve it?' I asked, voicing the question I was finding so hard to bury deep enough to ignore. 'What if I did cause rivers of blood?'

'You *were born twenty-six years ago, in New York. You didn't do anything,'* he said gently.

I let his words comfort me. He was right. Whatever old Persephone did, I didn't know if I would be capable of the same.

Old Persephone had loved Hades. And if I had forgotten it, tonight had reminded me - the King of the Underworld had a monster inside him.

I stayed there on my bed, alert and on edge, for more than an hour before I heard from Hades. My whirring mind was racing through morbid ideas of what I might have done in my previous life, when a tentative voice sounded inside my head.

'Persephone?'

'Hades!'

'I'm sorry, but they got away this time.' I felt my shoul-

ders droop with disappointment. *'I want you to stay in your room until Hecate comes for you tomorrow. And no more conservatory or training room visits alone.'* His steely voice gave no room for argument, and although I knew what he said made sense, I bristled at the idea of not being able to visit the conservatory by myself.

'What about Skop?' I asked. There was a long pause.

'When Dionysus volunteered the sprite as a guard, I don't believe he actually thought you would need defending from any threats. Skoptolis is not equipped to deal with this. He can stay with you, of course, but when I say alone, I mean without Hecate, a member of my guard, or me.'

I let out a long breath.

'OK. Do you think whoever is doing this will try to hurt me?' He didn't answer, and a little trickle of fear coiled through my chest. 'Fine. I'll add this to the list of things I need to survive,' I said, trying to mask the fear with my casual words, and failing.

'The next Trial is an intelligence test. You'll do great. But I would like to apologize in advance.'

'For what?'

'I strongly suspect you're going to see some of the worst the Underworld has to offer tomorrow.' The tension in his voice made me realize how hard that must be for him. His own realm was going to be used against me.

'I have my magic back. Have you seen those black vines? I'll kick the ass of anything your crappy Virgo throws at me,' I announced as loftily as I could. He didn't laugh, but when he next spoke his voice was soft.

'I don't doubt it, Beautiful.'

. . .

My forced bravado deserted me once I was lying in bed though, trying and failing to sleep. Skop's reassuring presence at my feet helped, but not enough to dispel the disappointment that Hades hadn't caught the culprit, or the constant wondering about whether I deserved the awful gifts.

Eventually exhaustion pulled me into an uneasy sleep, and I tossed and turned until I heard the faint sound of birdsong. Slowly, it got louder, and I stepped gratefully out of the darkness of my sleep-induced imagination into the Atlas garden.

'Do you know who is sending me these messages?' I asked almost immediately, inhaling the earthy scent of the stunning garden gratefully.

'*I do not. But I do know that you should not rely on Hades to fix this for you.*'

'What do you mean?'

'*You are gaining your power back, Little Goddess. One more seed and you will be able to deal with them yourself.*'

I knelt and ran my hand through moist soil, the feeling of it on my skin like home.

'But I don't know who it is or how to find them, or even why they are doing it. They say I am a murderer.'

'*You have been wrongly blamed for their losses. Regain your memories, and oust the true villain. That is the only way you shall find freedom from this.*'

'You said I would know where the river Lethe was when I got more power back. But I don't.'

'*Then you must win more seeds, and gain more power.*'

I nodded. Maybe it was time to eat the last seed.

TWENTY-ONE

PERSEPHONE

The next morning though, as I stared into the little box with the last magically preserved pomegranate seed in it, I couldn't do it. I couldn't pick one up and put it my mouth, no matter how much sense it made to me.

'What's the problem?' asked Skop impatiently, sat on the floor beside my dressing table stool.

'I don't know,' I said, staring at my reflection. But I did. The longer I looked at myself, the more sure I was that I could see tears the color of blood, leaking from my eyes and down my face. The image from that mirror, my skin cracking and rotting, the blood pouring from me... I knew for certain that the person I was now couldn't be responsible for causing rivers of blood. But I didn't know for certain what more power would do to me. They could turn me back into that person. I had vines that tried to steal another's magic. That seemed pretty dark to me. It was *wrong*.

Power corrupts. This was something I knew to be true. The kids with the most influence and strength at school had always been the cruelest. And the longer they stayed at the top of the pack, the nastier they became, pushing and testing the limits of their popularity. And that could only be worse in a place like Olympus. Hecate had told me how Hades had needed to lose parts of his soul in order to use his power to rule the Underworld.

I was caught in a desperate loop. In order to find out if the powerful Persephone had done something truly terrible, I needed to gain more power.

'The damned irony,' I sighed.

'You might need more magic for the Trial today,' Skop said.

'It's an intelligence test. I don't think I need more magic right now,' I said, tearing my eyes form the warping reflection in front of me and standing up. 'What I need is a shower and something to eat.'

After washing and dressing in my leather fighting garb, I found a pile of bacon the size of my head and a large wedge of warm bread on the dresser. I devoured it, absently noting that I may not have the headache and nausea of a hangover, but I sure had the appetite.

'So what do you think I can expect today?' I asked Skop.

'I don't know Virgo well enough to have any clue,' he said. *'They'd better not use me as bait again, or I'll be having words with Dionysus,'* he grumbled.

'I'm sure they won't,' I said, not really sure at all.

'I do know there are some pretty ugly demons here.'

'Ugly I can handle,' I said around my breakfast. 'What's the worst?'

'Cerberus,' he said, without hesitation. *'I like dogs, but he's a scary bastard.'*

'Well, I highly doubt I'll be meeting him today.'

'Yeah, it does seem a bit early in the competition,' he nodded.

'What? You mean I might actually meet him at some point?'

'Well, yeah. If you're going to live here, then you'll have to test your strength against Hades personal hell-hound at some point.' I gaped at him.

'Shit,' I said eventually.

'But I doubt you'll have to worry about that for a while. And Charybdis is one of Poseidon's worst monsters, and you survived him.'

I gave him a sideways glare.

'Don't remind me,' I muttered. I was still bitter that I'd won no seeds. Plus, I sort of wanted to see Buddy the hippocampus again.

'Yeah, he's like a giant asshole with teeth,' the dog said, and gave a little shudder. 'I wouldn't want to be reminded of almost being sucked into that either.'

'You're gross,' I told him.

A knock at my door made us both look up, and Hecate pushed it open.

'I heard what happened last night,' she said as soon as she came in. 'You OK?'

'I'm fine,' I told her. 'I just wish I knew who was doing it. First the doll, then the mirror... Hades seems worried they'll step it up.' Her face was hard, and with all her sharp silver jewelry and black leather I was reminded of how intimidating she was when we first met in the cave.

'They want to hope they die before Hades or I get hold of them,' she said, and a mix of fear and gratitude rolled through me.

'I don't want anyone else to die because of me,' I said quickly.

'Trespassing in Virgo, particularly in the palace, is punishable by death,' she said shortly.

'Palace?' It had never occurred to me that we were in a palace.

'Yeah. We're in the palace above the business part of the Underworld.'

'And the 'business part' is where we're going for the Trial today?' *And where the river Lethe must be,* I thought.

'Yes.'

'Do dead people actually live in the Underworld?'

'Sort of. It's complicated. Souls are the only part of the dead that live on, and they don't take up any space.'

'But you said yesterday that the undead could rise.'

'You can get bodies from anywhere.' I cringed at her words, but tried to stay on track.

'So what else is in the 'business part'?'

Hecate cocked her head at me, then sighed.

'OK, super fast lesson in the Underworld. Souls go to one of three places; Elysium and the Isles of the Blessed if they led an exceptional life, the Mourning Fields if they led a life of unrequited love, and the rest go to the Asphodel Meadows. The Underworld also houses Tartarus the torture prison, lots of very cranky demons and species that are essential to Olympus but too unpleasant to live out in the world, and a bunch of rivers.'

I blinked at her.

'That's quite a lot of stuff.'

'Yeah.'

'How many rivers are there?'

'That's your question? Not *what sort of unpleasant*

demons, or, *why is there a whole place for unrequited love souls,* but *how many rivers?'*

I shrugged.

'I like water,' I said lamely.

'Well these rivers aren't made of water and will all kill you. There are five, and they are sentient deities in their own right. For example, the river Styx circles the Underworld seven times and is made of hatred. And you want to stay the fuck away from her.'

'How can something be made of hatred?'

'If you become Queen you'll learn all about all the rivers. But they are not going to be the subject of today's Trial, as you couldn't be trapped in any of them without dying instantly so let's move on.'

'Fine,' I sighed. 'Tell me about the unpleasant demons instead.'

'I'm in charge of a bunch of them, and they're all assholes,' she muttered. 'Keres demons, for example, are the deities of violent death. Arae are demons of curses, Lamia are rotten vampiric demons who drink blood, as are Empusa but they're usually on fire too. Then you've got a couple of really nasty spirits, like Eurynomos, who is the demon of rotting corpses, and the three Furies, who are goddesses of vengeance and need seriously reining in most of the time. And then you've got some who are just weird, like Ceuthonymos, who's a spirit we can never pin down and haunts anyone who's not a Titan.'

'Right,' I breathed, forgetting completely about the river. 'Do you think I'm going to meet any of them today?'

'Maybe, yes. You've got *Faesforos?'* I patted my thigh as I nodded. 'Good. I made you that blade because it can be used against any foe. And that includes Underworld demons.'

'And I'm extremely grateful,' I told her. My nerves were beginning to hum. Blood drinking vampires and demons of rotting corpses? The Spartae skeleton was starting to seem pretty tame right now. 'This is an intelligence test though, right? I hopefully won't be fighting.'

'Fingers crossed,' she answered, without a trace of hope in her voice, and a half-assed smile.

She flashed us to Hades' throne room, and my eyes shot to his throne immediately, instinctively. He was there, smoky and translucent, and he gave me the briefest flash of silver eyes. Energy pulsed through me, and I rocked on the balls of my booted feet as I scanned along the row of gods. To my astonishment, Poseidon tipped his head to me as I made eye contact with him.

'Good day, Olympus!' sang the commentator's voice, and he glimmered into the space between me and the gods. 'Today Persephone will be facing one of Hecate's creations. She will need to escape the Empusa's lair!' I glanced at Hecate and wished I hadn't. Her face was a mask of dismay.

'Empusa? Please tell me that's not the vampire who's usually on fire?' I hissed to her, pulse now racing.

'Erm,' she whispered, her eyes filled with apology. But before she could say anything else, the room flashed white around me.

TWENTY-TWO

PERSEPHONE

The first thing I noticed was the smell. Sweet rotten meat and moldy earth swamped my nostrils and I was gagging before the light even cleared from my eyes.

'What the-' I started to say, but trailed off as I looked around me. I was standing in the middle of a cave, but unlike the rocky walls that glowed with daylight that I'd seen in Virgo so far, these walls glowed deep red. And they were casting their light over a floor littered with bones.

My stomach roiled as I gaped around at the room. Rows of alcoves were gouged into the rocky walls and there were hundreds of tiny figures lining them, made of something pale and ivory colored. More bone, I realized, as I stepped closer to the wall, screwing my face up as something crunched and sludged beneath my boots. *Don't throw up, don't throw up,* I chanted in my head, as a fresh wave of putridness assaulted my senses. I tried to remember the smell of meadow flowers and lavender and lilies and incredibly, the rotting smell faded a little, and I was sure I actually *could* smell lavender. Was that my powers?

Able to concentrate slightly better now, I pulled my attention from the rows of bone carvings to the rest of the small room. The thing that had caused all this must be in here somewhere. And so must a way out. All the walls looked completely solid though, and the room was only fifty feet around. All I could see on the floor were the remains of the prey of whatever lived here.

'Hello?' I called out cautiously, scanning the rocky walls for any clues to what I was supposed to do.

'Good day,' issued a silky voice, and I froze.

'Erm, where are you?'

A figure shimmered into being before me and my heart did a small gallop in my chest at the sight of her. I'd seen her before, when I was very first dumped in Hades' throne room, but not this close. She was beautiful, her barely clad body curvy and voluptuous, and her face angular and grand. But her hair was made of flames. Two short sharp horns jutted up from her forehead, and as I dragged my eyes over her I saw that one of her legs was made from wood.

'I saw you when I first arrived here,' I breathed.

'No. That was one of my sisters. We are the Empusa, pawns of Hecate. Welcome to my lair.'

'Oh. Thanks, nice to meet you,' I said, nerves making my voice hitch. 'Do you know how I can get out of here? Not that it's not...' I looked around, scrabbling for something polite to say about her disgusting lair.

'I have four riddles for you,' she said, saving me the trouble. 'If you can not solve them all, then you are mine.' Two fangs shot down over her bottom lip as an evil smile settled on her face. I shuddered as two thin lines of blood trickled down her chin, from where the fangs had torn her lip. Her fiery hair flickered and danced around her head, making her skin look like it was rippling. She gestured with an elegant arm and I followed it to see four holes appearing in a shoulder height section of the rocky wall. They were just big enough to put a hand in.

'Number one. I build my home with natural string, and defend myself with bite or sting. What am I?'

A home from natural string? That had to be a spider web.

'A spider?' The Empusa stared at me, her face unchanging. Did that mean I was wrong? Fear made my chest clench at the thought. I didn't want to die at all, but being eaten by this thing and left to rot here... I'd rather have been eaten by the giant sea-asshole, Charybdis, than have trinkets carved from my bones to adorn this place.

But she didn't move, and I frowned. I was sure the answer was right. There must be more to the Trial than just answering the questions.

I looked back at the four holes in the wall. Four riddles, four holes. Were they keyholes? Keys in Olympus were weird, I already knew that from those awful hourglasses.

So maybe I needed a spider key for the first hole? As I turned back to the lair my gut churned again. Please, please tell me I didn't have to find an actual spider. Please.

'Do I need to find a spider?' I asked the Empusa, my voice small. Her smile widened ever so slightly. Bile rose in my throat as I looked at the nearest heap of bones on the floor.

Then my eyes flicked to the rows of carvings. Was there one carved as a spider? I moved to the nearest wall quickly, and heard a deep rumble. A soft, sensual laugh bubbled from the Empusa's mouth and I looked at her.

'You'd better hurry, pretty little human,' she said, her eyes filled with glee.

A new smell hammered at the lavender barrier I'd

somehow concocted. *Sewage*. My gut constricted, causing me to retch as I swept my eyes over the room fast. Where was it coming from? A gurgling sound dragged my attention to the floor, and my pulse quickened as I saw a black sludge starting to ooze up from the ground, thick enough to displace the rotting bones.

'What is that?'

'Your doom,' the flame-haired demon grinned at me.

I didn't wait to find out what she meant. If I had four riddles to get through I didn't have time to let the sludge get any higher. I raced along the shelves, scanning every little carving, looking for a spider.

'Yes!' I hissed as I finally spotted a tiny bone carving in the shape of a spider, and reached out for it. As I picked it up though, heat burned through my finger tips, and I saw a flash of fire and blood. I yelped as I dropped it back on the shelf.

Another soft laugh came from the Empusa and I turned to glare at her.

'You are no creature of the Underworld. You may not touch my treasures, human.'

'I'm not entirely human any more,' I snapped, nerves humming as I hesitantly called up my vines. Relief washed through me when a green shoot began to ease gently from my right palm. The black vines were absolutely not what I needed right now. They tended to fly about angrily all over the place, and I definitely did not want to knock any of these carvings into the rising sludge. It was oozing over the toes of my boots now, and it reeked. Plus, if the black vines really did steal power like Hades said they did, the last thing I wanted was any of this Empusa's power inside me. *Yuk.*

I directed the vine towards the toppled spider carving, but as it got close it veered away, almost like when you try to put the wrong end of two magnets together. I concentrated, forcing the vine back towards it. But as it touched the bone, revulsion swamped me, the total opposite of the joy I felt when I connected with the earth and living plants. My breakfast rose fast in my stomach, and I snapped the vine away, heaving again.

'Life and death, light and dark... You will not master the balance,' the Empusa hissed. I looked up at her, sweat now trickling down my neck.

'Black vines it is then,' I hissed back, and a dark vine shot from my palm, smashing into the row of carvings. 'Shit!' I yelped, trying to control the whipping shoot. *Get your shit together Persephone, unless you want to drown in sewage,* I berated myself. With an effort, I pulled back the black vine, then sent it carefully towards the spider. Gingerly, slowly, I managed to wrap the vine around the bone carving.

A new, dark energy hummed along the vine and into my hand, spreading through my veins like fire. I saw no awful images, felt no searing heat, but I knew on every level that the power was wrong. It was fueled by fear and blood, and it didn't belong inside me. My whole damned body was sweating now, nerves and stress and fear pumping more adrenaline through me.

I could feel my temper rising, anger starting to simmer deep inside me as I hurried over to the four holes in the wall, the spider carving wrapped in my vine. The sludge was covering my boots completely now, and was half way up my shins. I found that lifting my feet out of it allowed me to move faster than trying to move through it; it was as thick as tar.

When I reached the wall, I carefully lowered the spider into the first hole, and willed the vine to let go. As it did a small click sounded, then rock began to fill the hole, growing all the way out of the wall and forming a small handle.

'Thank fuck for that,' I muttered, half panting as the brimming anger inside me abated. I gripped the handle, and discovered I could only turn it left ninety degrees, so that's what I did before turning back to the Empusa.

'Number two. My golden treasure never lacks a guard, and is held in a maze from which men are barred. What am I?'

'Golden treasure?' It had to be an animal of some sort, I thought looking at the carvings. My mind whirred, trying to think of an animal that had golden treasure. I didn't even know about half the animals in Olympus, so I'd have to hope we had the same animals in my world. What had gold treasure in a maze? 'A bee!' I shouted, as the answer came to me. I dragged my legs through the sludge, and started hunting through the shelves.

If I survived this, I was showering for a week. It took me until the sludge had reached my waist to find the fucking bee carving. The stench was becoming unbearable, my magical lavender no match for its ferocity. I carried the bee carefully over to the holes in the wall, my progress infuriatingly slow, and anger roiling inside me the whole time my black vine was cradling the carving. It was toxic, I was sure. The second I connected with the bones I could feel their dark, angry influence. I tipped the carving into the next hole as soon as I reached it and the hole filled in quickly, a second handle forming. I yanked it up and turned back to the Empusa, knowing I must have a wretched scowl on my face.

Just get it done. Just get it done. You'll be out of here soon.

The dark red light, the awful stench, the oppressive heat, the nauseating bones surrounding me; all were making the fury building inside me harder to dispel. This place was a damned hell-hole, and once again I was suffering for those bastard gods' entertainment. I needed to get out, before I lost my shit, which would almost definitely result in my death.

This wasn't an intelligence test, I thought bitterly. It was a test of temper.

'Number three. Although I only have two eyes on my head, my tail has a magnificent spread. What am I?'

I snarled in anger. There was nothing in my world that had a spread of eyes on its tail. How was I supposed to find something if I didn't even know what I was looking for?

But I had barely stamped towards the nearest shelf before I paused, my eyes snagging on a carving of what looked like a parrot. I'd seen other birds when I was looking for the last two carvings, and my mind flashed to the feather on Hera's mask at the masquerade ball.

'A peacock,' I exclaimed, and moved as fast as I could through the rising ooze to where I thought I'd seen the bird carvings. Sure enough, after a little hunting, I wrapped my vine around a detailed peacock carving. It was getting easier to control the vine, but harder to subdue the surge of rage that accompanied contact with the awful carvings. I made my way to the holes as fast as I could, but it was like I was wading through quicksand, and any speed was impossible.

The sludge was higher than my waist. When I finally dropped the peacock into the third hole there was a click, then the rock morphed slowly into a third handle.

Just one left, I thought, pulling up the handle then balling my fists. One more stinking, rotten, vile carving left to find, and I was out of here.

'Last, but not least,' the Empusa said, and something about her sinister expression made my skin crawl. 'I have the head of a leopard, the middle of a pig, the rear of a flamingo and the tail of a dragon. What am I?'

I stared at her. Surely there was no creature in Olympus that fit that description. Surely. The rear of a flamingo and the tail of a freaking dragon?

'The ugliest damned thing in the world?' I hissed, raking through my brain to come up with an answer. Wasn't a chimera what the Greeks had called a monster made up of other animals? But that was made of an eagle and a lion or something, not flamingos and pigs.

Panic was beginning to prick at my forced calm. I had to answer this right. My life depended on it. I could feel my power under the skin of my hands, humming with need, longing to break free of my fragile control.

Come on, Persy, it's an intelligence test, not a Greek mythology test. There was no way that creature exists, I reasoned. Which meant it had to be a trick question, or a different kind of riddle. The head of a leopard. Did that mean spots? Middle of a pig might mean pink? As were flamingos... A pink spotty thing with a dragon tail?

Another bark of frustration escaped me. Head, middle, rear and tail. Did that equate to start, middle and end? The start of leopard was 'L'. The middle of pig was 'I'. My heart raced as I thought through the riddle. Rear of a flamingo could mean the last letter, which was 'O' and if the tail of a dragon meant the same thing that was an 'N'.

'Lion!' I shouted the word, and this time the smile on the Empusa's face faltered. She hadn't wanted me to work it out.

With renewed vigor I forced my way through the stinking sludge, now almost at my shoulders, looking fervently for anything resembling a lion. Eventually, on a shelf almost too high for me to see, I spotted a carving with what looked like the ring of a mane around it. I sent my vine up towards it, and when the shoot made contact, I swear I could hear an actual lion roaring. All my muscles clenched as the dark, greedy, angry power flooded through me.

Kill her. Kill the vampire bitch.

The words were in my own voice, in my own head, but they didn't belong to me.

Fuck these riddles, these games, kill the demon.

The world whirled around me as darkness burned through my body, black and hot and brutal. I stared dumbly at the lion carving as images of my vines wrapping around the Empusa, dousing her stupid hair in the sewage, tearing her wooden leg away... A wave of sweet, rotting stench invaded my nostrils, mercifully snapping me out of the brutal vision.

The smell had been caused by the sewage reaching my neck, now only inches from my nose, I realized with a start. I heaved once more as I turned, hardly able to pull myself through the ooze now. Holding the lion carving high, fury and fear making my limbs shake, I lifted my other arm out of the thick black stuff, and fired a vine from my free hand at the handles on the wall. The vine smashed into one of them, and I willed the vine to curl around it.

Just as the sludge edged over my jaw and reached my mouth, I yanked, instructing the vine to retract, and take me with it. I was instantly pulled off my feet, the force of the vine tugging me through the disgusting sewage. It splattered around my face, and my eyes streamed with the acridity of it, but the vine pulled me on, and my head stayed above the surface.

But when I smashed into the wall, I realized with horror that the last hole was submerged. I plunged my hand into the rising muck, feeling frantically for it, but it was too deep.

I would have to put my head under.

A fresh surge of hatred for the people who had put me in here and forced me through this rose inside me and I very nearly smashed the lion carving against the wall in fury.

But I retracted the vine at the last second, rational thoughts forcing their way through the red mist. *Put the lion in the hole and it's over!*

With a huge breath, I closed my eyes and let myself drop through the heavy sludge.

It was so thick that I instantly panicked, the feeling of being crushed overwhelming. I scrabbled at the wall with my free hand, feeling for the handles to work my way down to the last hole. My heart was hammering so fast I thought my chest might burst, the weight around me pressing in hard, my eyes burning behind my eyelids.

I was going to die here, suffocated in sewage.

My fingers snagged on a sharp edge, and my body tried to take an involuntary breath as I realized it must be the hole. Acrid sludge burned my lips and nostrils as I drew the vine holding the lion desperately to my other hand, which was now gripping the hole. My lungs burned for air, every single instinct in my body warring with my instructions to stay calm and not breathe. I shoved the lion carving into what I prayed was the hole. The stuff was moving further up my nose, starting to fill the back of my throat, and it burned like acid. It was too much. My mouth started to open.

A handle formed under my fingers, and I yanked it.

TWENTY-THREE

HADES

I gripped the arms of my throne as Persephone appeared in the middle of the throne room floor, covered in the thick black sewage. She fell forward onto her hands and knees, heaving, and white hot fury roared in me, so close to breaking free from my godly constraints. *Look what they have done to her. They will all die.*

'Can't... breathe...' her words were ragged, and I leapt from my throne, but Poseidon got there first. In a flash he was standing in front of her, a cascade of water pouring from thin air over her body. Her back arched slightly and she began to take deep, shuddering breaths. My coiled muscles relaxed ever so slightly, but I glared at the back of Poseidon's head.

Watching her drown in that shit-hole, the lair of a creature created by Hecate, her only friend here, and supplied with prey by me, had been torture. My own realm had almost killed her, and Zeus had me powerless to help her. The monster inside me was hungry, and my brother was the subject of its attentions. Had she actually died in there...

Suddenly black vines whipped from Persephone's palms and she was staggering to her feet. Her wild eyes were filled with hatred, and the vines blasted towards the thrones. Artemis, Ares and Zeus leapt to their feet as her voice roared through the room, clear and crisp and furious.

'I'm sick of this! You are done playing with me!'

Poseidon threw up his hand and spoke as Zeus and I stepped forward.

'It is the Underworld sewage making her angry. She will be fine when it has all been cleansed from her.' His gaze was fixed on Persephone as the jet of water above her tightened and moved, forming a powerful jet. The black stuff began to sluice off her drenched body, her white hair clinging to her furious face.

'Why are you helping me?' she hissed at Poseidon, the vines still flicking fiercely through the air.

'Put the vines away, Persephone,' he answered her calmly. 'I'm helping you because my hippocampus liked you.'

Her eyebrows shot up in surprise and the tension in the vines slackened immediately.

'You give a shit what a hippocampus thinks?'

'Very, very much.'

She held his gaze a moment longer, then lowered her palms. The black vines disintegrated. I let out a long breath, and backed up again, glancing sideways at the other gods who had stood up. They all followed suit, Zeus flashing me a look that made my blood boil even hotter.

'I think it's all gone now,' Persephone said quietly, looking down at herself. All the slime had washed away. But the anger lingered on her face, hot and barely contained. I could feel it emanating from her. The shower of water stopped and Poseidon shimmered, then reappeared on his throne.

'And now to be judged!' sang the commentator, his normally irritating voice ever so slightly tense as he appeared at the foot of the dais. Persephone turned slowly on the spot, clearly knowing what to expect. The three judges, one cold, one fat and one wise, were seated behind her. *Five more minutes, Persephone, and you'll be alone. Just keep it together for five more minutes,* I willed.

'Radamanthus?'
    'One token.'
    'Aeacus?'
    'One token.'
    'And Minos?'
    'I agree with my colleagues. You will be awarded one token,' Minos said. The seed box appeared in Persephone's wet hand and she stared down at it.

'There you have it, folks! With four Trials still to go, little Persephone has won four tokens. Let's not forget that Minthe, the current leader, completed the nine Trials with a total of five tokens. Persephone only needs two more to win the position of Queen of the Underworld.'

    Persephone's eyes found mine, and I could see the realization dawn on her face. She could end this in just two more trials.

    'For her next Trial, tomorrow evening, our favorite little human will be facing an endurance test like no other. Of the twelve gods, four will have a surprise for her. Dress for the occasion!'

With that, the commentator vanished. I stared at the spot he had been standing in, my mind whirring. The gods had endurance tests planned for her? Well, I certainly wasn't one of four who had been selected. I threw a dirty glance at my brother and Zeus grinned back at me.

'Hades?' Persephone's voice in my mind made my whole body flinch, and as I looked at her I saw the barely contained power brimming over inside her, green light glowing from her body. 'Help me,' she whispered in my head.

I flashed to her, grabbing her burning hot hand, then flashed us both to the first place my brain connected with her. Our derelict breakfast room.

'Let it out, Persephone, you're safe here,' I told her. Something dark was dancing in her green eyes, and now her actual skin was glowing too. Vines erupted from her palms and she threw her head back as a blast of energy burst from her. The breakfast room was lined with windows fifty feet tall, and the glass smashed in every single one of them in unison.

As her power hit me I staggered slightly, not because of the strength but because of the way it felt. It wasn't just fury or wrath. There was more, something deeper. She needed to use her true power, I realized.

I moved quickly to the little platform her tree used to grow from, and made myself larger, forcing her attention onto me.

'Use the green vines. There is earth under here,' I said loudly, stamping on the cracked marble beneath my feet.

Immediately her vines turned green, bolting towards my feet. I moved fast out of the way as they smashed through the remaining tiles, churning through the hard, dead earth beneath. Then she gasped, and the green glow around her intensified.

Everything stilled to nothing as I watched my Queen, my beautiful goddess, turn the dark fury of the Underworld into awesome, unbound life.

Lightning fast, the trunk of the blossom tree began to grow from the middle of the platform, swirling and spiraling as it got larger, branches shooting from the trunk, then leaves and flowers following fast. Grass rose from the churning soil at the base, daisies sprouting amid the green turf. Pink petals began to dominate the sweeping branches as they extended over the table, and I could almost feel a phantom breeze ripple past me and through them.

Life. Color. Light.

I had longed for this tree for twenty-six years.

Her vines went slack suddenly, and she stumbled as they disintegrated. I flashed to her as her knees gave out, scooping her up and setting her down in one of the two chairs at the table. *Always laid for two but never used.* She took a shuddering breath as she looked up into my face and my heart swelled with so much hope and love that it actually rivaled the size of the dark pit of power in my gut.

. . .

I would never let her go again. I couldn't. She was light and life and love, and she was mine.

TWENTY-FOUR

PERSEPHONE

'W-what did I just do,' I stammered, staring up into Hades' intense silver eyes. He had an almost awestruck look on his face which was making me nervous, although I was too thoroughly drained for my body to react to my nerves. I could barely hold my own head up. I didn't feel like I was going to pass out though, which was something.

'You channeled your rage into earth magic. You regrew a tree that you used to keep alive here,' Hades said softly, and crouched in front of the chair he had put me in so that our eyes were level. I slowly tipped my head backwards and looked up. A pink blossom petal wafted down from the overhanging branches and landed on my wet hair. 'You used to laugh when they fell in your soup,' Hades said, his deep voice filled with emotion. I looked back at him.

'We ate in here?' He nodded. 'I knew I felt something about these chairs when I first saw them,' I muttered.

'You had them made for us. You said that there should be a place in my kingdom where I didn't have to be a king, so you made the chairs to show our powers equally. To share my burden.'

The intensity in his voice was almost too much to bear.

'Sounds like I was a pretty good wife,' I smiled, attempting to lessen the sadness. His face relaxed slightly.

'Now don't go getting an inflated opinion of yourself,' he grinned, rocking back on his heels. 'You'll start sounding like the other gods.'

His words wiped the smile from my face and he winced.

'I'm sorry. I know you must hate us all right now.'

'Hate doesn't come close,' I growled, but my burning rage from before was spent. 'Although I don't think I'm actually able to hate you. Something won't let me,' I told him.

'Even though you've just seen what my realm is made of, and it tried to kill you?'

'I don't want to live here, if that's what you're asking,' I half snorted. 'But I don't hold you responsible. I know you didn't choose to put me through this.'

'You did great, if it's any consolation. Underworld sewage is highly toxic, you would never have survived without controlling your black vines.'

'How did I change them from black to green?' I asked him. He cocked his head slightly.

'I don't know,' he admitted eventually. 'Before, if you got angry your power was all rage. This time though, I could feel your earth magic trying to get through.'

Hope and something that might have been excitement prickled inside me.

'So I might have better control of my angry power than before?' *Did that mean it was safe to eat another seed?*

'No god ever has full control over true wrath,' he said slowly. 'I don't know how you grew the tree. But you did.'

. . .

Nor did I. I had been ready to explode, the fury poisoning me from the inside out. But when Hades had stamped on the platform, my vines had taken over and the delicious feeling of thriving life had flooded my body, flushing the hate from my system.

'Do you have anything to drink?' I asked Hades. 'I kind of had my face filled with sewage. The aftertaste is pretty unpleasant.'

'Of course,' he said, leaping to his feet. I moved myself slowly, until I was sitting up in the chair. I gazed at the intricate detail on the arms and wondered how the hell I'd ever come up with something like this. But the more I looked, the more familiar it felt. The shape of the roses, the curve of the skulls, the patterns of the vines... Maybe I *could* see that same spark of creativity that went into my garden designs here.

'This should help,' said Hades, and I dragged my eyes from the chair and took the goblet he was holding out to me. It smelled like hot chocolate but it was golden in color. I raised my eyebrows at him.

'What is it?'

'Ambrosia.'

'Hecate said humans couldn't drink this,' I said, peering at the thick liquid.

'I think you've just demonstrated that you have enough power to handle it,' he said gently. 'But go easy.'

I took a slow sip. It tasted like the richest, most luxurious hot chocolate ever. Almost like melted chocolate, rather than that shitty powder stuff.

'Oh my gods, it's gorgeous.'

'Not as gorgeous as you,' he muttered, and dropped

down in front of me again. 'When you use your power like that... You look divine. It's all I can do not to tear your clothes off.'

His voice had become low and husky, and the warm drink was working its way through my chest now, my fatigue vanishing in its wake.

'Well, they are pretty messed up. And wet,' I said.

'I had noticed,' he whispered, and with a little pop, the damp fabric sticking to my skin was gone. I let out a tiny squeak as I looked down at myself. *The silk pajamas.* 'Maybe we could pick up where we left off?'

Desire danced in his eyes as he asked the question, and my body responded to him instantly. I took another slow sip of the ambrosia, warmth and energy spreading through me. I didn't know if it was the drink or the thought of Hades naked, but something was definitely revitalizing me. Tingles of excitement were rippling through me and I had a skipping feeling in my chest as Hades stood up. I stared at the beautiful god before me. He really was perfection.

I leaned forward to put the goblet on the ground, and as I straightened, I took the hem of my camisole on my fingertips.

His lips parted and his eyes darkened as he towered over me.

'You first,' I said.

His shirt was gone in an instant. It was as though he had been carved from marble, every curve and bulge of his chest screaming strength and power. My eyes were level with the waist of his low jeans, and the V of his abs dipping into the denim caused a surge of heat in my core, my muscles clenching. I reached out instinctively, desperate to touch his solid stomach, but he was just out of my reach. A tiny gold vine slid from my palm, curling towards him. I looked up into his face, unsure. He nodded.

The little vine touched his glowing skin, and merged with it, a shining gold tattoo sprawling up his ribs and across his chest.

Fierce desire exploded inside me, and before I knew what was happening I was standing, and he was lifting me and his mouth found mine. I buried my hands in his hair, with nothing in my head at all besides being as close to him as was physically possible as I wrapped my legs around him. His tongue flicked against mine and a pulse so fierce it almost hurt pounded between my legs.

'You are stunning, my Queen,' he murmured against my skin as his lips moved down my jaw. His words should have embarrassed me, but his voice was so loaded with passion, his intent and sincerity so clear, that my core clenched tighter.

'Your Queen?' I breathed.

'My Queen,' he repeated.

'I seem to remember you saying something about worshiping me.'

'I also said something about you screaming my name when I touch you, and watching you come over and over,' he said, moving so that I could see his darkening eyes. 'What I didn't tell you, is that I'm going to make you feel so incredible you won't remember your own name. I'm going to make you feel things you didn't even know were possible to feel. I'm going to bring you to the edge of ecstasy as many times as it takes for you to beg me to let you fall. And I'm going to fall with you.' A small noise I didn't think I'd ever made before escaped my lips.

He dropped to his knees, setting me down on the chair again, and began to kiss my neck, moving down slowly.

Heat rolled from him, and every time his lips touched my skin electricity fired through my body. As he reached my breasts he kissed over the thin silk of my camisole, my nipples hardening instantly. His tongue flicked over one through the fabric, and another wave of need crashed between my legs.

My thighs were still clenched around his solid waist and I gasped as I felt his hand under one of them, moving up towards my shorts. As his fingertips stroked higher I arched my back, pleasure and need making me dizzy. His fingers danced higher and higher, teasing me until I was squirming under him. I had my hands in his hair, and every time I pulled he grazed my nipple with his teeth through the silk. His fingers had reached my shorts, but he kept them over the surface of the fabric too, drawing closer and closer to the place I wanted him to be. *Needed him to be.* Waves of barely tolerable tingles shimmied across my skin from his touch and I didn't know if it was his magic or just how much I wanted him that was making them so powerful.

With excruciating slowness, I finally felt his finger brush over my sex, and a low moan left my lips. I heard his ragged breath as he must have felt how damp the silk between my legs was, and then he was kissing me on the mouth again, urgent and hungry. He tasted divine, and my mind blanked as his fingers danced like a feather over my most sensitive spot. The pressure was building with every movement, the desire inside me like a freight train, gathering too much momentum to hold on to. I kissed him back with a desperation I'd never felt before, as days and days of passion for this beautiful man, *this god*, flooded to where he expertly teased and touched me.

'Hades,' I moaned aloud, and a shattering wave of release crashed over me. His other arm wrapped tight around my shuddering body, and I buried my face in his neck, kissing any skin I could reach over and over as waves of pleasure hammered through me in shuddering aftershocks.

'Gods, you're stunning,' he murmured, his voice strained. 'I want to feel you do that again, around me. I want you, Persephone.'

'I'm yours,' I breathed back, gripping his shoulders.

But he moved back again, looking down into my face as he brushed a knuckle across my cheek. His eyes were glittering with fierce passion, but his words were soft.

'I never thought I'd see you again,' he said. 'Let alone hear you say those words. I-I don't want you to leave.'

I stared up at him, trying to concentrate on his words instead of the pleasure still rocking through my tremoring body, my desire to touch him, to feel him inside me, for him to take me completely.

'But you said I couldn't stay.'

'I know. But, I can't do it. I can't let you go again.'

Something inside me sparked, and it wasn't connected to my desire. It was deeper than that. *I was happy.* I was happy that he didn't want me to go.

But that wasn't the plan. I needed to get back to New York, away from murderous gods and amoral assholes.

And leave your powers, underwater worlds, flying ships and a fucking god who wants to spend an eternity worshiping you?

'I- I don't know if I belong here,' I said hesitantly. Hades said nothing, but emotion flickered through his eyes. 'But I do know that I feel something for you. Something I have never felt before.'

'We are bound,' he said quietly. 'But you have not fully accepted it. If you do, you will feel it.'

'I already feel something.'

He shook his head.

'It is not *something*. It is everything.'

I didn't know what to say. Guilt washed over me.

'I'm sorry,' I said, meaning it. I wanted, more than anything, to make him happy. Not just because of how much I wanted him physically, but because it was unbelievably important to me that he was happy. That must be the bond he was talking about, I supposed.

He stood up slowly.

'I'll make you a deal,' he said. 'If the bond awakens, and you feel it, I'll do everything in my power to keep you here. But if it is truly gone, then I swear you'll go back to New York, with no memory of me or Olympus.'

I sat up straight, pushing my legs together. This conversation was no longer about sex. And I didn't know what I wanted anymore. As much of me that wanted to return home to my brother and my gardens, also wanted to stay here, to find my powers, be with Hades and grow trees for eternity.

But the thought of the Empusa's lair, the people in the hourglasses at the ball, Hades' own indifferent reaction to what the gods did for entertainment, all made me pause. *That wasn't me.* And even if it was, there was no way in the world I could live in this place, with no outside, no windows, and death and demons beneath our feet.

'I need to think about this,' I said. 'It's a lot to take in, and I only just got my powers back. I don't know my place here at all.'

'Your place is by my side,' he said tightly, after a long pause. Part of me agreed with him, instinctively. The part that wished he'd kept his gorgeous mouth shut and not started this conversation. But not a large enough part of me to be sure.

'How about we talk about this if I survive all the Trials?' I said as casually as I could manage.

'You need to win the Trials.'

'What?'

'If you do not, I must marry Minthe.'

A bolt of jealousy ripped through me at the thought of him wed to someone else, and I screwed my face up.

'It's not that easy,' I said. 'I don't know if you've noticed, but your brothers really don't seem keen to make my time in Olympus pleasant.'

'You need to win,' he repeated. Frustration welled in me.

'I haven't even decided if I want to stay!' Hurt flashed across his face, and suddenly his shirt shimmered back over his chest.

'You've been through a lot today. You need to get some rest,' he said, his voice awkward and formal.

'But-' I started, then flinched and looked down as I felt my fighting clothes reappear around my body. They were dry now. 'Hades, please,' I tried again.

'I lost you once,' he said quietly. 'I don't know if I can do it again.'

'Just give me a little time to think,' I said and stood, reaching up to touch his face. His silver eyes flashed with desperation as he bowed his head and kissed me softly.

'Just try to win,' he said. I stared into his face, my mind whirring.

If I really could win, and I did, then I would have the upper hand. I would at least have the option of choosing to stay with him, as unlikely as I thought that would be. The thought of him kissing someone else, lifting someone else into this chair, touching them as he had me, caused an undercurrent of fury to blaze through me. But that didn't mean anything, I told myself. He'd just made me feel freaking incredible. Of course I would feel possessive of him right now.

Even without Hades in the equation though, I was discovering that I had magic powers that felt amazing, and had glimpsed a limitless world beyond anything I could have imagined.

There was no way I was in the right frame of mind to be making decisions this huge right now.

But if I won the Trials, I would have time, and surely more freedom to make a real decision. A calm, well-informed decision that didn't hinge on fear or lust.

'OK. I'll try,' I said, and something fierce glittered in his eyes as he pulled me into him, kissing me again. I couldn't help the wave of happiness as I kissed him back.

If this bond he talked about did awaken, then I would have to deal with it then.

TWENTY-FIVE

PERSEPHONE

'So... we were in the middle of something,' I said, breaking off the kiss and giving him a pointed look that I hoped screamed *take my clothes off, now. Yours too.*

'Until the bond awakens, I won't lay another finger on you,' Hades said, cupping my cheek.

'Why not?' Disappointment crashed through me and the words came out as a squeak.

'Because I don't do anything by halves. When I finally get to be with you, I want it to be the most mind-blowing thing you've ever experienced.'

'I'm pretty sure you could achieve that right now,' I told him, thinking about the orgasm he'd given me without even taking my damned clothes off.

He gave me a long, penetrating look, then sighed.

'You really should get some rest. Hecate needs to teach you healing tomorrow, before the endurance tests. I've no doubt my dickhead brother has something horrendous planned.'

I briefly considered begging him to finish what we'd started, but my pride kicked in just in time.

'Fine,' I scowled. 'Can we walk though? I don't feel like any more flashing today.'

'Of course.'

We didn't speak on our walk through the seemingly endless blue-torch lit corridors, but it wasn't awkward. He gripped my fingers in his, and it felt nice. Better than nice. My body was still humming with all the power and pleasure I had experienced in the last few hours, the horror of the Empusa's lair starting to feel like a long time ago.

When we reached my rooms, Hades turned to me, and his face was steely and hard, and heat began to simmer inside me again. Strength emanated from him, and gods help me, it turned me on.

'Do not leave this room without me or Hecate,' he said.

'I know.'

'And again, I'm sorry in advance for whatever Zeus has planned for you. For what it's worth, he's not making me put you through any endurance tests, but I don't know which gods it will be.'

I felt a stab of relief that Hades wouldn't have to suffer through causing me pain or anger. Both for his sake and mine.

'I'll be fine,' I told him. 'I'll learn everything I can from Hecate about healing.' It was probably a good thing he had decided Hecate should teach me instead of him. My desire and confusion when I was around him would definitely distract me, and healing sounded like a pretty important thing to get right. 'Are these bonds always this impractical?'

'Yes,' he smiled, and kissed me, his lips like feathers and fire at the same time. 'But they say love conquers all,' he said as he broke away from me, then vanished with a flash of white light.

'*Love,*' I repeated quietly as I shut my bedroom door.

It hit me then. The reason he wouldn't be with me without the bond. He didn't want to 'do things by halves'. He wanted me to love him, as much as he already loved me.

Could I love him? There was no doubt at all that I wanted him, and that I cared deeply about his happiness. Was that what love was? I pictured his face as I leaned against my door. There was something so right about it. About him. And I knew there shouldn't be. He was practically the definition of wrong, he was the Lord of the Dead, a god who didn't mourn the loss of life, who shed corpses made of light as he tore humans apart, who instilled primal terror in his victims.

Yet he'd created an entire realm, and new species because of his craving for life. He'd never chosen his role, but accepted it because he had to. His realm housed outcasts without judgment, and didn't allow invasions of privacy like gods reading your mind.

I respected him, I realized. I admired him as much as I feared him.

The softness of his touch, the tenderness of his kisses, the intense emotion in his eyes, they all contrasted so bluntly with the monster he showed the world. Soft and fierce. Light and dark. Life and death. The Empusa had told me that I would not master the balance, and she was likely right. Had Hades nailed that balance, and hidden the soft side of himself away but kept it whole? Or was he just as in danger of losing his balance as I was?

∽

'Is most of every god's life just parties?' I asked Skop as I adjusted the corset of yet another ball-gown. This one was bright red, the top half boned and tight like a classic corset, the bottom like weighted silk. White roses curled all the way from the hem up the right-hand side of my body. It was beautiful, but it was heavy and restrictive.

It is when they're hosting these events, yeah. I guess that's why they have them so often. I raised my eyebrows at him.

'Have any of the other gods been forced to marry like this?'

Not yet. Are you ready for tonight? I doubt I'll be able to help you much.

There was a bitterness to the kobaloi's voice again, and it was clear he didn't much care for being excluded from so much of my time with Hades. The suspicious part of me couldn't help wondering if he was reporting back to Dionysus. The trusting part of me wanted to believe he just cared about me.

'As long as you're not in danger again,' I told him, securing *Faesforos* to my ankle. My skirt reached the floor so the dagger would be unseen there.

Skop made a humpfing noise, but didn't say any more. I looked at my reflection, and took a deep breath. The red lipstick that matched the dress was far bolder than I'd ever normally wear but I needed to feel as fierce as possible tonight, and it somehow made me stand taller, and hold my head higher. *That's because Minthe was in red last time you saw her,* the petty part of my brain pointed out. *You want to look better than her.*

Are you ready? Skop cut through the thoughts.

'As I'll ever be,' I answered him.

. . .

Hecate had spent most of the day with me, trying to teach me how to access the part of my power that let me heal. When we were both pretty sure I knew what she was talking about, I'd very hesitantly made a tiny nick on my arm, and willed the skin to close. To my sheer delight, it had worked. And to my relief, she hadn't suggest we cause any bigger wound to test it on, but spent time talking about what it would feel like and how to draw more power to a specific area of my body if I needed to. I felt confident that I'd be able to help myself if I was injured, at least until my all-powerful god ex-husband got to me.

Knowing that Hades was looking out for me was a feeling I wasn't entirely used to, and liked more than I cared to admit. My brother had always been there when I'd needed him, but we didn't live in each others pockets, far from it. Sam would help when I asked, but otherwise he let me stand on my own two feet. Which, to be fair, Hades was kind of being forced to do. He wasn't allowed to interfere in the Trials, but he had broken the rules multiple times already to help me.

If I was actually about to die, would he intervene? *Could* he intervene? Hecate said that Zeus was stronger than the rest of the gods; I assumed that included Hades.

Hecate flashed into my bedroom and my hands jumped on the dresser.

'Can't you knock!' I exclaimed. 'You frightened the shit out of me.'

'Oh yeah, sorry,' she grinned. 'You look ace.'

'Thanks. Any last minute tips?'

'Yeah. Put up with whatever they put you through, no matter what, and you'll win,' she said with a shrug.

'Right. Easy,' I said, rolling my eyes.

'And don't screw Hades at the party. People will notice.'

I shot her a look and her eyes sparkled with mischief.

'You're as bad as him,' I told her, nodding at Skop.

'No, she's not,' he said. *'Trust me.'*

Hecate seemed much more relaxed than before the last Trial, and I eyed her curiously.

'Why aren't you worried about this one?' I asked her.

'It's an endurance test, and you're strong. If they need you to endure something, then it's not likely to actually kill you,' she said, flopping down on my bed.

'That's a good point.'

'Although they might kill someone else,' added Skop.

'Shut up,' Hecate said. 'Look, you'll go around all the gods at the party, and some of them will make you put up with something shitty for a few minutes. Done.'

'That doesn't sound like a good end to Round Two,' I said skeptically. 'I thought they liked more drama than that.'

'Some of them might be a bit nasty, I guess. But probably not as bad as drowning in Underworld sewage.'

'Yeah, not a lot could be worse than that,' I said, a shudder of anger taking me at the memory. I felt my magic simmer under my skin in response. I didn't know if that was comforting or alarming.

'What if whoever left the doll and the mirror gatecrashes again, with something worse than a phoenix?' asked Skop.

'Seriously?' Hecate glared at him. 'You're not helping, Skop. Hades' captain of the guard, a very stern Minotaur called Kerato, is all over it. There's no need to worry.'

The anxiety and nerves were building inside me, Hecate's blasé attitude not really settling me at all. I didn't believe for one second this would be easy. Zeus would want to end the round with a bang, I was sure of it.

TWENTY-SIX

PERSEPHONE

Hecate flashed us to a room that for the briefest of moments, I thought was Hades' breakfast room. But as I looked around, I could see stark differences. It shared the towering vaulted ceiling, and the tall arched windows covered by heavy drapes along one wall. But the platform with the tree in the center, and the table for two that should have been dwarfed by the room but somehow wasn't, were very much missing.

Instead, a long row of twelve marble thrones dominated the middle of the room, running parallel to the windows. There was a cold formality to the room that made me even more uncomfortable than I already felt. Where the masquerade ball had been almost ethereal, with twinkling stars on the rocky walls, atmospheric lighting and columns everywhere to hide behind, this room looked serious and solemn. It was lit by cool blue flames flickering in wall sconces, and waist high columns with flat tops provided somewhere for guests to put their drinks. And there were many guests. Faces that were now familiar peered at me from where they gathered in small clusters, all beautifully dressed in gowns and robes and togas that wouldn't have looked out of place on a catwalk back home. I clocked Selene, Eros, Hedone and Morpheus, and others I had last seen at the party on Aquarius as I scanned the room, smiling politely. The smile slipped slightly when I made eye contact with Minthe though, her eyes filled with malice. She looked stunning in a black strapless sheath dress, and my gut constricted as my confidence started to shrivel.

But then Hades' voice sounded in my mind.

'You look incredible. I love you in red.' I felt my back straighten, and my smile widen again.

'Where are you?'

'The gods are all here, we're just not allowed to reveal ourselves yet. My brother is a glutton for drama.'

'I thought you weren't supposed to talk in people's heads in Virgo without their permission?'

'Ah, I apologize. I assumed I did have your permission.'

'Well, you know what they say about assumptions,' I told him, accepting a drink from a satyr waiter who had appeared by my side.

'No. I have no idea what they say about assumptions.'

'Oh. That saying not made it from my world to here then?'

'It has not. Enlighten me.'

'They say assumptions are the mother of all fuck ups.'

There was a long pause, then Hades spoke again.

'The mother of all fuck ups is that pain-in-my-ass goddess, Eris.'

I snorted a laugh and Hecate gave me a slightly alarmed look as she raised her own glass to her lips.

'I guess the saying doesn't really apply here.'

'I guess not. I'll see you soon, Beautiful. Good luck.'

· · ·

Hecate and I separated, and I did my obligatory tour of the hall, smiling and nodding at everyone I spoke to whilst sipping my fizzy wine. As Hecate had said there would be, there were many more guards than I had seen before, posted at each of the large doorways at the ends of the hall and lining the walls between the windows. The hall felt weirdly empty, despite how many people and creatures filled it, and nervous energy was crackling under my skin with increasing ferocity.

'It's so lovely to see you again,' beamed Selene as I reached her.

'And you,' I smiled, meaning it. She had been warm and kind to me at the masquerade ball, and I sensed sincerity from her.

'Don't tell anyone, but I rather think you've become Olympus's favorite for this you know,' she said conspiratorially.

'Seriously?' I blinked at her.

'*Told ya,*' said Skop in my head, and I glanced down at him, his tail wagging. '*I knew they'd all love an underdog.*'

'Watching you come into your power is a pleasure,' Selene beamed. I opened my mouth but nothing came out. Selene was one of the nicest people I'd met so far, and even she thought watching me nearly drown in shit and be eaten by a sea monster was 'a pleasure'. What the hell was wrong with the people here? 'I'm sure you'll do fantastic tonight,' she said enthusiastically, filling the gap I'd left in the conversation.

I felt a tap on my arm and spun around gratefully.

An enormous minotaur that I had seen a few times

before in Hades' throne room bowed his head slightly at me, and I resisted the instinct to step backwards.

'*Dionysus drown me in wine, he's a big bastard,*' breathed Skop.

'You must be Kerato,' I said quickly, remembering what Hecate had told me about Hades' Captain of the Guard as I stared up at the minotaur. He was least nine feet tall, his hooves alone reaching half way up my shin. The beast blinked at me, his jet black pupils ringed with scarlet red. Hairy eyebrows cut above his eyes at an angry angle, and two curved black horns jutted from the sides of his furry skull.

'That is correct, my Lady,' he said gruffly. 'King Hades asked me to make myself known to you.'

'Thank you,' I said.

'Anyone wearing this sigil is part of Hades' guard.' He banged his clawed fist to the metal disc in the center of the gleaming armor that was strapped across his chest. A skull with a snake emerging from its left eye was carved on it. I couldn't help thinking that it looked like the sort of tattoo someone in a biker gang would have.

'OK,' I said.

'Good luck,' the minotaur grunted, then turned and marched back towards the doors.

'Quite intimidating, isn't he?' said a sultry voice, and I turned with a smile to see Hedone. She kissed me on both cheeks.

'He seems like he takes his job seriously,' I said.

'I've no doubt.'

'Where's Morpheus?'

'He couldn't make it tonight, but he wishes you luck.'

'Thank you. Hedone, what kind of creature is that?' I asked her as something with massive leathery wings and what looked like the legs of a lion stalked past us. His nose was a hooked, yellowing beak and his beady eyes swept over me as I stared at him.

'He looks like a Griffon hybrid,' she said. When I raised my eyebrows questioningly at her, she elaborated. 'There are wild and sentient versions of most creatures in Olympus, although some are more prone to staying wild. Like manticores. They are large winged cats with scorpion tails that live in forests, and it's very rare to find them sentient. But Griffons, who are lion and eagle, have enough human in them that most are sentient. It's rare to find them wild. His wings are large for a Griffon though, so perhaps there is some Harpy in there somewhere.'

'So a Griffon had sex with a Harpy?' I tried to keep the disbelief out of my voice as my brain went into overdrive picturing that union. The only harpies I'd seen here were mostly bird with human heads.

Hedone gave a soft chuckle.

'Where there's a will, there's a way,' she said.

'*There sure is,*' added Skop. '*I'm only three feet tall, and you should see what I've managed to bang.*' I rolled my eyes at him, but he just wagged his tail faster. '*It's all down to my enormous-*'

'Good evening, Olympus!' The commentator's greeting cut the kobaloi's sentence off, and it was the first time I had been grateful to hear the irritating blond man's voice. The room stilled, and I followed the collective gaze of the crowd to the middle of the room, where the commentator was standing at the left end of the row of thrones. 'Welcome to the last Trial of Round Two. And we have a bit of a twist for you! But first, please welcome your Gods!' The room dropped to their knees as one, myself included, as a white light filled the room. But I raised my bowed head enough to see Hades, his rippling smoky form on the far right of the row.

'Now, this evening Persephone will have to withstand four endurance tests, instigated by four gods,' the commentator boomed, as everyone rose to their feet. 'She can choose to go and talk to any god she likes in any order, but she does not know which gods will be testing her.' I cast my eyes over the gods' faces, searching for any giveaways in expression. I saw none. Not one even glanced at me. 'This evening though, there will be no judging,' said the commentator, and a ripple of chatter filled the room. *No judging? What?* 'Instead, for every test Persephone fails, she will lose one of her existing four tokens.'

Dread trickled down my spine. Lose my tokens? I'd already eaten two, for gods' sake. Would that mean I would lose the power I'd gained back as well? Plus there were only three more Trials after this one, and I needed six tokens to win. I did the math fast.

If I lost only one seed I could still win, but I would have to get at least one token on the next three Trials. And as I'd already proven twice, getting tokens was not easy.

Anger boiled through my blood as all my hopes of only having to do two more Trials faded away. Not only could I not win any more tokens now, they were actually going to take away what I'd already earned? And possibly my powers too?

'This is total bullshit,' I hissed under my breath. The chances of me getting tokens on every single other Trial were surely slim to none. And even if I hadn't just decided that I wanted to win these cursed fucking Trials, there was no way I was losing my new powers.

I was going to have to deal with whatever they threw at me and keep all four seeds, no matter what.

TWENTY-SEVEN

PERSEPHONE

'Persephone, come forward! Choose your first god!'

Every head in the crowd snapped to me as one, and I couldn't help gulping. My skin was fizzing with nervous energy now, and I was uncomfortably aware of my sweating palms.

Those palms have freaking magic vines in them, you can do this! I repeated the words to myself as I strode through the parting crowd towards the commentator. When I reached him he beamed at me, teeth pearly white and perfect.

'Now, who would you like to try first?'

'Hades,' I said, without hesitation. *Was that smart,* I thought as a ripple of laughter moved through the crowd. He was the only god I knew didn't have a test for me. But his name had sprung to my lips and now it was too late to take it back.

'Very well. Go ahead.'

Carefully avoiding looking at any of the other gods, I fixed my attention on Hades' smoky form and walked down the row of thrones towards him. I could feel the other

Olympian's eyes on me, but I ignored them. The best way to avoid being intimidated or manipulated by them was to be in charge, I decided.

When I reached Hades' throne and stood before him, he reached forward, his translucent smoke arm holding out a small silver goblet.

'Drink from the cup of death and see if you shall be tested,' he said, and his voice was the nasty, slithery tone I had almost forgotten existed. This was the Hades the rest of the world saw. I took the cup from him, searching his face for any signs of silver eyes, but he gave me nothing. *He couldn't show any favoritism,* I told myself, biting back the stabbing hurt his indifference was causing. Slowly, I drank from the little silver goblet. The liquid in it was sweet, but not a flavor I could place.

'No test from Hades!' sang the commentator. 'Choose your next god!' I handed Hades the goblet back, praying for a glimpse of his true self. I only just kept the smile from my face as the briefest flash of gleaming silver eyes shone through the smoke as he took the cup from me, and a surge of confidence followed.

I could do this.

'Athena,' I said firmly. She was seated two thrones away, Ares sitting between her and Hades. The god of war was again wearing the red-plumed helmet that hid his face, and this close I could see how thickly corded his massive torso was with muscle. I would really, really not like to get on the wrong side of him. Or face a test from him.

Athena was wearing the same white toga I had seen her in before, her hair braided around her head. As I stood before her, a small owl seated on her shoulder blinked its large eyes at me.

'Drink from the cup of wisdom and see if you shall be

tested,' the goddess said as she handed me a goblet identical to the one Hades had given me. I took a quick sip from the cup. This time it was bitter tasting, but nothing happened.

'Time to move on Persephone! Where to next?' The commentator's voice brimmed with excitement.

'Aphrodite,' I said, and looked five thrones down the line to where the goddess of love sat beside her husband, Hephaestus. If I was tested by Aphrodite, what the hell would that involve? What if she made me withstand something sexual? My nerves built as I approached her, panic that I might be put through something like that unwillingly rising in me. Hedone said that sort of thing wasn't allowed, I told myself, remembering the conversation I'd had with her before the ball about ego driving consensual sex in Olympus. The powerful liked to earn their good times, rather than take them.

Nonetheless, my hands shook as I took the cup from the goddess. She beamed at me, her vivid green eyes sparkling from under outrageously thick lashes, her hair jet black today, and cropped in a bob. She was wearing a skin-tight white dress and reminded me a little of Cleopatra. *Please don't be a test*, I prayed as I closed my eyes and took a sip from the goblet. The liquid tasted a million times better than the last two, but mercifully, nothing happened.

'Choose your next god! We're getting bored, Persephone!' I mustered up a dirty look to throw at the commentator, then handed the goblet back to Aphrodite.

'Dionysus,' I said, and moved back to where Dionysus was sitting, on the other side of Athena. I was unsurprised to see him once more in tight leather pants, a white shirt mostly open and only half tucked in. He had one ankle crossed over his knee, and dark sunglasses on.

'Drink from the cup of wine and see if you shall be test-ed,' he drawled, and leaned forward lazily with a goblet. I took it from him, for the first time knowing what to expect the liquid to taste like. Sure enough, it was a rich red wine, and freaking delicious. Before I'd realized what I was doing, I'd downed the whole damned glass. I licked my lips as I drained the last drops, and was just exclaiming how good it was, when I realized I wasn't in the hall any more.

That wasn't normal wine, I realized, spinning on the spot, panic flooding through me. I was in a forest. Except the trees around me stretched up so high that I couldn't see their tops, the light from the sky just streaking through gaps in the foliage. As I blinked around, I realized I could see little wooden structures high in the branches. I inhaled deeply, the smell of damp earth magnificent to me. Before I'd noticed I was doing it, green vines were snaking out of my palms, the lure of so much nature around me irresistible.

Then a low snarl snapped my attention to the nearest huge tree trunk. The gnarled wooden bark seemed to swirl and move in front of me, and I squinted at it. A wave of dizziness washed over me, as something black and lithe stalked from behind the tree trunk. Wings unfurled from its back, and I blinked furiously as the world tilted on its axis.

I felt drunk. Out of control drunk, not happy, silly drunk. I tried to focus on the thing now prowling towards me, and a flash of red above its back came sharply into focus all of a sudden. It was a glowing stinger, on the end of a scorpion tail. My conversation with Hedone earlier sprang into my mind, about winged cats with scorpion tails but I couldn't remember what they were called. A new disorientating wave of dizziness pounded over me, and I actually stumbled. Somewhere in the distance I heard a loud gong, then a voice rang out.

'Ten minutes, starting now!'

Ten minutes for what? I'd known before that I was here for something important but now... I struggled to piece together the last few minutes, but I could feel my memories slipping away as I stared at the huge black cat approaching me. He didn't look friendly. Maybe he lived in this forest? A woozy calm was settling over me, and I held my hand out, a green vine stretching towards the cat. He bared his teeth, and my vision wobbled again. A laugh bubbled from my lips. He was quite cute really, with his feathered wings and slinky steps.

Run!

The desperate thought pierced my cheerful haze, anxiety and fear smacking me in the chest so hard it was like I had been electrocuted. My feet started to move and I staggered backwards, my emotions flipping so far in the other direction that I was now too scared to take my eyes from the beast. There must have been something in the wine that was causing me to believe this thing was cute, because in reality it was damned terrifying. That bastard Dionysus had drugged me. My vision still swam, but I was sure the cat's teeth were growing, and its dark eyes were beginning to glow. There was no way I would be faster than it was. If I was its prey, I was in serious shit.

But its wings... They looked soft to touch, and were an ombre of reds. They were beautiful. Something that pretty wasn't dangerous, surely? My feet slowed.

It snarled again, dropping its shoulders low and pawing

the ground and I felt another shock in my chest as the placid calm was dislodged.

Of course its damned dangerous, look at it! Now get the fuck out of here!

Before the lethal calm could take me again, I turned and ran for the tree behind me. I heard the thing roar, and praying I was far enough ahead that it couldn't reach me in one pounce, I launched my vines from both palms at a branch thirty feet above me. They flew fast, wrapping tight around the branch as they reached it, and I tugged, willing them to retract. I was lurched off my feet, my hair whipping around my face as I flew up towards the branch. I looked down, just able to see the cat past my billowing red skirt as he leaped for me and missed.

Within seconds I had reached the branch, and only then realized just how high up I was. The forest around me began to spin again, and this time I didn't know if it was vertigo or the drugged wine.

Your vines have got you, your vines have got you, I chanted in my head, but as soon as my addled brain pictured me falling, I felt the vines slacken.

'No!' I shrieked, as I started to slip, and they tightened instantly, wrenching my shoulders as my descent stopped abruptly. Heart hammering against my ribcage and my breath shortening, I forced them to pull me back up, then started trying to swing my legs up, attempting to hook my feet over the branch. Eventually, stomach and arm muscles burning, I managed to get my legs firmly enough around the wood to pull my body up and over the wide branch, my vines staying firmly wrapped around it too. Panting and nauseous, I eased myself into a sitting position, dimly noticing how torn my skirt was.

All I had to do was sit and not look at the forest floor

below me until the ten minutes was up. It felt like I'd been here for an hour already, there couldn't be long left. A low roar snapped my attention to the main trunk of the tree and my vision wobbled even more as my blood turned to ice. The winged cat was prowling along the branch towards me, its massive claws gripping the bark like glue.

TWENTY-EIGHT

PERSEPHONE

Sense forced its way through the drug-induced fog swamping my brain as I scrambled backwards. It had wings, why the fuck did I think I'd be safe up a tree? The cat sprang forward, swiping at me with a huge paw, its glowing scorpion tail rearing back behind it. I ducked my body instinctively, fear of the cat overtaking my fear of falling, and it snarled as my right leg slipped and I cried out. Within a heartbeat my other leg gave way, not strong enough to keep me upright on the branch, and the world seemed to turn to slow-motion as the rest of my body followed my legs.

I couldn't breath at all as my fingers left the branch and weightlessness took me, the only thing in my head the certain knowledge that I was going to die. Then my shoulders wrenched again, harder, as the vines from my palms caught my weight and then I was swinging thirty feet above the ground, my whole body shaking violently and everything around me spinning.

I can't do this, I can't do this, I can't do this. The hysterical words pinballed around my head as the ground beneath me began to become obscured by the black dots overtaking my vision. I was going to pass out. And then my vines wouldn't stop me from falling at all.

Give up. I had to give up. *No, get to the ground!* The fierce voice sounded loud in my head, all the more shocking because it was my own thought, my own voice. *Extend the damned vines! You've already fallen from the branch, and you're still alive! You're stronger than this!*

Shaking my head, I willed the vines to grow, lowering me towards the ground. Looking down at the forest floor made the black dots come back, so I looked up instead, just in time to see the cat swipe at the exact spot my vines were coiled around the tree.

I willed the vines faster as his huge claws made contact, severing the vine from my left hand. I swung violently, but the right vine held strong, and now I was only ten feet from the ground and still moving fast. The cat swiped again, and weightlessness took me once more as I fell the last five feet to the moss covered earth. I landed awkwardly on my hip, and swore as I rolled and something hard cut into my thigh. Scrambling to my feet, I looked for the cat.

He was still up on the branch, but the dappled sunlight streaming through the thick canopy of leaves caught its stunning red wings as he extended them, then leapt from the branch. I couldn't outrun this thing, or hide from it, I thought, the pain in my thigh increasing. But as he landed gracefully opposite me, leaves swirling across the ground as his wings beat, the forest around me tilted and lurched hard, then vanished as a distant gong sounded.

. . .

I took a heaving breath of relief as the stark hall came into focus around me, the nauseating dizziness melting away fast. I'd done it. The ten minutes were up.

'Sorry, Persy,' I heard Dionysus' voice say, and blinked up at him on his throne in front of me. 'That's not how I wanted you to see my realm, Taurus. But I'm afraid I didn't have a choice. Nicely done though,' he added with a slow smile.

'Was the wine drugged?' I asked, trying to slow my breathing and willing my racing heart to slow down too.

'I happen to be the god of madness along with wine. Lots of Taurean wine causes hallucinations.'

'Wait, hallucinations?'

'Yeah. What did you see?' I felt my mouth fall open.

'You mean the huge cat with wings and a scorpion tail wasn't real?'

Dionysus chuckled softly.

'Had someone recently described a manticore to you, by any chance?'

'Y-yes,' I stammered, recalling the brief chat with Hedone I'd had before the Trial.

'Well, your sub-conscious remembered the conversation and your imagination did the rest.'

'So I was running away from nothing? I nearly killed myself in that tree for no reason?'

'I've seen people do a lot worse,' he said slowly.

A sharp pain in my thigh made me look away from him and down at myself. Through my torn skirt I could see a long gash on my leg, bright blood trickling down my bare skin. I summoned the power Hecate taught me to access earlier, concentrating hard on the wound. Thrills of excitement pulsed through me as the skin glowed a faint grassy green, then began to knit itself back together. The pain faded almost instantly.

Confidence filled me as I watched my thigh heal. My most crippling fear was heights, and I had just fallen out of a freaking tree and survived. Not just survived; I hadn't given up. Last time, at the chasm, I'd quit. But this time I'd pushed through the fear, and won.

One test down, one seed safe, and now I knew I could definitely heal myself.

Bring it the fuck on.

'Hera,' I said, standing up abruptly before the commentator could say anything. I strode past Hermes, then Zeus, and stopped in front of the Queen of the Gods. She was wearing a teal gown that would be classed as a toga, but had a distinctly modern feel to it. Her black hair was piled high in a complicated collection of braids, all held in place by a glittering tiara with a peacock eye at its center. Her dark eyes glittered as she leaned forward and handed me a goblet.

'Drink from the cup of marriage and birth, and see if you shall be tested,' she said as I took the cup. I steeled myself, and took a sip. It tasted like blueberries. Nothing happened, and I handed her the goblet back and she nodded.

'Who next, Persephone?' called the commentator.

'Poseidon,' I answered. He was at the far end of the row and I marched towards him. Poseidon had already tested me once this round; I could handle anything he might throw at me.

'Drink from the cup of the ocean and see if you shall be tested,' he said, and handed me a goblet. He was in full god-of-the-sea garb again, sporting a long beard and holding a smaller version of his trident. Waves crashed in his blue irises as I drank from the cup. I tried not to pull a face as briny water filled my mouth, salt making my throat contract. But nothing else happened, and I handed him the cup back with relief. Artemis and Apollo were in the next two thrones, looking significantly younger and more cheerful than all of the other gods.

'Make your next choice,' said the commentator.

'Apollo,' I said, and the sun god beamed at me. He was shirtless, wearing just a toga style skirt, and his skin almost glowed gold, making him look as though he'd been carved from the precious metal. His body was so perfect that my brain struggled to register it as real. His face was the same, the planes so refined, the symmetry exact. Hades' muscled torso and beautiful angular face filled my mind suddenly, seeming so much more *right* than the underwear-model perfection of Apollo.

'Drink from the cup of the sun and see if you shall be tested,' Apollo said, leaning forward to give me a goblet. His voice was deeper, and older-sounding than I had expected it to be. I took a sip from the cup, and yelped and dropped it as searing hot liquid covered my tongue.

Heat, as though I'd just stepped into an oven, engulfed me. I groaned as I looked about myself and the hall shimmered. I'd just found my second test.

The world came back into focus and I found myself standing on a bridge, bright blue sky above me. Instinctively I gripped the thick rope handrails either side of me, and looked around, sweat gathering fast at the nape of my neck. The bridge I was on crossed some sort of wide crater, and as I looked down dread gripped my whole body. Between the gaps in the wooden slats of the bridge I could see lava. I was standing over a fucking volcano.

The deep red liquid bubbled and oozed below me, areas glowing bright orange and even white with heat. The boiling surface was alarmingly close, no more than fifty feet down. The more I stared at it, the more my body became slick with sweat, and the more oppressive the heat became. I turned as carefully as I could, looking both ways down the bridge. It just led to a narrow path that lined the inside of the crater. But could wooden slats survive this heat? If they gave out, I was toast. Literally.

A gong sounded, accompanied by the commentator's voice.

'Five minutes begins now!'

Five minutes? That didn't seem long. Rather than comforting, I found the shorter length of time distinctly unnerving. Something awful was going to happen if I only had to spend five minutes here.

Taking a deep breath of hot, sulfurous air, I lifted one foot. Except it didn't move. My sandals were glued to the planks, and panic fired through my blood as I pulled harder. An ominous creaking sounded from the bridge, and I froze in my attempt to free myself. Did I really have to just stand here, while the heat burned away the wood beneath me? I'd die, surely?

As my heart beat faster in my chest, I tried to take deep breaths, assessing my situation. Sweat was running down my spine now, as well as the backs of my knees. I could hear the lava gurgling below me. If the bridge was already here, then surely it was resistant to the heat, I thought, rationally. A cracking sound drew my attention to the end of the bridge, just in time for me to see the last plank burst into flame. My breath caught.

Another sound cracked behind me, and I spun at the waist to see the plank at the opposite end go up in flames too.

Shit. Shit, shit, shit.

This was an endurance test, I told myself, as the next plank along caught alight. The idea is to frighten the participant into giving up. Not to actually kill them. I couldn't move from where I was, and there was nowhere to go. Which meant I had to hold my ground, no matter how close the flames got.

It turned out that was a lot, lot, easier said than done. By the time the planks four or five from mine were bursting into flames there was no part of me not drenched in sweat. I felt like I was suffocating, the heat a real, tangible, weighted thing bearing down on my entire body, crushing me. Every breath was hard, the temperature burning my lungs. And every plank that cracked and caught fire added to the heat and my mounting fear. My vines couldn't help me here. My healing couldn't help me if I dropped into the searing lava below. This was all about courage, and I was running out.

A plank three away from me on my right crackled with heat, then orange flames crept over it slowly at first, then burst to life, engulfing the dry wood. I turned slowly, knowing the opposite plank on my left would go next. Sure enough, fire flickered to life across the wood. Five minutes. I had to hold my nerve for five minutes, but I was estimating I only had about thirty seconds before the planks ran out and mine would go up in flames. And I had absolutely no idea how much time had already passed. The heat from the next plank on my left roared up, and I could smell the fine hairs on my arms burning. I closed my eyes, unable to watch as my mind begged me to quit, the fear bordering on winning over my willpower.

Just hold on, just hold on.

As if mocking my silent chant, heat suddenly exploded under my fingertips and I opened my eyes with a shout as I pulled my hands to my body. The handrail was ablaze, and within a second the rope had disintegrated. My legs shook under me as the second plank on my right burned out. The heat was making my body weaken, all liquid inside me seeming to have turned to sweat. I felt the fire leap on my left as the last plank caught.

They won't kill you, hold your nerve. This is the only way to win.

It had to be the only way to win. They wouldn't make an unbeatable test, would they?

The skin on my face seemed to tighten as heat scorched up to my right, and I turned my face, closing my eyes again. This was it. If the next time I opened my eyes I wasn't back in the hall, I'd be dropping to a fiery death.

TWENTY-NINE

PERSEPHONE

A gong sounded, and relief smacked into me so strong I actually felt my legs give out as the world around me shimmered. My knees banged against the cold marble of the hall and a desperate urge to lay down on the cool stone swamped me. I took a huge gulp of cool air as a satyr trotted up to my kneeling form and handed me a large mug of water. I gulped it down gratefully, and wiped the sweat from my forehead on my arm, only to find my arm wasn't much drier. It briefly crossed my mind that I must look a hot mess, literally, with my hair plastered down with sweat and my dress torn to shreds, but the sheer fact that I wasn't burning alive dispelled my concerns quickly.

'My realm, Capricorn, is known for seasonal extremes, and I'm known for heat,' Apollo said, a rich seductive tone to his voice. I looked up at him from where I knelt, my body still burning hot and skin stinging and singed. I summoned up my healing power, but instead of concentrating on a wound, I tried to focus on my skin as a whole. A pleasurable tingle danced over me, followed by the feeling of cool water lapping gently at me, first over my face, then my arms and chest and back. It felt so good a long sigh escaped my lips. Apollo's eyes darkened. 'I could do that for you,' he said quietly. I pushed myself to my feet quickly, the predatory look in his eyes feeling nothing like when Hades looked at me that way.

'Thank you, but I'm fine. Just thirsty.' I felt a touch on my leg through my shredded skirt, and looked down to see the satyr holding up a refilled mug. 'You're an angel,' I told him as I took it and drained it.

Two tests down, two seeds safe. Two more to go.

'Where to next, Persephone?' boomed the commentator. I looked wearily down the line, then back. Between Poseidon and Apollo sat Apollo's twin, Artemis, her young and eager face infinitely appealing.

'Artemis,' I said, stepping towards her. A bow as large as she was lay tucked into the side of her throne, and her hair was as gold as her brother's skin. She was wearing leather fighting garb similar to what I had back in my wardrobe, and I felt a pang of jealousy. A ballgown and sandals had to be the least practical thing in the world to perform these sadistic damned tests in.

Artemis was short, and she had to lean quite far forward to offer me her goblet.

'Drink from the cup of the hunt and see if you shall be tested.' She sounded no older than a teenager. I took the cup from her, and took a sip, the word 'hunt' wafting through my mind and setting alarm bells ringing. The liquid tasted earthy, like beetroot, and as I lowered the cup my limbs shivered involuntarily. Was this a delayed reaction to the heat? I looked up at Artemis, her innocent eyes now glowing with a wicked gleam. Shit. This was another test.

The world around me flickered once more, and an endless, hilly moor materialized under my feet. The grass was brown-tinged green and reached my knees, and the air smelled faintly dusty. It felt like it hadn't rained in a while. My green vines were itching at my palms, the desire to nurture and grow the needy life surrounding me almost overwhelming. But that shivering feeling took me once more, and this time I could actually feel something skittering across my skin. My breath skipped in my chest as the gong sounded.

'Ten minutes,' the commentator's voice boomed, and I stared down at myself in horror as thousands of spiders scuttled from the grass and up my body.

A strangled noise crawled out of my throat as I started waving my arms wildly, vines bursting my from my palms and whipping through the air as my panic grew. Within seconds the things had reached my chest and were on my bare skin, and I shook myself harder as I stumbled through the grass, slapping at my arms and body, trying to get them off me.

'They're more scared of you than you are of them,' I panted desperately, repeating the words my mom had told me every time I found a spider in the trailer. But they'd reached my neck now and my skin felt like it was alive and I couldn't stand it. My own vine smacked hard into my shoulder as I beat at myself, and the force made me fall onto my ass. The moment's pause was long enough for me to take in my once red skirt, now almost black with hundreds of spiders, most tiny, but some enormous. A beast with red stripes and massive hairy legs skittered up my skirt towards my bodice and I shrieked as I bat my vines at it, again hitting myself in the process. My heart was hammering so fast in my chest I wasn't sure it could take much more. I'd have a heart attack and drop down dead under a mountain of fucking spiders. I struggled back to my feet and started chanting again as I spun on the spot, looking for any sort of refuge. There was nothing, not even a tree on the horizon, just a sea of dry moorland grass. I felt the tickle of legs on my bottom lip and whimpered as I clamped my mouth shut.

They won't kill you, it's an endurance test, I told myself, employing the same tactic that had worked when I'd been over the volcano. *Just ride it out.*

But my skin was crawling with spiders and it was impossible to ignore them, panic and disgust battering at my willpower like colossal tidal waves. I wanted the things off me, I wanted to be anywhere but here. They were crawling up the side of my face now and I knew they would be in my hair. I felt a hot tear slid down my cheek as I squeezed my eyes closed, the contrast to the skittering spiders stark. Revulsion gripped my gut as I felt something inside my ear, and I almost opened my mouth to give up. I had two seeds safe, I could afford to lose one.

Don't you dare! My fierce voice was back inside my head, and I tried to shift my focus to it, tried to ignore the feeling that the spiders were burrowing into my head now, through my ears. If I lost a seed then I had to win one in every other Trial, which seemed highly unlikely. And whether I liked it or not, something inside me had changed. I *wanted* to win. I wanted to have a choice at the end of all this, I wanted there to be a possibility that I could stay in Olympus. S*tay with Hades.*

Come on Persy, what can you do? I channeled determination through myself, trying to focus. Were my powers any use here? The vines were shit at keeping the spiders off me, but there was grass here. I willed my green vines to connect with the earth beneath me, still keeping my mouth and eyes clamped shut, my body frozen in place. The creatures were moving up my nose now, and I was having to breath hard through my nostrils to dislodge them. I felt sick.

Until my vines hit the ground. Happiness coursed through my entire body, the sense of space and life surrounding me forcing out the fear of the spiders just a little. I sent the eager magic I could feel building inside me towards the earth, willing it to find the grass, to fill it with what it needed to flourish. I didn't dare open my eyes to see what was happening, but now I could only feel the spiders that were still trying to burrow their way through my ears and nose, and the ones that had gotten under my corset. The rest I was able to block out. *How long had I been here?* Taking as deep breaths as was possible, I channeled my fear into the ground as life for the yellowing grass, the joy from doing so offsetting the revulsion just enough that I could hold myself together.

When I finally heard the gong I made the mistake of opening my mouth in a relieved gasp. I just saw the hall fading into existence around me as spiders flooded into my mouth. I coughed and choked, my vines vanishing as I clawed at my tongue, but the spiders kept coming. More tears streaked down my face as a sob was ripped from my throat, then I felt a cascade of something warm and soothing pour over my entire body, washing the spiders away with it. Weird tingles flowed through my nose and mouth, and when they stopped, I couldn't feel any more scurrying feet.

I looked up, still frantic, and saw that Artemis was standing up in front of me, a lop-sided smile on her face.

'I think that's got them all,' she said gently. 'And thanks, for sorting out my meadow. Sagittarius could do with some more flowers.'

'Flowers?' I stammered, trying to stop my body shaking and keep my dinner down. She nodded at me, and gestured behind her. A shimmering portal opened up, and through it I could see a meadow brimming with wildflowers, some taller than me and in every color I could think of. The grass was a lush deep green, and dotted with tiny daisies.

'Did- did I just do that?'

'You did. And you endured my test. Well done.' Artemis sat back down and I took another shuddering breath, still rubbing at my arms and chest sub-consciously, and batting at my ears. I believed her that they were gone, but it still felt like I was covered in spiders. I would be burning this damned dress if I got through this. The satyr trotted up again and this time his tray had a small tumbler on it, filled with liquid. I took it carefully in my shaking hands and sipped. It was nectar. Immediately the shudders through my chest and limbs lessened. I felt my legs strengthening, and my pulse slowing. I looked away from the gods, towards the crowd, and saw Hecate at the front, giving me an over the top thumbs up, her thumb dancing with blue flame. Skop was sitting beside her, his tail wagging.

Three tests done, and three seeds safe. Just one more to

endure, and I was getting in my damned shower for the rest of time.

'One more test to find, Persephone, which god will it be?' The commentator's voice was jarring, and I put the tumbler down on the satyr's tray. I looked along the row of gods, and they were all facing me. My gaze settled on Hermes' twinkling eyes and red beard, where he was sitting between Dionysus and Zeus.

'Hermes,' I said, and strode towards him with as much dignity as I could muster. The gods only knew what my hair looked like now, but it really didn't matter. What mattered was getting this Trial over and done with.

'Drink from the cup of tricksters and see if you shall be tested,' beamed Hermes, handing me a goblet. The liquid inside looked like mud, but when I hesitantly sipped from it, it tasted like cherries. I held my breath as I waited, but nothing happened. I let go of the sigh as I handed the messenger god his cup back, and felt a little buoyed by his encouraging expression.

I had Zeus, Ares and Hephaestus left. Frissons of nerves rippled through me as I thought about my choice. It seemed very, very unlikely that Zeus would let the round end without getting involved. Surely the King of the Gods was hiding my last test? If he was, I wanted to find out now, and get it done.

'Zeus,' I said, stepping to my left so that I was in front of the god. A slow smile crossed his face and his formal visage rippled and morphed into the gorgeous blond from the coffee shop.

'Drink from the cup of the skies and see if you shall be

tested,' he drawled and handed me a goblet. I took the cup and started when electricity sparked through my fingertips. Oh, this was going to be a test alright. I looked into his eyes as I sipped the sweet liquid, and his lips parted.

'I'm afraid this might hurt a bit,' he whispered, and the hall vanished.

THIRTY

PERSEPHONE

I'd expected to find myself in an open space, or surrounded my lightning bolts like when Zeus had abducted me, but to my surprise I was in an underground cavern. In fact, it looked and felt like I would expect the Underworld to look and feel. I was standing on the banks of a river of liquid fire, which was running into a dark cave mouth in front of me. I turned slowly on the spot, thrown by how un-Zeus this felt so far. There was nothing else along the rocky river banks, and the high cavern ceiling sloped down towards the dark entrance before me. I peered into the river. It wasn't lava but actual fire, rolling and sloshing like water. It was mesmerizing, and I tore my eyes from it before I could get distracted. The only place to go was the cave, and I wanted this Trial over. So I strode towards the darkness.

The air was hot and humid as I stepped through the arched cave mouth, and the darkness barely receded, the only light coming from the burning river.

I knew instantly that something was wrong. Seriously wrong.

It was as though my senses narrowed to slithers, only specks of sound making it to my ears, and flashes of images to my eyes. Despite the heat the hair on my skin rose, and I stopped moving. I tried to listen for the gong, but all I could hear were fragments of something high pitched, that faded away before I could work out what it was. Things were moving in the shadows, the flickering red light never staying still long enough for me to see what they were. Fear began to churn through me, my stomach tense and uneasy as my black vines slid instinctively from my palms.

Suddenly the flames in the river leapt up, and I cried out and staggered backwards as the scene in front of me was illuminated.

There was a shallow pool of water with an apple tree in the center of it, and chained at the waist to the narrow trunk was what must have once been a man. He was so emaciated his body was barely more substantial than a skeleton, his pale skin paper thin and covered in blistering sores. He stood rigid against the tree, his sunken eyes hollow and staring, his thin lips withered and pulled back from his teeth.

'Water,' he rasped suddenly, and I gasped in fright. *He was alive? How?* I watched in muted horror as the man leaned down towards the pool of water, his skeletal hands trying to form a cup. But as he reached the liquid it shrank away from him, as though it were alive. He let out a wracking hiss, then moved fast, throwing his arms up towards a low hanging branch from the tree, grabbing for an apple. The branch jerked out of the way, his fingers just scraping the fruit as it whooshed out of reach.

'They cursed me,' he croaked, his hollow eyes fixing on

mine. I swallowed hard. 'I fed them my son, and they cursed me never to eat or drink again.'

'Fed them your son?' I breathed, very real fear now hammering through me, my vines hovering. Before he could answer, the flames in the river died down, and the pool and the tree and the awful man vanished.

This wasn't right. Where was the gong? And the commentator's voice with the time? What was I supposed to be enduring? Sure, I was scared shitless, but fear was Hades' power, not Zeus'. I needed to get out of here.

But what if this is the test? You can't afford to lose a seed.

With a snarl, I turned to the cave mouth a few feet behind me. Except it was gone. Panic mingled with the fear, fresh sweat rolling down my neck and making my palms clammy. I was trapped. The flames leapt again, before I could work out what to do, and where the pool had been before there was now a stone table. An enormous muscular man covered in dark hair lay prostrate on it, his abdomen ripped open. I heaved as a vulture swooped down out of nowhere, driving his hooked beak into the man's exposed guts, and he screamed. I turned my head so that I couldn't see, terror now taking over from fear as the giant's agonized shrieks continued. What the fuck was this place?

The flames died down again, and as soon as they did I dropped to my knees. There was no way I was walking through the darkness when I was surrounded by people being tortured. But crawling, I could feel what was before me before I reached it.

I'd barely moved a foot on my hands and knees, before the flames leapt again. My mouth fell open as a wheel made of fire burst to life high above me. It was spinning like a freaking firework, and strapped to its center, skin red raw and blistered, was a naked man. He was screaming the word 'Hera' as he turned and turned, the flames biting at his skin.

Something in my horrified mind jolted, a distant memory of my ancient history studies slotting into place. A man punished for trying to seduce Hera, strapped to a burning wheel to represent burning lust. And a man punished for serving his own son at a feast for the gods by being surrounded by food and water he could never reach. They were both sent to live out their eternal punishments in the depths of hell.

I was in Tartarus.

THIRTY-ONE

PERSEPHONE

I shouldn't be here. This wasn't part of the test, it couldn't be. Something somewhere had gone horribly, horribly wrong. I stayed where I was crouched, my eyes fixed on the grim burning wheel above me, my mind racing as fast as my out-of-control heart. I needed to get out of here. I was trapped in an endless pit of torture, and I needed to get the fuck out of here.

But there were no exits, no pathways, no freaking light. I was so far out of my depth I was drowning.

'Hades,' I whispered, his name coming to my lips unbidden. This was his realm, he was in charge. Surely he would find me here.

'Oh come now, don't be sad. We'll find plenty of people for you to play with down here, fledgling goddess,' a rich female voice echoed from the darkness.

'Who's there?' I called, unable to keep the wobble of fear from my voice.

'My name is Campe, and I guard Tartarus,' she answered, and the man on the flaming wheel soared backwards as a creature I could never have even come close to imagining slithered into the space in front of me.

At least five times my size, she had the body and head of the most beautiful woman, full round breasts and a heart-shaped face housing deep brown eyes and voluptuous lips. But from the waist down she was made of snake. Her enormous lower half was that of a coiled serpent, and as the end of her tail flicked up I saw that it was itself made up of what looked like a hundred smaller snakes. As I dragged my eyes back to her body my gaze was drawn to what was around her neck. It was the most hideous necklace I'd ever seen, each charm lining the golden rope the head of a creature.

'You are admiring my jewelry? It is made of the heads of the fifty most dangerous creatures in Olympus,' she purred. I blinked as I took in the heads, a lion, a bear, a dragon, and many other things I'd never ever seen, and hoped I never would.

'Why am I here?' I choked out.

'That's not my business,' she said, staring down at me. 'But we rarely get such fresh blood down here these days. You will be a delight to the residents.'

'Residents?'

'Oh yes. You've already met Ixion up here,' she gestured to the man on the flaming wheel, 'and poor Tantalus, who fed his son to the gods. But the Titans rule Tartarus. They are deep enough in the pit that they have not yet sensed you, but they will soon enough.'

The fear inside me was so strong that it had forced my tears and panic away entirely. I had reached the point bang in the middle of the crippling terror Hades caused that made me pass out, and the indecisive panic that burgeoning fear instilled. This was fight or flight, and there was nowhere to run.

I forced myself to my feet.

'I am a member of the Underworld palace,' I lied, with as much authority as my shaking body could muster. 'I demand you let me out. Now.'

Campe chuckled softly, the flames of the river dancing in time to the sound.

'A member of the palace? Those vines of yours certainly carry darkness, but you are not royalty.'

'I was,' I said, fiercely. 'And Hades will be pissed if you don't let me go.'

'Hades doesn't visit with us anymore,' she said, touching one hand to her cheek in a kind of mock sadness. 'Such a shame. I would be delighted if your presence brought him to us once more.'

So would I. In fact, I was banking on it.

'Why not?' I asked, deciding that keeping her talking was the best thing to do. It would buy time for Hades to find me. *Please, please let him be coming to find me.*

'He found himself a wife,' Campe said, bending at her huge waist and moving her beautiful face closer to me. The bloody head of a horned lizard bounced against her sternum. 'She became more appealing to him than torture.'

'I can't think why,' I whispered, staring at her morbid necklace.

'What is your name, baby goddess? It is uncommon to come into your powers so old, and you are clearly untrained.'

I scowled up at her. Would she recognize my name? Would it help me if she did?

'Persephone.'

A long hiss erupted from her, her genial expression

morphing into a glare. Her tail lifted, the splayed end rippling as the snakes writhed.

'You are Persephone?'

'Yes, I told you, I was once royalty. Now let me go.'

'Ohhh, how I've waited for this day,' she seethed, her eyes flashing with anger. 'I don't think I will wait for the Titans to wake after all.'

I had about a second's notice, granted purely by intuition, to get out of the way as her tail curled around her body and came smashing down towards me. I tried to roll away from the river of fire, but I stumbled on the rocky ground and found myself shaken to my hands and knees as the ground rumbled with the impact of her tail smacking the rock. I launched myself back to my feet, my vines helping push me up, then began to run blindly as a low, maniacal cackle rose up behind me. 'I wondered where you were all these years, and now you just stumble into my domain. What a delightful twist of fate,' Campe purred around her laughter.

It was too dark, and I couldn't see anything as I got further from the river, Ixion's wheel high above me providing the only slivers of light left. A piercing scream from my right almost made me fall in shock, and a row of men seated on golden chairs flashed into view. Their faces were masks of agony, twisted and contorted with pain. I changed course, but felt something cold and hard smack into me from behind, then I cried out as I was lifted from my feet by an invisible force. I twirled in the air as I rose, my black vines now flailing around me, seeking the unseen enemy. I floated through the stifling air, coming to a stop before Campe, level now with her gleeful face. I was being held up by nothing at all, just like Ixion's wheel. My heart was thudding in my chest as I desperately tried to think of a way out, but she had been right when she'd said this was her domain. Her magic far outstripped mine.

'You took him from me, you little whore,' she snarled, and confusion bit through my fear.

'Took who?' I gasped, as I floated helpless before her.

'The king. He was turning. He was becoming what he was destined to be, and the glorious beast inside him was almost free. Then you took him.'

'Do you mean Hades?' I kicked my legs in the air, trying to right myself, to stop the slow spinning.

'Of course I do,' she hissed, leaning her huge face close to me. She smelled like rotting flesh, the iron tang of blood laced through the scent.

A roar bellowed from beneath us and everything around me, including Campe, shook as it reverberated through the pit. Her face morphed, fear actually flashing through her eyes as her cruel smile dropped. 'He is coming,' she hissed, then slithered backwards on her huge snake tail.

'Hades?' Hope soared inside me.

'No. Cronos.'

Cronos? Wasn't he the Titan who had eaten most of the Olympians? The worst of the lot?

'Shit, shit, shit,' I chanted as I willed my vines down towards the floor, searching desperately for anything to cling to, to pull myself down. But they couldn't get a purchase on the constantly changing surface, and it was too dark to see anything useful. Another roar bellowed around me and a new, more primal terror began to creep through my veins.

'Release her at once!' The command made me gasp in

surprise, and I wheeled in the air, trying to see who had spoken. It wasn't Hades, but I recognized the voice.

'Kerato, how good of you to join us,' hissed Campe, who was still slowly backing away. Her tail was obscured by darkness now, her face and grisly necklace still flickering in the light of Ixion's wheel. 'Hades' lap dog is always welcome here.'

'I said release her, immediately,' The minotaur shouted. I couldn't see him in the darkness below me, but hope surged through me. I was no longer alone.

'If you insist.' My stomach lurched as I dropped abruptly, my vines frantically trying to find something to slow my fall and disorientation completely swamping me. Then a blast of neon blue light blinded me and I froze in mid-air for a split second, before gently tipping forward and floating down.

'You will explain yourself,' hissed another voice, and this time relief hit me hard. *Hades.* As my feet touched the ground I whirled, then stumbled as I saw him.

He was in full-on god mode. He was almost as big as Campe was, shirtless and solid, blue light streaming from his body, and morphing into crawling bodies at his boots. I watched in awestruck fear as the bodies climbed to their feet and began to line up in rows behind him. An army of the dead.

'Hades, you're just in time,' Campe purred. 'Cronos is on his way.'

Fear and rage as real as I'd ever seen filled Hades' bright blue eyes, the usual silver nowhere to be seen. The temperature soared, and a jet of blinding blue light smashed into Campe. She screamed as she was thrown backwards, the necklace around her colossal neck splitting and animal heads flying everywhere.

'Get her out of here, now!' roared Hades, and I felt my arm being grabbed by a clawed hand. I turned, Kerato's horned face inches from mine.

'Sorry, my lady,' he grunted, but as white light began to glow around him, he bellowed and staggered backwards, releasing his grip on me.

'Kerato!' I shouted, as Hades' light illuminated the red blood dripping down his shoulder around the tip of a protruding blade. Then a cackling woman's face appeared behind the minotaur, her youthful, deranged eyes dancing with malice. 'Leave him alone!' I yelled, whipping my vines towards the new threat.

Another roar ripped through the space, and the fire in the river suddenly became an inferno, leaping a hundred feet into the air. Red and blue light crashed together, and I tore my eyes from Kerato to Hades. His face was strained, both hands held high as though he was holding back something I couldn't see.

'He's here. Kerato, get her out of Tartarus,' he said through gritted teeth. But the minotaur's eyes were glassy and he was clutching his chest in silence as the human looking woman stepped around him. She was wearing a black toga and her bright red hair was piled high on her head.

'Yeah, he won't be taking you anywhere,' she said with a shrug, and poked Kerato's shoulder with her pointed finger. The minotaur crumpled to the ground. 'The boss wants you for something special.'

'Who are you?' I stammered, eyes flicking between Kerato's body and her.

'Ankhiale, Titan goddess of heat,' she took a low bow as she spoke, and her black toga burst into flames. 'I'm responsible for the interior decorating down here,' she grinned at me. She looked completely fucking mad.

'Ankhiale, if you lay a finger on her, I will make your life a million times more miserable than it already is!' roared Hades. She gave another cackling laugh.

'You think that's possible, oh Lord of the Dead? Give me a fucking break.' She was stalking closer to me, and I didn't know what to do. Should I use my vines, try to take her power? 'You won't be able to hold King Cronos back much longer, Hades. And you're breaking the rules, letting a pretty little thing like her down here. He won't obey you this time.'

Hades gave a wretched snarl, and I struck. With the tiniest flick of my wrists, I sent both vines at the woman, screaming as they made contact with her and heat seared through me like acid. But I held on, and the vines coiled around her shoulders, black tattoos blossoming under her flaming skin.

'What- how- get off me!' she shrieked, and gripped my vines in her hands. More heat, as hot or hotter than the volcano from earlier, burned along my vines and into my body, and the pain was almost too much to bear.

'*Get to me, now,*' Hades' desperate voice sounded in my mind. I did as he told me without question, letting the vines disintegrate as I whirled around. I let out a gasp of shock as I realized that the army of blue corpses were surrounding me, and as I pelted towards Hades, they followed, keeping their protective ring unbroken. I felt a blast of heat burn at my back and ran faster, throwing out a green vine and wrapping it around Hades' enormous leg and dragging myself towards him. The second my fingers landed on his body, the world flashed white.

THIRTY-TWO

PERSEPHONE

'W hat in the name of Olympus is going on!' roared Zeus, as the throne room materialized around us. I heaved deep breaths as shudders wracked my body, still clinging to Hades, vaguely aware that he must have shrunk because he was stroking a hand down my back.

'You're safe now,' he said quietly, pulling me tight to him. I felt like I was on fire, my stinging skin still burning, my lungs aching. Fear and confusion and pain were blistering through me.

'Answer me, Hades!' Zeus bellowed again, and I felt a crackle of electricity around us.

'Give her a damned minute will you!' Hades shouted. 'I don't know what happened, it was your cup she drank from.'

He tightened his grip around my shoulders, and I felt a tingle of magic wash over me, cooling my skin.

You're safe now. I repeated his words in my mind, until I began to believe them, my heart finally beginning to slow its sprint around my ribcage.

'Tartarus is the worst fucking place in the world,' I

mumbled into his chest, tying to suppress the sobs that the adrenaline and tension had brought bubbling to the surface.

'That's the idea. And you should never have been anywhere near it.'

With a deep breath, I pushed myself gently away from him, blinking up into his face. His smoky disguise engulfed him as I moved back, but I got a glimpse of his silver eyes, and the rage in them set my pulse racing again. This wasn't over.

'Are you suggesting someone other than one of us sent her to Tartarus?' said Poseidon's voice, and I looked towards the sea god. He, Zeus, Athena, Ares and Apollo were all standing up, every one of them looking alert and angry.

'Unless anyone cares to admit to playing a bad prank,' added Hermes. His usually playful smile was significantly absent. Nobody spoke.

'We will get to the bottom of this, brother,' hissed Zeus accusingly. Smoke billowed around Hades, tinged with blue light.

'Why the fuck would I do this?' roared Hades. 'Even if you rule out the fact that I don't want her dead, now Campe won't do a damned thing I tell her, and Cronos knows Persephone is here. You think I'd cause this shit in my own realm?' Icy cold air was streaming from him as his voice got louder, the slithering tone taking over. Zeus' expression changed from angry to wary as I watched. *Was Zeus frightened of Hades?*

There was a long pause, the tension practically tangible.

'We will deal with this in private,' snapped Zeus eventually, and sat down hard on his throne. The other gods followed suit, and Hecate appeared by my side.

'We gotta go,' she said with a glance at Hades. He nodded, and she flashed us out of the throne room.

We were back in my room, and the first thing Hecate did was give me a massive glass of nectar.

'Shit, Persy, Hades shouted something about Campe and Cronos. Please, please tell me you weren't in Tartarus.' I blinked up at her, and she shook her head and sat down on the bed beside me.

'*You have got to be joking,*' said Skop, jumping on my other side. '*You were in fucking Tartarus?*'

'A really big snake woman tried to kill me, then a goddess of fire killed Kerato while Hades held Cronos back, and then Hades got us out of there. That's the condensed version,' I said. A small sob escaped me as I remembered Kerato crumpling to the ground. 'He gave his life trying to help me,' I whispered, rubbing at my filthy cheek.

'Hades' guards are immortal, don't worry,' Hecate said quickly. Her face had gone pale again as she stared wide-eyed at me. 'Hades held back Cronos?'

'Yeah.'

'Persy, this is bad. Like really bad. Dying during a Trial is one thing, but becoming a Titan plaything in an eternal pit of torture?'

'Is that why Cronos wanted me alive? To be a plaything?'

Hecate didn't answer for a long while.

'Hades might know more once he's spoken to the others,' she said eventually. 'Have a shower, you'll feel better.'

I nodded and stood up, finishing what was in the glass and relishing the strength it gave me.

'Will you stay here?'

'Of course,' she nodded.

'Thank you. I really don't want to be on my own right now,' I admitted quietly.

'I'm not going anywhere, Persy.'

'*Me either*,' said Skop. Feeling eternally grateful, I walked to my washroom, pausing at the door.

'And you're sure Kerato will be OK?'

'Yes. It might take him a while to regenerate, but he's a demon. He'll be fine.'

'Ok. Good.' I turned and stepped through the door to my washroom, and froze in my tracks.

My apartment. I was in my bedroom, in my apartment in New York. My mind slowed almost to a stop as I blinked around the room. It looked like I had never left, the bed neatly made, a pair of blue jeans slung over the back of my easy chair, and my laptop open on the little desk, humming quietly.

I turned slowly on the spot, to see Hades standing behind me. I opened my mouth to ask him what was going on, but my words failed as I saw the look in his eyes.

THIRTY-THREE

HADES

As I watched her eyes widen in surprise to see me, I felt like someone had plunged a dagger into my heart. She opened her mouth, but didn't speak as she took in my face. My feelings must have been written all over it.

Devastation.

There was no other word that could describe what was churning through my ancient body.

'I'm sorry,' I said, my voice coming out brittle. Her features creased, a frown taking over her beautiful face. She had been through hell tonight, and she deserved to be treated like a victorious Queen. But we were here instead.

'Sorry for what?' she asked, her words painfully slow. She knew what I was going to say. I could see the fear in her bright green eyes.

'It's over.'

'What's over?'

'The Trials. Olympus, for you. It's over.' My voice was on the edge of cracking, emotion I'd spent over twenty years burying now building into a blazing pit of turmoil.

'No,' she said, and stepped towards me, shaking her head. 'No, you can't do this.'

She didn't know how close to the truth she was. If I didn't do it fast, I couldn't leave her here, in the mortal world.

But I had no choice.

'You wanted to come home. And now you are. It's over.'

Her eyes filled with tears as she punched out, hitting me on the arm.

'Stop fucking saying that! It's not over!'

Something white hot burned at the back of my own eyes. But gods did not cry.

'If I say you're done, then you're done.'

'Why? Why are you doing this? You said you wanted me to win, to be your Queen? You said Zeus had made sure I couldn't quit the Trials?' Tears were streaming down her cheeks, tracking filth from the pits of hell with them. The thought of her down there, in the darkest reaches of the most dangerous place in the world... The monster inside me roared. It had been awake since I lost her, since she had drunk from Zeus' cup. It had relished the fight with Cronos. And now I could barely contain it.

Cronos knew Persephone was in Olympus. Which meant she couldn't stay.

'I'll deal with Zeus,' I said quietly.

'So you could have sent me back all that time ago? When I actually wanted to leave? And you lied, told me you couldn't?'

'No. The other gods will back me on this. Zeus will have no choice but to abandon the Trials.'

'Will... will you marry Minthe?' Her words were barely audible, the pain in her expression unbearable.

I couldn't answer her.

'I can't believe you're doing this. I can't believe you actually made me want to win, want to be with you, and now you're fucking leaving me here!' She was shouting, her tears still streaming, her face furious.

I wanted to die. I wanted to throw myself into Tartarus's river of fire and burn to ash, rather than deal with losing her again. I couldn't do it. I couldn't see her like this, be the cause of her pain.

'She will cause the end of Olympus.' The words Poseidon had bellowed at me not ten minutes before echoed through my head. 'If she ever meets Cronos, we are all doomed.'

I had no choice.

'Say something, you bastard!' she shouted, and another piece of my shattered heart splintered away, lost to the hungry beast inside me.

'You can't keep a light this bright in the dark,' I whispered, gathering every ounce of control I had left, and drinking in her every feature. 'I'm sorry.'

With a heartbreaking wrench that destroyed the last of my fragile grip, I left.

Someone would die tonight. Likely many. The beast inside me had broken free.

<<<<>>>>

THE PROMISE OF HADES

ONE

PERSEPHONE

'Wait, wait, wait. Slow down. You seriously expect me to believe that you were kidnapped by Zeus and taken to *Olympus?*' My brother stared at me as I paced frantically up and down my small room, his hazel eyes wide.

'Yes! It's true. I was there for weeks.'

'Persy, I spoke to you on the phone yesterday.' He ran a hand through his sandy hair and shook his head as he glanced around my trashed room. 'Should I call mom? Are you OK?'

I stopped pacing and screwed my face up. Gods, I'd love to see my mom and dad. But they were nearly a thousand miles away in their RV, touring Atlanta. And if Sam phoned them and told them I was babbling about being kidnapped, they would likely use the little money they had to fly back to New York. The selfish part of me wanted nothing more, but the rational part of me answered Sam.

'No,' I sighed, and sat down. 'Don't call them.'

'Tell me again what happened,' he said, his voice gentle. 'And... What are you wearing and why is your hair white?'

. . .

I had called my brother the second my wracking sobs and blind rage had lessened enough for me speak. If I had any question or doubt about the strength of my feelings for Hades, the shock of him leaving me had completely dispelled them.

It felt like a piece of my chest was missing; breathing, thinking, walking - *everything* was now staggered and difficult. The sense of wrongness I felt when I looked around my room only served to widen the gaping hole inside me.

I'd never felt betrayal and rejection like it. I *couldn't* have left him like that. I couldn't have flashed myself away, knowing I would never see him again. My body and mind wouldn't have let me do it, I was sure.

Which I knew was irrational. Not a day earlier I had told him I didn't even know if I wanted to be with him. But the moment I had heard him say those words, *a light this bright can't be kept in the dark,* something had gripped my insides in a vice-like hold. Something bright and hot and intensely fierce. It carried his sadness, his passion, his love, straight into my heart and it had overwhelmed me. And it had flared to life only long enough to be doused out seconds later, when he'd flashed from the room, leaving me for good.

I'd cried so hard I'd almost thrown up. Then anger took over, fury forcing the tears out. Before I knew what I was doing I was launching my belongings around my room, cushions and clothes flying. Then I had noticed my purse on the bed, along with my leather biker jacket, and sense had bled through my rage. I'd dug out my cell phone and plugged it in to charge, then called Sam.

He was at my door faster than I thought possible, and I'd thrown myself at him, fresh tears filling my eyes as I took in his concerned face. A face I never thought I would see again. When I was done sobbing and hugging him, I had tried to tell him what had happened. Unsuccessfully, it seemed.

'I'm not from America. I'm from a place called Olympus, which is ruled by the Greek gods. I was married to Hades before, but I did something awful and they sent me here to have a new life as a human mortal, with no memories.' Sam stared at me, eyebrows high, and I took a deep breath. Was what I was saying even possible?

There was no way I could have imagined it all. Hades' silver eyes filled my mind. No way whatsoever. They were real.

'And Zeus kidnapped you?' my brother prompted.

'Yes. Hades disobeyed him publicly and created a new realm in Olympus, so to punish him Zeus let a bunch of women compete to be his wife, and he took me from New York to force me to compete too.'

Real concern was now clear on Sam's face.

'You were competing to marry Hades? The devil?'

'Yes. I'm wearing this torn, burnt dress because I was in the middle of a Trial that went wrong. I ended up in Tartarus.'

Sam stood up.

'We need to go to the emergency room. You've had a stroke or something,' he said, his voice strained.

'And you think having a stroke extended to dying my hair white and doing this to a ballgown?' I asked, waving my shredded skirt at him. 'I'm serious Sam, I'm telling the truth.'

'But, Persy, that's not possible. It's simply not possible.'

'That's what I thought at first, but it is! I had power, Sam!'

'Power?'

'Yes, I could make plants grow. And I had vines that came out of my palms!'

'Like fucking Spiderman? Persy, we need to go to the emergency room. Now.'

'No,' I said, shaking my head.

'Then what the hell do you want me to do?' He threw his hands in the air and glared at me.

'I need to get back there,' I whispered. Sam's mouth fell open.

'To the place where you were competing to marry the devil?' I nodded. 'You want to go back there?'

Something that might have been relief washed through me as I answered Sam's question.

'Yes.' I *did* want to go back. To Hades. I had to be where he was. I finally had one solid decision made in my head. Dread replaced my relief fast though. I was no longer trapped in the Underworld. Now I was trapped in New York.

I had no way of getting to Hades.

'I gotta call mom, Persy. This is fucked up, you're not well.' Sam moved to my side slowly, putting an arm around me as he sat down. I lifted my hand and peered at my palm, digging deep inside myself to feel for my power.

There was nothing.

'Sam, I've never fit in. Now I know why,' I whispered.

'Maybe you've invented being married to the devil to try to make yourself feel stronger?' he said gently. 'Perhaps you've been under too much pressure with the program at the botanical gardens or...' He trailed off, his face darkening. 'Did something bad happen? Has someone hurt you?'

'No! I swear to you, nothing awful has happened to me and triggered some sort of mental breakdown,' I told him firmly, and his face relaxed. 'But Sam, I *am* stronger. I was a freaking goddess. All this time.'

I felt a flare of something deep in my stomach, a stab of rage and pain, and I gasped as I realized it wasn't coming from me. *It was Hades.* I could sense his dark smoky power under the physical feeling. It was the same as what I'd felt before he had left, though the emotion wasn't sadness now. It was primal and animalistic, filled with fear and fury.

He was breaking. I could feel it.

'The bond,' I murmured, my skin crawling as the feeling spread through me. 'I have to help him,' I said, looking up at Sam, the urgency I felt making my voice crack. 'He made a mistake leaving me here, I have to help him.'

'Help who?'

'Hades. He's in trouble.'

'Erm, I'm sure the Lord of the Dead can handle himself,' Sam said, more calmly than his face suggested he was.

'No. No, I have to get back.' I leaped to my feet, yet more tears burning the back of my eyes. Pain and rage spasmed through me, and I almost cried out. Sam stood up fast, taking my wrist in his hand.

'Come on. We'll get help.'

I started to go with him, toward the door, but faltered as I realized what he meant.

'I'm not ill, Sam, I swear!' Frustration was welling inside me, my own anger mingling with the intense fury flowing into me from the bond to Hades.

My brother's grip on my wrist tightened, even as his face softened.

'I'm sorry, Persy, but we need to get you help.' He tugged me and I stumbled. He would never hurt me, but if he thought he was helping me I wouldn't be surprised if he picked me up and slung me over his shoulder. He was a lot bigger than I was.

'Sam, stop!'

My shout was cut off though, as blinding white light filled the room.

Sam let go of me as we both threw our arms in front of our eyes instinctively. Hope surged through me. Was it Hades? *Please, please let it be Hades.* I blinked furiously, and let out a cry of relief as a figure came into focus in front of me.

'Hecate!' I half sobbed, and threw myself at her. If it wasn't Hades, Hecate was the next best thing. She could take me to him.

'Erm, I don't do hugs,' she said, patting me awkwardly on the back as I wrapped my arms around her.

'P-Persy?' I heard Sam's almost whispered voice behind me, and let go of Hecate to turn to him. 'Persy, who is your outrageously hot friend and how did she appear out of thin air?' His face was pale, his hazel eyes huge.

'Outrageously hot, huh? I like him,' Hecate said, looking at me. 'He can come too, if you like.'

'I need to get to Hades, something awful is happening,' I said to her, ignoring my brother and gripping her shoulder urgently.

'Why the fuck do you think I'm here? Much as I like you, Persy, I wouldn't risk crossing every freaking god in Olympus if I didn't have a damned good reason.' Her face was serious, her eyes sparking with blue power. 'He's snapped, Persy. I've never seen wrath like it. So far we've been able to keep him in the Underworld, but he's too strong. If he gets out or Zeus discovers that he has lost control like this and put all of Olympus in danger...' She trailed off, her meaning clear. Ice seemed to snake down my spine, my skin fizzing with fear.

'Zeus would kill him?'

'Or worse.'

'Take me to him. Now,' I said.

In answer, the world flashed white.

TWO

PERSEPHONE

I f it weren't for the fiercely strong grip Hades had over my emotions, I would have begged Hecate to take me back to New York the second my eyes cleared.

We were standing in a cavern similar to the Empusa's lair, except it was much bigger, the walls glowing deep red and the smell almost unbearable.

There were bodies everywhere. Few of them appeared to be human, but all of them looked as though they had been ripped apart by an animal. Trying desperately to ignore my roiling stomach, I scanned the gruesome space for Hades but saw only corpses.

'Shit, he's moved,' muttered Hecate, then I heard heaving and retching. I turned, and felt the blood drain from my face as I saw my brother, spewing his guts up onto the cavern floor.

'Sam? Hecate, why the fuck did you bring him here?'

'I told you he could come with us, now shut up,' she said, and her eyes turned white as she glowed blue. 'Shit,

shit, shit, he's nearly at the mouth of Tartarus, she said, and grabbed and me and Sam, before flashing again.

The river of fire we'd been transported to flared into life beside us, but I didn't even notice it.

Hades was *monstrous*.

There was no other word for him. He was the size of a building as he moved towards the cave mouth, his back to us. His body seemed swollen with hulking muscle, and something black was moving under his skin, licks of smoke coiling from him. Blue light emanated from his body, but there was no army of defensive corpses forming around him this time. The light was forming a carpet of carnage in his wake, broken bodies with faces twisted in terror surrounding him as he screamed.

'Campe! I'm coming for you!'

I heard a thump behind me, and spun to see Sam collapsed on the ground.

'Hecate, get him out of here, he's human, he'll die!' As I said the words I felt my vines spring to life in my palms.

Without a word Hecate knelt to grab my brother, and they disappeared.

'You're next, Cronos!' bellowed Hades.

'Hades!' I yelled, as loudly as I could. He didn't falter, only a foot from the cave mouth now. 'Hades!' I tried again, and launched my vines at him. Just as his foot moved into the darkness, my black vines wrapped around his enormous shoulders.

Darkness consumed me completely.

Kill. Die. Fear. Burn. Blood.

The words hammered through my head and I gasped, dropping to one knee. There was no light. Only sparks of life flaring in my vision, calling to me. They needed to be extinguished. Everything needed to die. Fear always won. It could not be conquered. Death was the only certainty.

'Persephone?' The voice was strained, but light crept back into the edges of my vision as the sound of my name filtered through to me. 'Persephone, is that really you?'

'Yes,' I gritted out, unable to see him, but sure it was Hades speaking. 'You have to stop.'

'I can't. I can't.'

'Please. I feel it now. The bond. Can't you?' Hot tears streamed down my cheeks as wave after wave of hatred and violence crashed down the vines, flowing into me, poisoning me.

Kill. Kill them all. Tear them apart. Leave nothing. None of them deserve to live.

'The monster inside me is too strong. It will always win.' Hades' voice was suddenly hard and cold, and the little light seeped away again fast.

'No! You can fight it, you're not a monster!' I shouted, but the torrent of fury coming from him said differently. He was *worse* than a monster. He didn't just want to destroy, he wanted to torture. To ruin, to break, to brutalize.

I had to sever the connection to him, I had to remove my vines. I couldn't take his power, couldn't handle the fearsomely brutal desires. He had told me that he was too strong for me to ever steal his power, and he had been right. There was too much, it could flow endlessly into me and he would still be just as strong. It felt like he was filling me with his wrath, and every second I held on I lost more of myself. Why did my power do this? Why couldn't I take the fury away from him, instead of turning myself into something just as awful?

The gold vines. The thought powered through the cascade of furious darkness. *The gold vines did the opposite of the black ones.*

I willed the vines that I could no longer see to turn from black to gold, clinging desperately to the remnants of my infatuation with him, the strength of my connection to him, the desire to make him happy, content, loved. I recalled everything Hecate had told me about him, how he'd given up parts of himself to serve Olympus, how he had been forced to become this beast by his brother. I filled my head with the feeling of his lips on mine, his hands on my skin, his beautiful silver eyes, always so filled with emotion when he looked at me. He had created life. As much of him that craved death and destruction wanted life and light. I could give that to him.

I poured my power into my vines, praying it was reaching him.

'Persephone.'

I opened my eyes and gasped, shocked by the light. I focused on Hades, and took in a deep breath. He was still huge, but the blue glow and all the bodies had gone. The new light was coming from the gold vines stretching from me to him, morphing into shining tattoos that coiled around his shoulders and chest, covering almost all of his skin.

His eyes were fixed on mine, silver and stunning and haunted.

'Hades,' I breathed. 'You're back.'

'So are you,' he croaked, and thudded to his knees.

THREE

HADES

S*he was back.*

I was vaguely aware of Hecate, and her flashing us somewhere else, but I didn't let go of Persephone's hand, didn't
take my eyes from her tear-filled green ones.

She was back.

'I'm sorry,' I said, as she pushed me backward. I felt my legs
hit something and sat down hard. My head was still full of
darkness, but it was receding. The beast called to me, but
green and gold light burned hot through my body, drowning
out its voice, piecing my barriers back together, reinforcing
them with glowing vines. Her power.

'Sorry for what? Dumping me in New York, or nearly

getting yourself killed?' she snapped, and I blinked. She shoved something into my hands. 'Drink. Now.'

I did as I was bid, the sweet taste of nectar forcing the evil thoughts even further into the recesses. I realized I was still twice her size as I drained the tiny glass too quickly, and shrank myself down.

'I'll leave you to it, boss,' Hecate said, but I still didn't look at her. I couldn't take my eyes from Persephone. My Queen. My savior.

'Thanks, Hecate. And, erm, please be nice to Sam,' Persephone said to her.

'As if I'd be anything else,' Hecate responded, and there was a flash. Persephone looked back at me, and her face was stern. 'I'm only here because Hecate cares so much about you. You're an idiot,' she said, exasperation and fear mingling on her beautiful face. 'If Zeus found out that you lost control like that, what would he do?'

'He would give my job to someone else, and leave me in Tartarus for eternity,' I answered. And that's what I had wanted. There was no life without her. No point existing. And I was a monster. I was destined for that hell-hole in the end anyway.

'Hades, you are bound to me, and I to you. Even in New York, I could feel your suffering. Do you think it was fair to put me through that?' Her voice was strained, and I realized she was barely containing her emotion.

Electricity seemed to spark through my body as she spoke, and something the monster had snuffed out completely leaped back to life. *Hope.*

'You feel the bond?'

'Yes. I feel it. I feel you. And you were right. It's not something. It's *everything*.' I reached for her, but she stepped backward, out of my grasp. 'Hades, you need to understand. I felt what is inside you. And it is evil and cruel and toxic.' Her voice shook as she spoke, and I could feel the devastation closing in around me. The monster was stronger than the bond. *The monster was stronger than everything.* 'Instead of fighting it, instead of letting me help you, you left me. You left me and you let it win.'

She wasn't mad at the monster, I realized. *She was mad at me.* Shame washed over me as her expression hardened.

'You are the King of the Underworld. If I am to be your Queen one day, you need to start fucking acting like one.' My mouth dropped open. 'Everything here bows to you, the worst and most vicious demons, the cruelest gods trapped in Tartarus, all of it. That thing inside you is no stronger than they are.' I stared at her. She was right. Why had I never seen it that way? 'And if the one thing that would allow you to lose control of it is losing the woman you're bonded to, why the fuck would you do something as stupid as leaving me?'

'I... I had no choice,' I whispered.

'Hades, I am so sick of not knowing anything, of others making decisions about my life without me being involved, and being told there's no choice.'

'I'm sorry. I'm so sorry. I shouldn't have left you.'

'I *couldn't* have left you,' she whispered, her face a mask of betrayal.

'Well, apparently nor could I,' I snapped, rubbing my hands across my face. 'I don't know how many I killed. Most are demons who will regenerate.' Many weren't. Self-loathing roiled through my gut.

'Then why do it? Why did you leave me?'

I closed my eyes and let out a long breath. I had to make her understand. I couldn't let her think I didn't love her. I couldn't.

'You must never meet Cronos,' I said eventually, opening my eyes. She frowned.

'The titan in Tartarus?'

Apprehension and fear clouded her face and I reached for her again. She took my hand hesitantly, and a spark of something thrummed through my skin.

'Persephone, you can take power from others. If you were to take too much, from a far stronger being, you would not be able to hold onto it.'

'I don't understand.'

'There's no easy way to say this. Cronos is trapped, his power severely limited in Tartarus. If he were to use you as a vessel to channel his power...' I trailed off.

'What? What would happen?' Her eyes were filled with fear now.

'Your body would expel the magic,' I said tightly, rage and terror bubbling up again at the thought. 'Destroying you and everything around you.'

'You're telling me I'm a fucking bomb?'

'No. Only if you take the power of something exceptionally strong.'

'Like you?' she whispered. I shook my head.

'No. Stronger. Cronos is one of the original Titans, born of the sky and earth themselves. He is primordial in strength. You would be using his own power to destroy Tartarus.'

'Wouldn't that destroy him too?'

'A god can't be killed by their own power.'

She let out a long breath, then sat down beside me. I'd been so dazed that I hadn't even taken in my surroundings, and only then did I realize that we were in my own bedchamber, sitting on my bed.

'Is that why Poseidon hates me? Why he thinks I'm

dangerous?' asked Persephone, her voice small. I looked back to her, noticing she was still wearing the red ballgown, scorched and torn.

'Yes.'

'Why didn't you tell me all this before? I would never have tried to get my powers back,' she said. 'If I didn't have my vines, there would be no risk of Cronos using them.'

'If I had told you this before, you would have been over-whelmed. And by the time you had eaten the first seed it was too late.'

'Take my powers away again,' she said, her eyes wide.

'No. I'm never leaving you again. If you become Queen of the Underworld, you must have your powers back, or you would not survive here. And...' I reached out, cupping her cheek in my hand. 'And I need your magic. You are the only one who can save me, Persephone.'

FOUR

PERSEPHONE

H ades' words reverberated through all the other thoughts ricocheting around my brain. *You're the only one who can save me.*

I knew it was true. I was the light to his dark, the balm to his pain, the healer of his shattered soul. The invisible connection to him burned hot inside me, and the desire to help him, heal him, take away all his pain, was overwhelming.

'Could... could you love a monster?' he asked me, hesitantly. I stared into his eyes, the question stirring emotions I had never, ever felt before. I pictured him as I'd just seen him, towering and blue and fearsome, the poisonous cruelty pouring into me through my vines.

But that wasn't him.

'No. I couldn't love a monster. But I could love you.' He gripped my hand harder, his angular face pinched and more fearful than I thought he could look.

'You have seen what is inside me,' he whispered.

'And I charge you to never let it win again. I will do

whatever it takes to help you, Hades. You carry a burden heavier than most, but it does not define you.'

I was vaguely aware of the commitment I was making with my words, but they left my lips anyway, and the bond between us swelled and burned even hotter inside me. I knew with utter certainty that I had to be where Hades was. For as long as I lived, I needed to be by his side. He was my home. He was everything.

'I love you, Persephone,' he said, and his silver eyes were shining, all traces of melancholy gone.

I had never loved a man before, and I had nothing to compare what I was feeling with, but there was no doubt in my mind that this intense need for him to be happy, the need for him to be safe and with me always, was love.

'I love you,' I told him, and we moved together, our lips meeting.

Sparks of pleasure burst from the contact, his tongue seeking out mine with a sense of urgency that I relished. I needed him. I needed to show him how much I wanted him, needed there to be no gap between us, no distance for doubt or fear to fill.

His hands moved to my face, fingers caressing my cheek, then running through my tangled hair. I wrapped my own arms around his neck, deepening the kiss, heat and moisture pooling between my legs. Then he moved quickly, one arm around my back and the other under my legs, scooping me up into his arms. I gave a little squeak and he beamed at me, eyes gleaming with lust and promise.

'A bath, for my Queen,' he said huskily, and stood up. I kissed his jaw and neck as he carried me across the lavish room, and was rewarded with a strained grunt. I moved my kisses lower, across his collarbone. I could feel little sparks of pleasure through my whole body every time my lips met his skin. Was that the bond? If kisses felt this good... 'If you keep doing that I'll take you against that wall, and that's not how I want our first time to be,' he ground out, and I looked up at him.

'As long as you take me, I don't care,' I said, surprised at how husky my own voice sounded. I had wanted him for what seemed like forever, and I was ready. He gave a small growl, then kicked open a door in front of us. I gazed around at what looked like a freaking palace made of marble, slowly realizing it was a washroom. The bath was no ordinary bath though, it was a pool set into the stone floor, fed by a wall of quietly cascading water. A unit with two sinks and a long, ornate mirror lined the other wall.

Hades set me down on my feet, and stepped back from me, folding his arms across his bare chest.

'You can't bathe in your dress,' he said. Excitement quivered through me, making me ache.

'You'll need to undo it for me,' I answered, turning my back to him. Painfully slowly, he untied the lacing at the back, the bodice loosening around me.

'Done,' he grunted, and I turned back to him. The movement was enough to cause the loosened dress to drop to the floor around my feet, and his lips parted as he took in a breath.

'You are so beautiful,' he said. I knew he meant it, and confidence surged through me as I hooked my thumbs into the sides of my panties and slid them down. 'So, so beautiful,' he breathed, his eyes fixed between my thighs. Then they shot back up to mine, and he gave me a wicked grin as he snapped his fingers.

His jeans vanished.

I barely kept my footing as my gaze locked on him, hard and ready and freaking *glorious*. Desire was pounding at me now, slick and hot and untamable. But before I could throw myself at him he had scooped me up again, and was walking into the pool. Pleasure fizzed out from every point of contact our bare skin made, and I let out a wobbly moan of pleasure as hot water lapped at my skin as he moved deeper into the pool.

He set me on my feet once more when I was chest deep, the water moving against my hard nipples, then a bar of soap appeared in his hand. I cocked my head, about to ask him what he was doing but he spoke first.

'I want to wash away the horrors of this day, and give you some much, much better memories,' he said. Then he closed the gap between us, his soapy hands brushing over my shoulders, my back, down to my waist... I tensed with pleasure as his hands roamed, and when they reached my breasts he moved his head down and kissed me, my moan lost against his lips. His tongue flicked against mine in time with his fingers over my body and I willed them lower. The desire to feel him was now unstoppable, and I ran my hands over my own body, covering them in the foamy lather, then planted them on his rock hard abs. I felt him tense, his movements pausing for a split second, then speeding up, his finger and thumb now pinching at my nipples, causing pulses of painful pleasure in my core. I moved my hands down faster too, delighting in the feel of his solid muscles, his powerful body, the thought of everything he could do with it... My fingers moved under the water at his navel, and I soon felt coarse hair. Excitement made my breathing shallow, and I broke the kiss off to gulp down air, but as my fingers closed around him he kissed me again, hard and fierce.

I moved my hand along him in awe, and he suddenly wrapped one arm around the small of my back and lifted me from the pool floor. I gasped as he put his other hand under my leg, lifting me higher and making me let go of him to cling to his neck, wrapping my thighs around his waist. His hard length was pressed against me, and I gripped him tightly, leaning close to his ear.

'Take me. Please.'

'Tell me I'm yours,' he growled.

'I'm yours and you are mine.'

He lowered me slightly, and fiery pleasure spasmed through me as I felt him at my entrance.

'I'm yours and you are mine,' I repeated into his neck, almost delirious with need.

He lowered me again, pushing and stretching me exquisitely slowly.

'Once more,' he gasped, and I moved in his arms to look deep into his eyes.

'I'm yours and you are mine,' I breathed, and watched his eyes cloak with desire before he lowered me fully onto him. I threw my head back, crying out as my body clamped around him, filling me almost to the point of pain, but not quite. He moaned as his strong arms lifted me again, and shuddering pleasure rolled through me, obliterating every-thing but him.

Each time he moved me up and down I lost more of myself to his body, my mind taken over completely by the unbelievable feeling of rightness, the mounting power building inside me, growing with every thrust. It wasn't long before my whole body felt like it was alight with ecstasy, each time he filled me becoming more sure I would lose control.

'I love you, Persephone' he gasped, and I let go

completely, my orgasm crashing through my body. He cried out and tensed, and I pressed myself against him, kissing him hard as he came, my core still hammered by waves of pleasure.

Slowly the water around us stilled, and Hades pushed his hand into my hair, pressing my heaving chest to his as I shuddered.

'You were made for me,' I told him, my voice breathless.

'Yes,' he said, and kissed me softly as he lifted me off him, back to unsteady feet. 'We were made for each other.'

He led me to the wall of cascading water, where we showered, soaping and stroking each other's bodies like greedy teenagers. When we were done, he carried me back to his bedroom, and laid me gently on the massive draped bed. I looked around the room curiously. Like Hecate's, it was dark and elegant, with imposing dark-wood furniture and soft black fabric. But as I looked up, I gave a little gasp of surprise. Instead of the starry rock ceiling in my own rooms, his was glowing with golden vines.

'So I always think of you, last thing at night and first thing in the morning,' he said, laying down beside me.

'How did I spend so many years not even knowing you existed?' I murmured, stroking my fingers down his stubbled jaw.

'I'm sorry,' he said.

'You need to stop saying that. I've forgiven you.' And it was true. I still hated a hundred or more things about Olympus, but I knew that whatever Hades had done, he had done it for me.

'I promise I will never leave you again,' he said, raw intensity making his voice thick.

'Good,' I said, and happiness blossomed in my chest. 'Now, I believe you said something about worshiping me?'

'You wish is my command, my Queen,' he said, the wicked gleam back in his eyes.

He rolled on top of me quickly, the feel of his hot skin making mine burst to life with tingles. I stared up at his beautiful, godly body and he licked his lips slowly. I squirmed.

'I recall you telling me you would make me forget my own name,' I ventured, my breath half held.

'So I did,' he answered, and lowered his head. He took my nipple in his mouth, nibbling and sucking, and I arched into him, instantly ready for him again. He kissed his way down my stomach, trails of heated sensation burning in his wake. When he reached the apex of my thighs he slowed, his tongue teasing me, as he kissed and nipped the tops of my thighs, coming dangerously close but never quite there.

'Please,' I panted, and his beautiful eyes flashed, before his tongue finally settled right between my legs. 'Oh good gods,' I moaned as I sank back, pleasure consuming me.

He was right. A few minutes later, I couldn't have told anyone my name if my life had depended on it.

FIVE

PERSEPHONE

W e made love over and over, neither one of us able to get enough of the other. Every time the uncomfortable thought of Tartarus or the Trials entered my head, I kissed him instead of voicing my fears, and he kissed me back like there was nothing in the world more important. He made me feel incredible. He made me feel like I was worth a thousand times what I had spent most of my life believing I was. He made me feel like a queen.

And I was discovering that the advantages of being with a god went further than mind-blowing sex. Whenever we were hungry or thirsty, he snapped his fingers and whatever we wanted appeared out of nowhere. From coffee to cake, if I craved it, he made it happen.

'You know, we're going to have to face the other gods soon,' I said as I lifted a cup of deliciously hot coffee to my lips.

'They can go fuck themselves,' answered Hades, his eyes flashing dangerously. 'You're staying.'

'Then you'll have to try to be diplomatic about it. Will they make the rest of the Trials harder for me?'

'Probably, yes. But you must win them.'

'What if I don't?' I didn't want to ask the question, but I had to. 'What if I lose? Will I be sent back?'

'I don't know, but I would be forced to marry Minthe.' Rage instantly flared inside me, and I felt the black vines pushing at my palms.

'Not a chance,' I hissed.

'Then you must win.' He leaned over and took my hand, and I forced myself to keep my eyes on his, instead of flicking down his delectable naked body.

'Right. No pressure then,' I said. A thought occurred to me abruptly. 'I was never judged after the last Trial.'

'No. That will have to be rectified.' He let out a long breath, and squeezed his fingers around mine. 'Persephone, you must be careful. We still do not know who is behind these macabre gifts you've been getting, or how you ended up in Tartarus. Zeus swears he had meant to send you to his own realm, and I believe him. Even he is not so stupid to play games with stakes that high.'

'You're going to lock me in my room for the rest of the Trials, aren't you?' I said, with a sad smile.

'No. I'm going to lock you in mine,' he grinned back at me.

'Well, that doesn't sound so bad.' I set my coffee down on the bedside table, and began to kiss him, but we were almost immediately interrupted.

'Hades! You are required at Mount Olympus. Now!' The voice ripped through the bedchamber, and we both jumped. Hades' face darkened.

'He is the only one who can do that,' he growled. 'None of the others can get through my defenses.'

'Zeus?' I guessed, gulping. Hades nodded. 'Does he know I'm here?'

'Possibly. We shall go together.'

We dressed quickly, Hades conjuring up my fighting leathers for me. I gripped his hand tightly as he asked me if I was ready. I nodded, and with a bright flash, we were standing in Zeus' throne room, atop the mountain.

Zeus had not known I was back. That much was clear from the shock on the Lord of the God's face. He was enormous in his throne, purple light sparking around him and a lightning storm in his eyes. He was almost painful to look at, and I realized with trepidation that he had been ready for a fight with his brother.

'What is she doing here?' the sky god barked.

'She will finish the Trials,' Hades said, and let go of my hand as he grew. Pale blue light began to shimmer around him and I looked between him and Zeus, concern trembling through me. A fight between these two would be epic. And probably lethal for anyone not an Olympian.

'I heard you caused the death of sixty citizens. Explain yourself.' A sick feeling gripped my stomach as I looked at Hades. He had killed sixty people? *No, the monster had. Not him. He will never lose control again if you are with him.* I clung to the thought.

'I don't know how you came across that information, but what I do with prisoners in my own realm is no concern of yours,' Hades spat.

'Everything you do has become a concern of mine, brother. You can not be trusted.' Zeus' eyes were narrowed, his voice full of malice.

'You brought her back, Zeus. You started this, and now you will see it through to the end. I will call for the judging of the last Trial immediately.' The finality in Hades' voice carried a razor-sharp edge and the two gods stared at one another, tension crackling in the air. I scrabbled in my mind for some way to help, but Zeus spoke.

'I agree that she should finish the Trials. Call the judges.' I blinked, my mouth falling open. Hades stilled beside me, then slowly began to shrink to his usual size.

'I wasn't expecting him to back down so easily. What's going on?' I sent the thought to Hades silently, and his eyes flicked to mine.

'Zeus can hear everything we say like this in his realm,' he replied mentally. I looked at Zeus, alarmed, and he smiled at me.

'My realm, my rules,' he said with a shrug, and shimmered into the guy from the coffee shop. With a wave of his arm, his dais extended, and eleven other thrones materialized, then with a flash, the other gods appeared. I couldn't help glancing at Poseidon first, his face darkening with fury as he saw me.

'What is she doing here? I thought you took her back?' he hissed.

'She will finish the Trials,' said Hades, holding Poseidon's furious gaze. With a snarl, Poseidon sat down. Hades glanced at me, reassurance in his eyes, then strode towards his own throne at the end of the row.

'This is folly, Hades,' Poseidon called after him.

I couldn't help the fluttering feeling in my gut that the sea god was right. Wouldn't I want to get rid of someone who could accidentally end the world?

Now that I was out of the bubble of lust-induced bliss that was Hades' bedroom, the reality of what I had learned was beginning to sink in properly.

Someone had deliberately sent me to Tartarus. To Cronos. So whoever it was must know that my power was a way for Cronos to escape, and destroy Virgo. And if Virgo fell and Cronos was free, the rest of Olympus would not be far behind. Surely few people held that kind of knowledge? I looked at each of the gods in turn, trying to keep my suspicion from my face.

When my eyes landed on Zeus, I remembered that whilst I was on Mount Olympus he could read every one of my thoughts. Holding his gaze, I conjured up the thought of me punching him in the face, landing my fist on his nose repeatedly. He let out a low chuckle.

'Good day, Olympus! Due to an unexpected turn of events, we were not able to share Persephone's last test with you, and the judging was slightly delayed. But we are here with the little lady herself now, and the judges are ready!'

My vines itched at my palms as the intensely irritating commentator beamed at me from where he had appeared at the foot of the dais. I threw him a glare, before turning to where I knew the judges would be behind me. I was momentarily distracted by the breathtaking view of the clouds beyond them, but the commentator's voice sliced through my awe.

'Radamanthus?'

'You will lose one token.' Anger frittered through me. It wasn't my damned fault I couldn't complete Zeus's test, why should I lose a seed?

'Aeacus?'

'You will lose one token,' the pale judge said, nodding seriously. I clenched my teeth tightly.

'Minos?'

'You must lose one token, Persephone.' I could have sworn that there was the hint of an apology in the last judge's wise, dark eyes, but I glared at him all the same, until he vanished with the other two judges. The seed box was suddenly in my hand, hard and real. I'd won four tokens, and eaten two. I sighed as I opened the box slowly. One of the two remaining, perfectly-preserved seeds vibrated in the box, then vanished.

At least I hadn't lost any of my power, I told myself. And there were still three Trials to go. Minthe ended the Trials with five seeds, and I still had three. If I won all my remaining Trials, I could still win. I *had* to win. There was no way I could watch Hades marry another woman, least of all Minthe. Just thinking about her in his bed made my insides twist, a guttural sense of wrongness spreading through me. I shook the thoughts from my head, trying to focus.

'So the lovely Persephone loses one token, leaving her with three. Tomorrow we'll find out what's in store for her next, when we start Round Three of the Hades Trials!' The commentator beamed at me, before the world flashed.

I blinked around at my own room, relief washing through me as I saw Hades standing beside me.

'Hey, why couldn't you flash us out of Tartarus like that?' I asked, turning to him as the question struck me. 'Why did I have to touch you?'

'Because I was using just about all the strength I had to hold back Cronos. My power couldn't reach you.' His voice was hard and angry, and I stood up on tiptoes to kiss his cheek. His expression softened instantly.

'Well, thanks for rescuing me.' He brought his hand to my jaw, tilting my head towards him. But just as he leaned forward to kiss me, a male voice ripped through the moment.

'Persy, what the fuck is going on?' I spun to see my brother crashing through my bedroom door, his face white, and an exasperated Hecate behind him.

'You took arriving in Olympus a shitload better than he's taking it,' she said to me, following him into the room and holding the door open a moment. Skop bounded into the room, and a smile split my face. Hecate kicked the door shut and folded her arms across her chest as Sam froze, his eyes flicking between the little dog and Hades.

'Hey Skop!' I said, as the kobaloi leaped up onto the bed, his tail wagging furiously.

'I'm really, really glad you're back, Persy. Hades is a dick for taking you away.'

'Thanks Skop. I'm glad too, but it wasn't Hades' fault,' I said to him silently. *'We've made up.'* I couldn't keep the heat from my cheeks and Skop barked.

'You banged him! At last!'

'Persy!' Sam's urgent words snapped my attention back to him. He and Hades were staring at each other, more and more black smoke billowing from Hades' skin.

'No, don't put the smoke up!' I said quickly, laying my hand on his arm. 'Please, let him see you. He's my brother. He's called Sam.' I looked at Sam. 'And this is Hades.' Sam moved his mouth a few times, but nothing came out. 'This is Skop, and you've already met Hecate,' I continued. I was feeling guilty that I'd been holed up with Hades in a lust bubble for hours, when my brother had been somewhere in the Underworld, clearly freaking out. Although it sort of served him right for not believing me.

'Erm,' he said eventually.

'Nice to meet you,' said Hades stiffly.

'We shake hands in my world,' I prompted him.

'I'm a god and a king,' he said, looking at me. 'People bow to me, not shake my hand.'

'I know, but he's my brother and he's a little bit shocked. It might be easier to ease him into the god/king thing.' Hades looked from me to Sam, then reluctantly held out his hand. Sam stared at it for a few seconds, then stumbled forward and took it.

'You were telling the truth,' he whispered, looking at me.

'Yeah,' I nodded.

'Does that mean you really have magic powers?' His voice was filled with awe, and I looked at Hecate.

'How much have you told him? I'd have thought he'd be at least a little used to the idea of Olympus by now.'

'I haven't told him anything. He was irritating me, so I had Hypnos put him to sleep,' she shrugged. I closed my eyes and clenched my jaw a moment as Hades dropped Sam's hand.

'Hecate, not that I'm not grateful to see my brother, but why did you bring him here?'

'He said I was outrageously hot.'

'That is not a good reason,' said Hades.

'It's a fucking excellent reason,' said Skop.

I sighed.

As if I didn't already have enough to deal with.

SIX

PERSEPHONE

I asked Hades to conjure some nectar, and once Sam was sitting down, with the reinforcing drink working its way through his system, he was a lot easier to talk to. I couldn't help the beam of satisfaction I got from the amazement in my big brother's face when I showed him my vines. Usually Sam was the impressive one. He'd gotten a great job building apps for cell phones, completely self-taught, and had been the one to finally improve my parents' living space from the shitty trailer we'd grown up in, to an RV.

But as much as I loved him for that, I couldn't deny that it felt good to be the impressive sibling for a change.

I showed him how the vines changed color and told him about the conservatory and how I could grow plants, although I left out the part about my gold vines. I did not want to talk about magic sex powers with my own brother.

I told him about the Trials so far, Hades' face darkening with anger the more I spoke, and Sam's a mask of horror by the time I'd finished. With Hecate and Skop there though, I didn't mention what Hades had told me about Cronos and

Tartarus. I wasn't sure if they were supposed to know about it. Hell, I wasn't sure I *wanted* them to know about it. Being a walking, talking bomb that could destroy their world wasn't exactly something I wanted to share.

'So... Now you have to do three more Trials, and win them all to marry Hades?'

'Yes.'

'And...' His eyes flicked between me and Hades. 'Do you want to marry him?' He whispered the question. I felt a wave of heat come from Hades, and couldn't suppress my smile. What in the world did Sam think he could do to stop Hades if I didn't want to marry him? I loved him for asking though.

'Winning the Trials is certainly the best option I have right now. At least if I win, I have a choice,' I said carefully. More heat rolled off Hades.

You know, I only just decided that I'm in love with you. You can't just assume I want to marry you already, I told Hades in my mind. I made my tone teasing, but there was an element of truth in the words. Being parted from him would be worse than death. It would be tortuous.

But I'd literally only slept with him that day. Marriage commitments seemed a little premature.

You are mine, Hades said in my mind.

Yes. Body and soul, I answered. The air cooled. *But where I come from you don't just claim people if you want to marry them. We should discuss this later.*

Fine, he grunted.

'Sam, now that you know I'm safe, I think Hecate should take you back to New York,' I said, sitting down beside him on my bed and looking pointedly at Hecate.

'No way! You're safe right now, but you've got three more of these Trials to do!'

'And how would you help me?' I asked him gently. 'You're in more danger than I am here, you have no powers.'

'I'm not leaving you to these maniacs,' he said stubbornly. Another wave of heat rolled off Hades.

'Sam, you could be used against me. In my first Trial they nearly killed Skop because they knew I cared for him. Imagine what they would do to my own brother?'

'I can handle it.'

'No, you can't. When we first arrived here the sight of Hades in full god form caused you to black out. It nearly killed me, before I had my power.'

'He nearly killed you?' Sam gaped at me. 'And you're fucking considering marrying him?'

'It's not as simple as that!'

'Persy, I'm staying. If I can't help you physically, then at least I might be able to talk some sense into you.' He folded his arms, eyes fierce.

I sighed. Hades was staying eerily quiet. I turned to him.

'Can he stay just a little while?' Hades stared at me, silver eyes a swirling mass of tension. He turned to Hecate abruptly.

'You caused this mess. Clean it up,' he said to her. I opened my mouth but he carried on. 'Persephone will be moving into my rooms. He can have this room. If he leaves it once without you, I'm giving your job to that fucking skull you care for.'

'Yes boss,' Hecate said, flashing a wicked grin at me as my brother spluttered. My cheeks heated.

'You're staying in his rooms?' Sam half whispered at me, the disbelief back.

'Yep,' I said, my voice coming out awkwardly high-pitched.

This had to be the worst brother-boyfriend introduction ever.

~

My new living arrangements caused a raft of arguments. Sam kicked up such a row about being locked in the windowless bedroom on his own that eventually Hecate gave up and told him he could sleep on her sofa. None of us told him there were no windows in her rooms either.

Convincing Hades to let Skop stay with me in his rooms was a harder task. The little dog didn't make it any easier, hurling insults about the King of the Underworld into my head the entire time I begged Hades to let him come with me.

'He is the spy of another god, Persephone, you don't know how much you ask of me,' Hades said, exasperated. Guilt trickled through me as I recalled Hecate telling me how secretive Hades was about his realm.

'But he's one of my only friends here, and he's helped save my life,' I said. 'Plus he already knows loads about Virgo now. It's not like he'll be with you all the time, he'll be with me, and I'm not allowed to go anywhere or do anything.'

'*Fuck no. I'll be with him as little as possible,*' said Skop in my head.

'*You're lucky he bans mind-reading, now behave yourself!*' I snapped back at the kobaloi.

'He must sleep in the antechamber, and he must hear none of our conversations,' Hades growled eventually.

'Thank you!' I squeaked, and flung my arms around his neck. His tense shoulders relaxed under my embrace, and my brother made a strangled sound.

'You are welcome,' Hades said, but he didn't sound like he meant it. 'Now regretfully, I must go. I have neglected my duties and have a lot to... attend to.' I could see the guilt and pain in his face, felt his shame through the bond, and my heart ached for him. He could not escape the consequences of his wrath.

Had he saved me from facing mine when I drank from the river Lethe and forgot whatever it was I had done? Fresh frustration clouded my mind at the thought. I was fast reaching a point where I wanted to believe Hades was right about me being better off not knowing what I had done in the past. I had enough shit to wade through already, with the Trials and Cronos and Tartarus. Did I really need to know anymore? Would any good come of it?

How can you not know what you are capable of? Of course you need to know. The voice inside me was inescapable, and it was a blend of fear and justice. Whether I needed punishing or forgiving for my actions, both were important.

'Kerato will have regenerated soon,' said Hecate, and a small sound of relief escaped me as her words cut through my thoughts. The minotaur was OK.

'Tell him thank you from me, will you?' I said to Hades.

'Of course. I will see you in a few hours.' He leaned down to kiss me softly, then vanished. I felt a small pang of loss, but the bond flared inside me, reassuring and bright. I turned to Sam, determined to keep my mind off the myriad concerns rolling around my brain.

'Right. There are a few things you need to know about the Underworld. Hecate? Help me out?'

≈

Hecate had barely begun telling Sam about the twelve realms when the world flashed around me.

Panic engulfed me, every frazzled part of me expecting to come face to face with the flaming river of Tartarus and my vines tore from my palms before the light had even cleared from my eyes.

But the scene that came into focus before me wasn't dark and fiery at all. It was bright and warm and breezy. And beautiful.

'Zeus?'

I was in the breakfast room on Zeus's mountain.

'I wouldn't try using those vines on me,' his voice sounded behind me. I whirled, and gasped. He was shirtless, in the older, dignified form I'd seen him in a few times before. And this close it was impossible not to see how much better it was than the blond surfer boy form. If the angles of his face, the corded muscle across his chest, and the tightness of his abs weren't enough to make my breath catch, then the gleam in his eyes was. He oozed sex. Like it was actually pouring from his body.

'Stop. Now. I was told gods weren't allowed do this,' I said.

'I have no idea what you mean,' he said, stepping closer to me. I stepped backwards. 'I've brought you here to talk with you. On matters of grave importance.' He licked his lips, and my chest heaved. *Focus, Persephone!*

'You told me you wanted me to win last time I was here. Why?'

'Because my brother is not the god he used to be. The Underworld has changed him.'

'You did that to him, not the Underworld!'

'We all have our burdens, Persephone. Do you think it is easy for me to control the skies?'

'I don't believe it is as hard as controlling the dead,' I retorted. Zeus tilted his head, regarding me.

'I'll admit Leo has some benefits over Virgo,' he said eventually. 'Come with me.' He held out his hand, and I shook my head.

'No.' My left foot moved against my will. 'Bastard,' I snarled.

'I won't make you do any more than move your feet, feisty little goddess,' he smiled at me, then gripped my hand. With another flash we were gone from the mountain, standing instead on wooden planks. Wind suddenly rushed across me, blowing my hair around my face. We were moving, and as I looked around myself I stumbled. We were on a ship, and the sails billowing in front of me were shining like metallic liquid. Clouds flew past us on either side, spirals of glittering dust corkscrewing through the sky.

An overwhelming sense of freedom filled me, and I held my arms out as we soared through the sky. I felt like my worries were peeling away from me in the cool wind, the past, future and everything in between paling against the bliss.

With an abrupt flash, the wind stopped, and I blinked around at a courtyard garden. I gazed up at the most incredible trellis, covered in roses of every color I could imagine, the thorns shining gold.

'Beautiful, aren't they?'

'Yes,' I breathed, turning. Zeus was standing in front of a tall fountain, dragonflies the size of birds darting above his head. I could see Mount Olympus behind him, more of the flying ships cruising around it. 'Where are we?'

'One of the mansions that ring Mount Olympus. You created them.'

'What?'

'The gold-thorned roses. You created them.' I blinked at him, and he laughed softly. 'Olympus may have forgotten you, Persephone, but you left a legacy deeper than even Hades knows.'

'Why have you brought me here?'

'You need to know that the Underworld is not the only place that would welcome you.'

I frowned at him.

'You're trying to... make friends with me?'

'You are not meant to be kept underground, Persephone. You were born of light and nature. Not darkness and death.' Fear started to prick at the calm enveloping me. He was right. No matter my feelings for Hades, I couldn't live in Virgo. I couldn't live in the darkness, with that barren landscape the closest thing to nature I could get to.

'Are you telling me I can visit places like this when I am Queen of the Underworld?' I asked, a sick feeling in my stomach. That wasn't what he was telling me, and I knew it wasn't.

'No, Persephone. I'm telling you that you were never meant to be Queen of the Underworld. A Queen, yes. But not of the dead.'

'I love Hades,' I said, the words flying to my lips.

'I don't doubt it. But that doesn't change the fact that you can't live in the Underworld. Look at what it has done to Hades. And he is much, much stronger than you will ever be.'

No... No, I had to be with Hades. But he was bound to Virgo, he couldn't leave. Would the Underworld turn me into a monster like him? Was that what had happened before? Hecate's story burst into my mind.

'I can sacrifice something! Something important, to save my soul,' I said quickly.

'And be as miserable as that Titan witch your whole life?' Zeus' voice was low and he was moving closer to me. 'If you let me, Persephone, I can make you so much more.'

SEVEN

PERSEPHONE

Zeus' magic rolled over me, the sweet scent of roses, the kiss of the breeze, the heat of his body, all consuming my rational thoughts.

'More than what?' I asked, my pulse racing. 'What can you make me?'

'Anything you want to be. A goddess without constraints, a goddess living in the light.' His words were like a caress, and I stared into his purple eyes.

'A goddess living in the light,' I repeated breathlessly. How could I live any other way? I couldn't, *wouldn't* spend my life in the dark. Hades' own words filtered through my mind.

'You can't keep a light this bright in the dark.'

But I couldn't live without Hades either. Confusion was pouring through me in rivers as the terrible realization began to settle over me. This was why the idea of marriage had unsettled me. This was why my head was refusing to process a future with Hades, was putting off the decision until after the Trials. Because I couldn't live in the Under-world with him. I couldn't live in the dark.

What had I done? I'd let the bond awaken, let myself fall in love with a man I couldn't be with, with a man who needed me for his soul to survive. I would destroy both of us if I left, but the thought of those rock walls, the Empusa's lair, the fiery river of Tartarus and its tortured souls, the empty, barely-lit landscape... It would take my soul, I realized, tears burning hot behind my eyes yet again. The longer I stayed in that place, the more of my soul would die. It might take a hundred years, or a thousand, but my soul would eventually be lost to the darkness.

'Persephone, let me show you the life you should live. Let me show you what you truly deserve.'

'What do I have to do?'

'Win the Trials. Prove you are worthy of a crown. And when I tell the world you will be Queen of a brand new realm, *your own* realm, a realm filled with light and life and nature, you must stand by my side.'

A new realm? Was he talking about the realm Hades had created and was being punished for? I gaped at Zeus, the reality of what he was saying crashing through me as Hades' pain-filled face dominated my thoughts.

'You hate him that much?'

Zeus' smile slipped.

'You hate him enough to get the woman he loves to leave him and rule the realm he created to replace her? You cruel, cruel, vicious bastard!' I was yelling suddenly, all calm abandoning me and a rage gripping me in its place. Black vines leapt from my palms, snaking towards Zeus. 'You fear him, Zeus. You underestimated his power, and now you fear you can't control him.'

The sky god's expression twisted, his beautiful face suddenly ugly with anger.

'He was only able to create that realm because of that

Titan bitch,' he hissed. 'He's not that strong, and don't let him pretend otherwise. You could be stronger.'

'No, Zeus. I could not. And I would rather spend one day with him than an eternity without. I will be strong by his side, and I will make him stronger. And together you will be no match for us.'

Within a second he was three times his normal size, fizzing purple lightning flashing around him. Thunder crashed overhead, but my vines didn't recoil. They grew with him, whipping around me.

I wasn't scared of him. The realization buoyed me, and I pictured Hades standing behind me, his strength and love flowing into me.

'Are you threatening me, flower goddess?' boomed Zeus.

'Yes. Stay the fuck away from Hades. You've done enough.'

He laughed, a great, booming cackle.

'If I didn't respect you so much, I would smite you where you stand! You, who can just about make plants grow and throw some vines around, are trying to protect the King of the Underworld, one of the three most powerful beings in Olympus?' I opened my mouth to tell him that the Titans were stronger than him, but he began to shrink down quickly, and I faltered, surprised.

He was smiling, I saw, as he reached human size, the purple magic around him dissipating.

'I believe you have passed, Persephone,' he said, the wicked gleam back in his eyes. 'But you really did anger me there. You walk a fine line. Threaten me again, and I will end you.'

'Passed? What the fuck are you talking about?' I said, confused enough to ignore his threat.

Hera appeared beside him in a flash of turquoise, and my vines disintegrated as I looked between them.

'You have just passed the loyalty Trial, Persephone,' Hera said. I blinked at her. 'Well done. Hades will be lucky to have you if you can win the rest of the competition.'

EIGHT

HADES

Persephone was opening and closing her mouth, confusion and fury on her face, as she was flashed into my throne room. I couldn't stop the black smoke around me vibrating, anger causing the beast inside me to growl.

One day I would be able to stop Zeus. One day he wouldn't be able to play with me like I was his fucking toy. But right now... The Trials were overruling my command in my own realm, leaving him to do whatever the fuck he pleased with Persephone, with the backing of the other Olympians.

Like abducting her from her own rooms and forcing her to realize that she couldn't live in the Underworld with me.

Pain sliced through the anger and a wave of heat rippled out from me as Persephone's eyes snapped to mine. Slow realization was dawning on her face.

'You saw all of that,' she said inside my head as the commentator appeared at the foot of the dais. It wasn't a question, and her mental voice was strained. I swallowed my anger and replied.

'Yes. And I have never loved you more.'

'I'm sorry. I'm sorry I even considered his words, his magic is so strong, I-' I cut her off, unable to take the anguish in her voice.

'Very few can resist Zeus' power. And fewer still would outright threaten him. You sounded like a true Queen.'

'Good day, Olympus!' sang the commentator. Persephone turned to him. 'As you all just saw, little Persephone has successfully passed the loyalty test!' I flicked my eyes to Zeus, hatred bubbling through my veins. The world saw what he wanted them to see, not what had actually happened. There was no way he had let all of Olympus see Persephone standing up to him like that. Nor would he have broadcast any mention of the new realm. The only reason he had let us Olympians see what had really been said was because he wanted to taunt me, wanted me to see Persephone consider leaving or betraying me.

And although her fierce reaction had been more than I could have dreamed of, what Zeus had said was true, and Persephone knew it. She wasn't made for darkness and death. She would become muted and miserable as time went on, a shadow of herself. And it would be my fault. How could I let that happen?

Her words sang through my skull. *'I would rather spend one day with him than an eternity without. I will be strong by his side, and I will make him stronger. And together you will be no match for us.'*

Love so powerful it made my chest hurt fired inside me, and her eyes snapped to me again, softer now. She felt my emotion, through the bond.

. . .

'So now, to the judges!' The commentator's voice severed the moment, and the judges shimmered into the room. In turn they each pronounced that Persephone had earned one token, then the seed box appeared in her hand. She held it as though it were toxic, rather than a prize.

Before she or I could say a word, Zeus waved his arm and the room emptied immediately, leaving just the Olympian gods in their thrones.

'Where have you sent her?' I barked, leaping to my feet.

'Relax, brother. I've put her back exactly where I found her.' His expression was one of boredom but there was a glint in his eyes that said otherwise. My fury deepened.

'This is my realm!' I bellowed. 'You do not dismiss my subjects, I do!'

'Now, now, Hades. I would have thought you'd be pleased. Persephone stood up to the King of the Gods for you,' said Hera, standing. 'That's really quite a feat.'

'And now she knows that she won't be happy here. She knows what the rest of Olympus has to offer in comparison.' I couldn't keep the bitterness from my voice. A smug smile flashed across Zeus' face and my vision clouded. My monster was crawling its way up my chest, straining to get out.

'She loves you, Hades. If she wins the Trials this will be the best outcome you could have possibly hoped for,' Hera said.

'Unless she remembers what she did and loses her shit again,' added Zeus.

'Don't you dare,' I hissed. 'Her memories and the River Lethe are out of bounds for these Trials,' I spat, and I felt the temperature in the room plummet around me as I channeled my power.

'Agreed,' said Poseidon loudly.

'Agreed,' echoed Athena, Hermes and Dionysus. Relief tempered my anger a little. Zeus couldn't go against everyone. He shrugged diffidently.

'I wasn't suggesting that we did.'

My eyes flicked over the gods who had remained silent. I hadn't had any idea this damned Trial was happening, but in the short time I'd been alone I had been able to reach one vital conclusion.

Whoever was behind the macabre gifts Persephone had been getting must know what she had done before she drank from the river Lethe. And they must also be able to control the minds of the humans they were using to make up this Spring Undead faction. If they were also responsible for her unexpected trip to Tartarus then they knew about Cronos, which severely limited the list of suspects.

To the eleven gods in front of me.

All of them stared back, able to see through my smoke facade. Who would want to release the world's worst monster, Cronos, and start a new war, ending Olympian rule? Who would want to destroy Virgo? It made no sense. It had taken an age to build Olympus as it was now, countless fights and mistakes finally culminating in something they all benefited from.

I saw no reason why any of them would want to destroy it all. My gaze settled on Ares. Was he angry enough? Desperate for war enough? He glared back at me through the slits in his helmet.

The only thing I was sure of was that it wasn't either of my brothers. They had the most to lose.

'If you're not going to rant and rage and entertain me, then I'm leaving,' said Zeus, and before I could open my mouth he had gone. The others stood, Hermes and Aphrodite the only ones to nod at me politely before vanishing too. But one god stayed behind.

'How's Persy doing?' Dionysus asked.

'Why?' I snapped, suspicion filling me.

'Chill out, man, you know I care about her.' The wine god swiveled in his throne, kicking his leg up over the arm.

'You know exactly how she's doing, the kobaloi is keeping you well informed, I have no doubt.'

'Hmm,' grunted Dionysus, a goblet of wine appearing in his hand. 'Fancy a drink?'

'No.'

'Naked nymphs, you're dull. Get your ass over to one of my parties one day,' he said, and drained his goblet in one.

'I have work to do here, unlike the rest of you.'

'Hades, you have underlings. Share the load. You do not need to spend your whole life in a fucking cave. And nor does she,' he said.

'Coming from a god who lives in a tree,' I snorted.

'It's a very nice tree,' he said, standing up and stretching. 'And it's where she grew up. The first time.'

'What's your point, Dionysus? I am busy.'

'My point is that she doesn't have to live here for you two to be together.'

I scowled at him.

'You're saying she could live with you?'

'Yeah. She did before.'

'No.' The word had left my mouth before I had even considered the notion.

'She likes trees, man, she'd be happy-'

'I said no.'

The wine god's face hardened.

'It's not up to you. It's up to her.'

'Persephone is mine.' The words came out as a snarl, and blue light burst to life around me.

'Ease up, man, I know she is. I'm just trying to help,' Dionysus said, holding his hands up. But the fierce look in his eyes belied the casual words. 'Think about it,' he said, then disappeared.

As little as I wanted to, I found that I couldn't help thinking about what Dionysus had said. Persephone would love living on Taurus. It was nature and madness combined, a limitless island covered in giant plants and wild creatures. It was perfect for her. That's why Demeter had left her there.

I stopped by her room to make sure she was alright, but her brother was there, along with the kobaloi spy. In some ways I was relieved she wasn't alone. She had expressed her hatred for Virgo many times before, but now the subject had been laid so bare before us that we would have to talk about it. And I had no solutions. Only wildly conflicting emotions. The thought of making her suffer was intolerable. But so was the thought of living without her. Was visiting her on another realm whenever the Underworld could spare me really an option? In the early days I had tested the limits of my bind to Virgo, and found that I could never leave for long, or the monster became wild and even less tamable, and my control over the demons and Tartarus weakened.

I made my excuses and left, forcing myself to focus on more immediate problems. Persephone had two more Trials to survive and win, and she couldn't be sabotaged again. The thought of her in Tartarus made the monster roar within me, dark rage twisting my insides. I wanted to talk to Kerato about my suspicions. Every human member of the faction we had caught had known nothing about how their memories had returned, and if it was indeed a god directing them, then interrogating them further was pointless. We would learn nothing from them at all.

NINE

PERSEPHONE

'You know, you can't avoid me forever.' I sent the thought at Hades, hoping that wherever he was he could hear me.

'I'm sorry. I have much to attend to,' he replied immediately. 'Go to sleep, and we'll talk in the morning.'

I blew out a sigh and lay back on his enormous bed. It felt too big without him in it, his mighty presence altering the scale of everything around me. Hecate had brought me to his rooms earlier, and now I'd had too much time alone to think.

Whilst I was incredibly relieved to have passed another Trial and won a seed, I couldn't suppress my anger at the gods. I'd been warned of the loyalty Trial, I knew I wouldn't see it coming, but to force me to admit in front of Hades that I didn't want to live in his realm? It was cruel beyond belief.

He had come by after the Trial but his face was strained, his manner awkward. I hadn't known what to say to him. My mind screamed against the notion of being trapped in the dark for eternity, but the feeling didn't outweigh my desire for him.

'*The last two Trials are going to be the hardest,*' said Skop, interrupting my thoughts.

'Huh,' I said, hugging my knees to my chest. 'If Hades catches you on the bed you are going to be in deep shit.'

'*Persy, you should eat another seed. The more power you have, the more likely you'll survive. And win.*'

'We'll find out what the Trial is first,' I said evasively. I didn't want more power. I didn't want to make myself stronger.

I was already dangerous enough.

I did fall asleep before Hades returned, and almost instantly found myself in the Atlas garden.

'*Ah, little goddess,*' the voice whispered across the breeze, as a delicious calm wrapped itself around me. The sunflowers had grown, they were now as tall as I was. I brushed my finger along their petals as I made my way across the soft turf to the fountain.

'I have a question for you,' I said.

'By all means.'

'Do you know how I ended up in Tartarus?'

There was a long silence from the voice, filled by the sound of birds tweeting.

'I did not know you had been to Tartarus. That is an unpleasant place,' the stranger said eventually.

'It is,' I replied, running my fingers through the warm water and watching the lily-pads ripple. 'Will I die if I live in the Underworld forever?'

'No. Not if you are stronger than the evil there.'

'But if I become stronger, I become more dangerous.'

'Wrong. The stronger you are, the more control you have.'

'I want to stay in Olympus. But I don't want to live away from nature. It feels wrong.'

'That should not be your biggest concern now. You must regain your memories and right the injustice dealt to you. You must regain your power and learn who you are. Then you will know what is right or wrong. Then you will be able to make decisions about your future.'

I thought about that, the calm of the garden allowing the thoughts to organize themselves more clearly. It was true that the most urgent issue was surviving the Trials and discovering who had sent me to Tartarus. But did I need my memories back? Would it really help?

'What happens if I just stay ignorant? What if Hades and Athena are right?'

'Then you will forever be incomplete. Those who have used you, sought to harm you and Hades, will have won.'

Anger rumbled through me. Harm Hades? No. No, I couldn't allow that.

'Can't you just tell me what happened? Who my enemies are?'

'To know for sure, you must recover your memories. If you eat another seed, you will be able to find the river Lethe.'

The conversation was clear in my mind when I awoke, Skop still at the end of the bed and Hades nowhere to be seen.

'*Where are you?*' I projected at him groggily.

'I'm here,' he replied, and I sat up with a start. The voice hadn't been in my head, it had come from the adjoining room. I swung my legs out of bed, the only light coming from the softly glowing vines on the ceiling.

'Hades?' He was sitting shirtless in a large wingback chair, a tumbler of something amber in his hand. 'Are you OK?'

'I had a lot to clear up,' he said, his voice bitter.

'It wasn't you, don't forget that,' I said, padding over to him. He didn't answer, but I felt his body relax as I eased myself onto his lap. 'How's Kerato?'

'Good. It'll be a while before he's strong again, demons get stronger the longer they've been living.'

'Are all minotaurs demons?'

'No. Kerato became a demon to live here.' He looked at me as I wound my arms around his neck. 'Did Hecate tell you what she gave up in order to keep her soul?'

'Yes,' I nodded.

'Well, Kerato, and many others here, didn't have enough to give up. The Underworld owns them.'

'It doesn't own you,' I whispered. 'It owns the darkness inside you, but you are stronger.'

'*We* are stronger,' he corrected me, and kissed me gently. 'Persephone, Zeus was right. You could be so much more above ground. You are a nature goddess, with earth magic. This is no place for you.' The anguish in his words made the need to help him overtake my own concerns.

'I'll be fine,' I said. 'And anyway, I've decided not to think about it until after the Trials. My brain can only take so many life-threatening scenarios at a time, and the Trials are more urgent,' I said, thinking about what the stranger had said to me.

Guilt trickled through me at the thought of the Atlas garden. Should I tell Hades about it? It felt wrong keeping a secret from him, but as soon as I opened my mouth to speak, I closed it again.

Hades wouldn't tell me about my past, but the stranger wanted me to know. They were at odds. And I had first-hand evidence that Hades didn't always make the right decisions; he had felt obligated to take me back to New York when that was the worst thing he could possibly have done. He didn't necessarily know what was best for me, and until I knew what I wanted, it seemed a good idea to keep silent.

'I think focusing on the more immediate issues is a very good idea,' Hades said, and swigged from his glass. 'I believe the person who sent you to Tartarus was an Olympian.'

'You do?'

'Yes. Nobody else except my inner circle knows about Cronos.'

'What if whoever it is doesn't know about Cronos, and just hoped I'd die there? I mean, a trip to Tartarus is a pretty awful punishment, even if Cronos wasn't part of it.'

'No, it's too much of a coincidence.' I cocked my head.

'Hades, did Cronos have something to do with what happened before?'

'I swore to you I would never talk to you about what happened, please stop putting me through this,' he said tightly. *That wasn't a no.*

'Putting *you* through this?' I said indignantly. 'I think you'll find I'm the one being put through it.' I pushed my chin out, and he moved his hand to my jaw, stroking his thumb across my skin.

'I know. I'm sorry. Let me make it up to you?' His eyes were dark suddenly, and his chest was tensing. A wave of heat, smelling like wood-smoke, rolled over me and desire tingled through my whole body, my anger vanishing.

'I suppose I could be persuaded,' I mumbled, as he leaned forward and closed his lips over mine.

TEN

PERSEPHONE

'I must hold court today, I am days behind,' said Hades the next morning, rolling to the edge of the mattress and sitting up. I blinked the sleep from my eyes, and yawned.

'What do you do during court?'

'Judge the dead,' he muttered, his muscled back to me. I slowly pointed my palm at him, and a gold vine snaked out, creeping towards him.

'Sounds intense,' I said.

'Some days are worse than others. You should train with Hecate as much as you can today, and I'll see you at the Trial announcement tonight.' He started to stand, but my vines wrapped around his waist fast.

'Or I could see you some more now,' I grinned as I tugged.

His huge frame didn't move, and he twisted to look at me, a wicked gleam in his eyes.

'You're going to have to get much stronger than that if you want to move me,' he said.

'I don't need to move you physically,' I answered, and

sent my power through my vine, recalling as much detail as I could from the night before. His eyes darkened instantly, and he stood up, turning towards me and giving me an eyeful of his now aroused naked body.

'I believe you win this one,' he murmured, and pounced.

Eventually he did leave, after filling the table in his living rooms with waffles and piping hot coffee for me. Again I felt the initial pang of panic at his loss, until the bond fired, reassuring and solid. I could definitely get used to never feeling completely alone, I thought as I tucked into my breakfast. I could get used to magic waffles too.

Hecate and Sam arrived half an hour later. Sam was almost alarmingly bright and enthusiastic compared to the day before and I eyed Hecate suspiciously.

'What have you given him?' She shrugged and Sam answered me.

'Just some coffee, we were up all night talking about Olympus. It sounds freaking awesome, have you seen the giant trees or the underwater cities?' He was talking fast and I raised an eyebrow.

'You sound like you've had about ten coffees.'

'A few, I guess. What are we doing today?'

'Erm, training. The next Trial is announced tonight.'

'Can I train too?'

'No,' Hecate and I said together.

'Oh.'

'Skop, can you talk to Sam in his head?' I asked, a thought occurring to me. The kobaloi didn't answer me but Sam's face changed suddenly, his eyes widening as he looked down at the dog. 'I'll take that as a yes,' I smiled. 'Sam, you can practice talking back to him. You have to project the thoughts to him, concentrating hard the whole time.'

'You can talk to the dog in your head?' Sam shook his head in disbelief. 'This place is crazy.'

'Actually, he's not a dog,' Hecate said. 'He's a kobaloi. Which is a shape-shifting sprite.' Sam looked at Skop.

'How come you choose to be a dog then?' he asked. With a little shimmer Skop shifted, his naked gnome body taking the furry dog's place. Sam's mouth slowly formed an O shape as he stared.

'Because I won't wear clothes and your sister didn't like this,' Skop answered, pointing with both hands at his genitals.

'Yeah, I can't say I blame her,' said Hecate. Skop grinned at me from under his beard before shifting back to dog form.

'There's a drinks thing tonight at the announcement,' Hecate said.

'Great,' I said, rolling my eyes. 'Poseidon can glare at me some more, and Zeus can march around being a prick.'

'You did well turning him down,' said Hecate. I cocked my head at her. 'I wanted to screw him from the other side of a flame dish, so the gods know how hard it must have been for you.'

'What did you see during the loyalty Trial?' I asked slowly.

'Him coming on to you, you saying no,' she shrugged.

'That wasn't what happened,' I said quietly. 'He didn't try to sleep with me, though he was definitely turning on the charm. He tried to get me to renounce living with Hades if I won the Trials.'

'Really?'

'Yeah. He said I could rule the new realm if I left Hades.'

'Fucking asshole,' spat Hecate.

'I know. I told him I would rather lose my soul to Virgo than leave Hades. And then I told him to fuck off and leave us alone, that together we would be strong enough to stand up to him.'

Hecate let out a long whistle, her eyes as wide as my brother's.

'No wonder they didn't broadcast that. Nice one.' I grinned at the pride I could see in her eyes.

'Yeah, well, he threatened to kill me if I made him angry again, so... making an enemy of the Lord of the Gods can be ticked off my to-do list.'

I trained hard with Hecate most of the day, and not just on dagger work and close combat. She set up archery targets on tall stands around the room, and I practiced launching my vines at precise points on the targets, as well as using them to lift and throw the structures.

I did OK, but I knew I was at the limit of the strength I could achieve. No doubt I could learn to control them better and be more accurate, but I couldn't get any more physical power into the vines. *Unless you eat another seed.*

The longer I trained, the more power I wanted. Each time I failed to tug over a heavy target, and each time my vines thudded to a stop instead of powering through whatever they had hit, I ached for more strength. Which was exactly what I was scared of. *Power corrupts. The more you have, the more you want.*

But the difference was, I may need it, rather than just

want it. Right now the most important thing for me was to survive the Trials. Zeus and Poseidon both hated me, and they were in charge. Whatever was coming would not be easy. Plus, I couldn't bear the thought of Hades marrying another woman.

Other than a short break for lunch, we only stopped when it was time to get ready for the announcement. I was nervous about my brother, a human who was clearly important to me, being there but Hecate insisted she wouldn't take her eyes off him.

'Don't,' I said sternly. 'Because there are plenty of folk who would try to use him against me.'

'I know, Persy. He'll be fine.' We were back in Hades' rooms, and Sam was completely distracted by Skop, laughing at something so hard his eyes were streaming.

'And will you find him something to wear so that he fits in a bit better?'

'Yes. I will look after him. I promise.'

'Thank you.'

'No worries. He's kinda cute to have around to be honest. He's like you when you get all excited about stuff, except he's better looking. No offense, I'm just not into chicks. I can't wait for him to see a minotaur.' Hecate's eyes were sparkling.

I made a mental note to keep a firm eye on both of them, and Hecate left, telling me she would pick me up again in an hour. I made my way somewhat nervously into the dressing room off Hades' bedroom, not sure what to expect. He had told me that he had kept all my old clothes, and to help myself, but I'd yet to venture in there.

It was a large room with only the one door, and all three

other walls were lined with open fronted closets. The closet opposite me was filled with black garments, jeans and shirts and togas, clearly belonging to Hades. But the other two walls were a riot of color and fabric. I took in a breath as I ran my fingers along the rows of dresses, marveling that anyone could own such a huge number of beautiful gowns. Silk, organza, satin, velvet, cotton; every fabric imaginable hung in the closets, and beneath them rows and rows of stunning high-heeled shoes stood shining.

I closed my eyes and spun in a slow circle, deciding that the first dress I laid my hand on would be the one I would wear. I reached out blindly and gripped a soft, lightweight fabric, and opened my eyes. The dress had a high choker collar and no sleeves, and the top half of it was made of intricate ink-black lace, tiny flowers dotting the pattern. The bottom half of the dress was ocean blue, darker at the bottom than the top, and made up of lots of feather-light layers so that it puffed out from the tight lace.

It took me no time to shower in the epic bathroom, I was so excited to get the dress on. And I wasn't disappointed. I found a tall stack of drawers next to the dressing room door which was filled with lacy lingerie and fortunately, given that the lace top half of the dress was see-through, a few practical bras. The dress fitted me like a glove, and I swished and swirled in front of the mirror on the other side of the door, watching my white hair fall against the black lace. I barely recognized myself and it felt good to like what I saw in the mirror. It wasn't just the hair and the clothes. My new confidence ran deeper than that. Heat prickled through me, the bond sparking. I wasn't alone. A god loved me, and I loved him. And somehow that was changing me.

. . .

When Hecate came back to collect me, looking fierce in a white PVC corset dress and even more silver jewelry than usual, I felt ready to face the gods and all their guests. Including that douchebag, Zeus. I wanted to know what I would be facing next, nervous anticipation fueling my desire for the Trials to be over.

Sam was wearing a black toga, and even as his sister, I could see that it suited him. He was showing a smattering of chest hair and somehow looked even taller than usual.

'What do you think?' he beamed at me.

'Stay away from anyone Skop tells you to talk to,' I said seriously. 'He's a pervert and a pest.'

'Excellent,' Sam said, rubbing his hands together.

'I mean it, you should stay well away from the gods, Sam. Stick with Hecate.' He gave her a sideways glance, and I saw his eyes dip to the high hem of her skirt.

'Stick with Hecate. Got it,' he said. *Oh no.* Sam having a crush on the celibate goddess of necromancy could not end well.

'Ready to go?' Hecate said, and I nodded. I would have to have a talk with my brother later.

ELEVEN

PERSEPHONE

The announcement was being held in Hades' throne room, and Sam's face when he saw the huge colored flames made me wonder what my own had looked like the first time I was here.

'Geez, Persy, I can't believe this is real,' he breathed as he stared around himself. There were only a few guests already there, but a small group of tall women with skin like tree bark were fawning around an attractive man I recognized from previous meetings as Theseus, and seven or eight minotaur guards ringed the edge of the floating room. I scanned them quickly, looking for Kerato and spotted him by the throne dais.

'Stay here,' I told Sam, and made my way quickly to the Captain of the Guard. 'I'm so pleased to see you, Kerato,' I said as I reached him. He dipped his head low.

'And you, My Lady.'

'Thank you for trying to help me during the last Trial. I'm sorry you were...' I floundered for the right word.

'Killed?' he offered. The stern expression on his snouted

face didn't change. 'It is my duty. I will be as strong as I was before in around a hundred years.' I looked at him in shock.

'A hundred years?'

'Yes.'

'Well, that sucks.'

'A hundred years is not a long time, my lady. And Ankhiale is very strong. It could have been worse.'

I considered his words, a weird anticipation buzzing through me. The notion of a hundred years not being a long time threw stark light on the idea of being immortal. I'd known when Hades had told me that we were only married four years how small that amount of time must have seemed to him but... Endless life. Surely there was no point unless you had someone to share it with? The same question I was trying and failing to suppress popped up immediately. *Live without the man you love, or slowly lose your soul with him?*

I shoved the thought away.

'Well, I'm very grateful. You are a credit to Virgo and Hades,' I said to the minotaur, unsure if I was overstepping my role but the words coming anyway. Something flickered in the creature's eyes and when he spoke there was genuine warmth for the first time.

'I should like it if you won the Trials, My Lady.'

'I'll do my best,' I smiled back at him.

Slowly, more guests arrived, little bursts of light flashing around the room as we sipped from saucer shaped glasses and Sam gaped at everything.

'Can you all transport yourself around like that?' he asked Hecate.

'Nope, only powerful gods can do that. They've all been

given an invite that lets them flash here for this event, created by an Olympian.'

'So, how powerful are you?' There was definitely a flirtatious tone to my brother's voice, and to my surprise, Hecate echoed it as she answered him.

'You'll have to wait and find out.'

Oh gods.

'Is your brother into Hecate?' asked Skop in my head.

'If he is, you can be the one to tell him that she's celibate and he can't stay in Olympus,' I grumbled back.

'Woah, is that Poseidon?' Sam's awed voice drew my attention to where he was pointing, at the dais. Poseidon had shown up with his trident and watery toga, and his blue eyes found mine immediately.

'Yup,' I mumbled. 'And it looks like he still hates me.'

There was a wave of delicious ocean smell, then in a flash I was in a water bubble, the sea god directly in front of me. *Not again*, I groaned internally. I was fed up of being yelled at by gods.

'Hello,' I said tightly, bowing my head.

'I only have a moment before Zeus arrives,' Poseidon said, and I raised my eyebrows in surprise. 'I care more for my brother, Hades, than you may believe, and I see now that he is willing to put our world in danger for you. Rather than fight him, I have decided to help you. With combined strength and foresight, we will be strong enough to avoid any more disasters. We must not have a repeat of the endurance Trial. You must not end up in Tartarus again.'

'Hades told me that I must never meet Cronos,' I said. This time Poseidon looked surprised.

'Good. I am glad you are aware of that. Now, listen to me carefully,' he said, and leaned forward and opened his closed hand. A shining pearl lay in the middle of his palm. 'I have bewitched the hippocampus you bonded with so quickly in my realm.'

'What?' He thrust his hand out to me and I tentatively took the pearl from him. It was warm, and fizzed with energy.

'When you need his help, crush the pearl,' said Poseidon quickly. 'He will appear in the form you most require. But he was not designed to be out of the water for long, so you will only have about five minutes before he must return to Aquarius.'

'Buddy is in the pearl?' My mouth was hanging open as I looked between the sea god and the little gem.

'Yes. Use it wisely,' he said, then the bubble of water around us vanished and he turned to my brother. 'You are foolish to come here, human,' he said to Sam, then strode towards the thrones.

'He's awesome,' breathed Sam. Still too confused to respond, I stared at the pearl. Was Poseidon telling the truth? He had been so fearful and angry before, did he really now believe that he and the others could prevent me from causing any damage if they helped me?

What choice did the sea god have? My racing mind played out his options. If I died, Hades would fall to the monster inside him, then Olympus would be overrun by the dead. If I survived I could be used to release the most evil god in history and start a war. Poseidon was stuck between a rock and a hard place.

But I wasn't sure he knew how close Hades was to succumbing to the dark. Hades had lost me once before and the Underworld had continued on. Did Poseidon know how much stronger the beast inside the King of the Dead had become in my absence?

I eyed the pearl, full of suspicion. Hades said that if I

tried to take the power of something primordial in strength I would explode. This tiny pearl could be just that kind of weapon.

'*You look incredible.*' Hades' voice filtered through my thoughts and I snapped my head up, seeking him out. He was on his throne, his smoky form flickering against the skulls.

'*Thanks. You look smoky,*' I grinned back at him.

'*You know what I like most about that dress?*' he asked, his voice a purr.

'*No.*'

'*That I get to take it off later.*' Heat washed through me and I felt my cheeks burn. '*Are you blushing?*'

'*No! You sound like you've had a good day,*' I said, changing the subject.

'*For the first time in what feels like centuries, I had something to look forward to at the end of it,*' he said, the playful tone replaced by something much softer. Pleasure at his words made me take a deep breath, my chest swelling.

'*I wish I could kiss you right now,*' I told him.

'*When you are my Queen, you can kiss me whenever the hell you like.*'

'*If that's not a good enough incentive to win, I don't know what is.*'

'That dress looks like my grandmother made it,' a voice sneered from behind me. I turned, expecting to see Eris, the only person I'd met so far who would be so outright rude, but my eyebrows shot up when I saw Minthe instead. As she had been at the masquerade ball, she was dressed in scarlet red, but the dress would have looked more at home in a Manhattan nightclub than at a ball. It was skin tight, with peephole sides showing her toned waist, and a plunging neckline revealing ample cleavage. The skirt was short and she was wearing red boots that came high over her knees. She looked amazing.

My insides quivered as every instinct in me told me to roll-over, to avoid conflict, to let the pretty, popular girl have what she wanted because it would be less trouble for me in the end.

But I wasn't at school anymore, and yes, she might be wearing something more modern than me, but it was my dress Hades wanted to take off.

'Your grandmother must be very talented,' I said, and lifted my glass to my lips nonchalantly.

'Who's this?' said Sam, appearing over my shoulder. I clenched my jaw, annoyed, and lowered the glass.

'This is Minthe,' I ground out.

'I'm Sam,' he beamed, and stuck his hand out.

'You're a human,' she sneered, looking at his hand like it had come out of the Empusa lair.

'And you're rude,' he replied. I snorted a laugh.

'Minthe is the current leader of the Trials,' I told him. 'So not my biggest fan.'

'So you want to win? You're not being forced to compete?' he asked her. She looked at him incredulously.

'Forced to compete? Are you kidding? The Queen of the Underworld is a title most in Olympus would die for. And ironically, when I win I will never die.'

'Minthe is in it for the immortality,' I said to Sam.

'Whereas you're in it for love?' she said, perfect eyebrows raised. 'Spare me the act, Persephone. You've gone from being a pathetic, powerless little human to someone famous across Olympus, with magic. Don't pretend you're not in this for the same reasons as everyone else who's tried.'

'You know nothing about me,' I growled, gripping the stem on my glass tightly. My vines were writhing under my skin. She didn't care one bit for Hades, she would let him rot from the inside out whilst she gloried in being an immortal Queen.

'You're the same as everyone else. There is nothing special about you, despite what people say.'

'You're jealous,' said Sam, and we both looked at him. He gave a her a cold smile. 'You know Hades likes her and she has supporters, and you're jealous.'

I blinked. Nobody was ever jealous of me.

'Shut your mouth or I'll shut it for you,' she snapped at Sam, and the stem of my glass snapped in my grip. I didn't feel the glass cut my hand though, as a black vine snaked from my free hand. Minthe licked her lips slowly as she raised her own hands, the skin on her palms turning an earthy brown.

'Why don't you go and talk to someone else, Minthe?' Hecate appeared from nowhere, stepping between us. Blue light danced over her pale skin and power emanated from her. Minthe stepped backwards, and an angry look flashed over her face, as though she hadn't wanted to move.

'You and your Titan guard-dog are freaks,' she spat, then whirled around, her heels clicking on the marble as she marched away.

'I had that covered, you know,' I said to Hecate, resentfully. I was surprised to feel genuinely robbed of a chance to show Minthe that she shouldn't fuck with me.

'I know you did, but I'm allowed to be a bitch to people. You're not supposed to. This whole thing is being broadcast.'

'Oh,' I said. 'Then, thanks.'

'You're welcome. And you're bleeding.'

I looked down at my hand, the broken glass still clutched in it.

'Shit,' exclaimed Sam, taking the glass from me quickly. 'Is it bad? Let me see.' I smiled at him.

'It's fine. Watch.' I held up my hand to show him, and called up my power, concentrating on the cut. It glowed faintly as the skin closed, and delight spread across Sam's face.

'Now that is fucking cool.'

'Right?'

'You still need to make sure you don't get blood on your dress,' Hecate said, and a satyr tugged at my skirt. He was holding a tray with new drinks and a neatly folded napkin. I thanked him and wiped my hand clean.

'You know, I could get used to living here,' said Sam as the satyr handed him a fresh glass.

'Maybe you should wait until you see the bad stuff before making statements like that,' I said. A loud gong sounded and the commentator shimmered into the room at the same time Zeus appeared on his throne. 'And it doesn't look like you'll have to wait long.'

It was time to find out what my next Trial would be.

TWELVE

HADES

'Good day, Olympus!' boomed the commentator. I tore my eyes from Persephone, her tense anger after her encounter with Minthe rolling through the bond and firing inside me. And despite hating her feeling anything other than happy, I couldn't deny how good it felt knowing how much she resented Minthe. I was hers, and everything about her body and mind projected it and I liked it. In fact I loved it. The idea of being wed to that shallow mountain nymph was too unpleasant to consider.

'It's time to announce the penultimate Trial!' sang the commentator. My stomach tensed in anticipation, magnified by my awareness of Persephone's nerves. 'First thing tomorrow, Persephone will face one of the most exciting and unpleasant demons of the Underworld. One with an appetite for death and destruction.' My pulse quickened. I had known that this Trial would involve one of the nastier demons that inhabited my realm, but there were a few I prayed she would not have to face. A few that I really did not want to have to give up control over for the duration of the Trial, so that Zeus could play his twisted games.

It was impossible for me to guess what demon had been chosen. The depths of Virgo were home to some of the most dangerous creatures ever born, including some the other Olympians didn't even know existed. Many were too dangerous for me to give up control of at all, like the Furies, and some were too strong and willful to be drawn into these games, like Nyx. But Zeus still had a choice of many who would shred a person apart with relish, their power coming from the dead.

The commentator spoke again. 'She will enter the lair of Eurynomos!'

An excited buzz rippled through the crowd as Persephone's eyes snapped to mine, her face paling as my own stomach sank. Eurynomos was the embodied spirit of rotting corpses and one of the worst demons in the Underworld.

Before I could send a word of comfort to Persephone, Zeus stood up.

'See you all tomorrow,' he said, and waved his hand. The room emptied with a flash, and rage seared hot through my veins.

'I have asked you to stop doing that in my realm,' I hissed.

'And I did not agree. You are forbidden from communicating with Persephone before her Trial.'

'What?' I was on my feet, my muscles expanding instinctively. I would not be kept apart from her. Ever again.

'Eurynomos has been under your control for centuries. You will be able to give her an unfair advantage by telling her what you know about him.'

'I will tell her nothing,' I ground out.

'I know. Because you will not be able to.'

'Zeus,' I started, a roaring sound building in my ears and darkness spreading through my core. He would not keep me from her.

'Hades, it is for one night, and you can't deny that your information would help her. It is what is fair,' said Athena, standing up. 'She will be told, and kept safe.'

'Nobody can keep her safe except me.'

'Untrue,' said Zeus, but Athena cut him off.

'She's not going anywhere, you can guard her bedroom door if you wish. You just can't speak to her.'

The rational part of me warred with the shadowed fury. If they were all in agreement I couldn't do anything about it. This was a battle I couldn't win. But perhaps I could get something from it.

'I will agree on one condition,' I spat.

'You don't have a choice,' drawled Zeus, but Athena cocked her head at me.

'And what is that?'

'Leave her brother out of the Trials. He is to remain untouched.' Zeus rolled his eyes but Athena spoke.

'And you will not try to talk to her if we agree?'

'Yes.'

'Fine.'

'You spoil him, daughter,' Zeus said to Athena, then disappeared with a screech of purple lightning. She looked at me, her face soft.

'You are lucky that I'm his favorite,' she said with a small smile, then vanished too. As the other gods began to leave, their thrones vanished as well, the dais reforming with just my huge skull throne in the middle. I strode towards it, still hulking and angry.

·   ·   ·

Zeus would pay for what he done to her. *To us.* I wasn't sure how yet, but he would.

'A word, if I may, Hades?' Poseidon strode up to my throne, and I nodded, surprise knocking my anger back a little.

'What do you want?'

'Brother, I am worried. Someone sent Persephone to Tartarus deliberately, and very few know the true consequences of that.'

'If you are going to ask me to send her back again, I won't.'

'On the contrary. I have decided she is safer where we can see and control her.'

'Control her?' Alarm bells rang in my mind, a need to protect her flaring inside me.

'You know what I mean,' he said dismissively. 'I believe that the culprit is closer to home than we originally thought.'

'You think it is an Olympian,' I said sharply. It wasn't a question.

'Yes. And since you are clearly still in love with her, you are the only one I can rule out. Hence this conversation.'

'Who do you suspect?' If the sea god was in the mood to talk, then I should get what I could out of him, and revisit the statement about controlling Persephone later.

'Ares has not had a war in a while, Hera has wrath more lethal than any of us, Aphrodite's boredom knows no bounds, Athena makes wild plans beyond any of our understanding and Dionysus has been acting strange for weeks.'

'And Zeus?'

'He has the most to lose.'

'Or the most to prove,' I countered. 'And the most hatred for me.'

'He does not hate you, brother.'

'Really? So forcing me to marry against my will and exposing my realm to the world is an act of love?' My voice dripped with sarcasm.

'When Olympus discovers that it was you who created a new realm against Zeus' will, and that the Lord of the Gods can't undo it, they will lose respect for him. You know he can not tolerate that. You have brought this upon yourself.'

I hissed out a breath, unable to argue. A thought flashed into my mind.

'Oceanus may have a score to settle,' I said. Poseidon scowled.

'Oceanus is your friend and my mentor. I do not believe this would be in his interest.'

'You are right,' I said, feeling guilty for suggesting it. Oceanus was a Titan, and easily powerful enough to be the culprit, but he had never been malevolent. And I knew better than most not to judge Titans by their few monstrous ancestors. 'If Zeus has the most to lose, then could it be someone with a vendetta against him, rather than Persephone?' I said.

'That moves Hera to the top of the list,' Poseidon muttered. 'I'll never know why she married him.'

'He's as charming as he is fickle. How do I know it is not you, and this is not an elaborate scheme to dissuade me of your guilt?' I said, glaring into Poseidon's ocean-blue eyes. He chuckled softly.

'Brother, I certainly mean you no harm. It is true I fear what your lover could do to Olympus, but I am not so governed by pride that I will let my initial reaction stand. I want to help her win, for something in return.'

'What?'

'If she survives and she wins the Trials and gets her power back, let her live elsewhere.'

Anger trickled through my veins like ice.

'No,' I said immediately. Poseidon's face darkened, waves crashing in his irises.

'Hades, she can not stay so close to Tartarus and you know it. The more her soul deteriorates, the less control you or anyone else will have over her.'

'I do not seek to control her!'

'Do you mean to let the most powerful and evil being Olympus has ever seen go free?'

'Of course not but-' He cut me off before I could finish.

'Then make the right choice, Hades. She would be happier anywhere but here.'

The sick feeling in my gut spread, the knowledge that he was right worse than the anger roiling inside me.

'She can survive the Trials without your help,' I spat eventually.

'You are making a mistake.'

'This conversation is over.'

He gave me a long look, then the salty smell of ocean washed over me as he gave a bark of frustration and vanished. I closed my eyes, searching inside me for the remnants of Persephone's light, the barrier she had helped reinforce with her golden vines. I filled my head and my heart with her, and slowly the monster receded, sinking back into its toxic depths.

She had beaten many Trials already that should have killed her. There were only two left now, and then this nightmare would be over, one way or another.

But no matter how I spun it in my mind, I couldn't see a

happy ending. If she died... The thought of losing her was unbearable, and I cast it out before the beast could rise again. If she survived but lost the Trials, I could not marry that nymph. And if she triumphed... Could I really let her give up her soul to live with me in the dark?

THIRTEEN

PERSEPHONE

'What do you mean I can't see Hades?'

'It has been deemed that he would be able to give you an unfair advantage,' Athena said, her voice serene as she stood before me in my old room.

'I deserve an advantage!' I snapped. 'This is bullshit.' Power burst from the goddess and my knee buckled instantly, forcing me into a bow.

'Do not forget who you are addressing, Persephone.'

'I'm sorry,' I stammered, my heart hammering in my chest.

'Standing up to Zeus as you did wasn't just brave, it was stupid. Under any other circumstance he would have killed you where you stood. Do not think you can treat all gods in that way.' Her voice held a steely edge and I tried to lift my head to look at her.

'I am still learning your customs,' I said. *Plus Zeus was an asshole who deserved what I had said to him.* Athena regarded me a moment, then gave a tiny nod. My body relaxed, and I stood up again. 'Can I see Hecate and my brother?'

'No. Hecate knows as much about the inhabitants of this realm as Hades does.' I barely kept the scowl from my face. At least I had Skop, I thought, glancing down at the silent dog. 'Rest well in preparation for tomorrow,' Athena said.

'I don't suppose you can tell me anything? About what to expect?' I ventured.

'No. I can't. Goodnight, Persephone.'

The goddess of wisdom vanished before I could say anything else and I sighed as I slumped onto my bed. It felt small now, compared to Hades' bed. A flash of anger and regret pulsed through me as I remembered his words from earlier, about having something to look forward to all day. And now we were being denied each other's company.

'They're all assholes,' I said, kicking out at thin air.

'Dionysus is alright,' said Skop.

'You would say that, you work for him.'

'Doesn't mean I have to like him. I just do.'

'So he's not cruel or spiteful or egotistical?' I challenged. Skop snorted.

'He's all of those things. You can't have almost limitless power and endless life, and not think you're better than everyone else. Or become a bit fucked up along the way.'

'So why do you like him then?'

'Because the good outweighs the bad. Plus, your definition of bad is a little different to mine.' He wagged his tail.

'I don't doubt it,' I said wryly and stood up, my feet pacing automatically.

Nerves were making my skin fizz, and the thought of waiting until tomorrow for the Trial with no Hades to distract me was making me even more anxious. 'Do you know anything about Eurynomos?' I asked Skop.

'Only what Hecate told you, that he's the demon of rotting corpses.'

'Shit. I hoped I had mis-remembered that,' I said, pushing my hands through my hair. 'Maybe I should practice that thing I did in the Empusa lair where I blocked out the bad smell.'

'Good idea. Rotting-corpse smell could be quite distracting.' My stomach lurched, a combination of revulsion at the visual my brain conjured up, and my building nerves. *'You know what would be even more useful than practicing smell-blocking?'* Skop said, and I looked at the little dog, raising my eyebrows in question.

'What?'

'Eating another seed and getting more magic.'

I paused my pacing.

I knew he was right. There were two Trials left, and they were only going to get harder. Was the risk of more power corrupting me greater than the risk of dying? Survival instinct took over, the urge to make myself stronger filling me. *You're not just risking dying*, my internal voice reminded me. *If you survive but lose, you have to watch Hades marry Minthe.*

I had to win.

I stepped to my dresser, where the box of seeds stood. It magically appeared in whatever place I was staying, along with *Faesforos* and the old purse I had arrived in Olympus with. Flipping open the lid of the box, I took a slow breath.

Just a little more power. Enough to beat Eurynomos, and take on the last Trial.

And possibly find the river Lethe, like the stranger in the

Atlas garden had said. I shoved the thought down. I had to concentrate on the Trials.

I picked up a shiny, moist seed. What would more magic feel like? Just more strength? Or would there be new powers?

I put the seed in my mouth and swallowed.

Unlike the previous times I had eaten a seed, I did feel something right away but it was not what I had hoped for. It was massive fatigue. Within a few minutes I felt the need to lay down, my eyelids leaden, and almost as soon as my head hit the pillow I was out, my sleep completely dreamless.

I woke with a start the next morning when Skop picked up my hand in his wet mouth and shook it.

'What happened?' I shouted, sitting up quickly.

'You slept like the freaking dead and I had to stay up all night to check you were breathing,' he answered me, my hand still in his mouth. I tugged it back gently.

'Well, thanks,' I mumbled, blinking.

'How do you feel?'

'Good,' I said, swinging my legs out of bed. And it was true. My mind felt clearer and my nerves, though still present, weren't as overwhelming as before. Maybe being knocked out like that was exactly what I had needed. I'd had no chance to freak myself out. 'How long until the Trial?'

'An hour.'

'OK. I'm going for a shower,' I said, and made my way to my washroom.

Whilst I washed up and got ready, I did what I had meant to do the night before, practicing blocking out the smell of the soap by thinking about the smell of plants instead. Lavender definitely worked the best, which made sense as it was such a potent smell. I whipped out my vines a few times, checking the color and testing how they felt. Other than a keener sense of alertness, everything felt the same.

Dressed in my fighting gear, *Faesforos* strapped to my thigh, Poseidon's pearl in my pocket and my hair tightly braided out of my face, I felt more ready than I ever had before a Trial. I could kill demons. I was a goddess, dammit.

And I had one hell of a god to fight for.

When it wasn't Hecate who came to get me I felt a pang of nerves though. Athena returned instead, her white toga pristine. I hadn't realized how much confidence the fierce goddess of ghosts instilled in me until she wasn't there, and I missed her.

'You are different,' Athena said, tilting her head at me as soon as she appeared in my room. I bowed low as I answered her. I didn't want to piss her off again.

'I ate another seed.'

'That was probably wise.'

'Coming from you, I'll take that reassuringly,' I muttered as I straightened and she gave me a small smile.

'Are you ready?'

I nodded.

She flashed us to a cavern that glowed the same dim red that the Empusa's lair had, but it was much bigger. I turned slowly, looking around. It was completely empty, just bare rock everywhere.

'Good luck,' Athena said quietly, then vanished with a flash. The commentator's voice rang out immediately, and I felt a shot of adrenaline rush through me, my stomach lurching. This was it.

'Good day, Olympus! As you can see, Persephone is ready to start her next Trial, in the lair of Eurynomos!' I moved my hand to my side, nearer to my dagger. This didn't look like a lair. Where were the corpses and stuff? 'But let us not forget, good citizens, this is the penultimate Trial. We need some drama!'

My jaw clenched. Was me fighting a horrendous demon not enough for these fucking people?

'Persephone will be offered a choice. A test of her moral character.' I froze as the new voice boomed around me.

It was Zeus speaking.

'There is no catch or hidden agenda, and it is a rare opportunity indeed.' His seductive voice bounced off the bare cave walls and adrenaline surged through me. *Get on with it!*

Purple light began to crackle above me and I stared up at the ceiling of the cavern as something began to melt through it, entering the space.

Not something. Someone.

A woman's form began to take shape, emerging from the rock, facing down towards the ground as though she were laying on her front. She was wearing a red dress which hung from her suspended body, and she looked to be bound by ropes. Her hair also hung down, obscuring her face from view.

But I knew who it was without seeing her face.

'Get me the fuck out of here!' screeched Minthe.

'Persephone,' Zeus's voice boomed. 'We would like you to meet Eurynomos, demon of rotting flesh.' The walls rippled with red light, and shadows began forming on the flat walls where there shouldn't be any. I gripped my dagger instinctively, my vines itching at my palms. A whimper drew my attention back to Minthe, held against the ceiling by ropes forming a sort of net. Blackened fingers were snaking between the ropes from the rock, drawing closer to her.

'He is usually only able to take the flesh from the dead, but we've made an exception for today,' Zeus said, and Minthe screamed as a finger touched her bare shoulder. Her pale skin darkened instantly, as though she had been burned.

'Stop!' I yelled. 'This is my Trial, not hers!'

'So true, flower goddess. You need two more seeds to win. You may have both, right now, if you let Eurynomos have Minthe.'

'What?' My head spun at his words. I could win right now? No more tests and Trials and fear, just Hades.

But...

I looked up at the woman strapped to the ceiling, a flash of memory causing me to think of Ixion strapped to the burning wheel in Tartarus. My stomach lurched as another finger touched Minthe's leg, and she made a strangled sound.

'This isn't fair!' she screamed. 'I've taken my Trials! I've proven myself!'

She was right.

'If you choose to save her and succeed you will win one token, and therefore will need to win the last Trial to marry Hades,' boomed Zeus. 'If you choose to save her and fail, you lose the Trials. What is it to be, Persephone?'

There was no question in my mind. Maybe the fucked up gods and citizens of Olympus would kill for what they wanted, but I wasn't one of them. I couldn't live my life waking every day knowing I chose to let someone die.

'Let her live,' I said loudly.

'I was hoping you would say that,' Zeus said, and I could hear the delight in his words. The cavern began to rumble and shake around me, and I yelped as a huge part of the rock floor began to crack and split, causing me to stumble.

'I *was hoping you would say that too,*' hissed a high-pitched voice inside my head. '*It's so rare that I get living company, it is truly a treat.*'

'Eurynomos?' I called out loud, as more of the floor cracked around me.

'*Indeed. Now, if you want to save her you must cut her free.*'

I looked up at Minthe strapped to the ceiling. How was I going to get up there?

With a lurch, the part of the floor I was standing on shot up, and I dropped to my knees as I stumbled. The floor was falling away in huge pieces, leaving pillars of stone at different heights, barely large enough for me to stand on. The one I was on was one of the lowest, but some almost reached the ceiling. As I stared around I realized what I had to do. I had to jump from pillar to pillar, until I was high enough to cut Minthe's ropes.

Heights. Why was it fucking heights! They said I wouldn't have to face them again.

I peered over the edge of my pillar, pulse racing and heart hammering so hard I felt sick.

But the dark chasm I expected to see wasn't there. What I saw was much, much worse.

Bodies. Corpses in every stage of decomposition were

rising from the dark, filling the space between the pillars. Many were skeletons like the one I had fought at the start of the Trials, limbs and jaws clacking as they climbed over each other. But some still had flesh clinging to their bones, jaws and shoulders and ribs showing through their sallow, blue-tinged skin. I felt myself heave as their rotten smell rose with them, and called the lavender scent to wrap around me fast.

'Don't fall off the pillars, flower goddess,' taunted Eurynomos. 'They'll rip you apart, and then I'll eat your flesh.'

Shit, shit, shit. Terror surged inside me as I looked between the writhing mass of undead below me, and Minthe, shrieking above me. How the fuck was I going to survive this?

FOURTEEN

PERSEPHONE

OK, *human Persephone was scared of heights,* I told myself sternly, breathing hard. *Goddess Persephone has vines that can catch stuff and recently jumped out of a tree. Goddess Persephone can do this.*

'Will you get the fuck on with it!' screamed Minthe from above me. I flicked my eyes to her angrily as I tried to work out which rocky pillar was closest to me.

'Are you shitting me? I could have left you here to die!'

'Well you didn't, so get me the fuck out of here!'

'Stop swearing at me and shut up,' I snapped back, tucking *Faesforos* back into its sheath. A low rumbling moan was coming from the undead below me, and I guessed some must still have their throats intact. I let a green vine snake from my palm, aiming it towards the ceiling. The closest pillar was about a foot taller than the one I was on and a three feet leap away. I felt a thud beneath me, and my stomach lurched as a rotten hand appeared over the edge of my pillar. The undead were climbing.

My lip curled back as I kicked out at the hand, and I watched in muted fear as the corpse fell back onto the mass of skeletons below it. Another corpse replaced it immediately.

Minthe was right. I needed to get the fuck on with it.

My vine wrapped itself around the ropes holding Minthe up, and I tugged experimentally. The vine held firm. So I could jump, and the vine should hold me if I missed. Like a safety rope. A safety rope over corpses that would tear me apart before my flesh was eaten.

My hands were shaking as I bent my knees and gripped the vine, preparing to jump. Just a few weeks ago my knees would have given out already, but I was different now. I was strong. And I had to win. Filling my mind with Hades' face, I jumped.

I landed easily on the next pillar, the vine helping me get the height I needed, and a cry of triumph escaped my lips.

'There's like ten more! Gods help me, stop celebrating and hurry up!' shouted Minthe. I threw her a glare, and found the next easiest pillar to get to. They seemed to be in no order, but there was one about four feet away that was higher than mine. I felt the rock pound beneath me, and didn't need to look down to know that it meant the undead were still trying to get to me.

'Did you know that's how Spartae Skeletons were made?' Eurynomos' hissing voice filled my head. 'They are what's left when I've finished with the flesh.'

'Lovely', I muttered, crouching for the next jump.

'Hades lets me have the bad ones, you see. The ones who have sinned most foully.'

'That's nice,' I replied, and jumped. I didn't land so easily this time, the pillar higher and further than before, and my insides lurched as my back foot scrabbled on the edge of the rock.

'I don't miss him, you know. Hades never lets me have any fun, and I'm bound to his will. This Zeus character who controls me now though...' The demon tailed off and I couldn't help my interest.

'What about him?'

'He doesn't have what it takes,' Eurynomos hissed. *'He has power, but it's not dark enough to contain me. Not for much longer anyway.'*

A shudder ran through me at his words. Could he really break free of Zeus' power?

'Hades would just take control again,' I said flippantly, and decided on my next pillar. It was only a couple of feet away, but it was much higher than mine. A bony finger crept over the edge of my own pillar as I bent my knees, and I kicked at it. Eurynomos sighed loudly in my head.

'Yes, he would. But I might get a few brief seconds of blissful freedom first,' he said more brightly.

'And what would you do with that?' I leaped for the next pillar, and realized with a jolt that I wouldn't make it. Instinct took over and my vines shortened fast. Too fast. I flew up and over the pillar, dangling from my vine, the sense of weightlessness nauseating. I couldn't help looking down as I swung and black dots instantly clouded my eyes. Swarms of undead surged between the uneven pillars below me, and the thought of falling to them was the only thing I could process.

'Just pull yourself up, you idiot!' shouted Minthe. Her voice cut through my panic, and I did as she said, shortening the vine further. I began to zoom upwards, and I kicked myself mentally. *Why the hell didn't I do this before?*

'Oh no, no, it can't be this easy,' hissed Eurynomos, and then searing heat flashed down my vine towards me. One of the blackened fingers on the ceiling that had been

tormenting Minthe was gripping my vine, burning through it. Revolting images of the decomposing dead flashed through me as my vines turned black, the dark power of the Underworld filling me.

And then I really was weightless, the vine severed by the demon's touch. I whipped a new vine from my other hand out blindly, praying as I twisted through the air, all other thought gone. It hit something hard and I willed it to coil around whatever it was. I jerked, and then I was swinging towards a tall pillar, my vine wrapped tight around the top, and bony fingers were closing around my ankle. I kicked at the skeleton as I looked down, my insides lurching again as a squelchy, rotten fist gripped my boot. I smashed into the pillar hard, the momentum of my fall enough to jolt the undead's grip loose, and then I willed the vine to shorten, shooting me up to the top of the pillar and out of reach. I was panting hard when I got to the top, and I scrabbled up onto the rock, adrenaline making my muscles stronger.

Minthe screamed again, and the undead moaned louder in response. I needed to end this. But how, if Eurynomos was going to sever my vines? They were all I had. Maybe I could distract him.

'Where are you, Eurynomos? Why don't you show your-self?' I yelled. He chuckled in my mind.

'That is forbidden.'

'Are you too ugly to be seen then?' I eyed the next pillar and instead of sending my vines up to the ropes, I launched them from both hands at the top of it. It took more physical effort to climb the pillars like this than swinging from the ceiling, but at least the fingers couldn't get me. I pulled myself to the next pillar using the vines, and bashed my chin on it hard as I collided with the rock, my feet scrabbling for purchase. I dragged myself onto the top, scanning fast for the next one.

'*You might call me ugly I suppose,*' the demon said thoughtfully. I launched my vines at the next pillar. I reckoned I had another three or four to go, before I could reach the ceiling. I glanced up at Minthe, and saw that her eyes were squeezed shut. Now I was closer I could see the gaping wounds the fingers were leaving, burning through layers of skin. Bile burned in my chest. I had to get us both out. I jumped, trying to pull on the vines earlier so that I didn't hit the pillar so hard. It didn't work, and my shoulder took a pounding as I slammed into the next pillar.

'*What do you think?*' said Eurynomos' voice as I pulled myself up. I scowled through my panting.

'What do I think of what?'

'*Am I ugly?*'

Just as I straightened on top of the spindly pillar, he appeared, right in front of me.

My brain froze as I stumbled backwards in primal fright, and the only part of me to react to my feet slipping off the rock were my vines. They whipped towards the only thing to grab; Eurynomos.

His face twisted in delight as my vines made contact with his skin, and although my fall was halted, images so revolting I almost passed out flooded my mind. I could see him, on all fours, surrounded by corpses. His body was black and hairless, long and sinewy, and covered in sores that oozed dark red liquid that streaked his skin. Massive black eyes bulged in his elongated skull and his mouth was far too big, filled with razor-sharp, crooked teeth. The real demon, cackling before me, merged with the one in my vision, who was ripping flesh from bodies with his teeth like a rabid animal.

'You smell delicious,' he hissed, and I convulsed as I forced my vines to let go, to disintegrate. With another roar of laughter he vanished. '*Such a shame I'm not allowed to touch you until you fail to save the other one,*' he said, his voice mockingly sad. I was taking deep breaths, trying desperately not to throw up or pass out, my knees weak beneath me on the pillar.

'Get the fuck on with it, flower girl!' yelled Minthe. Anger surged through me at her words.

'I'm nearly killing myself to save you, you ungrateful asshole!' I yelled back. Weirdly the words brought strength though, and I realized my anger was pushing through the disgust and fear. My shaking lessened and I looked up.

I had to try something else.

I pulled *Faesforos* from my thigh and launched a vine at the ropes above me, near to Minthe's head. It curled around the rope and with a thought, the vine began to shorten, pulling me towards the ceiling fast. I knew I only had seconds before the fingers severed my vine, but hopefully that would be enough. As soon as I got close enough I slashed with my dagger. *Faesforos* cut through the rope like it was butter, and Minthe yelped as her right shoulder dropped.

'What happens if you manage to cut them all?'

'You'd better hope we get flashed out of here before you land in that,' I answered her, pointing at the undead clamoring below us, just as a finger closed over my vine. I winced but stayed focused, looking for a pillar to land on safely. I swung myself, adrenaline edging out the fear, the knowledge that I'd fallen from here already and survived giving me the strength I needed. When I judged I was swinging enough, I lengthened the vine again, kicking my feet towards the highest pillar and letting out a gasp of relief as my feet made contact and I was able to disintegrate the vine. The hideous images crawling from those blackened fingers were impossible to ignore.

'*Clever flower goddess,*' hissed Eurynomos. I ignored him, looking up at the ropes instead and preparing to repeat the maneuver.

Each time I swung from the ceiling I was able to cut more ropes, despite the rotten fingers getting faster at trying to sever my vines. And each time I did it, the stronger and more confident I became. The old saying 'what doesn't kill you makes you stronger,' clearly had some truth to it. After six swings there was only one rope left, and Minthe's face was a mask of fear. Her shoulders and shins were covered in wounds.

'You'd better not fuck this up,' she called to me as I prepared to swing again.

'Have you always been a bitch?' I yelled back.

'Yes. But I don't deserve to die like this.' Her voice was bitter and I couldn't help the surge of emotion I felt for her. She was a fighter, that much was clear, and she had been rendered helpless. I knew how awful it felt to have your fate in the hands of another.

'Perhaps you could be less of a bitch to me if I save your life?' She didn't answer, but her eyes locked on mine and I could see the very real fear under the attitude. 'Alright, I'm coming,' I breathed, and launched my vine up. Weirdly though, as I pulled myself to the ceiling, no finger appeared in the rock, snaking towards my vine. Suspicion filled me as I swiped *Faesforos* at the last rope, which was wrapped around Minthe's middle.

But it never made contact. Instead, Eurynomos appeared between us, my dagger tearing across his emaciated arm. He shrieked, a hair-raising noise that induced almost as much terror in me as one of Hades' rages.

'Pain!' the demon screeched, and I kicked at the air under me, trying to swing myself away from him. I looked desperately for a pillar beneath me to land on. 'Pain was what I needed! For a surge in power big enough to break free!'

'What?' I snapped my eyes to his warped, glee-filled ones.

'Free,' he hissed, and then he was on me.

Agony like I had never experienced, worse than being electrocuted by the man with the phoenix, engulfed me. I could feel my skin being torn from my bones as he bent his head to my shoulder, and I felt my vine disintegrate as I screamed. I began to fall, and the demon fell with me, my neck and my jaw searing with white hot pain as his teeth sank into my flesh. As darkness began to consume me, I heard Minthe.

'Fucking fight him!'

My back hit something hard, and I was vaguely aware of the clatter of bones and the squelch of rotting flesh. *You are a goddess.* Another wave of agony drew new screams from me, and I was drowning under Eurynomos' weight as he tore more skin and muscle from my neck. *You are a goddess. Fucking fight him.* I reached inside for everything I had and blasted my black vines at him.

They hit the demon so hard they went *through* him. I surged all the power I had through my palms, the black vines drawing on his foul magic and channeling it as my own strength. Eurynomos bellowed as huge thorned barbs appeared on the vines, and through the connection my vines had to him, I felt them pierce the inside of his chest.

As the vines grew they dragged him up, and I swung my arms, slamming him into the side of the cavern. The swarm of undead around me froze in place, only moving their heads to watch their master as I threw him into the opposite wall with as much force as I could muster. I drew my knees up, a dark rage fueled by the demon's power beginning to consume me. *Eurynomos would die.* He and all the others who sought to use me as a toy, torture me for entertainment, rip the fucking flesh from my bones. I was too entrenched in rage to notice that my skin was already knitting back together.

'Get me out of here!' Minthe's shrieks filtered through the toxic rage, and I stood slowly, my eyes still fixed on Eurynomos as I flung him between the cavern walls, his languid body bending unnaturally every time he hit the rock.

'One minute,' I hissed. 'I have something to take care of first.'

With my arms raised high above my head, the black vines glistening with the demon's blood, I held Eurynomos still above me. 'Tell me again how you are going to feast on my flesh?' I yelled at him. My voice didn't sound like my own, but I didn't care.

I didn't care about anything other than making an example of this evil creature. He moaned but didn't reply. *Couldn't reply.* I was drawing too much of his power from him.

With a final effort of will I tugged on the darkest part of him, drawing the magic into myself, and then with a roar I swelled my vines with it. Eurynomos screamed as giant thorns erupted from the vines, through his chest, skewering him from the inside out.

As the creature's life left him, so did the dark power

flowing into me, and I stumbled backwards as my vines weakened. Eurynomos' body crashed towards the floor and the undead parted as he landed hard in front of me, staring down at his pierced and bloody body. He began to glow a deep blue, then vanished. My black vines disintegrated and an epic wave of nausea took me. Before I could do anything else I was heaving, throwing up onto the rock floor, my body shaking uncontrollably.

'Get me out, please.' Minthe's pleading cut through my retching.

The acrid bile and the pain in my throat and neck made my eyes water as I tried to take deep breaths. *I had to get us out of here.* I shot a green vine towards the ceiling and my exhausted, shaken body didn't even register the height as I pulled myself up, grabbing *Faesforos* from my thigh as I went. I felt dazed, numb. Avoiding meeting Minthe's eyes, I cut the last rope binding her, and the cavern flashed white.

FIFTEEN

PERSEPHONE

A smattering of clapping met my ringing ears as I found
myself standing in Hades' throne room.

'Persephone,' his voice filled my head immediately. *'Are
you alright?'*

I nodded mutely at the vibrating smoky figure at the
end of the row of thrones.

'Persephone!' I whirled at the bellowed voice and saw
my brother trying to push his way through the small crowd,
frantic. Hecate was yanking him back, her face set and
hard.

'I'm fine, Sam,' I croaked, and he stilled, face pale. The
burbling sound my voice made wasn't right, and I tentatively
touched my neck. My stomach roiled as my fingers didn't
meet skin, but something lumpy and wet. I closed my eyes and
concentrated, willing the wound to heal faster than it already
was. I had no doubt it had been worse when Eurynomos first
attacked me, or I wouldn't be still be standing. I'd be dead.

'Alright for some,' muttered Minthe and I opened my
eyes. She was standing next to me, shaking. Deep dark burn

wounds covered her body, and her face was as white as a sheet. I frowned at her.

'What do you mean, alright for some? You think that was fun for me? That I'm lucky I got to experience that? I just saved your life, quit giving me shit.'

'I meant that,' she said quietly, and gestured to my shoulder and neck, 'I can't heal myself.'

'Oh,' I said. I cocked my head at her, then sent out a vine slowly towards her arm. She flinched when it touched, but said nothing as my vine turned gold, and I sent my healing power through it. Her lips parted in a small gasp, then the sores began to pale, then knit closed.

'Thanks,' she mumbled.

'I'm thrilled to see you two getting on,' boomed Zeus, rising from his throne with a cold smile. 'If you please,' he said and raised his arm. The commentator appeared with a pop.

'So, gutsy Persephone chose to save her rival instead of living with murder on her conscience! Let's see what the judges have to say about that!' He grinned. The judges fizzled into the space in front of the thrones.

'Radamanthus?'

'One token,' the judge said.

'Aeacus?'

'One token.' The gaunt judge eyed me suspiciously as he spoke.

'Minos?'

'One token. And my respect,' said the head judge, with a small smile. I raised my eyebrows in surprise, and the three of them vanished.

'As I'd hoped, it appears that we will have quite a show-down for the last Trial,' said Zeus loudly.

'How did you know I wouldn't take both tokens and end it there?' I asked, interrupting him. He glared at me.

'Because most humans are painfully predictable, you even more so,' he said, then looked back to the crowd. 'The last Trial will be the much anticipated Hell-Hound Run!' A huge cheer went up from behind me and I looked to Hades. Skop had said I would meet Cerberus at some point. I guess this would be it. 'The Trial will be a little different than it has been for the other contestants though. Previously, the goal has been to get past all three of Hades' pets in a chariot. This time, it will be a race between the last remaining competitors. The winner will marry Hades.'

I looked at Minthe, her jaw dropping in time with mine.

'But I've already survived the Hell-Hound Run, you can't make me do it again!' she protested, her voice aghast. Abruptly she seemed to realize what she'd said and dropped fast to one knee. 'Oh Zeus, I'm sorry, I am just shocked. Please forgive my outburst.'

'You shall both be allowed a team of two to ride the chariot with you. They may not be Olympians, but that is the only restriction,' Zeus continued, ignoring her completely. 'We start at midday tomorrow.' He clapped his hands together in an overly exaggerated gesture, and all the gods except Hades disappeared in a blinding flash.

'Shit!' shouted Minthe, stamping her foot as she straightened. My vine fell away from her.

'What happens in the Hell-Hound Run?' I asked her, aware that Hades was moving towards us on one side, my brother and Hecate on the other.

'As if I'd tell you,' she snarled, fixing her angry eyes on mine.

'Woah, don't blame me for this! Honestly, you are the most ungrateful person I've ever fucking met!' Anger swelled through me.

'You have no idea what's at stake for me. What I've given up for this.' Tears shone in her eyes.

'No, and I don't care! You want to use Hades for immortality, you won't make him happy.'

'Happy? You seriously think you can make the Lord of the Dead *happy*?' She gaped at me.

'I know I can.'

'Wow. You're more deluded than I thought you were.'

'And you're more of a bitch than I thought you were.' Dark smoke entered my peripheral vision and we both looked at Hades.

'Please send me home to prepare, My Lord,' said Minthe tightly, bowing her head. Hades flicked a smoke hand, and she vanished.

'Persy, what the fuck was that? I mean, you were badass, but I can't believe you really did that, my own sister-' My brother's words faded into noise as he barreled into me, wrapping his arms around me hard. My head was buzzing, the residual rage and shock of what I'd done to Eurynomos settling over me.

I should regret such an act of rage. I didn't have to kill Eurynomos. I could have left him trapped while I freed Minthe. But I had decided he would die, and nothing could have stopped me doing it. It had been an act of wrath. The thing I feared most about this other person, this goddess, inside of me.

But I didn't regret it at all. He was not a person, he was a demon. And that meant...

'He'll regenerate,' I said to Hades. I didn't phrase it as a question but as something I'd known before I'd killed him, a defense of my actions. But I needed to hear him confirm it.

Hades nodded.

'Yes. It may take a while, but yes.' A shudder of relief rocked through me. I wasn't a murderer.

'Persy, Slayer of Demons,' said Hecate, a smile on her face. 'I like that.'

'I could get used to it,' I grinned back. My grin slipped as I felt a surge of emotion through me that was not my own. Fear and desperation. *Hades*.

'I need a moment with Hades,' I said to Sam, extracting myself from his hug. 'Then we'll prepare for the next Trial and have a drink. A large one.'

'I'll get the cocktails ready,' said Hecate.

'What's wrong?' I asked as soon as the throne room was empty. The smoke surrounding him fell away and Hades rushed at me. He scooped me up in his huge arms, planting soothing kisses across my neck and shoulder, where Eurynomos had bitten me.

'If you hadn't killed him, I would have,' he whispered, pulling away and gripping my face in his hands. 'You were... incredible.'

'I wouldn't have killed him if he were a real person,' I said firmly. *You sure about that?* The voice inside me came from nowhere, and I forced it down. I was sure. 'I ate another seed,' I told Hades.

'I can see that. The thorns are back.'

'What else can I do now?'

'Heal yourself faster,' he said, silver eyes flicking to my neck. 'I wish I could stay with you, but I have to meet with the other gods, and it can't wait.' I felt his fury rise within him, and laid my palms on his chest. He took a deep breath. 'Zeus lost control of Eurynomos. I do not want to risk him losing control of Cerberus.'

'Will Cerberus try to eat me?' I asked, as casually as I could. Hades stroked his thumb down my cheek.

'He loved you once.'

'Really? I'm more of a cat person.'

'If you become my Queen again, we can get a cat.' My reaction must have shown on my face because a broad smile spread over his.

'You swear?'

'I swear.'

'Watch me ace this Trial,' I said.

After kissing me like his life depended on it, Hades left to meet with the others gods, promising to tell me all about the hell-hounds when he returned. And show me whatever my gold vines were able to do now.

He flashed me back to my old rooms, where Hecate, Sam and Skop were waiting, with the promised cocktails.

'We can only have a quick celebratory drink now, as we have a dinner invitation,' said Hecate, passing me a glass.

'I still can't believe you killed that thing, Persy, honestly, it was crazy!' Sam interrupted. 'And your neck... I thought you were going to die at one point.' He stopped speaking abruptly, a haunted look taking over his face.

'I'm OK, Sam. A demon is no match for a goddess.' I squeezed his arm encouragingly and took a long drag of my drink. It tasted divine.

'Well yeah, you proved that! You didn't tell me about the thorns.'

'I didn't have them until this morning. I ate another seed.'

'Good,' said Hecate. 'That might have saved your life.'

'*Told ya,*' said Skop.

'*And you were right,*' I answered him with a reluctant nod, then turned to Hecate. 'Who is the dinner invitation from?' *Please not Zeus, please not Zeus,* I prayed silently.

'Morpheus and Hedone. And I think they have good news.'

Hecate flashed us to Morpheus' rooms as soon I'd gulped down my cocktail, and boy did I get some room-envy.

His rooms were just like him, ethereal and floaty and just... magical. There was no better word. The rock walls glowed with stars but of every shade of blue, and they seemed to move like liquid across the rock. Just like his flowy robes. An enormous dining table was laid for five in the middle of the reception room and in the center was a large orb that glowed with yellow light, reminding me of the sun and casting a softer atmosphere across the whole space. Bookcases lined one wall, and an enormous tapestry covered the other. Before I could inspect it though, both Hedone and Morpheus were rising from the table to greet us.

'Persy, you were brilliant today!' beamed Hedone, kissing both of my cheeks. Familiar heat flushed through me at her touch and I felt a pang of sympathy for my brother. He would be completely bowled away by the goddess of pleasure.

To my surprise though, he kept it together pretty well, his cheeks only coloring slightly as she introduced herself. Morpheus seemed to fluster him more, the dream god's unearthly vibe leaving him stammering a bit.

'Please, sit,' Morpheus said, and we all took seats at the grand table. A satyr entered through the open door at the back of the room, carrying a tray of the delicious fizzy wine in saucer glasses.

'Sam, watch out for this stuff, it's not really meant for humans,' I said to him quietly.

'You can heal my hangover,' he grinned at me, and took a big sip. 'Fuck me, that's good!'

'Yeah, all food and drink here is.' I heard the pride in my voice as I spoke, as though I was showing off something that belonged to me. Somewhere along the line, my brain had seemed to have accepted Olympus as my home.

'Persephone, I've asked you here in a somewhat formal capacity,' said Morpheus, and we all looked at him. 'I would like to offer you my services in the chariot race.' I blinked at him. The chariot race. Zeus' words rushed back to me. *I could have two people to help me.*

'Seriously?'

'Yes. Did you have a team in mind already?'

'No, not at all, I hadn't even thought about it yet,' I spluttered. 'You would really risk yourself to help me?'

He chuckled.

'I'm as immortal as you can get without being an Olympian, the risk to me would be minimal,' he said gently. 'And I like Hades. So no offense, but I would be doing it for him, rather than you.'

I beamed at him, my heart swelling in my chest.

'Thank you! Thank you so much!' *I wouldn't be alone.* For the first time in this awful competition, I would have a friend by my side during a Trial. The thought was overwhelming.

'I'm assuming you were going to ask me too,' said Hecate. I snapped my head to her.

'Really?'

'Gods yeah. Same reason as Morpheus. I can't be dealing with a depressed Hades as a boss,' she shrugged. Her voice was as indifferent as her body language, but her eyes sparkled with something else. Excitement? She had been there, with me or near me, every single step of this journey. I'd seen her pale when discovering how dangerous my tasks were, seen the concern in her face when I'd been injured, seen her determination when we trained. She cared about me, I was sure.

'Will I be allowed to have two people from the Underworld to help me? Surely the hell-hounds know you two? I mean, Hades wasn't even allowed to talk to me before the last Trial.'

'Actually, I have the good fortune to never have to deal with the hounds,' said Morpheus dryly.

'I see them every day, but it won't matter. They'll be under Zeus' control, and there's nothing we can tell you about them that will help. And besides, Minthe has an advantage too. She's already done this Trial once.' Hecate said. That sounded more like a punishment than an advantage to me.

'But by that logic, if Eurynomos was under Zeus' control, why wasn't I allowed to talk to you or Hades last night?'

'Many of the demons in the Underworld can be bribed. If you know what to offer them, they'll do anything you ask. The hounds can't be bribed though, they're too well trained.'

'Oh. What does Eurynomos like?'

'Chocolate.'

'You're joking,' I said, staring at Hecate. She shrugged. 'You mean I could have avoided all that shit if I'd just offered him some fucking chocolate?'

'The Underworld is a fucked up place, Persy.'

SIXTEEN

HADES

'Will you put a fucking toga on, this is a formal meeting!' Zeus snapped as I appeared on top of his mountain, at the edge of his sky-high throne room.

'Will you learn to do what you're fucking supposed to, for once?' I barked back. Hera stood up from a long oval table and gave me a pointed stare. I clenched my jaw and changed my clothes to a black toga.

'Thank you, Hades,' Hera said and sat down again, gesturing for me to do the same. It looked like I was the last one to arrive. 'I do not want this meeting to degenerate into an argument,' she said, looking between Zeus and I as I yanked a chair back from the table and sat down, arms folded.

'So, I suppose as usual we are going to pretend that Zeus has done nothing wrong?' I asked. My brother bared his teeth at me but said nothing.

'Zeus acknowledges that Eurynomos was stronger than he first thought.'

'Nobody listens to me,' I spat. 'I've been telling you all for the last hundred years, each Eurynomos gets stronger

than the last. It's the same with all the infernal fucking creatures in Virgo!'

'Are you saying you are worried about keeping them
under control?' asked Athena.

'No. Absolutely not,' I lied.

'Then what are you saying?'

'That there is a reason they grow in strength. We should
be trying to deal with it.'

'We have had this conversation before, it is an Underworld problem, not ours,' said Apollo dismissively.

'I assure you, it is not caused by anything in Virgo.
Every sinner who crosses my path fuels the demons, and the
number of sinners grows every damned minute. Olympus is
filling people with greed and hate, and that is not my doing!'
Frustration was coursing through me. How many times did
I have to tell them? How could I make them see what they
were turning our world into, what the consequences of that
would be, without admitting to them how much of my soul I
had already lost to the darkness?

'If you become unfit to rule the Underworld, someone
must take your place,' said Zeus quietly. Every pair of eyes
fell on him.

'Are you volunteering to swap?' I asked him sarcastically. I knew he would never relieve me of this duty. And it
was too late anyway. Virgo was a part of me, I was bound to
the realm too deeply to ever be severed. If I fell, it would be
to the dead. I would become a part of the Underworld
itself.

'You would be a poor ruler of the skies, brother,' Zeus
said, still not meeting my eyes. 'But I believe I owe you an
apology.'

'What?' I wasn't the only one who looked shocked.

'The demons you preside over require more strength

than I realized and we failed to heed your warnings. But do not take my admission of your strength as a compliment.'

His eyes finally settled on mine, and they were sparking with electrifying purple energy. Every instinct in my body fired a warning, and power surged through my veins. 'The darkness in that creature was pure destruction. And you must be full of it to have such dominion over him. You are more dangerous than I thought you were.'

I could feel myself growing, the monster awake and ready. If Zeus wanted to know just how dangerous I was, I would show him. Too long he had dismissed me, bullied me. And now he had experienced just a taste of what I dealt with daily, he sought to use it against me?

'You chose one of the strongest demons in my realm for Persephone to face because you wanted to torment me, because you wanted to watch me lose her, and now you are shocked when you discover how strong it is?' I laughed, long and loud, and Zeus's expression darkened further as he grew to match me. 'Brother, you have no idea what I am capable of. What I have always been capable of.' Blue light was rolling from my huge body, forming an army of souls that began lining up around me. 'You made me a king, Zeus. A King of the Dead. And I have all the power that entails.'

'And it will never match mine,' Zeus hissed. 'Just because I can't control your fucking demons does not mean you are stronger than me. You would not be able to control my lightning!'

'Nor could I control Poseidon's waves, but I'm not the one fucking trying to! You behave like a spoiled child who wants to play with everyone else's toys and it will end us all!'

'You started this when you deliberately broke our rules

and created the thirteenth realm. This is your doing, not mine.'

'Stop fighting like children!' bellowed Hera suddenly, standing up again. 'Zeus, you have tormented Hades by bringing Persephone back, and now you must deal with that. Hades, your feelings for Persephone are clouding your ability to perform your duties, and *you* must deal with that. Now sit down, both of you.' Her voice rang out so loudly it actually made my head hurt, and the blue army of the dead shimmered and vanished.

Slowly, we both began to shrink back down. I caught the amused look on Dionysus' face and resisted the urge to lash out at him.

'It is extremely important that we do not have a repeat of what happened before. I am referring to when Persephone was sent to Tartarus,' Hera said.

'I agree,' I ground out.

'Then you will understand that you must not watch the last Trial with us, but guard the entrance to Tartarus instead.'

'What? No! If Zeus loses control of the hell-hounds they could rip her to shreds!'

'Then at least you won't have to watch,' Zeus said with a cruel smile. Before I could leap from my chair at him, Athena stood, thirty feet tall before my ass could leave the seat.

'Enough! Olympus is more important than anything else, and Persephone has the ability to cause the end of it, or plunge us into another endless bloody war. Cronos killed how many immortals before we defeated him last time? And many strong Titan allies who helped before are now gone, and we do not know where. We must not risk his being freed for anything, or anyone.'

'Brother, you can't put one mortal above the safety of the whole of Olympus,' added Poseidon quietly.

My insides churned as I stared between them, my muscles so tense they throbbed. I couldn't argue. What they were saying was true, and if all eleven of them were in agreement...

'What if the one who sent her to Tartarus last time is an Olympian?' I said, playing my last card. Athena visibly flinched and Hera made a scoffing sound. 'It's the only thing that makes sense, who else would know about Cronos? About what happened before?'

Every pair of eyes around the table bore into mine.

'You are so desperate you would accuse us?' asked Apollo, his voice hard. 'Why would any of us want a war after building this place so perfectly?'

Perfect? Was he not listening every time I told them how twisted the souls entering my realm were becoming? Frustration welled through me, teetering on the edge of rage. I had to make them understand. But before I could say anything, Zeus spoke.

'Even if it is one of us, you need to guard Tartarus. You are Cronos' keeper, and you must be there if anything happens.'

'I can flash there in an instant if needed,' I spat.

'An instant might be all Cronos needs. The decision is final.'

SEVENTEEN

PERSEPHONE

The meal Morpheus served us was fantastic. As we ate Sam asked more questions about the Underworld and Hades, but I struggled to concentrate on the conversation. The final Trial was almost here, and then this would be over. The thought of losing, of Hades wed to someone else, caused a surge of something dark and hot to roll through me, unsettling enough that I stopped myself even considering it. I had to win. There was no alternative. I still didn't know how I could live forever in Virgo, but I knew I at least had to be able to try. I ached to talk to Hades, and almost leaped out of my skin when his voice sounded tentatively in my head.

'Persephone?'

'Hades!'

'Am I interrupting?'

'No, never. I miss you,' I told him.

'Good,' he replied, and I swore I could hear a smile in his mental voice.

'Can I come and get you?'

'Please.'

. . .

Hades flashed into Morpheus' rooms a second later, and I was surprised to see him in a black toga instead of his jeans. He looked obscenely hot in it, the glimpse of bare chest making me want to reach out and touch him right there. He nodded politely at everyone, and I told him that Hecate and Morpheus were going to ride with me in the chariot. Genuine relief washed over his tense features, and he thanked them both.

'I must prepare Persephone as best I can for tomorrow, so we are leaving now,' he said.

'*Code for screwing*,' said Skop, and I glared at him. Hades fixed his gaze on the small dog, and his tail stopped wagging.

'Persephone has no need for a guard tonight,' he said. 'You may stay with Hecate.' Hecate made a noise of protest but a look from Hades made her fall silent.

'*This could be my last night with Hades*,' I told Skop quickly. '*Please.*'

'*If anything happens to you, Dionysus will kill me. And not demon-kill me, but actually kill me.*'

'*What's going to happen to me with the King of the Underworld there to protect me?*'

'*That's not the point, I'm not supposed to leave your side.*'

A long silence filled the room, the mute argument obvious to everyone.

'You can turn back into a gnome and drink this stuff with me if you like. I'm not bothered by your enormous dong,' said Sam, raising a glass at Skop.

'*Fine*,' Skop said after a second's hesitation. '*That sounds fair.*'

I shook my head with a smile. All it took was some

booze to buy his cooperation.

'I'll see you all tomorrow then,' I said, and kissed my brother on the cheek.

~

'I need the low-down on these mutts of yours,' I said to Hades, once he had flashed us to his rooms. 'And then I need the low-down on this extremely sexy toga of yours...' I made my voice as seductive as I could, but frowned when I saw his expression. 'What's wrong?'

'So many things,' he said, and his words were laden with strain.

'Tell me.'

'I can't-' he began, shaking his head, but I cut him off with an ineffectual shove to his chest. I ignored the electrifying feel of his skin on my hands and put on my fiercest face.

'I am not taking anymore of this '*I can't*' bullshit. I don't know if you noticed, but I killed a demon today. I have stopped asking you about my past, as you requested, and am doing everything I can to embrace my future. With you. As Queen of the god-damned Underworld. Do not fucking tell me that I do not need to know or you can't tell me, or I swear I'll lose that damned Trial tomorrow on purpose.'

I was expecting anger or rebuttal from him, but relief washed over his face, the tense anger softening and making him irresistibly beautiful. Before I could stop myself I stood up on tiptoes and kissed him. He kissed me back, softly, and too briefly.

'You are right, and we should talk. Now. If we keep kissing, then there will be very little talking.' Desire flashed through his eyes and I stepped backwards, nodding. He was right. If his lips were on mine a second longer I would be tearing off his toga with my teeth.

We sat down together in his living room, and he took a long breath. I didn't know if I was supposed to, but I felt nervous. I mean, what could he tell me that was worse than Cronos wanting to use me to destroy Olympus? Was he going to tell me what I did before, to get sent away? A weird mix of desperation to know and fear that once I found out I wouldn't want to, skittered through me and I wrung my hands together.

'If you win the Trial tomorrow, you will become my Queen. And when you ruled beside me before, I shared everything with you. It would be folly not to share what I know with you now.'

'I'm glad you're seeing sense,' I said tersely. He gave me a look that said 'don't push it,' and continued.

'You have seen the darkness in me,' he said. It wasn't a question. 'That darkness comes from the souls who pass through here who have sinned. I began to lose my faith in life, and the darkness took root. Each year, the number of terrible things I pass judgment on increases. The number of sinners increases. The crimes worsen. The greed and hatred of mortals appears boundless and infinite.' The look on his face caused a lump to swell in my throat. The strain he carried... *Infinite*. His endless future was to be exposed to the very worst of people. 'I am worried, Persephone, and I can not tell my Olympian brethren the true consequences of my concerns. The world they rule celebrates greed, exemplifies selfishness, encourages hatred. Eventually the darkness will win and the Underworld will claim me.'

My heart was hammering in my chest as I listened to

him. What was he telling me?

'If Zeus knew how strong the beast inside me was, he would find a new ruler of the Underworld, rather than risking me lose control. And he is beginning to suspect. But even if he does that, I will not be able to leave. Too much of myself is in the very rock around us, and too much of the essence of Virgo lives within me. My bond to this place is final and unbreakable.'

'What would you become then?'

'The thing you saw when you came back from New York. Forever. And I would be far too powerful to be free. Zeus would have to imprison me in Tartarus.'

'No,' I said, aghast. 'No, you couldn't live there!'

'It wouldn't be me anymore.'

'We can't let this happen. We'll make them understand, make them change how they rule Olympus!'

'Persephone, I have been asking them for centuries. It is too late. You can't just make the world nicer.'

'Then my magic will save you!' Tears were spilling down my cheeks now, memories of the mindless violence I had felt from him when the monster had taken over twisting through me.

'Yes. Your ability to nurture life, to share your light... It heals me. Only you can keep my soul safe.'

'Hades, even if I lose and you have to marry that witch, I will do anything to keep you safe,' I whispered.

'But Zeus was right about you living here. Eventually the darkness will put out your light. You are made to thrive in nature, not under the ground, encased in rock.' Pain filled his voice.

I stared at him.

'So... If I stay here and keep you alive, I die?'

'You will lose your soul to this place, just like everyone

else here. And with it, lose the power to heal me.'

A small sob bubbled out of my throat before I could stop it, and he wrapped his huge arms around me. I knew with every fiber in my being that I would rather die than watch him be lost to Tartarus.

'We'll find a way to stop it. We'll find a way to stop so much bad happening in the world.' I knew I sounded naive, but I didn't care. I had nothing else. Hades stroked a hand down my hair, his sturdy warmth an anchor for my churning thoughts.

'My Queen, we have many obstacles to face before we even get to that. As long as you live in the Underworld, in proximity to Cronos, the other Gods will interfere. They want me to guard Tartarus tomorrow, instead of watching the Trial with them.'

'What? Why?' I pulled out of his embrace to look at him.

'They are worried about another sabotage.'

'But you think it's one of them?'

'Perhaps, yes. And so does Poseidon.'

'Which one?'

'I don't know. Honestly, I can't see a reason any of them would want to start a war or destroy Virgo.'

Hades fell silent and I blew out a sigh, trying to reign in my emotions.

'What if Zeus loses control again?' I asked him.

'I have thought about this hard,' he said, and there was steel in his voice. 'It will make more sense if I tell you about my dogs first.' I raised my eyebrows, an invitation to continue. 'Cerberus is the most well-known. I found him as a pup in the depths of the Underworld, born to monsters now trapped in Tartarus. In those lonely early days he was my only friend.' I felt a pang of love for Hades so strong I almost interrupted him to kiss him, but instead I sat on my hands and listened carefully. 'Cerberus ended up being the first of three dogs, and though the other two are not as dangerous as him, they are both lethal in their own way. They are called Fonax and Olethros. When you lived here, you spent two years bonding with them, and though it was a test of patience, they came to trust you eventually. Cerberus took the longest to come round, but actually, he ended up the most fond of you.' A lop-sided smile pulled at the corner of Hades' mouth. 'Back then you had enough power to survive your early attempts at making friends with them. I'm praying you do again now.'

'Surely I've got a better chance than Minthe,' I said, optimistically. 'They might remember me.'

'The river Lethe is a powerful thing. I doubt that it was any less effective at wiping the dog's memories than everyone else's.'

'Speaking of which,' I said, casually. 'Where is the river Lethe?'

'Persephone, you must never go there. I swear to you, it will only bring you pain.'

Frustration simmered and settled in my gut.

'Do you intend to keep this secret from me our entire lives?' *What would be left of them when the godforsaken Underworld had stripped our souls bare.*

'Yes. As *you* asked me to.' I rolled my eyes. He was never going to tell me. For the briefest moment I considered again telling him about the Atlas garden and the stranger, but I knew he would disapprove, and I wasn't willing to close off the only access to information about my past I had. It wasn't that I didn't trust Hades, but I hadn't made up my mind yet. The need to know what the old me was capable of was impossible to snuff out completely. Plus the stranger said even Hades didn't know the full story. If there was a chance I wasn't guilty of whatever the gods thought I was, then at some point I had to try to find out the truth.

Just not before I survived the hell-hounds and won the Hades Trials.

'Cerberus normally does my bidding exactly,' said Hades. 'But if my asshole brother loses control of him, he'll be operating on instinct alone, and that is to guard my realm. I do not believe that he will attack if you are not near the gates of Virgo. The other two will be guarding something else, I don't know what, but the same principle should apply.'

'OK. So get away from the gates or whatever the dog is guarding if it all goes to shit?'

'Yes.'

'I can do that.'

'And win.'

'I *have* to do that. You said I could have a cat if I win.' Hades cocked his head at me, the tension easing from his face.

'As long as it's a scary, Underworld-appropriate cat.'

'Woah now, there were no caveats before! I want something cute and fluffy.' He scowled at me.

'No cat is cute.'

'That is simply not true.'

'Hmmm. I remain unconvinced. You'll have to win in order to prove it to me.'

I grinned at him, forcing the nerves and pressure down. If he couldn't watch the Trial, I wanted him to be as confident in me as possible.

'No problem. I'm a badass goddess now, in case you hadn't noticed.'

'Persephone,' he said, touching my cheek. His silver eyes

changed, the teasing gleam replaced with that heart-breaking intensity I had seen when I first laid eyes on him. 'I won't watch your light go out. Ever.'

'And I won't watch the darkness take you. Together we will be strong enough.'

His lips moved to mine, gentle and hot. He scooped me up, standing. He carried me to the bedroom, then sat down on the bed, his lips never ceasing their caress, his tongue teasing me. Heat was pooling inside me as the intensity of the kiss grew and my head filled with what I knew was coming.

My feet found the floor and I pulled away from him, standing up breathlessly. I tugged him to his feet and reached up to his shoulder, slowly pulling at his toga. It didn't move, and he smiled a delicious, predatory smile.

'You know, these aren't easy to take off.'

'Well, I need you to. Take it off. I need you to take it off,' I said thickly. 'If there's the slightest chance this is the last time I see you, then you need to be naked for as much of it as possible.'

With a small shimmer, his toga was gone. I sucked in a breath, biting down on my lip as my eyes flicked straight to his arousal. *Good gods.*

'Your turn,' he breathed, and I felt a whisper of air across my body as my own clothes vanished.

I stepped into him, and he wrapped his arms tightly around me as we fell backwards onto the bed, lips locked in a kiss more hungry than the last.

'I will never get enough of you,' I told him, as he rolled me over, so he was on top of me.

'I want you to see what I see,' he said, his eyes dark and

his voice thick with desire. I tugged my hand out of his hair, and a gold vine crept from my palm. Slowly, it reached his muscular arm, coiling around his hard bicep. Gold vine tattoos began to spread across his skin, and heat and desire and love rushed into me.

For a moment I saw myself as he did, glowing with glittering light, skin like honey and face perfect. A beacon in the dark. Then I felt him push against me, and every muscle in my body clenched with desire. Passion, his and mine, exploded inside me, concentrated between my legs.

'I love you,' he said, and then he was inside me, and the pleasure that rocked through him wasn't just mirrored in my own body, it flowed into me through the gold vine.

Being with me was more than physical to him, it was as deep, and as real and true as it was for me. Knowing how much he wanted me, loved me, *needed me,* was the most intense aphrodisiac I'd ever experienced. Our bodies moved together, utterly in sync, slowing when we got exquisitely close, speeding up when passion overwhelmed us. I lost myself not just in the pleasure, but in the shared feeling, the knowledge that we were made for one another.

The pleasure, the power, the bliss grew until it filled us, each touch of his lips on my skin, the feel of his hot breath on my neck, his fingers on my ribs and breasts as intense as his thrusts, until it was too much to contain. We let go at the same time, and there was nothing but him and sensation, my body part of his.

He held me as I shuddered against him, my nails digging into his back as he pressed his face against mine.

'You are mine, and I am yours,' I breathed into his hair.

'Always, my Queen.'

EIGHTEEN

PERSEPHONE

'Why can't you just show me a map?' I asked Hecate as she tried to explain to me what the Judgment Hall was and what it looked like. She'd been trying to teach me the key monuments of the Underworld for what felt like hours, and I was still having trouble laying it out in my head.

'Argh, Persephone, pay attention! Everything in the Underworld moves around all the time, the rivers are alive. The only constants are the things I'm trying to tell you!'

'Morpheus is driving and you'll be with me, why do I need to know?' Under any other circumstance I would love to have learned about Virgo, but with less than an hour before the Trial began, nothing was getting through my nerves and into my skull. I was practically vibrating with energy. Possibly against my better judgment, I had eaten the last seed. Unlike all of the other times I could feel the difference, swirling energy pulsing through my veins, desperate to latch onto something. I almost felt like I needed to grow my own body, become bigger, in lieu of being able to make anything else burst to life.

'You need to know in case anything happens, or you get lost,' ground out Hecate.

'I'm sorry, I just can't concentrate. I need to do something. Do you want to train?'

'No, you need to save your power.'

'Hello?' called Morpheus from the other side of Hecate's closed door. My brother groaned from where he lay on the other sofa, a pillow over his head.

'Serves you right,' I told him as Hecate leaped up to open the door.

'Heal my hangover, please,' he moaned. I rolled my eyes, and sent my vine out towards him. He jumped in surprise when it coiled around his limp wrist, then yelped as I sent my magic toward him.

'That feels weird as fuck!'

'Yeah, well, it works so quit moaning.' The vine disintegrated as Morpheus strode into the room. His swirling skin was positively glowing.

'Are you ready?' he asked me enthusiastically. 'Because the chariot is, and I want you to see it before we start.' A bolt of excitement shot through me and I jumped to my feet.

'Definitely.'

'Can I come?' said Sam, struggling to a sitting position, the pillow sliding off him.

'No,' I said. 'Shit, who's going to stay with him whilst you're with me?' I asked, whirling to Hecate, panicking suddenly.

'Calm down, Hedone has volunteered.' With a sigh of relief I looked to Sam.

'Just in case I do die, give me a hug,' I told him. He pulled a face as he stood up, wrapping his arms around me.

'I saw what you did to that gross thing in the cave, you're going to do great,' he said. 'And once this is done, we can talk about what happens next, yeah?' he added quietly, looking down at me.

'Yes. I promise.'

'Good. 'Cos cool as it is here, I need some sunshine.'

'You and me both,' I said, squeezing him.

'Good luck, Persy.' He kissed me on the top of my head and let me go. A fresh wave of trepidation rolled over me as I moved to Hecate, and she flashed me, Skop and Morpheus out of her rooms.

I found myself in a bare, rocky cavern, the walls glowing with artificial daylight. Set in the middle of the narrow space was a wooden chariot and I felt my eyes widen as I took it in. It looked sort of like the pictures of ancient Greek ones I'd seen in my classes, except the front was raised and peaked exactly like the front of a small boat, and there were no wheels. In fact, it looked a bit like someone had cut a boat in half and made the bottom flat. The decoration and the grand spiral trim across the wood looked every bit ancient Greek. There was no back to it at all, the wooden planks making up the base just stopping dead. Six foot-long spikes jutted out of each side of it, and attached at intervals on the high sides were chains with angry looking spiked balls. My memory flashed on the skeleton and the flail I'd used in my very first Trial. It seemed appropriate to have a flail in my last Trial too.

'It's awesome, Morpheus,' grinned Hecate, walking around it slowly. 'Persy, whatever you do, don't fall off the back.'

I blinked at her, then nodded mutely. It looked like it would be a pretty tight squeeze for three people.

'Shall we take her to the start line?' Morpheus looked at

me. His eyes were alive with excitement. The tiniest bit of me resented him for it. For me, this was not a game. It was life or death, and more than he knew besides.

But more of me was grateful for his help. I mean, where the hell would I have found a chariot? Least of all had the time to learn to control one.

'Definitely,' I told him.

'Step aboard.' He gestured at the wooden vehicle.

This was it. I patted my dagger at my side, and stroked my hand over the pocket I had put Poseidon's pearl in, checking it was still there. I'd worn the leather corset today, deciding protection was more important than maneuver-ability. My hair was braided out of my face and my boots were laced tightly. I had nothing left to do. I was ready.

With a big breath, I gripped the side of the chariot and stepped onto the planks. Morpheus strode up beside me, positioning himself at the front, where the wooden sides met in a sharp peak. The prow, I supposed.

Hecate hopped on behind me.

'Hold on,' she grinned, and the chariot lifted off the rocky ground.

I suppressed the yelp that tried to escape my throat, and gripped the side hard. Just like the ships soaring around Mount Olympus, the boat shaped chariot was flying, on mind-power alone. We hovered for a moment, and Morpheus looked back at me, his skin sparkling.

'Ready?'

'Uhuh,' I replied, pulse racing and heart hammering. With a whoop from Hecate, the chariot raced forward.

～

For a terrifying moment I thought we were going to smash straight into the cavern wall, but as we approached it, an opening started to form in the rock. We burst through and shock stilled my nerves as the most incredible view materialized before me. With a jolt, I registered what I was looking at.

The Underworld.

All the time I had been living in Virgo I'd been flashed between rooms, and although I'd seen many places; my bedroom, the throne room, the training room, the conservatory, the ballroom, the breakfast room, even Tartarus, I'd never been able to imagine Virgo as an actual realm. It had just been a series of caverns and pits to me, and the way it was all connected had just been a vague description from Hecate.

But the view I had as we soared through the air in the chariot...

It was as though we were in a giant cavern, one as large as a city, and as mountainous as the Rockies. We were flying over a river of blue light, similar to the light that came from Hades when he was in god mode. The river was gouged from the dark rock and it seemed to have sources everywhere, waterfalls of light pouring down the many slopes into the main, rushing body of water. On my left and dominating the landscape was a towering mountain, and at its peak, a palace. *Hades' palace.* I felt my jaw drop further. Huge skulls, visible for miles, were carved into the walls and fierce gothic-style towers and balustrades were wrapped with thorned rose carvings. The very tip of the palace reached up past the ceiling of the cavern, and I realized with a start that that must be where the rooms with windows were, the rooms that were above ground. The breakfast room.

As I dragged my eyes down from the palace I saw a glowing band wrapped around the middle of the mountain, shimmering gold. As I squinted into the light I realized there was an island floating just off the mountain.

'That's Elysium, and the Isle of the Blessed. Where the good guys go,' said Hecate, reaching past me and pointing.

'I can't see clearly,' I said, and she laughed.

'The only way you can see into paradise is by dying, so be careful what you wish for. Over there you can just see the river of fire, Phlegethon, that leads down to Tartarus.' She pointed at the flicker of red far in the distance. 'And down there are the Fields of Asphodel and the Judgment Hall. Where the dead come to be judged.' She pointed below us. I peered hesitantly down, over the side of the chariot. My head swam for a moment, but I dragged my healing power up and around me, forcing out my body's reaction to the height. I simply couldn't let vertigo affect me in this Trial. It wasn't an option. I was a damned goddess, and I was in charge of my own body. My vision steadied as I channeled my power, and I took long breaths as I focused.

Below me was a massive washed-out meadow. Hundreds upon hundreds of figures ambled slowly around, and though we were too high to make out details, I could see no color. A gleaming white temple sat between the blue river and another one that glowed purple until it merged with the blue.

'What are these rivers?' I asked.

'The big blue one is the Styx. She's hatred and honesty. The purple one is Acheron, who is woe.'

'Nice,' I mumbled.

'The river Cocytus is over there today. That's lamentation.' She pointed at a green glowing river streaming through an uneven section of rock far to our right.

'And the Lethe?' Hecate shrugged.

'She's always a bitch to find.'

'What color is she?'

'Can't remember,' Hecate grinned at me. 'And I've given up trying to. That's her power, after all.'

'It's quite beautiful,' I said, staring out at it all. 'If a little dark.'

'Yeah. I think so too. See over there? That's the main entrance, for folk who can't flash. That's where Cerberus guards the gates and the ferryman collects the dead.' She was pointing to the top of the cavern, at the opposite end of the river Styx to the palace, where the river seemed to disappear into the rock.

'OK. So where will we be racing?'

'The starting point is the Judgment Hall,' said Morpheus without turning around. We were dropping in height, the spectacular view disappearing as high outcrops of dark rock grew up around us as we moved lower.

'Where are the demon's lairs, like the Empusa and Eurynomos?' I asked Hecate.

'They move around, but they're all hidden throughout the rock.' I stared down at the dark, jagged surface as we raced over it. There could be any kind of creature right below us, and I wouldn't know.

'How do you find them?'

'I'm tethered to them, like Hades. They are bound to us.'

'Would... Would they be bound to me if I became Queen here?'

'No. You'd be giving yourself to Hades, not Virgo.'

I thought about what Hades had told me the night before. He said he was part of Virgo, that he and the Underworld were one now. So maybe Hecate was wrong, and if I gave myself to Hades in marriage, I would be wedding the

Underworld too. If I became his Queen, perhaps I *would* have dominion in this place.

Did I want that? Did I want to know what was hidden in the rock, in this dark and toxic place? If it was a part of Hades, then I must embrace it. But it felt so very far from any part of me.

I was saved from my thoughts when the gleaming white temple loomed before us. It was massive, at least three stories tall, and just like all the throne rooms it had no walls. The left and right sides had a tight row of columns holding up the triangular roof, and the other two sides were completely open, allowing Morpheus to glide the chariot into the building. We landed gently on the white marble floor and my gaze fixed on the chariot we had pulled up next to.

NINETEEN

PERSEPHONE

I t looked exactly how I would expect a chariot belonging to Minthe to look. Where the wood of mine was a rich and natural hue, hers was painted a dark, angry red. Instead of square Greek spirals, hers was decorated with a fierce looking eagle, the wings of the bird stretching intimidatingly around each side of the chariot. There were big pointed spikes jutting out of each side like mine, but where I had flails she had ropes with red sacks tied to the end. I frowned at them, then scanned the rest of the temple as I stepped off the wood and onto the marble. I could see row upon row of stepped benches, set up like bleachers along the right side of the space, and the dais with the twelve thrones was on the other side. In front of the dais was the grand table that the three judges were always sitting at when they appeared. I couldn't see any other people.

'Where is everyone?' I asked as Morpheus followed me out of the chariot.

'I'm not sure. I'll go look,' he said, and strode towards the dais. Hecate followed him.

'They're waiting for you,' Minthe's voice rang out, and

she stepped out from behind one of the pillars. She was wearing an outfit similar to mine, but the leather was a rich burgundy color and her hair was loose around her shoulders. 'They can't start without their precious human underdog,' she said, her voice dripping with menace.

'Seriously, you're still going to be this shitty to me? After I saved your damned life?'

'I've wanted immortality longer than I've been indebted to you,' she spat. 'If your pathetic conscious didn't allow you to kill me in order to win outright, then I deserve every chance I've got at winning the prize.'

'The *prize* is a man,' I said angrily. 'With a heart and soul and feelings and-'

She cut me off with a hiss.

'Save it, Persephone. You may not be capable of killing me, but I don't believe you're so sweet and innocent that you think the King of the Dead is capable of love.' Fury swept hot through me and I felt my lips curl back from my teeth.

'You don't deserve him,' I hissed.

'Not true. Whoever wins the Trials deserves the prize.'

'Stop calling him a fucking prize!' I shouted, and my vines burst from my palms toward her. Chunks of dark rock flew between the columns, knocking my vines away before they reached her and I whipped them back with a snarl.

'My powers belong down here,' she said, and the rocks flew back past her, out of the temple. 'Yours do not.'

I felt my vines falter at her words. They were true. I was out of my depth. I didn't belong here.

She could make the very rock of the Underworld fly about with her mountain magic, and all I had was freaking plants. *Plants that heal the soul of the man you love. The man who loves you.* I clung to the inner voice, and my vines flicked taut again.

'I won't be bullied, Minthe. Not by you or Zeus, or anyone else.'

'I'm not a bully. I'm a competitor, just like you.'

She was right, this *was* a competition. And she was goading me, I realized. Trying to damage my confidence, trying to throw me off before we started.

Two could play at that game. I pulled my vines back, straightening my shoulders.

'Good luck, then,' I said, as sincerely as I could manage. She frowned at me. 'You're not going to win, but I hope you survive, so that dealing with that demon wasn't a complete waste of time.' Minthe cocked her head at me.

'I owe you nothing, Persephone,' she said quietly. But I could hear in her voice that she knew the words weren't true.

'May the best woman win, Minthe,' I said, and strode after my friends.

~

Morpheus and Hecate couldn't find anyone to ask what we were supposed to do next, so I sent a tentative thought to Hades.

'Where are you?' I asked him.

'We will arrive in ten minutes,' he answered immediately. *'My egotistical brother wants the gods to make an entrance.'* The strain was clear in his mental voice.

'OK. See you soon.' I bit my bottom lip, and added quickly, *'I love you.'* There was a slight pause, and then he answered, the tension in his tone gone completely.

'I love you too, my Queen.'

Biting back my grin, I told the others we had to wait and we made our way back to the chariot. Only a few moments later, spectators began appearing in the bleachers. Within five minutes, the space was full. Creatures and humans of every size, shape and color crammed in together, and the chatter was at fever pitch.

'Fucking tourists,' grumbled Hecate. 'There's a reason Hades keeps this place secret.' I raised my eyebrows at her and she leaned back on the side of the chariot. 'If you glamorize the Underworld, who the fuck is going to be scared of ending up here? Damned idiots.'

I could tell Hecate was more nervous than she was letting on, not least because of the amount of times she was saying the work fuck in a sentence. I was pretty sure we shared the habit of swearing profusely when nervous or angry.

'Is that a cyclops?' I asked, pointing at a giant woman in the bleachers with one large amber eye and sharp spikes sticking out through her hair, covering her head.

'Yeah. Don't see 'em often, they're usually in Hephaestus' forges, and his realm is forbidden.' She scowled. 'As this realm is supposed to be.'

There was a bright flash of white light, and we both turned to the dais. Eleven of the twelve gods were there, all looking exceptionally grand. There were all in togas, even Dionysus, and they all wore large crowns. Hera's was the most eye catching, adorned with peacock feathers, and Athena's was the most plain, just a gold band.

'Good day, Olympus!' boomed the commentator, his voice seemingly amplified by the rock around us. I spotted him next to the judges' table, and started as I realized the three judges were now there, eyes intent on Minthe and I. 'Please welcome your host for these incredible Trials one last time!'

Black smoke suddenly billowed through the area, and

the crowd gasped as it began to gather in front of the dais, a small tornado forming. It began to solidify as blue light flickered through the air, lighting up the smoke like a strobe light. An enormous two-pronged trident made of gleaming onyx emerged from the swirling smoke, then the smoky form of a man followed it, at least ten feet tall.

'This is the grand entrance you were talking about?' I said mentally to Hades as the crowd erupted into cheers.

'It was not my fucking idea,' he ground out.

'You look impressive,' I told him. The smoke figure raised the trident and blue light shot from the end like fireworks. The cheers got louder.

'Impressive? I'm supposed to be terrifying, not impressive. I could make every unwelcome person in this hall feel their worst fears right now,' he hissed. 'Instead, Zeus turns me into a jester with tricks and lights.' His words were laced with bitterness, and I understood his anger. Zeus was turning the King of the Dead, Lord of the Underworld, into a spectacle, whilst showing the world the realm he had always striven to keep private.

'Maybe give them a little taste of what you can do,' I said, and saw his smoke form pause.

'Really?'

'Just a little. Don't make anyone actually mess themselves.' I heard a tiny chuckle, then cold rippled over me and the cheers died out abruptly. Tendrils of something pricked at my skin, and discomfort and fear started to seep into my mind, but my healing magic leaped up around me. Within a second, the fear had been forced out, barred from me completely.

When the room was silent, Zeus stood. His expression was tight.

'Thank you, brother, for that welcome,' he said tersely.

Hades flickered, and reappeared on his throne. His smoke form looked languid and relaxed. I didn't know if he got pleasure from frightening people or what that said about him, but I *did* know he got pleasure from defying Zeus. And that was worth freaking out a few morbid spectators.

'Thank you, Zeus,' Hades said, his voice slithery and creepy. It was so weird now to hear him speak like that, his rich, warm tones nowhere to be heard. 'The race is along the Styx, to the gates of Virgo. You will encounter all three hell-hounds on the way, ending with Cerberus. Each dog is guarding a gem. Green for Persephone, red for Minthe. Collect all the gems first and you will win.'

A massive swell of nerves rolled through me. His cold, impassive voice was so completely at odds with how I knew he felt, but he sounded for all the world like he didn't give a shit which of us won. Doubt stabbed at my mind, until I heard his voice, his real voice, in my mind.

'Win for me, my Queen.'

'I will.'

'I have to leave now. A smoke dummy will be in my place so that the crowd don't know.'

Hecate and Morpheus were climbing onto the chariot and two people had joined Minthe. I couldn't look anywhere other than him though. I didn't want him to leave.

'OK,' I said, stumbling as I stepped onto my chariot. My eyes were locked on his smoke form, adrenaline now rushing through my body. *'I love you.'*

'I love you,' he replied. I felt him leave, the bond pulsing with a faint sense of loss inside me as he moved further from me.

'Shit,' muttered Hecate beside me, and I dragged my eyes from the fake smoke figure now on Hades' throne.

'What's wrong?' I asked her.

'That,' she said, pointing to Minthe's chariot. 'That's what's wrong. Fucking look at them!'

I took a deep breath, anxiety making me feel sick as I took in Minthe's team mates.

The woman at the front of the chariot was wearing a toga and looked about a hundred years old, but that wasn't what I noticed first. She was see-through. Like actually transparent. And the other woman on the chariot was at least six feet tall, wearing a wonder-woman type outfit made of gleaming armor, and holding a crossbow. Her blonde hair was in a knot on top of her head and the muscles cording her arms and shoulders put my brother's to shame.

'What are they?'

'The woman at the front is an Eidolon. That's a ghost in your world.'

'I thought you controlled ghosts?'

'The ones down here, I do. Not the ones that are free. Like her.'

'And the woman who looks like a body-builder?'

'Definitely an Amazon warrior. But they never leave their tribe in Ares' realm so she must be an outcast.' I raised my eyebrows at the fierce looking woman as she examined her weapon.

'Amazon warriors? Is there anything Olympus doesn't have?'

'Not really. Most history from your world is based on Olympus. What Athena planted as Greek mythology.'

The woman noticed me staring at her before I could answer, and bared her teeth at me.

'Are you ready to face the sting of my bolts?' she called, lifting the crossbow threateningly toward me. My old instinct would have been to flinch away or look to Hecate to help, but my power crackled and hummed in response to the threat and before I could stop myself I lifted my hands.

'Just try it,' I shouted, and black vines whipped from my palms, stopping just short of her and flicking back. The woman's eyes narrowed, but she kept her mouth shut and lowered the weapon.

'Save it for the race, Sanape,' said Minthe, tugging her elbow. Sanape glared at me, then turned away.

'I'm glad to see so much of the old Persephone survived the mortal world,' said Hecate quietly. 'You can't get by in Olympus without a decent dose of courage.'

'You call it courage, the rest of us call it attitude,' said Morpheus with a grin. 'Are you both ready?'

I nodded, and the chariot rose slowly into the air, my stomach lurching with it.

This was it. The final time I would have to fight for my life and the right to marry the man I loved. The man it turned out I had always loved. The man I had been waiting for my whole life, without even knowing it.

Hades' face filled my mind, and strength coursed through me, my power crackling under my skin.

I was going to win this, and become his Queen.

TWENTY

HADES

Not being able to watch Persephone was torture. But
even if something terrible did happen, I wouldn't be
able to help her, I was bound by the rules of the Trials.

I snarled as I looked out over the rocky landscape to
where I knew she was. Perhaps if the chariots got high
enough I would be able to see them from here. I knew I was
too far away, but I clung to the thought all the same.

Something *was* going to happen, I was sure. There was
no way that whoever was trying to punish her or get to
Cronos was going to let their last chance go without trying
again. At the thought of Cronos I looked along the flaming
river, flowing into the mouth of the cave that led to Tartarus.
Where Persephone had come back, and stopped me
walking into Tartarus while the darkness had control of me.
Where she had saved me.

Movement caught my eye and I froze, only relaxing
when I realized it was the flickering flames of the river
Phlegethon against the rock walls. I was still holding the
onyx trident, a relic I rarely used any more. It had been
made for me by Hephaestus, to celebrate the three brothers

taking their roles in sky, sea and earth. A trident for each of us. Poseidon hardly went anywhere without his, but I no longer needed the amplification of power it could give me. If anything, I needed less power, not more.

Except today. If anyone was coming for Persephone, they would have to get past me, and I'd take all the strength I could get. I tipped the trident towards the cave mouth.

'You hear that, Cronos? You're not getting your hands on her today, or any other day,' I said, then blew out a frustrated sigh. Being stuck here was 'bullshit', as Persephone had called it.

'Where's the fun in that?' purred a voice.

I had the trident in both hands, pointed directly at the cave mouth in a flash, my form growing fast as a small figure sauntered out of the cave. Nothing should ever be coming out of Tartarus without my permission. The monster reared up inside me, fear and strength swelling me as my heart began to pound.

Ankhiale stepped fully out of the cave, and gave me a low bow. Her red hair burst into flame as she straightened and smiled at me. My blood ran cold as I stared at her.

'How? How have you escaped?' If she was free, did that mean... 'Where is Cronos?'

'King Cronos is safe and sound,' she said. 'My friend couldn't break through his bonds. But he didn't have too much trouble with mine.'

Blue light burst to life around me, and the monster crawled higher up my chest. Ankhiale was ancient. She was one of the strongest Titans in Tartarus. Nobody but me should be able to free her from Tartarus.

'Who?' I demanded. 'Who freed you?' Even as I barked the words though, I knew. Fear squeezed my chest, the darkness twisting and snarling to be free.

'That's not important, little Hades,' she said, and cackled as she grew, eclipsing my size in an instant. Heat so intense it made me wince slammed into me. My eyes flicked to the rows and rows of blue soldiers surrounding me, more getting to their feet from the pool of blue light flowing to the ground from my body. 'What is important is that in a few hours, Cronos, the true King of the Gods, will be free and this shit-hole you call home will be obliterated.'

'Never,' I growled. 'He will never be free while I live.'

'I'm afraid that's not true,' she said, cocking her head and giving me a mocking smile. 'It's your lovely wife who needs to die, not you. You will live on without her, a mindless monster doing your master's bidding.'

'No!' I roared, rage blinding me, horror at the thought of Persephone's death too much to bear. I couldn't lose her. I would do whatever it took. Ankhiale threw her head back and laughed, as flames burst to life across her skin.

'Yes, little Lord,' she said, and launched herself at me.

TWENTY-ONE

PERSEPHONE

'Just some clarifications of the rules, folks, and we can get this race started!' sang the commentator. 'There will be no mental communication allowed during the race. Minthe, follow the red lights, Persephone, follow the green lights. Stay on your own course. This will ensure you don't face the first two dogs at the same time. Only Persephone and Minthe may get the gem from the dog. If anyone else helps, the team will be disqualified and severely punished. After Fonax and Olethros it's a straight race to Cerberus and the finish line!'

I blinked as a dancing green light shimmered into life in front of our chariot, hovered a moment, then bounced out of the temple. An identical red light did the same thing before Minthe.

'Follow the light,' repeated Morpheus. 'No problem.'

'On the gong, you may start,' said the commentator, and the crowd cheered.

'Come on, Persy!' My brother's voice carried over them all, and I looked down to see him and Hedone waving from the front row of the bleachers.

. . .

As the gong sounded and the commentator bellowed, 'Go!', rage flared inside me, Hades' primal power surging through the bond.

'Hecate,' I gasped as the chariot shot forward, and I gripped the wooden sides. She didn't hear me over the roar of the crowd, or the rushing of air as we pelted out of the temple, soaring over the glittering blue river. Another swell of fear and fury rolled through my body, mingling with my own adrenaline-fueled energy.

'Duck,' Hecate yelled, and a crossbow bolt thudded into the wood just an inch from my white knuckles.

'Something is happening to Hades,' I shouted, and the chariot swerved slightly as Morpheus looked back at me, his face anxious.

'He can handle himself, Persy, now get down!' she shouted back. Her eyes turned milky as blue light shot from her palms, and my mouth fell open in dumb confusion as I watched the light hit the red chariot ten feet from us. Sanape stumbled, but kept her firm grip on the crossbow.

'Hold on!' shouted Morpheus, and the chariot swerved hard to the left as the red and green lights ahead of us parted abruptly. Minthe's chariot soared off to the right, and I spun to Hecate.

'Something bad is happening, I can feel it!'

'There's nothing you can do from here, Persy!' she said, gripping my arm and looking into my eyes. 'He's one of the strongest beings in Olympus, the best thing you can do for him is concentrate on surviving and winning this.'

I nodded. She was right. Hades could handle anything, and little would be worse for him *or* me than losing the Trials and not being with him.

A geyser of blue liquid shot up past the chariot and Morpheus jerked it aside violently enough for me to almost lose my hold of the wooden side. Heart in my mouth, I tightened my grip and widened my stance.

Dying. Dying would be worse than losing.

'OK. Full focus, I got it,' I told Hecate, breathing deeply in a bid to try to settle my stomach.

My braid whipped over my shoulder as I turned to the front and concentrated on what was before us. We were following the dancing green light along a narrow offshoot of the Styx, and I turned briefly to see the red light in the distance, Minthe's chariot whizzing along after it over a different blue stream of the Styx. The rock around us was uneven to the point of mountainous, and as I looked ahead again, I realized the light was moving lower, forcing us closer to the river. Uneasiness washed over me. Now that my fear of heights was under control, it was actually better to be higher up, as we could see further across the Underworld. The lower we got, the more the rocky slopes obscured our view. Something dark loomed before us and the light swerved towards it, along the glowing river below.

It was a large ridge, and the river was flowing into a cave mouth set low into it.

'Wanna bet either Fonax or Olethros is in there?' called Hecate.

'Bring it on,' I called back, the false bravado not helping my nerves at all.

I couldn't help holding my breath as we entered the darkness of the cave. I was instantly reminded of when I'd been in Tartarus, everything lit by the glow of the flickering river, only this time it was blue instead of red. The bouncing green light ahead of us whizzed along the banks of the Styx, and Morpheus led us after it.

'Any last minute tips on dealing with hell-hounds?' I asked Hecate, my pulse racing.

'Don't get eaten?'

'Thanks.'

My heart skipped a beat as the chariot dipped suddenly, and a new color seeped through the darkness. Purple. Hecate had said the purple river was Acheron, which was woe. 'What happens if we fall in a river?' I asked as mildly as I could.

'The Styx would strip your skin bare in an instant. It's filled with the hatred of every dead soul in Olympus and is toxic as fuck.'

'And the Acheron?'

'You'd become so overwhelmed with sadness you would instantly go mad.'

'Right. Good to know.'

'Just don't fall in the Phlegethon. You don't want to know what happens if you do that.'

I shuddered just thinking about the flaming river.

'Guys,' called Morpheus over his shoulder. The green light was slowing down, drifting toward an island of solid rock between the two flowing rivers. As we and the light got nearer, details began to emerge from the gloom.

There was a gate across the island, barring the entrance to a small one-story building. It was a dirty, tired looking hut, built of worn and ancient stone that had discolored. The roof barely clung to the walls and looked to be made of straw or mud. The gate however... The gate was gleaming. Made of criss-crossed iron bars, it looked like something you'd see outside a fifth avenue apartment block, grand and imposing. The green light bobbed towards it a couple times, then settled a few feet higher than the gate's peak. The chariot slowed and we all stared.

There were things tied to the iron bars. Hundreds of things, bits of old paper, cups, jewelry, rags, weapons, all sorts of stuff.

'Do you think the green gem is on there somewhere?' I whispered, the absence of the rushing wind now making it eerily silent.

A low rumbling growl met my words.

'If it is, go and look now, before...' Hecate trailed off as a dog twice the height of me emerged from the darkness, stepping out of the iron gate like it was some sort of portal. He looked a bit like a greyhound, if a greyhound was jet black, blessed with too many teeth and had a tail made from fire.

I gulped.

'Olethros,' whispered Hecate.

'Remind me what that means?'

'Destruction.'

'Excellent.'

Olethros barked once, and the flames from his tail streaked across his lithe body, lighting spirals of fire that danced over his sleek fur.

'Why is everything in this fucking hellhole on fire?'

'Go, Persephone,' said Morpheus. 'We must not forget we are in a race.'

'That's easy for you to say,' I muttered, as my vines snaked from my palms, my gaze still fixed on the dog now prowling up and down the length of the gate. 'How the hell do I get past him?'

'We can't help you, Persy.'

'Right.'

I took a big breath, and whipped my vine toward the rocky island, far from the iron gate. Olethros froze, his black eyes fixing on my flickering vine. 'Come on, doggy,' I coaxed. 'Take the bait.' He lowered on his huge haunches, his ears flattening against his head. 'That's it...'

He pounced, and dammit, he was so quick I didn't have time to whip the vine out of the way. His long snout closed over the vine, but not hard enough to sever it, and he jerked his head. With a yelp, I was pulled from the chariot.

I had a split second to react, before I would slam into the ground at the hound's feet, and I threw my other hand out, shooting a vine desperately at the iron gate. It caught and coiled around the iron bars just in time, my body bouncing like it was on a bungee-cord between the twelve-foot-tall dog and the massive gates. Olethros shook his enormous head and I bit back a cry as my shoulder was wrenched hard from its socket. I willed the vine the dog had hold of to disintegrate, then shortened the other, pulling myself fast towards the gate whilst sending my healing power to my shoulder.

But now I was a moving target, and Olethros snarled as he raced after me. I crashed into the gate and wasted no time scrambling up it, each diamond-shaped gap between the bars as long as my legs and difficult to pull myself up. I sent my vines from my palms ahead of me, helping to drag myself higher and making sure that if I fell I wouldn't fall far. I felt Olethros smash into the gate a second later, the whole structure shaking hard. My heart was hammering against my ribs, but adrenaline had caused my focus to sharpen, and I was scanning every bit of junk I was passing as I climbed higher.

After what felt like an eternity I cast a glance down, checking I was out of the hound's reach, before slowing to a stop. He was jumping, snapping at me, giving big echoing barks that made my head hurt. But he couldn't reach me. I took a second to get my breath back, then looked along the gates, desperately seeking out anything green. Knowing the asshole gods, they would have put the thing I needed to get low down, well within the dog's reach. The spirals of fire covering Olethros were getting bigger and unease rippled through me. He would be completely on fire soon.

But then the fire-light from his body reflected off something bright and colorful, and my eyes widened as they fixed on the object. A pendant, tied to the iron gate only ten feet off the ground, set with a massive grass-green gem.

Reaching to my left, I awkwardly untied the nearest thing to me with one hand, which was a warrior helmet, complete with faded red plume. As soon as the cord came loose it fell, and I sent silent thanks into the gloom as it clattered to the ground, drawing the dog's attention immediately. His ears pricked as the clattering continued, and I couldn't help giving a fist pump as the helmet began to roll noisily away from the gate. Olethros followed.

I didn't waste a second. Using my vine to control my descent, I launched myself from the gate to the ground, then ran to where the pendant was. I scrambled the few feet up the gate as quietly as I could, holding my breath as I reached the gem and frantically started to pull at the cord. I heard a growl in the distance, and my sweating hands fumbled with the knots. I couldn't untie the damned thing. I needed something to cut it.

'You're an idiot,' I cursed myself as pulled *Faesforos* from its sheath and sliced through the cord like it was nothing. The pendant dropped to the ground before I could catch it, and I jumped from the gate after it. I crouched to grab it, elation surging through me as I put it safely around my neck, then straightened. My heart skipped a beat.

Olethros was bounding towards me and he looked pissed. I tipped my head back, finding the chariot above me, and threw both palms out towards it, praying like hell that one of them would catch. Almost as the hound reached me, I felt resistance on one of them and pulled. I shot upward, but Olethros was fast. He jumped at the same time, snapping at my leg, his razor sharp teeth tearing through the muscle of my right calf. I screamed as white-hot pain raced up my leg, and my skin went tight and cold over my whole body. Dizziness swamped me as I kept rising, then there were hands pulling at my shoulders. Hecate was dragging me onto the chariot, the small space barely big enough for me to sit.

'Heal yourself, quickly. That bite will turn nasty fast,' she said urgently. I concentrated, trying to block out the searing pain and drawing my healing power to my leg. Warmth replaced the tight icy feeling, then soothing magic tingled over the wound, spreading throughout my body. My magic was removing the toxins I knew were spreading from the bite.

'I think it's working,' I panted.

'Good,' she answered, and her grip on my shoulder relaxed. I felt strength returning to my limbs, the tightness in my chest easing and the dizziness receding. Last time I had been poisoned I couldn't heal myself. Now... Now I was strong. Strong enough to fix myself. *Strong enough to fix Hades.*

· · ·

'Let's go, Morpheus,' I said loudly, getting slowly to my feet. I wobbled, but Hecate and the side of the chariot kept me upright.

'You got it,' he said, and the chariot took off after the little green light, into the darkness.

TWENTY-TWO

PERSEPHONE

We chased the green light out of the mountain and found ourselves flying through a high-sided gulley, the Styx and the Acheron flowing side-by-side below us.

'Incoming!' called Morpheus, and I squinted to see the red light fast approaching, Minthe's chariot behind it.

She was on her way to Olethros, which meant she had her first gem too. Shit.

My vines sprang from my palms, ready, and Hecate raised her hands, her eyes turning milky, as the red chariot got closer.

The lights neared each other, forcing our chariots within striking distance of one another. The flails on the side of ours leaped to life, whirling fast on their chains, stretching beyond the spikes. But the red bags on the end on the ropes on Minthe's chariot rose too, and as a crossbow bolt whizzed by my head, the mountains around us rumbled. Minthe's eyes caught mine as she raised her arms, and rocks exploded from the bags. I threw myself down, below the side of the chariot, yelling for Morpheus to do the same. He did, as a wall of blue light burst from

Hecate, stopping about half of the rain of sharp stones from landing in the chariot. But the rest got through, and the chariot began to tip forward in a nose dive toward the ground.

'Morpheus!' I shrieked, and the chariot leveled sharply, tipping me onto my ass. My heart leaped into my mouth as I lost my grip, but my vines instinctively coiled around the wooden edge of the chariot and steadied me.

'They're past,' called Hecate, and I got quickly to my feet.

'Are you hurt?' I asked as Morpheus pushed himself up.

'A little,' he said, and a trickle of blood that shone a weird silver color ran down his temple. 'But it'll heal. I need to concentrate.'

'OK,' I said, and turned to watch Minthe's chariot get smaller as they approached Olethros' cave. 'Well, I'd say they won that encounter.'

Morpheus did a perfect job of weaving between the geysers of glowing liquid that the rivers shot up at us as we raced after the green light, and eventually we moved up out of the ravine. My breath caught as wind rushed over us, the view of the sprawling rock landscape covered in glowing streams truly magnificent in its own other-worldly way.

The green light darted off toward another steep incline, and we zipped after it, until it reached a long, flattened ledge in the rock. It slowed abruptly, and my pulse quickened. Had we reached the second dog?

'Fonax is the ancient word for bloodthirsty, Persy, you need to be really careful. He doesn't look as bad as Olethros, but trust me, he's worse.' I nodded at Hecate as we moved lower, toward the ledge.

'If Minthe could handle him, so can I,' I said determinedly.

But when Fonax came into view, pacing the ledge with predatory grace, my insides skittered. He was a smoky gray color, broad, and much smaller than the last hound, probably waist high on me. He paused, sniffing the air as we neared him and I noticed that his short snout was dripping with something red, and his eyes were gleaming scarlet. Then he growled deep in his throat, and I saw his blood red teeth as he bared them in our direction.

'What do you mean, he doesn't look as bad as Olethros? He looks just as bad!' I exclaimed.

'He's smaller, and not on fire,' she protested.

'He has red eyes and teeth. That's pretty fucking creepy.'

'This is a race, ladies,' called Morpheus, interrupting us. I clenched my jaw, and scanned for anything at all on the ledge that might be hiding a gem. I spotted a large iron ring on the ground, and could just make out what looked like a trapdoor beneath it.

Deciding to deploy the same tactic as before, I asked Morpheus to get us as close to the trapdoor in the ledge as he safely could. Fonax started barking as we approached, and waves of icy fear slammed into me. Hades had said his dogs could instill fear in people, I remembered. But if they were like him, I could block it out with my power. I focused, using my healing magic to create a shield around my head, blocking the visions I knew would come if I didn't protect myself. Confident it was working, I snaked my vines out, then flung one as far from the trapdoor as I could.

Fonax raced after it, and I sent the vine from my right

hand to the iron ring on the trapdoor. I held my breath as I jumped the ten feet from the chariot to the ground, and landed hard on one leg, failing to use my vine properly to slow the jump. I cried out as my ankle twisted and I fell. The shout was all Fonax needed to realize I'd tricked him. He spun, turning a hundred and eighty degrees in a heartbeat, and raced toward me. I yanked as hard as I could on the vine on the trapdoor, both trying to open it and pull myself to my feet. It creaked but didn't open, and I stumbled toward it, crying out again when I put weight on my left leg.

'Open! Fucking open!' I forced my power into the green vine, desperately pulling on it as the hound got closer, his gleaming red eyes terrifying.

With a lurch the trapdoor finally gave way, and I threw myself into the dark space without a moment's hesitation, tugging the door shut behind me with the vine. Nothing down there could be worse than Fonax reaching me. As the trapdoor closed above me it severed the vine that was attached, and I tumbled through the darkness until I landed on something relatively soft.

Panic rose in my chest as I rolled, struggling to right myself. I had no idea what I was on top of and the thought was nauseating.

Dirt. I moved my hands around hesitantly as I came to a stop on my ass, and was pretty sure I was sitting on piles of sandy dirt. I paused as my fingers skimmed something solid. I needed light. Cautiously, I sent a gold vine from my palm, hoping the glow it gave off would be enough to see by.

It was, just. I was in a small, dirt-filled space, the ceiling not much taller than I would be, standing up. I moved the vine down and saw that I had run my hand over a broken doll. As I looked, I saw more bits of junk, half buried in the sand. I immediately began to dig, searching for anything green in the dim golden light.

Another volley of barking began above me, making me jump in surprise, then a fierce scratching sound began. Fonax was trying to get through the trapdoor.

I dug faster, sending my power to my ankle to try to heal it. As soon as the power flowed to my leg, waves of fear crashed into me, flames and screams rushing into my mind. Corpses, the bodies of those I had killed... My hands stilled in the dirt as the scratching got louder, and sweat broke out across my forehead as terror began to claw its way up my chest.

I forced my healing magic back to my head, abandoning healing my ankle. Slowly the screams died away, and my pulse slowed slightly.

Breathing hard, I flexed my shaking hands, trying to block out the frantic scratching and barking. If my healing power could only protect me from the fear or heal my ankle, not both, then I would have to make do with my busted ankle. The fear would cripple me.

I rolled onto my knees, and resumed digging in the dirt, tossing ancient crap out of the way, and seeing nothing green.

The scratching overhead stopped abruptly, and an ominous creak replaced it. I paused, glancing up at where the trapdoor was. A resounding crack made me gasp in shock, then a slither of light streamed through the wood.

'Shit,' I said, and turned back to the dirt, moving as fast as I could on my hands and knees, my glowing vine close to the ground. 'Come on, come on, come on,' I muttered frantically, trying to ignore the thought that was repeating itself over and over in my head.

Even if I found the damned gem, I had no fucking idea how to get back out of the trapdoor and past the hound.

By the time the time I found the green stone, embedded in a ring barely big enough to fit on my finger, most of the trapdoor was in shreds. I staggered to my feet as I shoved the ring on my pointer finger, my ankle wobbly and sore, but not agonizing. Sweat was rolling down my back, and my mind racing with bad ideas. I had no way of getting past Fonax and out of this space. Claustrophobia added to my growing panic, the low ceiling and dark gloom closing in on me.

A crack louder than any of the previous drew my attention to the trapdoor, and my heart almost stopped in my chest as a large piece of wood dropped into the space, followed immediately by Fonax.

He was glowing, the same red as his eyes and teeth. His ears were back, his shoulders hunched, and his lethal gaze fixed on me.

'H-h-h-hello,' I stuttered, holding my hands out. 'Who's a good boy?' I said. He snarled, dark liquid dripping from his teeth. I tried to reach out with my mind, like I did to talk to Skop, but there was nothing there. 'You don't want to eat me, Fonax. Your master will be super pissed with you if you do that,' I whispered, as the hound stalked closer. My gold vines were turning black as they swirled about me, preparing for a fight.

· · ·

Fonax pounced. Fortunately for me he couldn't get much height in the cramped space, and my vines hit him square in the chest. I wasn't filled with enough hatred or anger for them to go through him, like they had Eurynomos, but they knocked him off course, and began to coil around his front legs and chest. He snarled and growled as he fought to get free of them, his powerful body pushing me backward in the dirt as I fought to cling on. He stopped fighting for a split second, then seemed to throw everything he had into lunging for me. My vines only just held him back as his teeth snapped at my midriff.

'Oh no you don't,' I said, and felt his power start to flow down the vines, into me. Dark black tattoos began to spread across his fur, and he yelped and struggled. Unlike before, when I'd used my black vines, I seemed to have more control over the flow of power. I wasn't immediately rushed by the hell-hound's dark energy. 'I'm sorry, Fonax, but I have to win this,' I told him, edging my way around him, toward the trapdoor. 'I'm just going to take enough of your power that I can escape.'

But as the dog's bloodthirsty energy flowed into me, the more I felt like taking all of it. I would need it after all, to get past Cerberus. More power couldn't be a bad thing, could it? I felt Fonax stop fighting, and looked into his angry red eyes.

No. That was the Underworld talking, not me. I didn't need his dark, vicious power. I had my own.

Slowly, I released one vine, whipping it back to me and sending it up, out of the trapdoor. I felt it coil round something solid, a rock, I guessed, and tugged on it. It held. 'I'm going to leave now,' I said, feeling powerful. I felt like I could conquer the world, let alone one dog.

Kill. Blood, death, kill.

The words ricocheted through my skull, and I shook my head. *That's Fonax, the bloodthirsty hell-hound, not you,* I told myself firmly.

'Stay there,' I said aloud, and let the other vine disintegrate. He didn't have enough power to come after me, I was sure.

I was wrong. The second my vine vanished, he went for me, closing the gap between us in a heartbeat. His jaws clamped onto my thigh and I screamed, the same white-hot pain I'd felt from Olethros searing through me. I yanked on the vine, and my feet left the floor, tearing my leg from Fonax's mouth, and leaving a chunk of my flesh between his jaws.

Rage blurred my vision, the voice in my head now louder than my own thoughts.

Kill! Burn! Blood!

I burst up through the hole where the trapdoor had been, my vine dragging me along the rocks, the pain interrupting the fury flooding through me.

'Persy!' yelled Hecate, and I rolled to see the chariot just a few feet from me, by the ledge.

But I didn't want to get back on the chariot. Now I had a score to settle, with an ungrateful, murderous hell-hound. I pushed myself onto my knees, dimly aware of the massive amount of blood pouring from my thigh. 'Persy, stop the bleeding, now!'

I ignored her, crawling back towards the trapdoor.

'Persephone, what are you doing? Get back on the chariot!' Morpheus shouted. But fury had taken over, Fonax's bloodthirsty Underworld magic coursing through my body.

'Persy, if you don't stop the bleeding, you will die, and

Hades needs you!' Hecate's words finally pierced the fog. *Hades*. Hades and Minthe and... The race. The Trials.

I turned, the pain penetrating through the rage, obliterating all other thoughts. *Heal*. I had to heal myself. Fonax was trapped in the space under the trapdoor, and I'd taken most of his power, so when I sent my magic at my leg, no crippling torrents of fear hit me. Slowly, painfully, the wound began to close.

'Persephone, you have to get back on the chariot, we can't lose this much time,' Morpheus said, his voice calmer. I looked sideways, my head swimming, and saw that he had pulled the chariot up alongside the ledge.

'OK,' I stammered, dragging myself up onto my feet. I limped to the ledge, each step agony, still sending as much power as I could to my thigh, and Hecate pulled me onto the wood.

'Tell me you got the gem,' she said, wincing at my leg as I propped my back against the side of the chariot. I felt it lurch into motion as I held up my hand to her, showing her the ring.

'Yeah. I got the gem.'

TWENTY-THREE

HADES

'Let me go!' I roared, for the hundredth time. Ankhiale rolled her eyes at me, just as she had every other time.

'Good gods, you're irritating. If you're careless enough to let me trap you, then you should handle the consequences like a real man.'

I glared down at the metal band glowing around my wrist, furious that she'd managed to get it there. If I'd known she'd had it I would have fought differently.

'I know who gave this to you,' I hissed. It was a manacle forged by Hephaestus, and there were only three in existence. They were able to bind a god of almost any strength, and due to their exceptional power were only ever used in extreme circumstances.

And the only gods they were entrusted to were the three strongest; Zeus, Poseidon and myself.

I shook my wrist, pouring the little power I could still access into the metal, but the manacle didn't move. It was chained to an iron stake in the ground, pinning me in place. I knew it was useless. I used my own manacle to transport powerful prisoners to Tartarus, until it was no longer needed to trap them and limit their power. I knew how unbreakable the magic was. And I knew that only one of my brothers could remove it.

'Well yeah, it's pretty fucking obvious,' Ankhiale said, stepping through the ring of flames she'd created around me. I couldn't survive her fire without my power. My mind was racing, fear for Persephone overruling all else. I was useless here. 'That pathetic water-loving brother of yours isn't strong enough to free a Titan from Tartarus,' Ankhiale smiled at me.

She was right. Poseidon would never have enough dominion in the Underworld. But Zeus...

'He orchestrated the Trials here so that I would have to relinquish control of the Underworld to him. It was nothing to do with finding me a wife. It's why he found Persephone.'

She nodded, her flaming hair falling about her face, her blood red lips pulled up in a grin.

'The longer the Trials have gone on, and the more control you have allowed him, the more power he has gained here. He's the strongest of all of you. All he needed was a little time, and a little deference from you. And the girl.'

'I *am* the Underworld,' I spat. 'He can not beat me in my own realm.' She chuckled.

'It would appear he already has, little Lord,' she said, gesturing at my wrist. I instinctively drew on my power, but the response was just a pathetic swell of fury, coursing uselessly through me. I couldn't channel it into magic, no matter how hard I tried.

'Why would Zeus free you? He hates you, and all other Titans.' I couldn't make sense of it. The very last Olympian who would want Cronos to be free was Zeus, surely?

'Ego and hatred are powerful emotions, Hades. The world has forgotten how evil we Titans are supposed to be. They are allowed into the academies to learn magic along-side the other citizens, they are allowed to work and live in the realms, treated the same as everyone else. And now, to top it off, you've given one of our most powerful, the mighty Oceanus, his own realm in Olympus.' I stared at her in disbelief.

'You're saying Zeus is freeing Cronos to show the world that Titans are bad?'

'He doesn't think Cronos will actually make it to free-dom. He thinks he can use me, and your lovely ex-wife, to let Cronos wreak a touch of havoc, reminding the world of what Titans are capable of, before he swoops in and saves the day. And then all will hail our mighty King Zeus.' She gave a mocking bow. 'But he's a fucking fool,' she hissed straightening suddenly. 'As soon as Cronos gets his hands on that little flower goddess of yours, Zeus will not be able to contain him. Nobody will!'

TWENTY-FOUR

PERSEPHONE

Morpheus kept us on course as we raced along the Styx, to the gates of the Underworld and Cerberus. My leg was still stiff, but the wound was completely closed now, and any loss of blood I may have experienced was being offset by the power still coursing through me from Fonax. I was keeping the voice commanding me to kill at bay by clinging to the image of Hades' face, but the more I thought about him, the more intense his fear felt through the bond, which in turn was making me more anxious and angry and susceptible to the dark power.

'Please tell me we're almost there,' I yelled over the rushing wind.

'Over there,' shouted Hecate, and pointed. We were making our way over ground that was gradually sloping upward and I could just make out a dark hole in the rock above us, that the glowing blue river seemed to be streaming from.

It only took a few moments more to reach it, and I flexed my fists as we entered the darkness.

· · ·

We flew into a long cavern, and my jaw fell open as I stared around myself. The river veered off to the right, immediately obscured from view by the walls of the cavern. But the walls weren't made from rock, they were made from *wings*. A hundred feet tall and the same again in length, they stretched the length of the cavern, struts that looked like ribs holding them up at intervals. They were slightly transparent, and I could see huge flames flickering behind then, casting everything in a fiery orange glow. We slowed as we flew further into the long hall, and I saw what the wings were attached to. At the end of the room was a huge iron gate with thick bars, and towering above it, a statue of a demon, the wing walls curving from its back. It looked like a grotesque gargoyle, with fangs and horns and sagging stone skin and I shuddered.

'Wow,' I breathed. The gates of hell were terrifying. Impressive, but terrifying. 'Where's Cerberus?' I asked. The second the dog's name left my lips, a rumbling growl began to roll through the air. Morpheus brought the chariot to a stop, just a few feet above the ground.

'I don't know, but here's Minthe,' muttered Hecate, looking behind us. Her red chariot was pelting toward us, and as she neared I saw that her arm was wrapped in fabric, blood seeping through the material. She couldn't heal, I remembered, and Olethros' bite was toxic.

'Are you alright?' I called to her, as they slowed. Sanape growled and leveled her crossbow at me, but Minthe barked something at her.

'Fine,' she shouted back at me. 'May the best woman win!'

I nodded at her, as respectfully as I could, and turned back to Hecate, who was giving me a strange look.

'You do actually want to win this, right?'

'Yeah, but not by letting someone else die,' I snapped.

'Her health is not your problem. It's extremely good for you that she's injured.' A loud snarl cut across her words, and all the hairs on my skin stood on end.

'I'll win because I deserve to, not because she dies,' I said quietly, vines snaking from my palms. 'Where's Cerberus?' I asked again, before she could say anything else on the subject.

'He doesn't normally guard the inside of the gates,' she said. 'Persy, if you get bitten by him, you're not going to have long to fix it. His power over fear is as strong as Hades' is, and that almost killed you once.'

'OK,' I nodded. 'I won't let him bite me.' My stomach clenched in anxiety, and I flexed my fingers, my vines turning black. 'I'm ready.'

As if on cue, a creature melted through the iron gates, and I felt my knees go weak.

He was a combination of the other two hounds, in the worst possible way. Thirty feet tall, his dark body was covered in dancing flames. At his shoulders his neck split into three, and each broad, snarling head had angular eyes that looked like blood-red gemstones, and dark red liquid dripped from lethal fangs. Terror gripped my chest as I stared at the beast, fear spreading through my body all the way to my bones. Cerberus' ears pricked up, and all three heads barked. The sound rocked through me, and I clapped my hands over my ears as dread coursed through my veins. *Fire, flesh, blood...* I was drowning.

'Persy!' Hecate caught me as my legs buckled.

I snapped my magical shield up, and for a moment it did nothing. But then light broke through the dark spots in my eyes, the desire to run and run and run fading. My legs steadied, and Hades' face filled my mind, fierce and passionate. I was here for a reason, I couldn't run.

I had to win.

'Where's the gem?' I said, breathing hard. Morpheus pointed, and my insides clenched again. Glinting in the orange light, on a silver chain around Cerberus's middle head, were two gems the size of my fist. One green, and one red. I gaped, looking between Hecate and Morpheus.

'How the hell am I supposed to get onto his neck? He's on fucking fire!' They both stared back at me, Hecate's eyes filled with apology.

'We can't help you, Persy,' she said eventually.

'But Minthe has a plan, so you'd better come up with something fast,' said Morpheus, and I spun to see the other chariot powering toward the giant dog.

There was no way I could land on top of him, I'd be burned instantly, I thought, trying to play out scenarios as fast as I could in my head. But from underneath him, perhaps I could use my vines to reach the silver chain collar.

'Take me down,' I asked Morpheus, and he nodded, the chariot immediately dropping to the rock. I wasted no time, sprinting toward Cerberus. He snarled as I approached, then his right head moved up sharply, snapping at Minthe's chariot. Taking advantage of the distraction, I threw myself to the ground and slid. One huge flaming head came down, fangs terrifying as they chomped at me, but I made it underneath his massive chest before he could reach me. He barked again, the sound so loud I thought my head might explode. I wriggled around on my back, looking up at the underside of his body as his clawed paws stamped around me. The flames didn't extend under his chest, and I saw a pendant on a chain that was stretched over his barrel shaped ribs, bouncing against his black fur. Squinting, I made out the image of a skull, with a rose wrapped around it. Without thinking, I leaped into a crouch and jumped for the pendant. The second my hand closed around it, Cerberus howled.

It was so much worse than his bark. The sound instilled a terror that I had simply never felt in my life, waves of fear beating against my shield, impulses to run and hide and cry pulsing through my mind as I fought them.

After what seemed like an age, the howling mercifully stopped. Gasping, I inched forward, trying to get under his heads to see the collar, and I realized with a start that he was no longer on fire.

The pendant... Had it somehow stopped the fire? Mind racing, I changed course, running instead for his tail. If he wasn't on fire, I could climb up his back.

But so could Minthe.

As I emerged from underneath him, I twisted, launching my vines at the base of his tail and pulling myself up fast. His left head turned, snapping at his rear end, but he couldn't reach me as I landed at the base of his tail. My stomach twisted as I looked up and saw Minthe, wrapped tight around the neck of his right head. Tears streaked her pretty face as the head thrashed, and blood still seeped through her bandage. But she was closer to the collar than I was. And I had to win this.

Focusing on the central head, I ran up Cerberus' enormous spine, my arms flailing either side of me like a damned tightrope walker. The only thing that kept me upright as the dog stamped around was my speed. I threw myself at the middle neck as my foot finally slipped, but I missed. I fired my vines as I slid, and one coiled around Cerberus's neck, catching me as my body followed my foot, dangling between his middle and left heads. The third head snapped and snarled, and I swung myself desperately out of the way. I could see the gems glinting on the collar, high above me. But then I saw Minthe, her head appearing over the top of his central neck, gripping the chain collar. She saw my vine and paused, her gaze following it to where I was dangling. Her hand appeared by her head, a knife in it. *She was going to cut the vine.* I sent another one up fast, and it coiled around the collar. A blast of hot breath was my only warning that the third head was coming in for another go at eating me, and I pulled on both vines hard, willing them to shorten. The giant jaws missed me by inches. Cerberus howled again, and I winced, pain and a feeling of utter hopelessness lancing though my head.

I only had seconds before Minthe reached her gem. But she hadn't cut my vine. I looked up at her as I grabbed for the underside of the collar, and saw that she had one arm wrapped across her face, the other clinging to the top of the collar. I was only a few feet from her now.

I scrabbled at the collar, trying to twist it to reach the green gem, but it was thicker than my arm and wouldn't budge. The left head chomped at where Minthe was and I heard her whimper. She couldn't block out the fear like I could.

I yanked on the chain, pulling myself up and around the other side of his neck, closer to the gem. The right head swooped at me, and I launched a black vine at it, adrenaline powering through me.

I was so close.

The vine collided with Cerberus' temple, then began to coil around his ear. I couldn't make the dog weak by draining his power, or Minthe would have a chance too. The only reason she hadn't already got her gem was the fear crippling her. But I could at least keep one of the heads distracted. Cerberus shook his head violently, trying to dislodge my vine and making me wobble, but I held on. Using my legs I hauled myself up next to Minthe. She was trembling but her breathing was slowing.

'Do you really love him?' I heard her say, her voice weak. I froze.

'Yes.'

The left head barked suddenly, twisting toward us. I moved fast, lunging for the green gem. My fingers closed around it, and I pulled.

TWENTY-FIVE

PERSEPHONE

B lue light flashed all around us, and suddenly Cerberus was shrinking. Minthe yelped at the same time I cried out, then the chariot was right next to me, and Morpheus was yanking me onto it.

'Well done!' he yelled, as I fell on my butt on the wood.

'What's happening? Did I win?' Light was flashing around me like a strobe, totally disorientating me. I blinked down at my hand, the green gem huge and glowing. Had I done it? Had I really won?

But we were moving.

'Morpheus, where are we-' I cut off as I turned, confusion turning fast to fear. 'Where's Hecate?' Morpheus was facing ahead, and as the flashing lights lessened, I realized that we were speeding out of the orange glowing cavern.

I sprang to my feet, dropping the gem and gripping the chariot edge. 'Morpheus!' I yelled, wind rushing over me as we burst back out over the rocky landscape, the glowing rivers snaking across the Underworld below us. 'Morpheus, what's going on?' Black vines pushed out of my palms.

'You'll see in a moment,' he yelled back, without turning to me.

'See what? Where's Hecate?'

'This was her idea! But she'll be punished worse than I will, so we agreed I'd take you alone.'

'Take me where?'

'The river Lethe.'

~

This was wrong. Every tense muscle in my body was screaming at me as I reached out desperately in my mind for Hades or Hecate, but nobody responded.

I'd spent so much of my time here trying to work out how to get my memories back, but not like this. I'd just got the gem from Cerberus, I'd just won the damned Hades Trials, I should be celebrating with Hades, not flying to the one place I wasn't supposed to go!

'Morpheus, I want to go back. I want to see Hades.' I tried to keep my voice level, but it came out strained.

'You've come too far, Persephone. You must see this through.'

'Why are you doing this? I want to talk to Hecate.'

'I told you, she's holding back the others, this was her idea.'

'I don't believe you.' And I didn't. Hecate would not spring something like this on me. She loved Hades, and if Hades said I wasn't to get my memories back, then Hecate would support him.

We were swooping low through a gully, flying over the purple river, and a glimpse of sunshine yellow caught my eye in the distance. The river Lethe.

'You can't make me do this,' I said.

'I don't want to make you do anything. I'm trying to help you.' I thought about using my vines, but if he crashed the chariot we would both die, and I had no idea how to control it if I managed to disable him. It would be safer to get away once we were on the ground. I reached out desperately with my mind again for Hades or Hecate, but there was nothing.

As soon as the chariot touched down on the rocks on the bank of the yellow river, I launched my vines at Morpheus, but he spun to me, the air in front of him shimmering and bending and an image coming into view. My vines fell to the floor as I recognized my brother's face, a sleepy expression across it.

'Sam?' I realized I was looking at the Judgment Hall, but the crowds were gone, only my brother and Skop remaining. Skop was in naked gnome form, and he looked equally as out of it. 'What's happening?' I demanded. Hedone stepped into the image, a sad look on her face.

'This is a portal, like the flame dishes. One of my godly gifts,' said Morpheus. 'Hedone's gift is bewitching those around her with her irresistible charm. Men like your brother and Skop are particularly susceptible.' Anger surged through me, and my vines whipped up again.

'I thought you were my friends!'

'I'm sorry, Persy, but our cause is bigger than any of us individually. It has to be this way,' said Hedone, through the portal. She looked genuinely sad and I blinked at her.

'What cause? Why are you doing this?'

'The gods need to be taught a lesson. They need to know that they can't treat mortals like toys, wipe their memories, force them into action for their own entertainment.' Hedone's voice became hard as she spoke.

'What's that got to do with me? And where's Hecate?' Hedone pointed and the portal swung, showing Hecate's prostrate body on the marble.

'Hecate!' I yelled, and the portal swung back.

'She is only unconscious,' said Morpheus. 'At this stage we have no reason to kill her.' Fury was bubbling through me now, the remnants of Fonax's Underworld power surging through my veins.

'Kill her? I can't believe this! You were supposed to be my friends! Hecate's friends!' The betrayal stung to my core, and was making my eyes fill with tears, but I couldn't let them fall. I couldn't look weak. They had my real friends, and my brother.

'It wasn't supposed to play out like this,' Morpheus said. 'It was supposed to be simple, but so many things have gone wrong.' There was a bitter edge to his voice. 'Hedone implanted the memory of what you did in the humans so that they could scare you into getting your power back, but she lost control of one and he showed up with the phoenix at the ball. So, we changed tactics. But Hades got to you in Tartarus before Cronos could when we sent you there before.' I felt like ice was trickling down my spine, my head pounding with anger and shock.

'Why? Why are you doing this?'

'That is why we are here, at the river Lethe. Cronos and Hedone believe that you will be more cooperative if you know the truth. You will understand then why we must do what we are doing, the magnitude of our task.' His eyes were wide, and his skin was swirling with light as his words increased in volume. 'Drink. Drink from the river. Restore your memories.'

'No,' I said. For weeks I had yearned for my lost past, but not like this. If my memories were linked with Cronos and these maniacs, then Hades was right, I wanted nothing to do with them.

Morpheus sighed.

'Hedone, my sweet,' he said. Hedone moved, a long dagger appearing in her hand from the folds of her dress. Her eyes were filled with apology as she handed it to Sam. Horror filled me as my brother gazed at the blade.

'Sam, my love, place the tip of the dagger on your chest for me? You'd make me so very happy,' she beamed at him, her voice like honey. Sam smiled stupidly at her as he lifted the blade to his chest. 'Now when I say push, you must push. It won't hurt, it will feel like bliss.' Sam's smile widened.

'No!' I screamed, as I stepped towards the portal, flinging my vine towards the dagger. But the image just shimmered as my vine passed harmlessly through it. My heart hammered so hard against my ribs I thought it might burst free, and I felt sick as the hot tears finally spilled down my cheeks. I looked at Morpheus, hopeless dread gripping my body. I couldn't get to Sam to save him.

'Drink, Persephone,' he said. 'Now.'

I knelt slowly next to the river, my mind racing. Would Hedone really kill Sam? She didn't look like she'd wanted to, but her voice when she had spoken to him had been as smooth as silk, laced with seduction. Not a hesitation or wobble. I couldn't take the risk. I reached down, cupping my hands and dipping them into the glowing sunshine-yellow liquid. A rush of memories blasted through me, memories of mom holding me as I cried, memories of Sam helping me pick up books in the corridors at school. Memories of

Professor Hetz and the botanical gardens, and of my apartment.

I took a shuddering breath as I lifted my hands out of the river, water dripping slowly from the bowl my palms had formed.

'I don't want to do this,' I tried one more time, as I looked up at Morpheus. He shook his head slowly at me.

'This is out of our hands, Persephone. It is bigger than you or I. Drink.'

Gooseflesh covered my skin as I closed my eyes and lifted my cupped hands to my face, and drank.

'Persephone, how can you possibly be a better queen to Hades if you don't even know the Underworld properly?' I blinked at the voice, spinning around on the spot fast. I was in a dining room that looked a lot like the breakfast room in Hades' palace. I froze as I saw myself, sitting at a table with a man whose face I could not see. It was not Hades, that much I was sure of. I was wearing a black corseted dress, and my hair was as white as it was now, but I looked younger.

'I've made friends with the hounds now! And I've seen most of Virgo. Just not the really nasty bits,' the me who was sitting at the table told the man.

'If you truly want to help Hades, it's the worst parts of his world that you need to understand the most,' the man said. His voice was familiar, and I stepped closer cautiously.

'That does make sense,' younger me said slowly. 'You know, I have asked him to take me to Tartarus. But he always says no.'

'You're a Queen, Persephone. You have your own mind.

And in my experience, it's always better to ask for forgiveness than permission.' The arrogant mischief in his voice finally clicked into place, and I let out a breath as I rounded the table.

Zeus.

He didn't look much like he did now, but his purple eyes were unmistakable.

'I suppose you're right,' younger me said, voice filled with juvenile excitement. 'If you think it means I can help Hades rule better, I should do it. He'll understand. I'll take Cerberus with me, just in case.'

The image before me swirled and with a jolt, I was standing at the cave mouth before Tartarus, the flaming river burning beside me. Younger me was cocking her head at the inky blackness, and beside her was Cerberus, ten feet tall and swirling fiery spirals dancing over his fur. All three heads looked at younger me, then the closest nudged at her shoulder before turning, trying to walk away from the cave. Cerberus didn't want me to go in.

'Don't be silly. I'm Queen of the Underworld, everyone in there has to do as I say,' younger me said to the dog. Cerberus whined, but turned back to the cave. His tail drooped.

The scene before me whirled again, and I was in Tartarus. Ixion turned on his flaming wheel above us, and I stared as younger-me stood before a swirling mass of light and shadow. Cerberus was growling, deep and fearsome, but a voice drowned him out.

'I promise you, my Queen, I have been falsely judged. Zeus, Lord of the Gods himself, made sure that Hades was tricked and I was sent here for eternity. I am a god of light, and being trapped here in the dark is a torment too awful to endure.'

Nausea rolled through me. I recognized the voice. It was the stranger from the Atlas garden.

'Why should I believe you?' asked younger me, and the mass of light pulsed brightly.

'Because I speak the truth. I swear it.'

'Hmmm. You know, I can find out myself.' Slowly, younger-me lifted her hands, and vines snaked out of them. 'I can taste your power, find out exactly what sort of god you are,' she said, confidently.

'No,' I whispered. The vines turned black as they reached the mass, and a wave of power rippled through the deep red cavern. Younger-me gasped, dropping to her knees, and Cerberus howled, long and loud. The mass pulsed brighter, and the voice spoke again.

'You can take my power, but you can't contain it!' The words were spoken as a delighted realization, and a moan escaped younger-me's lips. Then a burst of bright blue illuminated the whole cavern, and a column of pure, blazing power smashed into the mass, tearing the vines from it. Hades, smoky and blue and enormous, scooped up younger me, and the scene flashed once again.

'It's too much,' younger me cried in Hades' arms. We were in a tiny rock room, barely any light around us.

'Let it out. It's safe down here, we're deep under the ground,' Hades said, his face a mask of pain.

'I can't. I can't. If I let go, his power will be free.'

'No, you only took a little. Let it go now, before it kills you.'

At his words, younger-me's body began to glow a deep blood red and with an agonized cry, waves of power burst from her skin. They smashed into the rock, and I saw the fear cross Hades' face as the walls began to crumble. He tightened his grip and flashed again, and then we were hovering in the sky above the ocean, islands dotting the blue.

I was looking at the realms of Olympus. He flashed again, and we were lower, looking over a series of small domes that were floating on the surface. They looked like the domes of Aquarius, but above the surface of the water instead of below.

Bile rose in my throat as rock burst from the waves, less than a mile from one of the domes. It grew and grew, and a whimper escaped me as I realized what it was. Red and black bubbled at the rock's peak, then a deafening boom echoed through the air.

It was a volcano.

Hades' face was white as he hovered in the sky, waves of red energy still pulsing from the body of my younger self, clutched in his arms. Lava spewed from the volcano, and I felt weak as I watched it rain over the nearest three domes. Tears flooded from my eyes as the screams began, and as desperately as I wanted to turn away, I couldn't. People fell as they ran through the streets, the fiery liquid chasing them down before they stood a chance of escaping. Buildings crashed to the ground as the lava melted them, crushing fleeing people.

A new scream pierced my ears, and I tore my eyes from the domes to see my younger self shrieking in Hades' grip.

The waves of red power had stopped and her gaze, *my gaze,* was transfixed on the fiery death and destruction below.

'Let me help, we have to help!' she was screaming, and I choked on a sob.

This is what I had done. I'd caused a volcano, and the death of hundreds of innocent people.

TWENTY-SIX

PERSEPHONE

The scene flashed again, and mercifully I wasn't taken down to the domes. I was back on the banks of the river Lethe, Morpheus towering over my crouched figure.

'Three of the domes above the surface were destroyed, and two below were cracked and flooded when the volcano rose from the sea bed,' said Morpheus, his voice gentle.

A strangled sound escaped my throat and more burning tears blurred my vision. Bile was burning my throat.

'I killed them. That's why Poseidon hates me.'

'You are not responsible for their deaths. Zeus is. He sent you down there, hoping you would die.'

I blinked up at Morpheus. 'Why?'

'He hated to see Hades happy. Zeus' ego is over-inflated to the point of mania. You were making Hades strong, and he couldn't handle it.'

'How do you know all this?'

'Cronos. He saw it in you when you connected with him.'

'You've been letting him talk to me. In my dreams,' I

said, clinging to the words, forcing out the terrible, terrible knowledge I now had. That I couldn't face.

'Yes. I can't free him myself, but I can give him some access to humans, via their dreams.'

'The Atlas garden. You created it.'

'No. Cronos did. He is not who the world makes him out to be. He is strong and beautiful and a far, far better ruler than Zeus. This is why you needed to know the truth.'

'But to free him, you need me to die,' I said, struggling to my feet.

'Yes. But now you understand why. Zeus will destroy Olympus, and everything good in it, to prove his power to the world.'

'I don't understand.' Urgent thoughts were beginning to batter through my grief and revulsion, and I clawed at them mentally, using them to stabilize my spinning emotions. 'Where is Hades?' He should be here. He would be able to feel my pain through the bond, he should be here. 'And how did you send me to Tartarus before? Only Hades can do that. He thought an Olympian was involved.'

'And he was right. I may be powerful, and a resident of Virgo, but even I can only talk to Cronos via my dreams. I can't enter Tartarus, much less send someone else there. But the most powerful god in Olympus can, once Hades relinquished some control to him.'

'What? But that makes no sense, why would-' Morpheus cut me off with a vicious laugh.

'Persephone, Zeus is a dangerous lunatic! His hatred for Titans is no longer shared, and the citizens of Olympus are starting to accept them. How better to remind the world of their evil than to let Cronos out? Zeus thinks he can step in and save the day, and the world will remember why they worship him. But he is mistaken. Cronos is far, far stronger than him. He has forgotten the war too quickly, his inflated opinion of himself now so deluded that reality and fantasy have merged. He approached me not long after you were banished, when I was worried about Hades. My king was a shadow of himself. Zeus asked me to keep an extra eye on Cronos, should Hades neglect to, and I agreed, hoping to support my king. And I discovered that Cronos was not who I thought he was. He was fair and wise and everything Zeus was not. So when Zeus asked me to help him with this new plan, I agreed, but because I want Cronos in Zeus' place. I told Cronos what Zeus has planned, and even now Zeus still believes I am working for him. His ego will not allow him to believe otherwise.'

Fear and disbelief were overriding everything else in my head as Morpheus spoke. *Zeus was behind this. The only god more powerful than Hades.*

'Where is Hades?'

'He's tied up with a friend at the moment. But don't worry, Cronos has a proposition for you.'

'Why are you doing this? What's in it for you?'

'Love for Olympus, Persephone. Zeus needs to be removed, for the good of the world. Hades may not have told you, but the Underworld is seeing crueler people every year, and they are a result of his twisted society. Cronos will make the world a better place. And you're about to meet him.'

Protesting was useless as Morpheus watched me climb back on the chariot. With Sam, Hecate and Skop at his mercy, he knew I would do as he asked.

But the rational part of my brain knew they would die

anyway if Cronos got his power into me and I went off like a bomb. I had to do something, but no matter how desperately I scrabbled around for a solution, nothing came. If Zeus had the other gods distracted, or convinced nothing was wrong, and Hades was trapped somewhere, then nobody was coming for me. I was on my own.

I barely saw the Underworld flash by below us, my mind was so focused on trying to come up with a plan that didn't involve everyone I loved dying. But as the flaming river came into view, my pulse raced even faster, my stomach lurching as we began to descend.

'Ah. There's Hades,' said Morpheus, from the head of the chariot, and my insides seared hot as the bond fired and I leaned over the chariot.

A little way off from the cavern that led to Tartarus, on a barren, uneven piece of rock, was a flaming ring twenty feet across. And at its center, on his knees, was Hades. His face snapped up to mine and I almost lost my grip on the chariot, his emotion rocketed through me so hard.

He was scared. And furious.

I reached for him desperately in my mind, but I couldn't hear him, couldn't get to him. There was no blue light around him, and his black trident lay useless nearby. Something had stripped his power, I realized. As the chariot soared over him, Ankhiale stepped out of the fire. She tilted her head and gave me a little finger wave, and a roar of frustration escaped me.

He's immortal. They can trap him, but they can't kill him. I clung to the thought, repeating the words over and over as we descended, and Hades and the fire witch disappeared from view. Pain surged through my gut again, my emotions mingling with Hades' as we lost sight of each other.

Morpheus set the chariot down at the mouth of the cave that led to Tartarus, and turned to me.

'Off you go, my Queen. Cronos is expecting you.'

'Only Hades, and apparently now Zeus, can enter or leave Tartarus,' I said, refusing to move my feet.

'I think you'll find that the winner of the Hades Trials, and Hades' Queen-to-be, also has that privilege,' he smiled at me.

Shit. What the hell was I going to do? Adrenaline was racing through my body, focusing my mind and building my power inside me. Which was exactly what I didn't want. My power couldn't help me here. In fact, it would be what killed me and everyone else in Virgo. And if Cronos was as bad as history and Hades said he was, possibly the whole of Olympus.

'I shouldn't have eaten those fucking seeds!' I yelled, and Morpheus blinked at my outburst.

'It's too late for regrets, Persephone. You will be a martyr. The little goddess who saved the world from a maniac.'

'You're the fucking maniac.'

'Ah, I see now that the shock is wearing off, the attitude is surfacing,' he said. 'I recommend being more polite to King Cronos.'

'Hades is your king, you filthy traitor,' I snarled.

'Not for much longer. Now go.'

I stared at him, desperation and fury boiling over inside me, with no outlet. With a hiss, I shot my arm out, and slapped him as hard as I could across the face.

'You're a fucking disgrace to the Underworld,' I spat, then stamped off the chariot, onto the rock. I didn't turn back as I marched towards the cavern. I couldn't face seeing if he would punish my brother or friends for my behavior, but I hadn't been able to help myself.

The orange flames of the river cast flickering shadows over the walls of the cave, and I walked fast. The last time I had been here, Hades had succumbed to the monster, and was about to set foot in Tartarus and take out his fury on the worst of the Underworld.

Perhaps I should have let him. Perhaps he would have killed Cronos. I knew in my gut that that wasn't possible though. Hades had described Cronos as primordial in strength. He was truly immortal, unable to be destroyed. Memories of when I was last in Tartarus swept through me, the utter darkness, the screaming tortured souls, the endless fear. Panic threatened to engulf me, blackness swimming across my vision, but I bared my teeth as I pulled the thought of Hades into my mind.

I had to be strong. I had to work out a way to escape this.

At the mouth of Tartarus, I paused, squeezing my eyes closed and praying. *Please don't let me through, please don't let me through.* But disappointment melted through me as my foot entered the darkness without a hitch. I took a shuddering breath, and stepped through completely. The darkness was as terrifying as I remembered it, but this time power surged hard through me, blocking the fear and the smells. I couldn't block the sounds of screaming though, as I walked carefully forward, alongside the flaming river. With a screech and a flash, Ixion appeared above me, shrieking. I gulped back my trepidation and took another stride forward. All I had now was myself, and I was not going to cower in fear. Cronos would meet the goddess I knew was inside me, not a naive girl or a terrified woman.

He would meet the goddamned Queen of the Underworld.

'Cronos!' I bellowed, summoning every ounce of courage within me. The flames in the river roared up, and a deep rumbling shook the ground. Illuminated on my right suddenly was a row of grand chairs, and a man sitting on one of them cried out when he saw me.

'Help me, please,' he screamed, and I recoiled as I saw the remnants of flesh and blood stuck to the vacant chairs. The man and the chairs melted back into the darkness before I could say a word.

'Cronos, I'm here!' I yelled again. The rumbling grew louder, then the mass of light I'd seen in the memory from the river appeared before me. Shadows intertwined with the white light, spinning and turning in a mesmerizing dance.

'Little goddess,' Cronos said, and a man stepped out of the light.

He was so beautiful I gasped, my lungs not working properly for a heartbeat. His eyes and his hair and his eyebrows were made of what looked like pure daylight, and instead of being creepy, it was stunning. He held his hands out and light shone from them too.

'I will not free you,' I choked out, my eyes streaming in his brightness.

'I wish, so very much, that you did not have to die. I would have liked for you to rule beside me.' The calm, soothing voice I had come to trust in the Atlas garden washed over me, and I clung to my anger, refusing to let him addle my brain.

'I will not free you,' I repeated. 'You can't make me use my vines.'

'It really is such a great shame to lose one as beautiful as you. But needs must. And the world's needs are greater than our own.'

'You were imprisoned here for a reason, and you will stay here,' I said, wishing desperately that I could grow, like Hades and the others did. Standing before Cronos, I felt tiny, despite his physical body being barely larger than mine. His presence was immense, as though he was light itself, more element than being.

'Little goddess, I have an offer for you to consider. I have become fond of you, and I would rather do this with you willing. It will hurt less.' My hands shook as I stared at him. He wasn't scared of me. My words had no effect on him at all. What the fuck was I going to do?

'You can't make me use my vines,' I said again. 'If I have to fucking stand in front of you like this forever, I will.'

'If you cooperate with me, I will allow Hades to live, free of his obligation to the Underworld,' Cronos said. I froze. 'I will free his soul of this place, and he will finally live the life he has always craved.'

TWENTY-SEVEN

HADES

I had to get to her.

Cronos was the strongest being still in existence in Olympus, and only my power over Tartarus gave me dominion over him.

Persephone didn't stand a chance. Fury swept through me, my head pounding with pain.

'You'll pay for this, Ankhiale! When I've got my power back, you'll fucking pay!' I bellowed. She stepped from the flames, shaking her head.

'Hades, you won't get your powers back, you fucking moron. You'll be consumed by them instead.'

'What if I offer you a deal?' I tried, changing tactics. 'What if I give you more than he can?' She laughed.

'More than Cronos can? Please. You're half as strong as him. What could you possibly-' she cut off abruptly, screwing her face up as a small flash of light sparked behind her. I frowned, then struggled to my feet as a shimmering burgundy powder appeared from nowhere, showering her whole body. A slow, easy smile spread across her face, then she giggled. 'There's six of you,' she slurred, then slumped to the ground.

'What the-' I started, then squinted as a small, naked gnome ran towards me. 'Skop?'

'Hedone thought she'd charmed me, but despite her being hot as holy hell, I am immune to such powers,' he said, talking fast as he reached me. I thrust the manacle out to him, one desperate hope left in me.

'Get my trident into the keyhole,' I said urgently. The trident could only be wielded by me, so it should be enough to unlock the manacle.

'I pretended she was in control, but secretly told Dionysus everything. He couldn't send me into Tartarus with Persephone, so he sent me to you instead. Armed with wine powder, but it won't last long. Ankhiale will come round in five minutes.'

'Zeus is behind all this,' I told the kobaloi, as he dragged the Trident toward me. It must have weighted three times what he did, and his bearded face showed the strain. Energy was building inside me, hope coursing through my veins.

'Dionysus worked that out when I told him you weren't really with Persephone. Zeus took the other gods to Leo to *give you two some time alone*. I believe Dionysus and Poseidon are confronting him now.' He had dragged the Trident to my feet and I ducked into a crouch, scooping it up with one hand.

'Help me,' I said, and together we wrestled the end of the long weapon into the manacle. With a roar, I forced the trident into the metal, and with a loud crack, the cuff opened.

Power flooded my body, the monster rearing loud and white-hot inside me, screaming up my chest, ready to end anyone or anything that stood between me and my Queen.

TWENTY-EIGHT

PERSEPHONE

Cronos could free Hades. Free him of his eternal obligation and let him live as he truly wanted to. If I was going to die anyway, surely this was a deal worth making?

What if you can stop him though! Don't give in! The fighter inside me screamed. But my heart ached as I thought about Hades consumed by the darkness, the idea of him living trapped in Tartarus as a mindless machine of violence unbearable.

I barely felt the vines snake from my palms.

As though on magnets, they burst toward Cronos.

'Wait!' I shouted, but it was too late, it was as though I no longer had control of them. A slow smile spread across Cronos' face as they reached him, and the storm of light around him shimmered a dark orange.

'It appears you have made your choice, Persephone.'

'No! No I hadn't decided yet!'

'Your power responded to your heart, little goddess. You would do anything for him.'

My vines coiled around his arms, and I sent every ounce of power I had in my body into them to keep them green. As soon as they turned black, they would take his power. Sweat rolled down my back as I concentrated.

'But the thing is, I lied.' My eyes snapped to his. 'Hades has been my keeper for a very, very long time. Do you really think I would not repay him for his actions? After you have destroyed it, I will rebuild Tartarus, and it will be much, much worse than this. The Olympians have little imagination when it comes to torture. And Hades will spend at least as long as I have in the darkness.'

Fury raged through me, my passion and my instinct to protect him too great to suppress.

'It's Zeus you're angry with, not Hades!' I could feel my power reacting, the image of Hades' face fueling my strength, as it always did. I couldn't let him live that life. I had to do something. And my vines agreed. With a ripple, they turned black.

'No!'

Cronos let out a long breath and closed his eyes as black tattoos began to spread across his shoulders.

'No!' I screamed again, desperately trying to disintegrate the vines. But it was as though they were glued to him, he was too strong. And then the power flowing down them from him hit me, and everything stopped.

Time itself stood still as power consumed me, so vast I could make no sense of it. Within seconds it was overwhelming me, I was drowning in the infinite; swirling through a mass of light and shadow that never ended.

. . .

'Persephone!'

That voice... I knew that voice. That voice was the most important thing in the world to me. More important than anything else. I clung to it, the dizzying vortex around me slowing.

It was Hades.

As I came back to reality I saw Hades, hulking and furious, a canon of blue light beating uselessly at my vines. Legions of blue bodies were climbing up Cronos' expanding form, but Cronos wasn't reacting, his arms open wide, black vine tattoos spreading further across his body.

'Persephone, stop the vines! I can't flash you out while you're connected to him!' Hades roared, but I couldn't speak. Tidal waves of power were rolling through me, leaving me utterly breathless, images of worlds beyond my wildest imaginings flashing before me.

'Persy! Persy, tell me how to help you!'

Skop. I could hear Skop's voice.

'Worship me.' I was vaguely aware that the words were coming from my own lips, and Hades' eyes locked on mine, filled with dread as more blue light powered from him, into Cronos. 'Olympus will know true fear. True power. True death,' my voice thundered.

Stop! My mind railed against the words I was saying, but the little voice in my head, the one that really belonged to me, was too small, too quiet, too weak. Cronos was taking over. His power was filling me, burning away everything else.

Pain, that had been indistinguishable from the torrent of emotion and power at first, was growing. Burning agony exploded suddenly in my head, and I cried out.

Desperation took over Hades' face, before blackness filled his silver eyes in a rush. The monster was taking over.

'You're too late, Hades!' said Cronos, his calm, soothing tone gone. 'I am becoming weak. Which means she has most of my power already.'

My head swam, a storm raging inside me.

'Never!' bellowed Hades, and raised his gleaming black trident. I could only just see them both, my eyes streaming as another pulse of agony ripped through me, the flood of images pouring through my mind blurring with reality. I could hardly breathe.

I started to fall to my knees as Hades brought his trident down on my vines with a roar.

I felt the reaction from Cronos before it occurred. The full wrath of Hades was enough to loosen his control. It was enough.

The second I felt the magnetic pull weaken, I willed the vines to disintegrate with everything I had. I tumbled forward as they disappeared, but instead of falling onto the rocky ground, I fell into Hades' arms and the world flashed white as Cronos screamed.

TWENTY-NINE

PERSEPHONE

I gasped for air as an awful sound reached my ears, my insides twisting and churning as white-hot pain burned through my veins.

'Persephone,' choked Hades, and I realized the sound was coming from him. I blinked up at his face, trying to force out the cascade of power ripping through me long enough to focus. I was lying in his arms, bare wasteland around us.

'Where are we?' I gulped.

'The surface,' he said, and I realized tears were streaming down his beautiful face.

'You need to take me somewhere I can't kill anyone,' I said, panic causing another swell of pain to grip me.

'Use your gold vines. Give me the power,' Hades said, gripping my jaw in his hand.

'Will-will it kill you?' I ground out, my head swimming again.

'No, it won't kill me,' he said, desperation in his eyes. I knew he was lying.

'It will fill you with darkness,' I whispered, knowing the truth of my words. He didn't respond.

Pouring Cronos' power into Hades would cause him to lose his soul as surely as if Cronos had broken free.

'My soul doesn't matter, as long as you live,' Hades breathed, pulling my face to his. Another wave of infinite power sent me into a spasm, and I could feel the pressure building inside me, tortuously painful. I couldn't contain it. I knew I couldn't. I was going to die. And I couldn't take Virgo or Hades with me.

'I love you,' I said, and an unexpected calm cut through the storm swirling inside my mind. 'I'm so glad I found you.' More tears rolled down Hades' face, his breath hot on my cheek as he kissed my face, over and over.

'Please, please, Persephone, give the power to me.' I pushed my numb hand into my pocket, and closed it around Poseidon's pearl, and lifted my other to Hades' wet cheek.

'Don't let the monster win. Ever. You're stronger than it is.'

'Persephone, I love you. Please, please. You can't leave me again.'

I pulled him to me, pressing my lips against his for the final time. Then I crushed the pearl in my hand.

Freezing ocean water cascaded over us and Hades cried out in surprise. I pulled myself to my feet, my vision blurry and my whole body numb as Buddy whinnied into existence beside me. And as I had hoped, he wasn't a seahorse. He was a *winged* horse.

'I love you. You have to let me do this,' I said, looking into Hades anguished face.

'I love you,' he choked, and I pulled myself awkwardly

onto Buddy's back. He began to gallop immediately, then his huge wings snapped taut, and we launched into the sky. The waves of pain were increasing now, and I gripped his mane as tightly as I could as we soared higher.

'When I tell you, you've got to get out of here, Buddy,' I whispered to the horse, and he neighed loudly. Poseidon said he could be out of water for five minutes. And to make sure I killed nobody when the power overcame me, I needed to be as high as I could be, as far from everything and everyone in Olympus as possible.

We flew on, higher and higher, and when I could barely see Hades on the rock below, and the pressure inside me was so painful I knew I couldn't bare it any longer, I let go. I let go of Buddy, I let go of the power, I let go of myself. Completely.

A clarity I had never known descended over me as the horse vanished, and I hovered, weightless, suspended in time and space. I stared around myself, gaping, as the pain stopped immediately. A swirling mass of light and shadow was surrounding me, and with a jolt, I realized the power hadn't left me yet.

For the few moments before it overwhelmed me, at that suspended point in time, the power belonged to me. I had magic and strength unparalleled. And as it glowed and swirled around me, understanding came to me.

It wasn't all dark.

Daylight and shadow, light and dark; they both swirled together.

Hades' words sang through my mind. 'You can't keep a light that bright in the dark.' But what other purpose did a bright light serve, if it wasn't lighting the dark? One could not exist without the other. One had no purpose without the other. Light was destined to live with the dark.

· · ·

I knew what I had to do. I knew it with bone deep certainty. I needed to light the dark.

My vines burst from my palms, gleaming gold, and as I began to fall through the air, I shot them at the surface of Virgo. They slammed into the ground, and I heard Hades shout over the rushing wind, as I drew every bit of light I could from Cronos' power and channeled it into the rock. Life flared bright inside me, rushing through my body, and I focused on Hades' face, on love and light and growth.

And I felt the dark around me, inside me, changing. The shadows in the swirling mass were receding, the light forcing them out. The torrents of power that had been battering against me now flowed through me and into my golden vines like a river of life, and as I approached the surface, green invaded my blurred vision.

Too late I realized I was going to hit the ground, and with my vines connected to the earth I couldn't use them to brace myself. But instead of hard rock, I hit something soft. I was on a cushion of blue light, and as it lowered me gently to the floor, Hades ran toward me.

His face was a mask of awe and shock, and as I channeled the last of the glittering power into the ground, I called out to him.

'A light this bright was made for the dark. They belong together.' My vines disintegrated as he reached me, and he barely slowed, scooping me off my feet and kissing me so hard I couldn't breathe.

'You're alive,' he said, over and over between kisses. Exhilaration rocketed through me, and as the remnants of the godly power left me, my own emotions finally took hold of me again. *I was alive. And so was he.*

'We both are,' I gasped, and kissed him back, just as hard.

Eventually he set me back down on my feet, staring into my eyes like he'd never seen anything so mesmerizing.

I'd done it. I had actually saved us. I had channeled that immense power into something good, and light. I hadn't let it overwhelm me. I had been strong enough to save us. Disbelief was making me giddy as I stared up at Hades. If I had truly filled his realm with light, then there was a chance for us. A real chance.

'I love you. I love you so much. Look what you've done to this place,' he said, gripping my shoulders and turning me around slowly.

We were standing in a glade, willow trees waving softly in a gentle breeze. Birds tweeted somewhere in the distance, and butterflies flitted between meadow flowers dotting the lush grass.

'Is the whole surface like this?' I asked, breathless. I wasn't sure how much I'd done.

Hades pulled my back close against his chest, wrapping his huge arms around me, and flashed. We hovered, high above the surface, where I'd been with Buddy just moments before. There wasn't a dusty, barren bit of rock anywhere. Streams meandered across the landscape, trees of every type and stature, flowers of every color and species filling the space. I could see a huge forest in the distance, and beyond that a green-covered valley, waterfalls cascading down one side.

Hades flashed again, and we were back in the glade. I spun in his arms, looking up into his eyes.

'This is still part of Virgo, so can you live here?' Hades

raised his eyebrows at me, then closed his eyes. I felt his power rolling over me.

'We are far from the dark, where my power is most needed, but... you are right, this is still Virgo. It is still my realm.' Excitement lit up his stunning eyes as he opened them, and hope made my chest swell to the point it ached. 'Yes. Yes, I think I can.'

'We can live up here half of the time! We will get respite from the darkness, but you will still be in control of the Underworld!' Elation made my words fast, my voice high-pitched. *We could be together. We would be safe, together, light and dark as one.*

He pushed his hand into my hair, stroking his thumb down my jaw.

'Persephone, you... You complete me. You make me strong. You make me whole. You saved us.' Happiness gripped me, and I felt a lump in my throat as I stared back at him. 'I love you,' he said, his voice the softest, most sensual thing I'd ever heard.

'In that case,' I whispered, letting the happy tears come as I stood on tiptoes to kiss him, 'it's a damned good thing that I'm your new Queen.'

THIRTY

PERSEPHONE

As I realized what my words meant though, panic swelled through me. The Trial... Morpheus!

'Sam and Hecate! Hedone has them hostage! We have to stop Morpheus!'

We may have survived, and Cronos may still be trapped in Tartarus, but this wasn't over yet. Guilt swamped me as the emotion and power crashing through my brain started to clear, and the full impact of everything I'd learned in the last hour began to filter through. *The volcano. Zeus. My brother and Hecate.*

Hades' face darkened, and the world flashed around us.

I gaped at the scene before me in the judgment hall, my power-addled body and brain simply not keeping up.

'Persy!' My brother charged toward me, lifting me off my feet as he reached me. 'Thank god you're OK.' I squeezed him back as I stared over his shoulder.

· · ·

Tied up with chains made from some sort of glowing metal, were Morpheus and Hedone, and they were both sitting on Minthe's red chariot. Kerato and two other guards had spears pointed at them and Morpheus bared his teeth at me.

Minthe and Sanape were standing nearby, and were both covered in blood. The spirit who had been driving their chariot appeared to be tending their wounds.

'What happened?' I breathed, as Sam let me go. 'Where's Hecate?'

'I'm here,' she said from behind us, and I whirled, relieved to see that she looked fine as she strode forward. 'I'm sorry, boss. She knocked me out.' Her eyes dipped to the floor as she reached Hades.

'They managed to manacle me, so I'd be a hypocrite to reprimand you,' Hades said, an edge of steel to his tone.

'They manacled you?' Hecate gasped. 'Zeus is a fucking asshole, I swear if he ever-'

'Who detained Morpheus?' Hades said, cutting her off.

'Minthe,' answered my brother. 'It was pretty amazing actually.'

'Yeah, we owe her,' said Hecate. 'Ask her yourself, we were both out of it, so she can tell you best.'

'Minthe?' called Hades, and the mountain nymph looked over at us, wincing. I glanced quickly at Hades, then hurried over to her, my gold vines snaking from my palms before I reached her.

'Let me help you,' I said, expecting an argument. But she just raised her wrist for my vine to coil round. 'Did you really save my brother?' I asked her as Hades stepped up behind me.

'That slutty bitch Hedone thought I was too injured to be a threat. That'll teach her not to underestimate me,' Minthe snapped as my healing power began to flow into her. She closed her eyes, a look of relief washing over her face. Her tone was less angry when she spoke again. 'I was laid on the floor by the chariot, my arm and knee fucked, when I saw the portal and you and Morpheus through it. I heard everything. So I asked Poly,' she gestured at the spirit woman, 'to get help. Then Sanape and I jumped Hedone as soon as the portal was closed. Morpheus turned up not long after, but Sanape is a seriously good shot.' Sanape gave me a vicious grin and I glanced over my shoulder at Morpheus, restrained in the chariot. Silver liquid was dribbling from his temple. 'Kerato and the guards got here with the chains just in time, I'm not sure we could have held them much longer.'

'Thank you,' I breathed, and threw my arms around her before I could stop myself. She stiffened in my embrace, and then muttered,

'You can stop the healing now, I'm good. Help Sanape.' I let her go, and did as she asked, the Amazon woman looking reluctant to receive my help, but accepting when Minthe gave her a long enough look.

'Minthe, the Underworld owes you a debt,' said Hades. She looked at him, then bowed her head.

'I owed Persephone a debt. It's now clear.' She had a hard glint in her eye when she looked back at me.

'Yes, yes of course it is,' I said.

'I can't bestow immortality on you, as you know it is forbidden for any single god to do that. But I can make you rich. You will have diamonds to last you a lifetime,' Hades said.

Minthe's mouth opened slowly, her eyebrows raising.

'Thank you, King Hades,' she breathed, dipping her head again.

'You too, Sanape,' he said, turning to the Amazon. She

dipped her head less reverently, but pride was stamped across her expression.

Hades turned, and strode to the chariot. I released the vines that had now healed Sanape, and followed him, nerves skittering through my stomach. Hedone was asleep, looking peaceful as she sat back-to-back with Morpheus.

'You can only save her from her punishment for so long,' Hades said, and his voice was like ice.

'I'll keep her asleep as long as I can,' answered Morpheus, not looking up. 'This is not her fault. She wanted to hurt nobody.'

'Unlike you?'

'I am fighting for a higher cause. I am fighting for Olympus. Cronos said there would be casualties.'

Blue light flared around Hades, and all the color drained from Morpheus' face abruptly. He seemed to shrink in on himself, and I saw gooseflesh raise on his skin. A small whimper escaped his mouth.

'You are as bound to your role as the dream god as I am to mine,' hissed Hades, 'and only that will save you from Tartarus. But you will perform that role as a prisoner to your own fear, for the rest of your immortal life, Morpheus. What you see in your mind now, is what you will see every minute of every day and night.'

'No,' he whispered, finally lifting his haunted eyes to Hades. 'No, please!'

'Take him to his rooms, and bind him,' Hades said, and Hecate stepped forward.

'With pleasure, boss,' she said, and with a flash, they both disappeared. Hedone fell backward without him to lean on, and moaned softly.

'Kerato, confine her in the palace until Aphrodite can deal with her, as she is one of her deities.'

'Yes, my Lord,' the minotaur said.

'What did you make Morpheus see?' I asked Hades quietly, as the minotaur pulled Hedone groggily to her feet, and the chariot lifted off the temple floor.

'It doesn't matter,' he answered.

But it did. The punishment was hitting me hard. Because I had an awful feeling I was going to live the same life. I was going to see all those people I had killed over and over again, every day. Those screaming, innocent people, running hopelessly from the lava.

My thoughts were either clear on my face or made it through the bond, because Hades pulled me to him, tipping my face up to his.

'Cronos did that, not you. You were a conduit, a vessel, a weapon. Not the cause. Do you understand?' I nodded, trying to believe his words. 'And you are no longer that person. Look at what you did up there. You controlled the power this time, and saved the lives of thousands. Possibly more.'

This time, his words did hit home. Saved the life of thousands. He was right. New Persephone saved lives.

I would never forgive myself for what I knew I had done, but at least I was making a start on setting it right.

A bright flash was followed quickly by the smell of the ocean, and then Poseidon was stood before us, Dionysus at his side.

'Skop!' The gnome sitting on Dionysus' shoulder shifted

into a dog as he jumped down and ran to me. I crouched and pulled the dog into a hug. 'I'm so glad you're OK.'

'And boy am I glad to see you too,' he said.

'Zeus escaped,' said Poseidon, and I stood up fast, my attention on the sea god. 'He severely wounded Ares and Artemis, and Hera has withdrawn completely, and won't talk to anyone.'

'Shit,' hissed Hades.

'Shit doesn't cover half of it,' said Dionysus. 'He's got that fire Titan of yours with him, she came and busted him out of Ares' hold.'

'But he hates Titans!' I exclaimed.

'If Ankhiale knew that Cronos wasn't going to be free, she will move to the next strongest god,' Hades muttered. 'And Zeus won't turn down allies now.'

'So, does that mean you're at war?' I asked slowly.

'No. Zeus hasn't declared any such thing, but he will need to face a trial and punishment. Just like Hades did, when he broke the rules,' Poseidon said with a pointed look at Hades.

'Is that why he has run?'

'Yes. He'll be back, I've no doubt. With an elaborate excuse for all of this, and a new plan to inflate his ego further.'

'He is a dangerous maniac, and he can no longer rule the Olympians,' said Hades. Dionysus nodded.

'Hear, hear. The man needs to chill the fuck out.'

'We will deal with succession later. For now, I'm here to see Persephone,' said Poseidon. I gulped as the Lord of the Oceans turned to me. 'Your handling of Cronos' power bears the marks of a true Queen and goddess of Olympus. I am pleased to welcome you to our ranks.' My mouth fell open. 'And thank you for taking care of my hippocampus,' he added, before giving me a twinkling smile, and vanishing.

'Well done, Persy,' said Dionysus, as I blinked after Poseidon. 'Make sure you visit soon, there are some folk on Taurus who remember growing up with you now,' he said, with a big grin. 'And your fella needs a drink. I got lots of that.'

'I-I will,' I stuttered, and felt a smile take over my face. My future in Olympus was looking a whole lot better than I could have possibly imagined.

THIRTY-ONE

PERSEPHONE

I took a deep breath as I stared at my reflection in the grand mirror. Happiness so intense it made me want to scream washed through me. I was wearing an actual wedding dress.

I twirled, letting the white lace spin around the satin slip beneath. The dress had been made for the occasion, and the top was a classic white corset, but the bottom... The bottom was miles upon miles of white lace that I had designed myself. An intricate pattern of roses and skulls. Earth and nature, dark and light, life and death.

It had been a month since Cronos had almost killed me and I'd used his power to turn the surface of Virgo into a nature-filled haven for the two of us. Hades used his power to build us a modest hut, to see if we really could live above the ground. He had been nervous at first that the longer he was above the surface of Virgo, the less control he would have over his realm and the dangerous demons he was linked to. Mostly, he feared losing his grip on Tartarus.

But it was a full two weeks before he felt any difference in his power, and so for the following two weeks, we returned to his rooms in the palace, below the surface. His control strengthened again immediately.

I saw no reason we couldn't live like that for eternity, spending half our time in the light, and half in the dark. Especially since I had some pretty epic plans for the house in the glade.

I looked down at the ring on my finger, a thrill of anticipation whipping through my body. *Married.* I was actually getting married.

It hadn't taken much to convince Hades to do the 'human' down-on-one-knee proposal. In fact, I'd just asked Hecate to tell him that was what he was supposed to do. And he went one step further. The culture in Olympus was to have one ring, for both the engagement and wedding, but because he knew that there were usually two rings in my world, he'd made a special ring for me. It was a silver band, tiny swirling vines engraved on it, and it had a section cut out all the way through, where a second tiny gold ring fitted, the ends meeting in little Greek spirals. It was the most precious thing I'd ever owned.

'Are you ready?'

I grinned as I turned, and Hecate beamed back at me. She was wearing a blue dress, and it was the first time I'd ever seen her wear something floor length. Like me, she had white roses weaved into her hair.

'As I'll ever be.'

'Here,' she said, and passed me a saucer of fizzy wine. 'A toast. To the new Queen of the Underworld.' A stupid smile stretched my cheeks as I clinked my glass with hers and sipped. The freaking Queen of the Underworld.

'I'm really, really not happy about this,' came Skop's voice, and he waddled into the room, Sam striding beside him.

'You look great,' I told him, and he scowled at me from under his beard.

'I'd rather be a dog than wear clothes. This is the most unnatural thing I've ever done,' he answered, pulling at the ill-fitting pants he had on. I laughed.

'You can be a dog if you like, but it'll make drinking and dancing a little hard. And before you ask for the millionth time, no, you can't be naked at my wedding.'

He gave a big, over-the-top sigh.

'If it was anyone else, I'd refuse,' he grumbled, rolling his eyes.

'Thank you Skop. You're the best,' I beamed at him.

'Don't you forget it. Best personal guard ever. Saved your damned life and you won't even let me be naked,' he muttered.

'You look amazing,' said my brother, leaning forward to kiss my cheek and saving me from having to respond to the kobaloi.

'Thank you. It's a shame mom and dad can't be here,' I said.

'Definitely for the best that they're not,' he grinned at me. 'And anyway, now you're all immortal and powerful and stuff, you can visit them next week.'

'Yes. I want Hades to meet them. But I'm not sure who or what to tell them he is. Maybe a lawyer?' Sam snorted.

'Right. A terrifying, football-playing, body-building lawyer.'

'We've got to go, Persy,' said Hecate, cutting across our

conversation. 'This is not something you want to be late for.' More excited nerves rippled through me and she smiled as she reached for my hand.

I linked my arm through my brother's as the doors to the breakfast room opened, and the harps began to play. The blossom tree was in full bloom, and light streamed through the huge arched windows, gold frames sparkling and lush green beyond. But my eyes were locked in place on the reason I was there.

Standing next to our tree, at the end of the aisle, was Hades. He was wearing a black toga lined with silver and the sight of him took my breath away. His eyes found mine as I stepped into the room, and as I saw delight wash over his beautiful face, his voice sounded in my head.

'You look... unbelievable.'

'So do you.'

'I can't believe you're marrying me. Again. I'm the luckiest man in the world.'

I beamed at him as I walked down the aisle toward him. He was my everything. 'I love you.'

'And I love you, my Queen.'

THE END

WANT TO SEE WHAT HAPPENED WHEN HADES PROPOSED? GET ACCESS TO AN EXCLUSIVE CUT SCENE BY SIGNING UP TO MY NEWSLETTER HERE.

EXPLICIT CONTENT

THANKS FOR READING!

Thank you so much for reading this take on Hades' and Persephone's story.

I've been obsessed with Greek mythology for as long as I can remember, and I can't tell you how much I love sitting down every day to bring characters from that rich world of craziness to life. The moral message, the mutual sacrifice, the intense love between Hades and Persephone, that perfect balance of two such different beings, has always been right up there with my favorites of all the myths, and I have LOVED writing this story.

'Love conquers all' is the theme behind everything I write, and that comes in no small part from the love I get from my own husband. He's my biggest fan, despite having never read anything I've written (he's not a reader - I'll get him to listen to the audiobooks one day). But he listens to me and supports me and helps me in all the other ways I need it and I am eternally grateful.

I am also in awe of how much help and support complete strangers have given me during my journey as a writer. Reena, I can't believe you actually sent me the ring, from Greece, that inspired Persephone's wedding ring!! (Picture on next page!) You make my books better and I'm so thankful for your help and support and friendship! Brittany, thank you for your sharp eye and experienced early opinions! Mum, thanks for proofreading everything I write, even if it's a bit steamy. And for trying to keep the naughty books away from Grandad...

I will keep writing about all the incredible gods from the ancient Greek world until I run out, and I'm pretty sure that won't happen. Next up is Ares, and I am very, very excited about it.

Hecate turned out way more fun than I had originally expected, so I have a follow on novel for her planned too.

Thank you again, fabulous reader, for making it possible for me to keep writing!!

Eliza xxx

The ring Reena sent me from Greece - Persephone's wedding ring!!

You can get exclusive first looks at artwork and story ideas, plus free short stories and audiobooks if you sign up to my newsletter at elizaraine.com and you can hang out with me and get teasers, giveaways and release updates (and pictures of my pets) by joining my Facebook reader group here!

You can read the series that follows straight on from this one, **The Ares Trials***, on Amazon.*

Anger management isn't so bad when your shrink is gorgeous. It's less great when you turn up to find him dead on the floor, and an armored giant dressed like a freaking ancient warrior standing over his body though.

Ares, the God of War, has lost his power and the only way for him to get it back? Me. Apparently, I'm a goddess. One with the power of *war*. I mean, it does explain a lot.

To my relief, Joshua, my shrink and only friend, isn't really dead. He's been kidnapped and taken to Olympus—the world where I'm supposed to belong. I vow to do whatever it takes to find him. But Ares has other plans for me. He wants my power, and the easiest way for him to get it is to kill me.

When Hades suggests a compromise, I'm forced to work side-by-side with a giant, murderous warrior god. One with far too many secrets. Ares might be the brute everyone thinks he is, but I'm no angel. He awakens a power within me that I've failed to control my whole life.

And I soon discover that Joshua isn't the only one that needs saving.

Made in the USA
Las Vegas, NV
02 January 2023

64614403R10381